Pithole Kate
and
The Lust for Liquid
Gold

The Tumultuous Times of America's First Oil Strike Pennsylvania 1861-1866

Rosemary Neidel-Greenlee

©

October 15, 2022

KDP Amazon

December 2023

ISBN 979-8-9889132-0-7

Dedication

To my mother, Marian Amsler Neidel who peaked my curiosity about the location where we both grew up. A teacher, she knew the history of the early oil fields, followed the growth of the oil industry, and told me some of the stories about those who inhabited the area during the first oil rush. From her, I developed a sense of place.

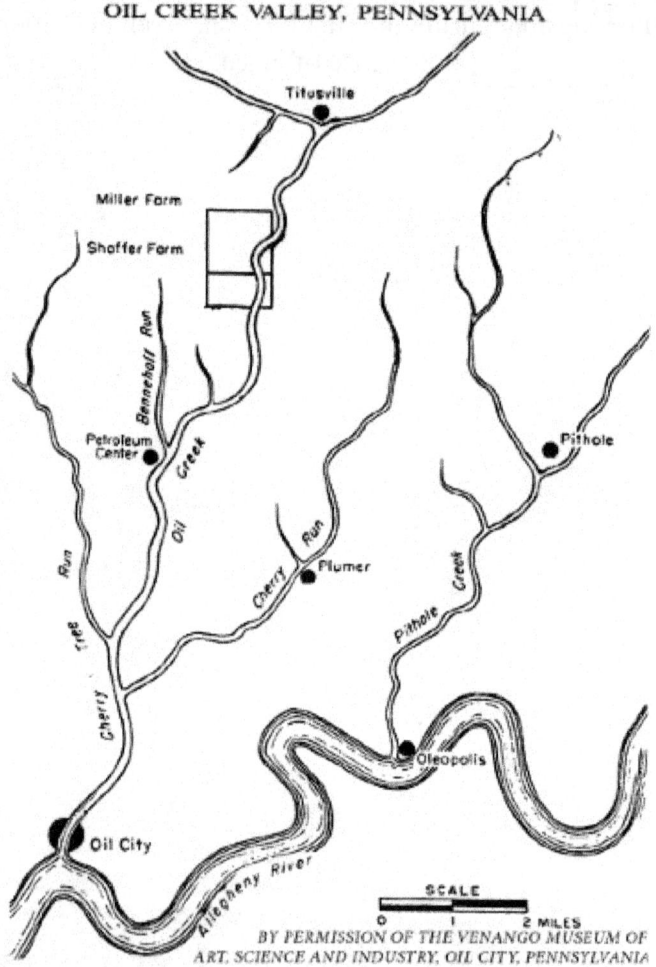

OIL CREEK VALLEY, PENNSYLVANIA

BY PERMISSION OF THE VENANGO MUSEUM OF
ART, SCIENCE AND INDUSTRY, OIL CITY, PENNSYLVANIA

TABLE OF CONTENTS

Along the Banks of Oil Creek

Miller Farm once made the oil men sorry,
For there ended the railroad from Corry,
But helping trade, and likewise this ditty,
It was afterward continued to Oil City,
From whence, the first Oil Region metropolis,
It reached to Pithole, through Oleopolis,
Where the first great oil gushers did appear,
Was near the hamlet still called Pioneer,
And many of the famous early wells once stood
Within the limits of this neighborhood...

--William Temple Bell (1843-1916)

Lucky Luke

Late March 1861, Cornplanter Settlement
Northwestern Pennsylvania

Luke turned his back on fog-shrouded Oil Creek that usually shimmered rainbows of colors on the surface near the shallows and into the tall cattails that marched up the banks from water's edge. Now, white chunks of jagged ice crowded the sodden, muddy banks laid white with mushy, melting snow whose cold collided with unusually warm air. The morning fog signaled the end to a grim, gray winter when the sun seldom shined. He turned toward the river.

Nine–year-old Luther, nick-named Luke, a third- generation German immigrant had awakened and eagerly peered out from the open door of their log house to discover everything familiar to him--the woodpile, the river docking area, and the leafless towering tree near the frozen horse watering trough--all hidden from his view.

In his excitement to try out his new fishing pole, Luke dressed quickly, asked to go outside before breakfast, then slipped out the cabin door and headed for the river.

"Elias told me to fish the river and leave that oily creek to those oilmen, and their greasy barrels." His footfalls made a soft squishing sound as he moved toward the riverbank.

Luke's eighteen-year-old brother, Elias was Luke's hero. He knew that what Elias told him was true and he believed Elias knew everything. In October, Elias had taken Luke with him when he hunted grouse, wild turkey, rabbits and sometimes squirrel. Elias had taught him to handle his rifle--how to carry, aim and shoot, and then clean it. He was teaching Luke skills that John Obadiah, their father was unable to carry out.

"Here ya go, Luke," Elias had said last evening after supper. "I fixed you a good sturdy fishin' stick. Air getting warmer, ice is meltin', so you'll be ready to fish with me here pretty quick."

Luke remembered the feeling of pleasure that had washed over him when Elias had invited him to fish with him on the big river, not just the creek…

The sudden snorting of a deer interrupted Luke's walk toward the riverbank. Its white tail erect, the doe moved parallel with him, toward the edge of the waterway. Luke stood stock still watching her ease her way over the ice to the open water where she dipped her shaggy brown head to drink.

An early morning breeze ruffled Luke's blonde hair as he quietly passed the huge stone blocks of the Oil Creek Iron Furnace that lay abandoned since 1849. He moved noiselessly toward his favorite fishing spot along the north bank of the Allegheny River some 100 miles north of Pittsburgh, Pennsylvania.

Cautiously, he walked to the river's edge, pausing his scrawny frame to survey the ever-shifting surroundings created by up-river ice melt and down-river currents. Repeatedly warned by his parents and older brother about the dangers of the river, he moved slowly onto a sheet of ice, undisturbed so far by passing chunks of solid river water floating in the open channel.

"I am being careful, like Elias told me."

Several feet from the muddy riverbank on the edge of the ice, he grasped the end of his fishing pole, a four-foot-long River Birch branch with a length of light-weight homespun twine attached to a small scrap of iron sinker and metal hook at the end, and cast the line, up-stream. He watched it float past him, then pulled it out, and flung it in again, just as he had watched his brother do. He knew that he should have bait on the hook, but the ground was still frozen so digging for night crawlers was out of the question. Even though it was just for fun, just for practice, Luke felt like a grown-up, grasping the pole in his hands and casting his line.

From a distance, he heard Elias calling.

"Luke, come on! Ma's got vittles for us, right now."

Just as he turned to make his way to the shore, he sensed the support under him give-way. Surprised, he first felt his feet then his legs sink into the dark, icy slush.

"Elias-help! I'm going into the water! Help!"

He felt his torso slipping into the cold, dark Allegheny River. The frigid, unrelenting waterway was swallowing him up to his neck, except for one arm. His breaths were coming in short shallow gasps and his left fist clutched his most prized possession. Desperate, he let loose of the pole, and grasped on to a jagged, chunk of up-thrust ice. A sudden shock of betrayal shot through him. The great, wide river, always before had been his friend. Now it became his nemesis--gray, forbidding and terrifying.

Behind him, he could hear awakening birds twittering in the nearby undergrowth, and the startled deer snorted. Those familiar sounds were replaced by a strange, high-pitched ringing in his ears as he gasped for air, and struggled to pull himself onto solid ice.

"Luke, hold on! I'm comin' for ya!"

Unable to get a grip with his numb hands, Luke clung to a sharp icy spike, wrapping his left arm around it. He rolled his head skyward to keep his mouth above the frigid water. His left hand was cold and turning white, the other, submerged, motionless, and lifeless. He glimpsed the gray, rolling clouds of fog overhead. The ringing in his ears faded; his breathing slowed; and the sky got dimmer, darker. Then everything went black, then silent.

Meanwhile, Elias bolted forward, running as fast as he could. At the edge of the muddy bank, trying to distribute his 160 pounds over the fragile surface of melting ice, he flung himself facedown-- belly-flopped. He slid so rapidly across the distance that lay between him and Luke that he over-shot his target. He plunged headfirst, up to his waist into the frigid water, right beside Luke.

Elias struggled to wriggle back away from the open water, but was shaking violently from the frigid plunge. His soaking wet, blonde hair hung in his eyes and blurred his vision. His right hand slid out from under him, as he struggled to lift his torso up and back away from the river's death grip. He blindly reached out with his left hand, found Luke's arm, and grasped it. A flash of terror shot through Elias as he struggled for traction and leverage to pull Luke to safety. Would the river claim both of them?

Suddenly, Elias felt someone grasp him firmly by both ankles. He was yanked backwards, so vigorously that he pulled Luke with him--out of river's deadly clutches. As he righted himself to a sitting position and gathered Luke to him, he saw a pair of wet deerskin boots and leather fringe on the bottom of a skirt. From the shore, he heard a dog bark, and saw a shaggy brown dog with a white neck ruffle running toward them--Makwa. Then Elias looked up and into Gala's familiar blue eyes.

The lithe Seneca girl of the Turtle Clan wordlessly helped him to his feet. When they were sure Luke was breathing, Elias lifted him onto his shoulder, cold muddy water dripping from his clothing. They trudged toward to the boys' cabin, some twenty-five yards away.

Just then, a figure ran toward them.

"I heard what happened. Can I help?"

"Thanks, Jesse." Elias paused to catch his breath. "I'm hustlin' home with Luke. He's frozen to the bone--that's durn freezin' water."

3

Elias felt the cutting cold penetrate his own body to the bone. He started to shake violently, whether from the bitter cold or from the shock of the close call, he was not sure which. It did not matter, as long as they were safe. He would be forever grateful to Gala and her unflinching willingness to help the very people who had moved onto her ancestral land.

...

Back in the warmth of the cabin, Luke heard the murmur of far-off voices, then felt his body shaking from his head to his feet. His teeth chattered uncontrollably. He realized that he was being held and rocked by someone, then the distant voices faded, and returned-in-and-out, close by, then far away. He felt so tired and numb with cold that he could not open his eyes. He felt the rocking, heard the soft voices that disappeared, then he knew nothing.

Elias hovered near the fireplace and with head bowed, watching Luke's purple lips and limp body. He was wrapped in a patch-quilt his mother had made from scraps of leftover material. Molly Margaret continued to place large round river rocks, heated on the hearth, as close to Luke's body as she dared without burning him. Elias watched the rhythmic rising and falling of Luke's chest, as the old family clock on the mantle ticked out the hours of watching and praying.

As the sun moved overhead and the fog cleared, Elias heard his mother's soft voice.

"Elias. Please come here and hold Luke close to your chest. He's still so cold. Your body is warmed up enough now to help Luke. I'll heat us some stew so when he wakes up, he can be warmed by that hot broth."

Elias was now Luke's only sibling, the two others born in between them having died before the family's move to Cornplanter. Elias could vaguely remember those sisters. When he had asked his mother about them, she stopped sweeping the floor. Her eyes had filled with tears, and she sat down on the wooden bench near the hearth and stared at the fire.

"They died of diphtheria while we were still living in Fryburg near Grandpa's place. First one died--Johanna and then Magdalena the next day. Folks were so afraid of that dreadful diphtheria that no one dared come to the funeral. We buried them on the place, right away."

With her long, slender fingers, Molly had caught the tears

4

from her eyes with a handkerchief from her apron pocket, then dabbed her straight, elegant nose. Elias felt sad that his question had upset his mother and was sorry that he had asked. He knew that life on this frontier was as unpredictable and precarious as the thawing spring ice on the Allegheny River.

Elias lifted Luke's cold body and pressed him to his own warm chest. He was eager to assist his mother with a problem that he had, in his view of things, helped to cause. Elias suffered remorse and overwhelming guilt for giving Luke a fishing pole before the ice was off the river and the creek. He knew he had been careless. But, he reasoned, his mother had not cautioned him against it, nor had she placed blame on him now. More than anything, he dreaded his father's reaction when he would hear about the accident, and that would happen all too soon.

"Ma', when is Pa' due back from his trip?"

"No tellin,' son. Any time now, if the weather holds and it doesn't squall again. If this warmer air keeps up and the river ice melts, he may come back by steamboat from Pittsburgh this time."

Ambivalence gripped Elias about his father's impending return. He wanted him to have a safe journey, but at the same time, he dreaded the continuing clashes between him and John Obadiah...

Recently, he and John Obadiah had argued seriously and had locked in disagreement. That unpleasant experience left him feeling anxious about his future. His father proved to be a determined man of principal, controlling and unyielding, who was known by his family, both here and with his relatives who lived near Pitch-Pine, to be difficult. When it came to his elder son, Elias, he had been adamant.

John Obadiah's discussions had become one-sided and delivered with increasing passion and emotion, especially when fueled with his drinking home brew or hard liquor. Discussions with his father led to arguments that became lectures, and his face would flush red and sweaty. Elias had tried to remain attentive, but found himself escaping the contentious confrontations by imagining that he was sitting in the sun by the river with a fishing stick in one hand, and a piece of beef jerky in the other.

"I want you here with me, Elias, not up that creek, tangling with some of the unsavory characters like those rough-speakin' crude teamsters who have been drawn there by the hopes of makin' a fortune."

"But Pa', I mean to help out--be able to buy some things--

5

trade more with the Seneca's for grain, instead of buying off of the paddleboats--more expensive."

"Not if it means you leavin' here. I've got you a steady payin' position with the steamboat company--good payin' all but for about three months, due to the freezin' of the river. With my position of managin' the landing flats for them, I can keep you workin' steady in the warm months, and the pay's good--in gold, not paper."

"But I know that I can make more working up the creek than down here with the steamboat company. And up there, they work through the winter."

Elias remembered John Obadiah shifting in his chair and leaning forward, settling in for another extended argument and lecture.

"Dealin' with those freshets is dangerous work. Look what the lumberin' did to me, and I was only 20 years older than you are now. I prit'near died the day that tree fell and crushed my legs and lost my right leg. You know that. I couldn't just sit around, not workin'. When I heard about the steamship company had some openin's, I came here from Fryburg and got a sittin' job. Not what I used to do, but I am workin' for a livin'."

Elias had kept silent. Arguing with his father was useless. Instead, he talked with people whom he encountered in his work on the Cornplanter flats. Old-timers told tales of strip-mining bog ore from the river's edge and melting it with the heat from burning coal in huge iron furnaces along the river. In the 1840s, those pioneers sold the pig-iron down the river in exchange for necessities--salt, flour, tools, boots and yard-goods. Men in the oil business, crewmen on the steamships, and rafters who poled long lines of lumber and barrels of oil downriver described life on the water-highway and settlements well beyond Elias' imagine. He heard news from faraway places--Pittsburgh to New Orleans. Elias valued the descriptions and stories of men who saw the world beyond Elias' limited scope of Cornplanter.

His father's lectures had continued. "And now I hear that the oil people will keep usin' the freshets to float their barrels down the creek so the boats can move them to Pittsburgh. The steamboat traffic is pickin' up--they're puttin' more paddlewheels on the run. No, you're better off right here in Cornplanter for now. Besides your mother and I need you to help with the store."

The store was one of a number of businesses that stood at the south end of Cornplanter's muddy, bottomless, crooked streets. Fall rains created sticky brown substance that required folks to build pine plank sidewalks and wear knee-high boots as daily equipment. Thigh-high waders were a necessity during the Spring melt that produced mucky lanes where horses and men sank three feet into the murky mud. From what he'd heard, Elias knew there were better places to live than this settlement that at times was attracting more people than could be supported.

Running their small business was slow when supplies could not be delivered by riverboats in Winter due to ice, and at times of low water in Summer. In fact, Elias thought the store was more work than it was worth. He wanted a different life than this existence, scratched out of the mud and bursts of river traffic from the rafters who piled into their place, dragging dirt with them. There was dirt everywhere and he found it an endless effort to keep the wooden flooring of their store clear of mud.

As soon as the Allegheny got cleared of ice, these lumbermen, clad in red-plaid wool shirts and sporting bushy, unkempt beards, knives strapped to their sides would arrive in groups, on large wooden flat boats from up-river. They caused a lot of commotion. Sometimes he had felt overwhelmed by their demands--where to get a space to sleep; did he have the supplies they needed--lanterns, short handled axes, beef jerky, pickled pig's feet; and asking about which family was serving dinner for travelers that evening. These times were hectic for Cornplanter, but the income from these visitors was good, but sporadic. From them, he'd heard a lot of talk about oil money.

"But, Pa', there's a lot of money to be made in that oil area. We're sitting here, only fifteen miles from where Colonel Drake sank that well August before last. It sure started a lot o' oil fever-- all that creek property being bought up or leased out, and the oil barrel business booming. Things are changing here in Venango County, Pa', and I want to be part of it."

John Obadiah Kahle would not entertain such ideas. What he did believe in was hard work, and that doing it would get you closer to God. Besides, it was a tightly held, lofty family value that was deeply rooted into their German ancestry.

Now, Elias was dreading to face his father's tyrannical torrents of volatile verbiage. He would have yet another browbeating coming at him about the near-drowning accident. Elias felt trapped between his dreams for the future and his crippled father's diabolical derision and domineering demands...

7

The odor of soup heating on the hearth nearby returned him to the present. The smell of cooking made his mouth water. He suddenly realized that he'd had nothing to eat since pulling Luke from the river--just lost his appetite, partly because he was so worried about Luke, and very cold himself, but for another reason that he tried to deny. It was because he had seen Gala again.

The very sight of her made him feel good, even though he'd almost drowned, was shaking with cold, and flooded with guilt over Luke's close encounter with death. Gala, he loved. He was sure of it. But that too was a problem, and he and his father had gone head-to-head like rutting rams in continuous combat. That argument over his relationship with her had been far worse than the argument over wanting a job in the oil field...

"I see your spendin' time with that Seneca squaw again, Elias," John Obadiah had accused one day at dinner. Molly had cooked pumpkin pudding, Elias' favorite, and he had taken his first bite when his father spoke of Gala. He almost choked.

"Well, Pa, I assist her when she comes onto the flats, just like everyone else who comes here by boat. What's wrong with that?"

"You can't fool me, Elias. You linger and take your time with her when she's there. You best not get any ideas in your head about her."

"Pa, I'm almost a full-grown man. And she's somebody I've known since we moved here--been coming here to trade on these flats since I can remember. Besides, there are so few ladies around here my age, that I have no acquaintances who are young women."

Molly had come to his defense.

"Well, John, we do live in a place that has few opportunities for a youngster such as our Elias. Cornplanter has a gristmill and the miller has only sons. J. F. Hopewell is the oldest resident, but his offspring are grown adults now, not Elias' age. W.J. Kramer has a wagon factory and Cummings Brothers, a machine shop on the 3rd Ward, but no offspring the right age. Hasson and Company have that hardware store farther up the creek. The McFarland Brothers have a general store, as does, McComb, and they have children, but those three are more Luke's age, not Elias'."

John Obadiah countered.

"What about the Kerr daughters? Those two young ladies

seem a sturdy lot."

"Pa, getting to know young ladies is not like buying a horse. You don't go by the fact that they are sturdy or how many teeth they got. I have no interest in Abigail and Suzanna. I've been knowing them for several years, and I can't say that I've ever taken to either of them."

"Oh, Elias, we know that someday you will want to marry. Most men do." Molly began clearing the table.

"Well, Molly. I don't want him gettin' involved with some' idol-worshippin,' Indian squaw. Those Senecas are just a bunch of heathens."

"Pa, that's not true. Gala and her grandma follow the Code of Handsome Lake and some Christian preachings are a part of it. And that's not an idol that Gala wears. That's a totem. It represents her clan, the Turtle Clan."

John Obadiah seemed not to have heard Elias' statement and went on as if he had not spoken.

"That's not going to happen in this family. Do you want to have some half-breed grand-youngen'? I don't. I forbid such a match!"

With that, he had risen from his chair, knocking it to the board floor with a clatter, grabbed his crutches and stormed out the front door that closed behind him with a bang.

Elias could feel his face flushing with anger. His father's vehement reference to Gala as an "idol-worshipping-Indian-squaw" made his gut ache. His father's judging people he did not know in such harsh terms left him disgusted and discouraged.

There were times that he hated his father and his domineering ways. He looked to his mother for support, but when she failed to meet his eyes, Elias felt alienated from his family. He asked to be excused, and left the table, abandoning his pumpkin-pudding. He walked away leaving his favorite food uneaten. The memory of that argument made him feel angry and anxious about his future…

. . .

Elias pulled himself out of this memory and realized that he was salivating in response to the enticing odors of venison stew wafting from the hearth. Just then, he felt Luke move has legs against his own thigh. He watched as his eyes fluttered open. His little brother seemed confused, looking around at the room as if for the first time.

"Luke, how do you feel?"

Hearing that question, Molly whirled away from the pot of cooking food and in her excitement dropped the ladle on the hearth with a resounding clatter. She clapped her hands, beaming with relief.

"He's awake! Praise the Lord in Heaven!"

"What happened?" His voice was a whisper. "Why am I on your lap, Elias?" He slowly turned his head toward the sound of Molly's voice. "Where are my clothes?"

With that question, the once limp Luke sat up straight, and swung his bare feet to the rough timbers of the floor. He slid out of Elias' lap and started to walk. He wobbled and Elias caught him as he sagged and fell backward.

"Whoa, little fella. Take your time. You fell into the river, and we've been warming you up."

"Yes, Luke. Here's some hot broth for you. It will warm up your insides." Molly handed him a metal mug of steaming potage.

Luke sat quietly, slowly sipping the hot liquid. Suddenly, he seemed to recall his fishing accident, and icy plunge into the Allegheny.

"My fishin' pole! Where is it? Do you have it, Elias?"

"No, Luke. By now, your fishing pole may have floated down the Allegheny as far south as Franklin and Fort Venango--way past French Creek. I'll make you another one as soon as the ice is off the river. You had a very close call with that ice breaking under your feet, and we don't want that to happen again."

Now, Elias thought, Luke had survived the near fatal accident, he had to endure telling his father what happened and the truth about who really saved them both.

John Obadiah's Homecoming

April 1861

For the next week, the unpredictable spring weather in Northwestern Pennsylvania was warmer than usual, and the river ice melted more rapidly than in previous years. Elias was sweeping out the store when Jesse leaned through the open door.

"Hello, Elias. I don't want to track mud into your place, but I'm here with news."

Elias set aside his corn-shuck broom and walked to the entrance to greet his friend.

"You got news, Jesse, what news?"

"The first paddlewheel is on its way up river from Pittsburgh."

"That so? Wonder if Pa's on it." Elias felt his neck muscles suddenly tense.

"I reckon so--better than the stage to Butler and then horseback the rest of the way--especially with your Pa's leg and all."

"When's the steamboat due here?" Elias asked.

"Depends on the ice-melt farther south. If there's no big jams, they said it may be here tomorrow, or maybe next."

"Thanks, Jesse. I'll let Ma' know. She's been wondering when Pa'll get back."

Elias hurried to the cabin and announced the news to Molly, and watched her reaction.

"Well, that's news, all right. He's been gone a good while, and if ice is almost done, the paddlewheel can make it through."

Just as they were talking, Luke came to the cabin door where he sat on the step and removed his muddy boots, then scrambled to his feet.

"I heard the steamboat is coming up from Pittsburgh."

"Yes, and the word is, that he's on it," Elias said.

Molly considered the news and took a deep breath. "Sit down, boys. Let's talk. We need to have a home-coming for Pa."

First, they discussed a special dinner of chicken and dumplings. Molly planned to pick out a fat hen. Elias would kill it with a hatchet on the stump near to coop. And Luke was assigned to help pluck the feathers. They'd roast potatoes from the root vegetable storage crib.

That being settled, Molly paused as if to clear her mind for the next part of the plan, and looked them straight in the eyes, first at Elias and then at Luke.

"We need a plan to keep things as peaceful as possible, once Pa is back. I've been thinking about it--your accident on the ice, Luke. Pa's likely to come down hard on you both, and there's no sense in that. Elias, I think it best that we just don't make any mention of it. Can we agree?"

Luke looked at Elias, who sat staring at the floor. It was a full minute before anyone spoke. Elias felt a wave of relief flood over him, like a cool river breeze on a hot summer day. He broke the silence.

"Ma,' I guess you know I've been worried about Pa's reaction when he gets wind of it. I know I'll be in the doghouse. 'Fact, I've been thinking about what I need to do because I know he'll yell and be nasty for hours. I am grateful for your words. I feel relieved."

"Luke," Molly shifted her gaze from Elias. "Son, you're old enough to hear what I have to say. It needs saying…"

Luke nodded and Molly continued.

"I want you boys to know that Pa' was not always like this mean and short-tempered--flying-off-the-handle. Things changed with him after his logging accident, when you were only a baby, a year old, Luke. Those huge logs pinned him under the water for so long, nobody who saw it, thought he'd survive. He was hurt bad--no doubt and a little different after that--pretty short tempered, couldn't sleep, and when he did, sometimes he'd be swinging his arms and kicking with the leg he had left. Sudden loud noises would make him jump--startle him, and make him angry, things like that. I'm telling you these things so you'll understand. He's changed after that accident."

Molly's eyes filled with tears.

"Couldn't walk, couldn't work, angry a good bit at his lot. And then, the girls took sick with the diphtheria and died. It hit your Pa' real hard…said he felt cursed."

Luke felt sad, and moved closer to Molly and put his arm around her. Elias did the same. The three of them just sat there, Molly with her eyes shut, hugging her two sons. After a few minutes, she stirred.

"I got to get our dinner started soon. So, we're agreed on not mentioning the ice accident, right?"

Both boys nodded.

"The only thing, Elias, do you think anyone else besides Gala knew about it? That morning was real foggy and it happened early before most folks were stirring."

"Yes, Ma.' Just one other person. Jesse was on the east creek bank and came running, but Gala got there first. I know Gala wouldn't tell it."

"Well, Elias, you talk to Jesse. I hope he kept it to himself. I hope he hasn't discussed it with anyone. He knows your Pa and his bad temper. We need to keep him calm for all our sakes."

"No one has mentioned it to me. What about you, Luke?"

"Not to me either, Ma'."

The two boys stood, nodding their agreement. Elias returned to his work at the store, and Molly turned her attention to preparing dinner. Luke, feeling stunned, sat on the front stoop, watching gray squirrels scrambling up and down the oak trees, chasing each other and chattering loudly, and sending small pieces of bark, flying.

He felt as if something very important had just happened. He had been taken into the circle of adult confidence, and he felt confused, but proud at the same time. He decided he'd talk to Elias about it later. Elias always knew what to say, what to tell him. Elias would listen.

…

It seemed to Elias that the entire settlement of Cornplanter heard the steamboat whistle, an extended and loud blast that echoed across the Allegheny River from one long river ridge to another, announcing the boat's forth-coming arrival as it maneuvered through chunks of ice floating in the deep, open channel. The inbound vessel rounded the last long curve before the locals who were crowded on the river landings could sight it. Gathered on the west side of Oil Creek, the enthusiastic citizens shouted a warm welcome for the long-awaited appearance. After the many months of virtual inaccessibility, their connection with the outside world was secured.

On this clear and sunny Spring day, the first steamboat of the season raised a real ruckus. As the gathering expanded to the Third Ward near the Old Moran House and Samuel Hopewell's Tavern, Elias watched women wearing ordinary housedresses running across the wooden Oil Creek footbridge toward the excitement. With no time to prepare, their long hair was unfurled and streamed out behind them like the wake created by the arriving steamboat. Parents ran past the still vacant lots laid out by the Michigan Rock Oil Company, trying to keep up with their screaming children. Barking, excited dogs encircled them all. On the east side of the creek near the entrance to the Kahle's store, a huge horse tied to the hitching post whinnied, and tried to rear, pulling hard against its tether. With the booming blast from the oncoming vessel, the somnolent inhabitants of Cornplanter suddenly sprang to life.

As the large white river craft with the name *NEW CASTLE* painted of its side approached the mud-brown flats of the tiny town, it belched out bellows of sooty smoke. The boat's slowing paddlewheels splashed sparkling sprays of icy river water onto excited bystanders who had just awakened from the winter season's somber slumber. Water birds scattered and running people gathered, maneuvering to catch a glimpse of boat passengers who were arriving on the vast vessel that towered high above the town's low landing flats.

Elias, Molly and Luke watched as the steamer tied up at Vandergrift's Landing and a crewman lowered a wooden gangplank to the mud flat. Enveloped by the crowd, they pressed forward to greet John Obadiah who leaned on his crutches and swung his body forward, alighting on his left leg.

Elias noticed that his father had dressed in his only suit that sported a black vest and the 3-button white shirt with a standup collar. A wide black bowtie had been carefully looped in a loose knot and secured with a stickpin that Elias had never seen before. His father's black top hat covered the familiar graying-brown hair that appeared to have been recently trimmed for this occasion. Elias thought his tall, well-dressed father looked younger and more rested than when he'd seen him last, before his long trip down river.

"Pa'!" Elias moved to his father's side and took his dark blue carpetbag as Luke gathered his heavy winter coat. Molly moved between the boys to welcome her husband and the family pushed through the crowd on the landing, crossed the wooden footbridge, and followed the dirt path that led to their cabin. They had planned an early dinner to leave time before bed to hear about John Obadiah's journey.

...

When the roasted chicken and fried potatoes from the root

cellar had been eaten, the refreshed traveler sat back in his chair, smoothed his neatly trimmed mustache and stretched out his left leg. Elias thought he seemed happy to be back home.

"Luke, fetch me the carpetbag. I brought you each something from Pittsburgh."

Luke dropped his fork onto his metal plate with a loud clatter and jumped to his feet with enthusiasm. In just moments, he returned with John Obadiah's travel bag.

"Lots of stores there and it was hard to decide what to buy-- so many choices." That said, he handed Molly a small paper-wrapped object and she immediately opened her gift. A fine hairnet edged with ruchings of red ribbon tumbled on to Molly's lap, and she gasped with delight. The netting matched the color of her long blonde hair, and she smiled broadly at such a treasure.

"Thank you, John Obadiah! I will try it on while we talk."

For Elias, his father had selected a black bow tie with a silver stickpin, similar to his own. Elias thanked him, then turned to watch Luke open his gift. As Luke unwrapped a small, heavy object, his father watched.

"You're old enough to have your own knife, Luke, so now you can stop borrowing Elias' knife."

They all laughed since that had become a point of humor within their family. Elias knew where he could find his knife on cold, windy winter evenings. Luke would be whittling with it--just as he was on this occasion as well. Luke thanked him with a hug and sat down to explore the coveted gift. With that, John Obadiah grew more serious and continued to describe details of his trip.

"I've got news from Pittsburgh. Brought some newspapers for you. Some things are more easily read about, than discussed. The most important, and alarmin' news is the big division in our country. I didn't realize that it was as bad as it is. Some folks are talkin' war, and some states have left the Union--just voted to secede. You heard about South Carolina quitin' back in December. Well, then Mississippi, Florida, Alabama, Georgia and Louisiana followed-- that whole block of the South. And dependin' on who you talk to, some hate the new President Abraham Lincoln, and some love him and believe in what he's aimin' to do."

Elias sat forward in his chair.

"Pa, what is the President aiming to do? I heard this conflict is all about the states having their rights--that the Washington government has no business in telling them what to do."

Elias paused and took a breath.

"Others from up the river say it's all about setting the Negros free--the slaves, I mean. One rafter called Mr. Lincoln a 'Negro lover,' and that he should leave well enough alone..."

"Well, son, those are weighty questions. One opinion I overheard, and this was a gent' from South Carolina at the hotel where I say stayin',' is that Jeff Davis and his lot want slavery to be allowed all across the south part of this big country-territories too-- out west way past the Mississippi River. There's a line called the 36-30 parallel. Cut's the whole big landmass in half. Another fella- -had a long gray beard and a thick accent--Southern, I guess-who with him was talkin' about slave owners fearin' an up-risin'--a race war they call it--between them darkies and the whites."

John Obadiah paused and looked over at Luke who continued whittling as if he was not hearing the conversation.

"Worst of all, they said was that there would be the mixin' of the races--the Negros with the white folks. Not just livin' among them, but marryin' each other--black and white. Said whites are the superior race, not to be tainted by Negro blood. They both agreed on that."

Molly's brow wrinkled and Elias listened silently. Luke sat on the floor near the hearth and continued to whittle quietly on a piece of pinewood with his new knife.

"Lots of things are changin' in the country, I tell ya'. Worst part is the talk of war--the south has ideas of keepin' things the way they are--with slaves and all. They call it 'a national benefit,' and in Pittsburgh, those folks call it 'ridiculous.' South Carolina has seceded since Lincoln's election, then the rest of the South followed. No more than Mr. Lincoln got sworn in just this month than all hell's breakin' loose. Looks like the South has its own country by electin' a president, Jeff Davis. That *Pittsburgh Post-Gazette* is full of what's happenin' so I brought some of the most recent papers."

Molly sat up straight and smiled.

"Oh, thank you, John Obadiah. I am anxious to read about the happenings. Ever since I read *Uncle Tom's Cabin*--you know the book that Miss Harriet Beecher Stowe wrote--I've felt disgusted about slavery. Sounds as if things are coming to a bad place with all those states pulling out of the Union."

Elias listened and said little. During his father's absence, news had circulated, mainly by raft-men who had arrived at the flats as soon as enough ice had come off the main channel of the

Allegheny. They spoke of men in several counties to the north in the Wildcat District, Warren, Forest, McKean and Elk, who were getting organized to fight.

Elias had heard stories from several of the earliest rafters, about these rugged up-river Warren County men who rafted their lumber to New Orleans, then walked some 1000 miles to get back home. That was until the steamboats had come into service on the upper Allegheny with its low waters, dangerous shallows and numerous islands that made navigation harrowing at times. Elias knew that these men were a hardy lot and they were planning to go to war.

He recalled the pronouncement of one of the rafters who had come on to the Cornplanter landing just last week. A broad-shouldered, ruddy-faced Warren resident named Martin had an announcement.

"One man, Tom Kane who lives in Warren wants to gather the sharpshooters who are hunters and lumberjacks from the forests who got quick reactions and used to hard livin'. Tom's brother, Doc Kane is the famous Arctic explorer. He's helpin' Tom. They've got a surgeon up there examinin' volunteers, lookin' for sound and hardy men. Got to prove to be excellent shots, too." That conversation plus a recruiting bulletin Martin had shown him and Jesse gave Elias something to think about, but he kept it to himself...

John Obadiah turned toward Elias.

"Well, boy, the ice is mostly gone off the river all the way from Pittsburgh to up here. Just some clingin' to the north shore where it got piled up and doesn't get much sun. Oh, and when I met with the new manager of the paddleboat company, he told me that they've put more boats--maybe three or four--besides the *Venango* and the *New Castle*--on their north route, due mostly to the increase in shippin' of more and more oil from here. They say more passengers are buyin' tickets for our oil region, too. Sounds as if you and I are gonna to be busier than last summer."

He went on.

"Since that Michigan Rock Oil Company came in here February before last and divided the land 'round here into lots for sale, things have changed. That new general store built by J. D. Reynolds from Clarion and McComb from Pittsburgh is just one example. The Hasson's Hardware on the east bank and The Mead House, and there's the brick buildin', first one not made of timber, another store that Williams and Brother are about to complete."

John Obadiah continued.

"You see, those wells that been drilled up along Oil Creek, some of them have come in, like the wells on the Buchanan Farm. Then last spring, Brewer and Watson spring-pumped for oil and produced twelve barrels a day 'til water contaminated the well. They suspended their operation until they could get engines set up to do the drillin'. Had to come down from Erie with that equipment. Of course, their oil gets shipped out'a here."

He paused.

"That's why all those storage buildin's and warehouses are risin' up on the flats near the landin's. Last year, we shipped over 17,000 barrels of crude down the river to Pittsburgh. And word is that this year, they'll be a good bit more oil comin' down that creek, lots more. That's what is bringin' all these wildcatters and speculators to Cornplanter."

John Obadiah paused to drink the last of his home brew, giving Elias an opportunity to ask a question.

"Pa, what is going to happen with this crude oil? How did all this drilling get started? Does anybody know what to do with it?"

"From the time I was about Luke's age, I heard about what they called rock oil. Your great grandfather, Fredrick Rickenbrode who immigrated from Wurttemberg talked about rock oil that came from drillin' for salt water. Those salt wells were used to make salt for folks to buy. That rock oil came into those salt-water wells and near ruined the salt makin'. Back then, that oil in the salt wells was considered a nuisance to those drillers." He paused and took a deep breath.

"Those early settlers were curious, though, about rock oil, and learned from the Indians, the Senecas. For years, those people used crude oil for medicine called it 'Seneca Oil' that they gathered from Oil Creek by spreadin' out their blankets on the surface of the creek where the oil floated. The blanket soaked up the oil as the blanket was bein' dragged off the creek. Then the Indians would wring out their blankets to get some oil. Wrung it out into pits that lay scattered for acres--held up by wood logs. Some said these cribs were spread in a pattern. Never saw it myself, but early folks talk about it."

Luke looked up from his whittling.

"Why did they want the oil, Pa'? They didn't have machines to oil-up, like the paddlewheels, did they?"

John Obadiah smiled one of his rare smiles, and Elias was

18

surprised to see that several of his teeth were missing. Maybe the result of the logging accident. Elias didn't dare ask.

John Obadiah looked at Molly who was busy sewing. She looked up and shook her head in agreement.

"That is a good question, youngen."

"Old Grandpa Fredrick said he followed the Indian's practice. They used it for medicine, salve for wounds, sprains, bruises and sore joints; painted their faces with it. It was told to me that they collected oil from the creek, poured it into one of those pits in the ground and would set fire to it for special ceremonies."

Elias glanced at Luke whose mouth was open and his eyes bright and alert.

"They lit a pit on fire? I would want to have seen that!"

"Well, I don't think that Grandpa ever saw that either, Luke, but I bet it was a spectacle. You remember that oil will catch fire quickly. It can be real dangerous."

He paused for another swallow of his home brew, and finding the beaker empty, used his crutches to stand on his foot, then hobbled into the storage closet nearby.

Luke looked thoughtful.

"Do you know if Gala ever saw them light a fire in an oil pit, Elias?"

Molly's head jerked up for her sewing, and Elias gave Luke a hard look, shook his head from side-to-side, and put his right index finger to his closed lips. He hoped that John Obadiah had not heard Luke.

A moment later, their father regained his seat, seeming to have missed a question that could have started another fire, a real explosion, right here in their house. Instead, he continued his story about early oil use.

"Said around here that Old Man Cary, one of the first white men to settle on Oil Creek was an interprisin' gent who collected oil by skimmin' it off the surface usin' a blanket—just like the Senacas did. Then he'd tote it off south to Pittsburgh--a five-gallon keg slung on each side of his horse. Rode for 80 some miles--not an easy trip. He'd trade the crude for necessities for his family. I think that was the beginnin' that led to all this oil excitement."

Then John Obadiah went on.

"Grandpa kept handy some oil he used for medicine. I saw it one time. 'Kier's Petroleum' came in an 8-ounce bottle with a wrapper that told how to use it._ Bottled in Pittsburgh where Mr.

Kier started a real business of it some years back. Now it's sold everywhere. Grandpa said he bought it from some travelin' huckster--sellin' snake oil from his wagon. Grandpa said it was good for both animals and people. He rubbed it on cuts and places where the saddle rubbed the skin off of his horse, Topsy. He said that it worked on Topsy and on him, too. Supposed to cure liver complaints, consumption, cholera, morbus, bronchitis and such. I've read the paper of instructions that comes with it."

Elias went outside to the woodpile for another log to revive the waning fire. He did not miss noticing the peacefulness of the homecoming dinner and conversation. Everyone seemed to enjoy being together, and actually were discussing things. Good thing his father had missed Luke's question about Gala. That would have ruined this peaceful evening.

Relieved, he took a deep breath and exhaled slowly, watching his exhaled breath turn white in the cold night air. He looked up and saw that the sky was clear and the stars bright. He felt fortunate. For once it was not the usual straight lecture from Pa that made him feel guilty or foolish about things. Why couldn't it be like this more often? Why not? Elias returned to the hearth with another log and placed it on the red-hot coals. After a few moments, the log caught and bright yellow flames curled upward.

"Getting' back to what you asked, Elias, there have been attempts to use crude to replace whale oil for lamps--whale oil sells for 'bout $15 a gallon--but there's too much smoke in burnin' petroleum. Hurts folks' eyes and makes furniture dirty. Also, a couple of professors got involved. One at Dartmouth and another gent, a Professor Stillman in New Haven--Yale have been experimentin' with breakin' the oil down--refinin' it to improve how it could work in oil lamps like the yellow dog lantern--that one with two spouts coming out the sides. In fact, there is a refinery at Pittsburgh that is refinin' the crude that we are shippin' to them on the river flatboats." He paused. "Maybe it'll come to sellin' under the price o' whale oil. Heard tell that several refineries will be started here, too."

"So, Pa', you still think this oil business is just a 'fluff in the pan?'"

"Well, Elias, looks like a whole lot of speculation to me. I've got a wait-and-see attitude. Far as I can see, they're not sure what large volumes of oil's any good for…"

"Pa,' Captain Reynolds says that he uses crude on his

paddlewheel, the *Venango*. They smear it on parts of machinery that move with other metal parts. Keeps the friction down and makes things act more smoothly. Captain Reynolds said that the crude out of Franklin works better than some from other areas. He said a blacksmith named Evans was trying to get a water well dug near his house when he got oil mixed with the water. It was not long after he'd heard about Colonel Drake's well hitting oil. Evens made his own tools--bought iron on credit so he could go deeper. Used a spring-pole and hit oil at about seventy-two feet in the sand rock." Elias paused. "Made me think that when I get some of my pay together, I want to buy some shares in either a Franklin well, or one of these on Oil Creek."

"Elias, I think that'd be a waste of your cash. Don't be foolish. These speculators are gents with deep pockets. For you, just good hard work'll get you somewhere. No gamblin' in this risky oil business. Good thing about workin' for the steamboat company is steady pay and in gold or silver too, not paper. It's not like the price of a barrel of crude. First it sold for $20 a barrel last year when that Titusville tanner, William Barnsal drilled through rock with a spring-pole--didn't wait for an engine."

"Pa', what's a spring-pole? Can people use it for digging a well?" Luke was curious.

"Well, son, it's a rough metal drillin' piece rigged to a green pole, you know a limb that's just been cut from a live tree, so it can bend, snap back, and won't break. You tie the drill bit to a rope and drop it into a hole. Then you bounce the pole with your foot-by workin' a rope and platform tied to the other end, and the drill bit bites into the dirt, deeper and deeper until oil comes out of the hole. Gotta use a sand-pump to get rid of what's being dug up. It's a spout about 3 inches across that sucks out the diggin's. That's the less costly way of drillin' for oil, but it takes a long time. Took Barnsal three months of drillin'. It's called 'kickin' down a well,' and it's for men with strong muscles and a slim purse. Gotta have a lot of patience, too."

John Obadiah gestured with his hands to help Luke understand his explanation about the spring-pole.

"Could we drill with a spring pump--Elias and I?"

"Don't think we're in the right area. Those fellas who kicked down wells were farther up Oil Creek where they might hit oil after two or three months of hard work, when they get to about 200 feet deep, and then the hole might be dry. Cost was about $3000 for

Barnsal, and it takes a lot of work…"

      Luke was sitting on the edge of his chair, eager to hear more. "Did Mr. Barnsal get much oil from his well, Pa?"

      "Barnsal had the second well on the creek and got twenty-five barrels a day and sold it for $18 a barrel--but that was last year. Then Jonathan Watson, manager of a lumber and mercantile business in Titusville did the same thing, but farther south on Oil Creek. He used a spring-pole. Now this was only the third well on the creek, and he hit pay dirt-his well started runnin' at sixty gallons a minute! That much oil caused the price of oil drop down to 60 cents a barrel. Price went way down due to more wells bein' drilled. Like I said, it's risky business, even when you do hit oil. Some folks have invested a lot of money for drillin' equipment--cost about $1000, leasin' land or buyin' it, then another $1000 to sink a well and have only dry holes--no oil."

      "Some of those drillers just gave up and walked away, leavin' expensive machinery like one set of drillin' tools weighin' 1,800 to 2,600 pounds--worth about $350. That's two wrenches, rope auger, sinker bar, temper screw, rope socket, jars, two bits, and a round reamer. And that's just sayin' nothin' about the rest of it--drillin' machine, sucker rods and valves, and the cost to lease the land. Then if you do hit oil, ya' gotta get it out of the valley and down river. Some of the speculators who ran off didn't stop to surrender their leases with the farmers, either. There's a lot of expense and loss."

      "What do the farmers get out of the leases, Pa?"

      "Well, Elias, some get one-eighth to one quarter interest in what's produced. Sometimes, a fortune--most of the time nothing but a lot of trees and pasture land destroyed." John Obadiah paused. "It's Oil Creek humbug--bein' said by some. Why even the colonel's well--Drake Well produced only fifteen barrels a day, then fell off slow 'til end of the year-- produced for just four months."

      Elias enjoyed hearing his father talk about his trip and the oil business that flourished around them. For a while, at least, there was peace, and he liked hearing new ideas. On one hand, he felt glad that his father was back from his travel. On the other hand, down-deep, he knew that this pleasant interval with his father might be short-lived, and this familial peace broken by saying the wrong thing. It was like walking on guinea hen eggs.

      "Well, Pa'. All this talk about the wells. What one would you buy shares in, if you could?"

"Don't you go getting' some high-falootin' ideas about getting' rich, Elias."

Elias felt his face flush and his fists clench. He saw his mother stand as if to change John Obadiah's negative focus, avoiding a predictable diatribe by her husband. She finished clearing the table.

"Luke, you'd better finish your chores. It's getting late. Later than I realized."

Elias felt relieved that his mother had made a smooth intervention just when things could have gotten heated between him and his father. Elias did have ideas and dreams, and he and perhaps his mother were not about to have anyone squelch then, especially John Obadiah.

Elias' Dilemma

During the third week of April 1861, word came up the Allegheny that Fort Sumter in South Carolina had been attacked by rebel forces and fallen into Confederate hands on April 12. Although the news was delayed by days in reaching the isolated oil area, that information alarmed the Cornplanter settlement, and for many, it changed the focus and pace of their lives.

The citizens of Venango County, the heart of the oil excitement were true to the Union. News of units being formed for the Pennsylvania Reserves circulated and was updated with the arrival of flatboats from the north and steamships from the south. Bulletins recruiting for the state reservists floated downriver from the Wild Cat Country, advertising the commitment as a six-month obligation. In small towns around the county, enthusiastic newspaper editorials were urging citizens to form war committees where women gathered donations of money and prepared hospital supplies. They talked of nursing the wounded and sewing items of clothing for those volunteering to serve. Men working on the steamboat flats and the oil field discussed going to war, joining up. In the entire region, the pace of activities quickened and that included the mud flats at the oil storage area and steamship landings at the confluence of Oil Creek and the Allegheny River.

Not all Cornplanter inhabitants turned their attention from oil production to war preparations. Anxious oil producers were talking with John Obadiah, asking questions about steamboat schedules, shipping capacity, incoming supplies to be delivered, and oil waiting to be shipped off. They worried about the possibility of the river traffic being interrupted by the War of Rebellion. Steamship passengers asked questions about schedules and travel tickets, and citizens and business owners, about mail delivery and shipping expense. More flatboats were coming and going from that point on the river, which escalated the mix of river and creek traffic to a new high.

With tow boats, barges, flat boats, guipers, bulk boats and steamboats, plus the oil fleet tied up at the confluence of the commerce, there were so many boats that, at times, a pedestrian could cross the Alleghany River going boat-to-boat from the South shore to the North shore or visa-versa.

At the start of this busy season when the main river channel was ice-free, dock manager, John Obadiah had delegated more responsibility to Elias. As he observed his father dealing with the increased workload, he thought that the faster pace was making it difficult for his disabled father to keep up. Elias accepted the added responsibility while thoughts of the war swirled through his head.

The declaration of war and its possible impact on oil production and the shipment of greater volumes of crude weighed heavily on both father and son. Since the number of wells along Oil Creek had grown over the past two years, production of oil was increasing. These wells were tapping oil at 200 to 300 feet from the first and second sand-rock. The production of oil from major wells such as the Burnt Well on the Buchanan Farm, the Philips Well of the Tarr Farm, along with the Sherman and the Empire Wells glutted the market with a product whose application, to a large extent had not yet been determined.

In their early days, those wells collectively produced a daily yield of 1000 to 4000 barrels. Two years later in the spring of 1861, the daily production had grown to 8000 to 10,000 barrels per day. With the rising volumes of crude, the price of a barrel of oil plummeted from one dollar a barrel to ten cents a barrel. The effect on speculators and small-time operators was devastating. They were walking away from their partially dug wells. Some of them joined the Pennsylvania Reserves or a local unit preparing for war.

However, the downturn did not deter some drillers with deep pockets. They, together with the producing well owners moved forward. Oil storage at the well sites became stressed and the warehouses at the Oil Creek-Allegheny River flats had limitations as well. This historic production of oil required selling it off for shipments downriver, no matter the price. It had to be moved.

One day as Elias went about his work accounting for shipments of oil for the steamboats, he heard loud talking at the edge of Oil Creek. It sounded like an argument and seemed to be increasing in volume and intensity. He paused from his tasks and looked in the direction of the creek. He adjusted the tilt of his hat to shade his eyes from the early morning sun.

"You heard me! You owe me another ten barrels."

"You agreed to a boat-load of crude and that's what you got in bulk. Your boat is full."

Elias walked closer to the disputing men. Talk like this was rare and most deals were handled in a less confrontational manner.

25

It was with pride that people of the region managed business--on trust and honesty. He was surprised at the scene, and curious to see who was involved.

The oil storage tanks were close to the creek and the buyer's boat had run up alongside a tank from which the small boat had been supplied oil by the bulk. From where Elias stood, the boat appeared to be full. Yet the argument ensued.

The buyer argued.

"But I measured the amount that this boat can carry and its short by ten gallons, I tell you!"

Elias recognized the oil producer who was well known around the waterfront to stand his ground. He appeared unmoved, his hands on his hips. The producer's worker waited near the tank and held a large hose that dripped brown with the oily product under contention.

"You know, Sam, water in this settlement is more expensive than this here crude we're arguing about. The price is so low, I don't get your point."

Samuel McKissick took off his hat and threw it to the ground.

"I know what the price of a barrel of crude runs at the well. I want that two barrels you owe me!"

The producer shrugged and waited. When the bearded buyer launched into his argument again, the seller nodded to his employee who released a full stream of oil into the McKissick's boat. Elias watched in fascination as the overloaded craft sank slowly into the waters of Oil Creek and listed to its portside, dumping the entire contents of the oily cargo. The oleaginous would-be-shipment, now a buoyant blob, like a floating island, surged into the fast-flowing waters of the Allegheny River and disappeared down-steam. The irate buyer waded into the creek to rescue his partially submerged dinghy that was slippery with crude. The producer held up his hands, palms up in a sign of resignation and amazement.

Elias looked around for John Obadiah but did not spot him among the milling masses on the crowded flats. He wondered what his father would have thought of this episode. These days, no one could predict what might transpire on the busy landing flats that dealt with some speculator's entire fortunes.

…

At the height of activities on the flats, just after noon,

someone spoke to John Obadiah.

"How're your boys doing after that close-call with them almost drowning in the river?"

When he heard details of the ice incident, the landing flats manager stopped from checking in-coming freight, dropped the inventory papers, and stared straight ahead.

Suddenly, everything got quiet, so eerily quiet in the midst of the busiest time of the day that Elias looked up from counting Columbia Oil Company barrels to see what was causing the work-pause.

Elias watched his father snatch his crutches and get off the wooden stool where he'd been sitting. Something about the way he moved gave him a sinking feeling. His countenance, a scowl, John Obadiah hobbled toward Elias.

"Elias, what's this I hear about you and Luke fallin' through the ice out there?" He swung his right arm in the direction of the nearby riverbank.

"Why did you keep that from me? I been back home here for 'bout two weeks now, and nary a mention of it. Was it some kind of secret--that you both 'most drowned?"

He took two more steps closer to Elias who was standing near a huge pile of coiled rope.

"You and Luke were foolish enough to go out onto the meltin' ice of this here river?"

Elias stood wide-legged, arms crossed in front of him, listening respectfully to John Obadiah whose face, he noted, was flushed.

"I'm beginnin' to wonder if I can trust my own family!"

His father's voice was rising to a high enough volume that people had stopped what they had been doing, and looked toward them.

"Well, Pa'," Elias began, "I didn't think it was of consequence--not worth your worry. It was over and done within a few minutes…"

Elias saw strangers and curious on-lookers encircling the two of them. John Obadiah leaned on his crutches and his eyes looked like slits to Elias. He knew from that sign that things were going to escalate. Elias tensed, waiting for the next onslaught.

"I know why you kept it a secret--'cause you were rescued by a woman--that Seneca squaw that hangs 'round here. Why was she there so early in the mornin'?"

Without pausing, he continued in a louder voice filled with more emotion.

"I told you to stay clear of her--sneakin' 'round behind my back, in my absence..."

Elias wondered who told his volatile father about the entire incident, and had the details correct, right down to the fact that Gala was involved--certainly not Gala, nor Jesse. Must have been someone else out there that morning. But who? Cornplanter is a small place, he thought, but he'd not heard gossip about Luke's falling in, neither had Ma'. Whoever told, waited for two weeks after John Obadiah's return from Pittsburgh.

"Well, Pa', it was a good thing she was nearby. It was early in the morning and foggy. It seemed to me that no one was there except Luke and me."

"What was Luke doin' out there on the river bank so early?"

Elias spied Luke and Gala among the bystanders. He looked straight at him and signaled for him to leave the landings and go home. He watched Luke melt into the rear of the crowd and head for the Oil Creek footbridge.

"Luke was fishing, Pa' No harm in that..."

"Fishin'! With what? I thought his fish pole got used for kindlin' wood last winter. Where'd he get a fishin' pole?"

Elias felt his palms getting sweaty, and his face flushed.

"I made one for him..."

"You gave him a fishin' pole? While there was meltin' ice on the river, boy?"

"Yes, sir, I did. Luke loves to fish..." Elias felt trapped--like a wild rabbit caught in a snare. Being made a fool in front of all these people--friends, dockworkers, neighbors, and boats' crews was almost more than he could bear.

"Well, I see you were tryin' to cover up a really bad mistake, to keep you from lookin' a fool. And keepin' it a secret from me that you're hangin' 'round that Indian squaw. You are too stupid to be my son! I ought to disown you here and now before you bring home some half-breed young'un into my house. You stupid..."

With those crushing words, John Obadiah picked up one of his crutches and swung it at his son's head. Instead, it hit Elias' right shoulder. Instinctively, he took a step away and the second swing missed its target completely.

Suddenly a snarling, growling dog broke through the circle of onlookers. Elias saw Mohwa, his head down and white teeth bared, hurl himself at John Obadiah. The dog's coat was bristled from head to tail as he sank his teeth into the swinging crutch. He growled and pulled at the wooden prop while John Obadiah held onto his support piece and cursed at the dog. It looked like a tug-of-war.

He heard several men in the crowd murmur and a woman steamboat passenger gasp. The circle of onlookers opened wider. Elias moved toward Gala's dog and spoke quietly to him. Instantly, Mohwa released his grip on the would-be weapon. Then he heard an almost inaudible command from deep in the crowd of onlookers. The dog looked up at Elias and then retreated through the forest of legs.

Elias thought that his father looked dazed. His eyes glittered and he was working his jaw. Saliva dribbled from the corner of his mouth. He watched, transfixed as his assailant, balanced between a nearby railing and his remaining crutch slid his hand to his side. Deftly, he pulled out a knife from its sheath strapped to his left leg. He screamed obscenities at Elias. Then he positioned the knife to throw it. Clearly, he was the target.

Elias saw the crowd move as one, away from his angry, out-of-control father and him. Just then, two men he recognized as neighbors moved toward John Obadiah from behind and seized both of his arms, restraining him.

"Drop the knife!" someone in the crowd shouted.

Elias froze for several seconds reasoning whether he should help his father to their cabin, or make his escape. When the attacker continued his wrathful, verbal assaults against Elias, and struggled against his restrainers, he was clear on his decision.

He saw someone suddenly pushing through the crowd. Jesse approached his raving boss with a deerskin pouch full of water. He moved right in front of John Obadiah and poured the cold river water onto his head. It ran down his torso to his leg until it trickled to his boot, forming a wide puddle on the brown muddy surface of the steamboat flats. The knife fell with a thud several feet away from John Obadiah.

"That'll cool him off--bring him to his right senses." Jesse turned to him. "You'd best get out of here, Elias. No reason for you to stay. I'll deal with your Pa'. Don't worry. I'll see to it that he gets home safe a little later. Good luck to you."

He beat a hasty retreat from his fuming father and the astounded audience. He escaped to the footbridge and ran toward the cabin.

...

Luke sat on the edge of the hearth with Molly who had her arm around his slight, shaking shoulders. His blue eyes were red from crying.

She spoke to Luke in a quiet voice.

"I'm sorry that you were on the landing when Pa' got so angry--the very thing we were trying to avoid. Good you told me what happened, because I expect Elias at any minute. Don't know about Pa'. I hope he won't follow him, if he's still acting so crazy…"

In just minutes, Luke heard someone running hard, pounding the ground, then quick, heavy footsteps on the small stoop. The door burst open and Elias entered, sweating and breathing hard. He hurried to the hearth and hugged his mother and then Luke.

"He's acting mighty crazed, but Jesse's going to stay with him there for a while, hoping that he'll come to his senses."

Elias looked into his mother's eyes and then Luke's. "The time's come. I knew it would sooner or later. We all did. I'm leaving."

Elias quickly climbed the wooden ladder to the upper sleeping berth, and returned with a pack that looked to Luke like a rolled-up blanket. He had a deer skin water pouch, his long rifle, and a hat, a black hat with a buck-tail insignia.

"What's that?"

"My new hat, Luke. I made it about a month ago. Called a 'bucktail' hat. I'm going to join some riflemen from up north, Warren County, in the next few days. They're woodsmen--hunters like you and me, good shots with the rifle. They'll be rafting down the river, headed for Pittsburgh to join the army."

Luke's jaw dropped and then his already reddened eyes and damp lashes produced more tears that trickled down his face in muddy streaks, then onto the front of his shirt.

"You're leaving, Elias?" he stammered. He felt crushed and frightened. It was as if the bottom had just dropped out from under him. Elias, his big brother, protector, and teacher was leaving. He felt sick, and his stomach began to ache.

"Where are you going to be, Elias?"

"Luke, I don't know. In war, I recon you go where they tell you."

Luke looked at Molly whose eyes were welled up with tears.

"Luke, Elias can't stay here with your Pa' so riled up. For some reason, Pa' blames everything on Elias, whether he's done anything wrong or not. It's not good for Elias--not good for any of us--but it's far worse for Elias. Safest for him to go away for a while--maybe for a couple of months."

Molly quickly stood and produced a packet of food and a red flannel shirt.

"I just got the last of the sewing done on your shirt, son, and here's your favorite beef jerky and some cornbread. It'll keep for days and still be good. Just see to it that it stays dry."

Wanting to ask more questions, but feeling too overwhelmed, Luke wiped his runny nose on his shirtsleeve and tried to stop crying so he could listen. How could things change so quickly? Why was Pa' being so mean?

His mother was talking.

"Elias, I'll send word to Uncle Matthias at Fryburg like we discussed. Don't worry about Luke and me. We're going to be all right. Just you write and let us know where you are. I'll watch for your letters when they come up from Pittsburgh on the steamboat. Jesse gets the mail off the boat. I'll check with him and tell him Luke and I are looking for your letters. And we'll write you--just have to know where to send them."

As he listened, he realized that Elias and his mother had things planned out ahead of time. He thought about the fact that they had not included him, but in a way, he felt grateful. Keeping secrets was difficult for him.

His mother stood and faced Elias.

"Elias, I know the Bucktails are near ready to leave Warren, but where are you going to stay until they get here to fetch you?"

"I'll be camped out a little south of the river flats, down around the bend. Those guys, the Bucktails will be looking for vittles when they get here, so folks along the way will be feeding us--same here in Cornplanter. Gala's going to be coming into town, so we'll know when they're about to leave and move south. She knows Martin, and he's in charge of one raft, so they'll pick me up--out of sight of Pa'."

Luke felt Elias' eyes on him.

"Luke, you and Ma' don't know where I am, do you? As far as anyone is concerned, I'm just 'gone,' and you don't know where."

Numbly, Luke nodded in agreement. That secret, he would keep. He'd never tell. ___

Through eyes blurred with tears, Luke watched Elias embrace their mother. Then, he felt the strong arms and warm breath of his beloved brother as he kissed him on the head. He wondered if it would be for the last time.

Then Elias was gone.

...

Last season's cattails, fuzzy and shedding, lined the base of the long-forested river hill that ran almost to the water's edge at the Allegheny River just south of Cornplanter. Neither Elias nor Gala had slept. Light from the waning moon had shown directly on them and reflected off the river waters as well, making sleep all but impossible on their last night together. Their mounting sorrow about Elias' departure was fueled by separation anxiety. Neither Elias nor Gala had traveled more than twenty-five miles from Cornplanter in any direction.

Gala tried to control her concerns for his traveling far away into what appeared to be the government's growing conflict with the Confederacy. She braced herself emotionally for his actual disappearance from her life. Her feelings of increasing sadness were welling up this morning, and she feared that her reaction to his last touch would cause him more grief. Clearly, he had had enough trouble.

She had witnessed John Obadiah's outburst and attempted attack on Elias that day on the docks. How humiliating for him, and for her too, "that Seneca Squaw," as Elias' father had referred to her. At that point, she had shrunk back away from the crowd and retreated quietly from the terrible trauma. John Obadiah's depiction of her was based on his prejudice against her people, the Senecas, not on any information about her.

In fact, she had stayed with her grandmother, a white woman living about a mile from the small Cornplanter settlement. From that loving relative, she had learned to read and write, cook and sew like any girl in Cornplanter. It was true that she lived part of the time with her Seneca family farther north and in the mountains. She felt grateful for the knowledge and skills she gained from both experiences--learning the Whiteman's ways and the ways of the Seneca's. She felt better prepared for the future, whatever that was now, she had difficulty imagining, especially in a life without Elias. She prayed that he would return to her.

"Elias, listen! I hear singing! It must be the Bucktails' raft

32

coming now."

Elias ate his last bite of bread and got to his feet quickly. He stretched out his hand to her, and together they climbed out onto a half-submerged boulder where they'd hung her sleeping blanket as a marker for Martin. From upstream, they could hear hardy male voices accompanied by someone strumming a guitar.

"John Brown's knapsack is strapped upon his back!
John Brown's knapsack is strapped upon his back!
His soul's marching on!
Glory, Halle-hallelujah! Glory, Halle-hallelujah!"

Suddenly, a raft glided into sight, carried by the current of the main channel. It was a large flatboat with the stars and stripes flying, mounted on a green Hickory pole topped by a buck tail. She could hear singing.

Gala could feel goose bumps on her arms and the hair at the nape of her neck rose at the sound of the fife and drums and the sight of the men, soldiers going to war.

"Gala, give them the signal. I will get my rifle and belongings," He disappeared into the bushes on the riverbank behind the boulder.

She picked up her red and brown blanket, waving it high over her head. A man at the front of the raft took off his cap and waved back. With a shout, the singing accompanied by the fife and drums ceased and several of the rafters manned long poles, maneuvering the flat boat at the north shore, toward her location on the rock.

As they approached, she could see that the men on board the big wooden flatboat were all wearing red flannel shirts and hats with the buck-tail insigne, that gave the group of soldiers their name, The Bucktails. Martin and several hardy-looking soldiers handled the long poles that they were using to direct the raft toward the shore.

When Elias climbed on to the rock and stood beside her, the men all shouted, cheered, and took off their caps, waving them in the air.

"Hello! We found you! Welcome aboard!"

Ruddy-faced, and smiling, Martin jumped off of the boat while others held it in place. He shook hands with Elias, patted him on the back, and offered his hand to Gala.

"He's in good company with us, the Bucktails."

She forced a smile, and looked Martin in the eyes. "Please take care--all of you."

She turned to Elias who took her in his arms for their last embrace, and all the soldiers were silent for a moment, bowing their heads as if in reverence to the parting couple. Then a loud shout went up and echoed off the hillside.

"Three rousing cheers for the Elias! Rah! Rah! Rah! Three rousing cheers for the Union! Rah! Rah! Rah!"

With that Martin jumped aboard, and took Elias' belongs and gun with him while Elias turned to Gala and looked into her eyes.

"Wait for me. I will return."

She could only nod. She could not trust her voice. She did not want to cry, not now. That would happen later, she thought.

Then Elias turned and jumped onto the barge with the Bucktails. They pushed off, and maneuvered into the main channel. Once well underway again, they burst into song, with the drums rumbling and echoing off the sides of the long river hills as Elias waved his hat to Gala who stood on the boulder, alone. As she waved farewell, her left hand moved to her swelling abdomen.

Her eyes filled with tears as the raft bearing her beloved Elias disappeared around a bend in the Allegheny.

"You didn't need to know, Elias. You have much on your mind and many changes in your life now. I carry your spirit with me. I am happy in my sorrow of losing you to the army."

She stopped before climbing down from the boulder, turned her back to the river, and looked up to the top of the familiar river ridge in front of her. Many trees were light green from the Spring rains. As she scanned the growing forest, she spied a blackened stretch nearer to Oil Creek. Even from this vantage point, she could see the devastation of the land. The destruction was glaring--a harsh, black gash in the light green spring growth of the un-touched forest. What would her great warrior ancestor, Chief Cornplanter say to this land laid bare by mining of oil on this sacred space? She stood in silence, grieving for her people and their loss. Then, looking up, she raised her hands over her head toward the open sky.

"I pray that this land will heal. I pray that Elias will return to me."

Silently, tears ran down her smooth tan cheeks.

Katherine's Desolation

Village of Brooklyn, New York April 1861

An early spring rain sprinkled fine drops onto Katherine's light brown hair that emerged from under the black veil covering her face and head as she gracefully maneuvered her slim body around piles of thick, round rope, stacks of cavernous crates and palates piled high with building materials on the damp docks of the Brooklyn Navy Yard. Pausing for a moment to look toward the water, she saw small surface waves kicked up by the light breeze that came into the harbor from the east.

The drifting gray clouds and green foamy water created a feeling of gloom and despair. The death of her mother, her only parent created an irreplaceable loss that had resulted in the sudden and dire reversal of circumstances for fifteen-year-old Katherine. Her future had been turned upside-down in a matter of hours following her mother's funeral just three months earlier. Katherine stood staring out to sea, lost in the memory...

...

The wild wintery weather had dominated, governing this day that seemed out of control and that had fallen upon them like a torrent of icy water during a spring thaw in the Catskills. The cold January wind had whipped black coats and sent heavy capes twisting, as the mourners clutched their flapping garments to steel themselves against the Arctic blast. The heads of neighbors and friends bent downward in an effort to keep warm as the wind renewed its strength, rushing across the Hudson River, ascending the slopes, and washing over the Green-Wood Cemetery located at one of the highest points in the Village of Brooklyn.

For Katherine, the scene sliced into her mind, and then planted itself there, causing her head to throb, and her throat to burn. She gripped the cold iron rail that surrounded the black pit before her. She felt her eyes fill with burning tears, blurring out the dark wooden coffin that bore her mother's body. She had no feeling in her toes. The high button leather shoes that her mother had had made for her just weeks before, lost their protection against the bitter cold.

She tried to wiggle her toes-first on left foot, then on right-but was unable to feel anything.

In February 1854, just two months after Katherine's father had enrolled his eight-year-old daughter in school, horrifying news had rocked the household. News came that the Captain's ship had capsized during a storm, off the French coast with all hands unaccounted for, including Captain Emile Van De Mer. At the shock of that dire message, his, wife, Yevette Van de Mere had cried aloud. Her unrestrained anguish had alerted Katherine who was a room apart, practicing her piano scales and the young girl had crept toward the sobbing sounds. She witnessed her mother's slight slender body, heaving with racking sobs, while being comforted by a faithful family servant. Her father's disappearance at sea continued to haunt her, and left a permanent rent in the fabric of her young life.

The shock of her mother's death had created not only overwhelming grief, but disorientation of being set adrift in her young and previously protected life with no parents nor family close by. Terror, her fear of loss of control, present and future, contributed to her unrelenting tremors as well. She had sensed foreboding and danger, but was unable to focus on its origins, its roots.

She had felt a sudden sharp poke in her back and turned quickly to see a large, portly man swathed in black withdrawing his walking stick he had used as a prod to alert her. He was prompting her to accept the short-handled shovel he held out to her. Katherine shook her head and gestured for him to undertake the terrible task. He nodded in agreement.

With his large bulky body, her stepfather, the barrister, Petrus Plugge hoisted a shovel-full of dark, clotted dirt and deposited it onto the casket's lid. It landed with a resounding thud, like the first clap of thunder in a sudden rainstorm, the sound even rising above the whistling of the winter wind. To Katherine, it was a grim announcement of the finality of its intension, to bury her mother's casket.

Burning bile had risen into her throat. Her ears began to ring as she steadied herself against the fence. How would her life change now with both parents gone? She could only guess, but the knot in the pit of her gut filled her with dread. Her corset felt too tight, causing her breaths to come in short, shallow gasps. If only she could loosen it. She felt desperate.

Then, buffeted by the unrelenting blasts of winter wind, she had backed slowly away from the gapping gash in the ground, her mother's final resting place. With head bent down and away from the cold waves of air, she slowly followed her stepfather who lumbered toward the waiting carriage draped in black.

She remembered as they had departed the cemetery, her feelings of sadness that no one would be coming home to her, not Pa-pa', and now, not Ma-ma'. She had felt deserted-desolate and abandoned, but above all, apprehensive...

...

The April rain was increasing on the docks of the Brooklyn Navy Yard, as if urging her to move off of them or under a shelter. She shook herself to quit her reverie. She turned away from the open sea to leave, but another memory forced its way into her consciousness. The wooden docks that tethered bobbing boats and a fleet of fast steam-powered ships triggered pleasant memories...

...

She recalled that in 1850, when she was five years old, she had come here with her father. Holding her small hand, he had walked her around the moored sailing ships that smelled of fish, while seagulls swooped and called to each other as they searched for food. She had looked up at him in wonder, in awe. He seemed strong and invincible, and had a kind smile and gentle touch, yet a firm, warm grip on her small soft hand.

As the salty water slapped both the underneath of the support pieces of the docks and the water craft tied up there, he had good-naturedly questioned her.

"Now, Katie, which one is our ship?" She'd begin pointing with her tiny finger and reading ships' names painted on the bows—syllable-by-syllable. It was an exciting game, passing one ship after another, all tied up at the long docks.

"This one, Papa'? The Al-bit-ross?" And they would both laugh, shake their heads and say, "No, not that one." The game continued until they came upon her father's vessel. Then she would shout it out.

"This one, Papa', this one! The *West Wind*!" He'd hugged her close and picked her up, carrying her across the narrow gangplank and onto his ship...

Now back to the present-April 1861, the rain trickling from her black hat to her veil then on to her straight nose brought Katherine back from her reverie. She hastened her steps toward her destination at the end of the dock. When she arrived at the door of the Assistant Harbor Master, she adjusted her veil, and opened the door slowly.

"Good day, Miss Van de Mere. I have been expecting you. Come in from the rain and have tea with me."

As she removed her heavy travel cloak and shook off the rain, she looked into the wrinkled, smiling face of her father's old friend, Ebenezer Elliot. He took her black travel wrap, and offered her a wooden chair near the warmth provided by the pot-bellied stove that dominated the center of his sizable office.

These several recent, but brief visits to Ebenezer were a lifeline for Katherine. For two months since her mother's death, she had been cut off from her familiar surroundings and pleasant past. She desperately wanted to ask for help, but was unsure of how to go about it. Failure of such an attempt and detection by Barrister Plugge could land her in the Refuge in the East River or the Women's Asylum for the Insane. So, she restrained herself and found solace in short visits to this familiar place with its good memories. But time was of the essence and the risk of detection, great.

Over a cup of hot tea, she asked, "Any word from Cousin Fredrick, Ebenezer?"

Ebenezer held her in his gaze. "Not yet, Miss Katherine...not yet. The North Atlantic is rough water this early, but leastwise, some ships will be arriving in a fortnight or so."

Having gotten an answer to her most urgent question, she finished her tea and rose to depart.

"My carriage is waiting in the street and my time is limited. May I call again soon, Ebenezer?"

He nodded and smiled.

She felt hopeful for the first time in days. Her visits here gave her the strength to carry on, for a while at least.

...

Several weeks after her visit to Ebenezer at the Navy Yard, Katherine sat on a straight-backed chair at her place of employment, her step-father's business. Her overseer, Madame de Brunt, the manager of the establishment had called her into the office. Madame De Brunt was mentioning that their boss, the Barrister Plugge, an expert on maritime legal issues was scheduled to appear in court for the day. Katherine quickly took advantage of her step-father's being a distance from Manhattan and wheedled permission from the manager to take a buggy ride.

"I need to take some air."

When Madame de Brunt hesitated and the request was followed by silence, she begged her boss.

"Well, I am taking quite a risk for you. You understand?"

Katherine hurried to the street and hailed a carriage. She headed south to the Navy Yard once again. She tenaciously clung to one hope, her only hope, and here she was again, back at the Navy yard, she mused, eager for news that seemed never to come. Even at her young age and her formerly sheltered life, she realized that she was in dire circumstances, caught in a web that held little promise of releasing her, like a housefly at the mercy of a skulking spider.

Just thinking about her complicated situation filled her with mounting anxiety. To deter the oncoming feeling of panic, she depended upon the comforting words of her late father. Memories of him helped to sustain her, and one of his wise sayings had stayed with her from earliest childhood.

"It's always darkest before the dawn. It's always darkest before the dawn," she said aloud, since no one was nearby to overhear her. She used that saying as a mantra to get her through each day--each hour. Repeating it in her mind infused her with hope and damped down her continuing state of near panic. She was hopeful of help. Hopeful of escaping her situation. Hope was what kept her returning to this familiar place of comfort. The carriage halted and the driver placed a small wooden step at the carriage door for her.

As she hurried toward Ebenezer's office, she realized that the shipyard was more active than during her last visit, just a fortnight ago. This time, it had a very different feel for Katherine.

On a distant pier in front of her, soldiers, men dressed in various descriptions milled about a number of uniformed officers as they managed equipment, baggage and weapons. As she watched, men kneeled, maneuvering supplies into bulky brown bags.

When she came upon them, she read the shoulder patch on a uniform: THIRTEENTH REGIMENT NEW YORK MILITIA.

They looked like a swarm of bees, as in a hive, busily preparing for activity of some sort. They were so engrossed that they seemed not to take notice of her walking among them. She thought that several looked no older than she, young smooth faces lacking wrinkles and void of facial hair. She had heard about them. At her step-father's place of business, she had overheard discussions among clients about President Lincoln calling out the New York militias to join the federal forces in the War of Rebellion. These milling men apparently were among those busily preparing to follow the President's orders.

Amid the din of organizing soldiers, she thought about other differences in the Yard from when she had come here with her father. Then, all of the vessels they saw were sailing ships with tall, stately, wooden masts and white sails, reminding young Katherine of the fluttering miller moths that tumbled from her father's belongings on his return from a European voyage. Of today's moored vessels, at least half of them were steam-powered with huge wooden paddlewheels, not totally dependent on the whims of the winds, but powered by coal and steam. Taking in the scene playing out before her, she was lost in thought.

A persistent question, something that she'd not voiced to anyone kept returning to her: would it have been different for her father if the *West Wind* had been a more modern ship, a paddlewheel steamer? Was he alive somewhere? He was considered missing, but no report had come to her mourning mother about his body being recovered, washed onto a lonely beach somewhere along the French coast. For Katherine, not knowing haunted her, suspending the unknown in her mind-like a persistent harbor fog that obscured the visions of her future and would not go away. If her father were here now, everything would be drastically different.

When she arrived at the door of the Assistant Harbor Master, she adjusted her veil, and opened the door slowly. Ebenezer arose from his seat at a large wooden desk to greet her.

"Good day, Miss Katherine. I have been expecting you to return sooner. I am very glad to see you. Come in and have tea with me."

He took her black travel wrap, and, as before offered her the wooden chair near the pot-bellied stove. She welcomed the warmth that emanated from its heavy iron furnace.

As she took her seat, she noticed a difference from her previous visit. This time, her friend's smile had faded quickly and he stood and paced while she sat and listened. He seemed to forget his offer of tea altogether. Perhaps the accelerated activity of the shipyard was having an effect on Ebenezer.

"Miss Katherine, I have some news. It's not the news you are seeking, but I must relate it to you, as I am sure it is of your concern." He paused and looked at her quizzically.

"Your step-father, Barrister Plugge came by here just yesterday, and said some things that caused me concern-concern for you. And I beg that you not think me officious. What I am about to say, I say because your father, Captain Van de Mere and I were good friends and because, as his friend, I extend to you, his daughter, my friendship. I care about your welfare, Miss Katherine."

Just hearing the name of her step-father caused her body to tense and she clenched her fists so tightly that she could see they turned white at the knuckles. She felt her left eyelid begin to twitch. She sat forward in her chair.

"He came here? Why? What was his business?"

"He was querying me in regards to the latest news of Mr. Lincoln's signing the Proclamation of the Blockade--the blockading of southern ports, one of the strategies in this struggle to re-unite our country. The President signed it just two days ago. I saved you yesterday's *New York Times* so you could read about it, in case it escaped your notice." With that, he handed her the folded newspaper.

She read aloud, "April 20, 1861: 'Government has done well by declaring Southern ports under blockade. Such a course has been repeatedly urged by the *Times*. The blockade should be maintained at every point by a competent force. Such force exists in the greatest abundance in our commercial marine, of which Government can readily avail itself...'"

"Ebenezer, what does this have to do with my stepfather?"

"Yes, well, I'm coming to that." He took a chair across from her and continued.

"He is looking to buy an interest in one of the shipbuilding companies here at the yard. He spoke with some authority that Mr. Lincoln's declaration came well before the Union's ready--only three ships that are fit to enforce a blockade, right now. Said Navy Secretary Gideon Welles will be expanding the Navy's fleet right away. Not sure where he got his information, but I do remember that he knows a good number of people in high places--this city and the nation's capital. He queried me, asking if the government had yet offered a contract to any of the builders here in Brooklyn. Said to let him know when I get word."

He paused and took a deep breath and adjusted his wire-rimmed spectacles to sit farther back on his nose, making his gray, neatly trimmed mustache twitch as he did so.

"I told him that I had heard nothing, or at least not yet. Then I said, 'So, you've got some cash-some gold--for such investment?' And he said he had and what he said next concerned me the most. He said that as soon as you sign over the deed to your property with the house, he would have even more, because he plans to sell that property."

"What! He said that?" she felt confused. She struggled to remember. "Ebenezer, I had no idea that I was listed on the deed to that property. No one told me, certainly not the Barrister, not even Mama'."

"Perhaps, in her illness, she either forgot, or did not know it herself. Your father purchased that place when you were a wee thing, so he apparently did put your name on the title then. Maybe your Mama' just forgot."

"So, the Barrister is planning to get me to give up more of what is rightfully mine?"

"Apparently, and it brought to mind that it was a peculiar thing to admit to me. I thought it strange."

He paused.

"What do you mean, 'give up more?'"

When she did not answer, he went on.

"And why do you not know about his plans, Miss Katherine? Is he going to sell the house right out from under you?"

"Had he been imbibing in spirits? What time of day was it? He carries a silver flask in his waist pocket, so perhaps his tongue had been loosened."

"Yes, perhaps. He did come in late afternoon. Quite so. But, why do you not know about his plans, Miss Katherine? Is he going to dispose of your house without your knowing?"

Suddenly overwhelmed with confusion and alarm, she was speechless. She felt her heart pounding and her breaths came only in shallow gasps. 'It's always darkest before the dawn...' She recited her mantra to herself three times until she regained her voice and her eyelid stopped moving in spasms. She felt her friend's eyes on her. He waited patiently and his face had an expression of pity.

Finally, the dammed-up emotions she had kept in check for

42

weeks spilled over the top, and she began to confess a portion of what had happened to her.

"As you know, Mama' died in January last, and since then, I have been at the mercy of Barrister Plugge. On the very day of her burial, he informed me that Papa's savings for Mama' and me were gone. I was so shocked that I knew not how to respond. He said that I would not be going back to the Brooklyn Female Academy, and that I had to go to work--for him. He put me out of the house, Ebenezer. And please, no one else but you knows, only you. I have said nothing to anyone."

"But Miss Katherine that is a terrible fix in which he placed you. And why have you said nothing to anyone about this?"

"There is more to what he did to me, but I dare not speak a word of it. He said that if I did tell what happened, no one would believe me."

Katherine remembered the words of the Reverend Quackenbush's wife to whom she had appealed for help back in January, the month of her mother's death...

"You evil child--saying such things about Barrister Plugge! Unspeakable! He is such a pillar of our community... an elder of the church... an influential member of society! Hush, child, or you could become an orphan in the almshouse or end up in the Lunatic Asylum on Blackwell's Island in the East River! Think of your poor mother. She would turn in her grave at such prattle! That talk will only get you in deep trouble! Were it not for your dear mother, I would relate your charge to the Barrister."

To Ebenezer she said, "The Barrister told me, in his words, that 'no one would believe a mere child who is crazed by her mother's recent death.' He said that he would have me committed to The Women's Lunatic Asylum--shut away by legal order--and you know, he has the knowledge and wherewithal to do so."

She could feel her eyes fill with tears that brimmed over the edges, then streamed down her face. She shook with sobs as she retrieved a lace-trimmed handkerchief from the pocket of her skirt.

In a shaky voice, she continued.

"That is the reason for my visits to you as of recent. I desperately need to hear news of Cousin Fredrick and know when he returns here."

That said, she pulled a beige envelope from a pocket in her skirt, and handed it to Ebenezer.

"Please take this letter. It is for Fredrick when, or if he gets here. It is good that I prepared it as I now think that my visits to you will be curtailed. In fact, my tormentor knows not of my short episodes of freedom. Since he has papers for my signature, I may be locked in until I sign."

She saw the expression on Ebenezer's face, and realized that he now understood the urgency and brevity of her previous trips to the shipyard. He turned and secured her letter for Fredrick in the company safe behind him.

"I now understand that you are in desperate straits, Miss Katherine. I am so sorry. Where are you staying, may I ask?"

"Somewhere not far away, but I have little free time, and am closely watched by the manager of my stepfather's business. Therefore, my brief visits with you are a respite for me--to get away from that awful place, and to stay in touch with such a friend as you. Now, I must take my leave as I have a carriage awaiting me."

She jumped to her feet and reached for her wrap and veil, but then hesitated.

"Ebenezer, when do you think we may get word from Fredrick?"

"My dear Miss Katherine, the sailing season is just beginning. The rough waters of the North Atlantic keep most from setting sail until later in the spring. Pray, do have patience." He looked at her over the top of his spectacles and hesitated. "We could hear from him in a fortnight or so."

Ebenezer helped her ready herself for the outdoors, and accompanied her to the door.

"I will keep watch for news from Fredrick. Will you return here next week?"

"I do not know, and please, not a word of this to anyone."

"You have my word. The wind's picking up, so don't tarry on the dock. Looks like a storm's brewing up out there."

Katherine felt the rocking of the carriage, and heard the voice of the driver ordering the horse to a halt. All too soon, they had returned to the place of the Barrister's business. A business that she was sure he had kept hidden from her mother. Mama' would never have agreed to such goings-on as these. And now, I am enmeshed in it. It is so disgusting.

She felt humiliated, degraded. Her palms began to sweat as she hoisted her skirts and alighted from the carriage. She paid the driver and bid him adieu. Unnoticed by the occupants of the main level of the establishment, Katherine slipped around to a side entrance, and climbed the back stairs to her second-floor room. She hoped that the creaking, wooden steps would not give away her comings and goings. Amid shrill laughter, she could hear men's voices, the clinking of glassware and silverware-typical afternoon sounds that would gradually build during the evening as more customers appeared.

As she untied her shoelaces and loosened the strings of her corset, she reviewed her conversation with Ebenezer. His saying that Fredrick might arrive within several weeks made her feel hopeful. She could hold out against the promises of new assignments, "new experiences of the business" only so long. So far, her faking of illnesses, abdominal cramps and frequent throbbing headaches, convinced the manager to limit her assignments to entertaining clients by playing the piano and singing, bookkeeping and wine selection and ordering supplies, liquors and wines. At least, the actual nausea and vomiting of several weeks ago had subsided.

Now she needed to invent other maladies. She knew what was yet in store for her, and she felt like a trapped, helpless animal, a desperate critter with no way out of a one-way tunnel.

Fredrick's Voyage

April 1861, The North Atlantic

Shaken awake by the sudden violent motions of the ship, Fredrick Van de Mere clutched the frame of his rack to keep from rolling out. The sounds of shrieking winds and crashing waves brought him to sudden wakefulness. With considerable effort, he righted himself in his bunk. Just as he placed his feet on the deck, he pitched headlong into the next rack. Momentarily disoriented by what felt like the ship heaving, he scrambled into action. He knew that with another heave like that, the ship could swamp. The very thought alarmed him and he hurriedly pulled on his boots, and rain gear, and in the total darkness staggered along the bulkhead toward the hatch that opened to the main deck.

"Who has the helm," he said aloud as the ship swayed and the wind almost jerked the hatch cover from his hands. He struggled to close and latch it securely while the rain stung his bare hands and face. Water gleamed black and ominous on the shiny, open deck. Dark foaming swells of the North Atlantic pitched the 290-foot, three-masted steamship like a wooden toy boat in a Brooklyn storm drain after a sudden summer downpour. Fredrick clutched the icy rail, steadied himself against the ship's sway, and edged his way toward the bridge, sleet stinging his face as he waded through seawater four inches deep.

He could make out a dark, solitary figure hunched over the helm of the *SS Pelican* as it rolled with the rising swells and bucked against the fierce headwinds. The shrieking winds covered the sounds of his approach as he battened down the hatch and moved toward the helmsman.

"Steady as she rolls…"

Captain Mandville turned toward him momentarily.

"Ah, Van de Mere--we've hit a real squall, this. Can't trust the North Atlantic this time of year."

"It's a rough one, I'd say."

"Since you're about, check on the Second Mate Brun. He went amidships to secure the rigging--been gone a while now."

"Aye, aye, Captain."

Fredrick released the latch and the wind pinned him to the bulkhead momentarily. He struggled to free himself just as the ship pitched violently. When he regained his footing, he battened down the hatch and waded through swirling, salty sea foam that washed over the deck like soapy, sudsy water poured from a metal bathing tub. Grasping the bull rope along the gangway, he made his way onto the open deck to a pile of rigging, not properly stowed, apparently due to the sudden squall. No doubt that was the concern of the Second Mate and he had set out to take care of it. Fredrick scanned the deck, looking for signs of his shipmate. The rain drenched his face and occluded his vision. He blinked and realized that sleet was clinging to his eyelashes, eyebrows and his mustache. As he tried to clear his vision, he moved forward slowly looking for any sign of the Second Mate, the ship's navigator. Finally, he spotted a prone figure in a rain slicker-face-down on the flooded deck.

Fredrick lurched forward and grasped the Mate's left arm, raising his face from the water. When Brun failed to stir, Fredrick dragged the limp body, heavy with water toward the base of the mast. He steadied himself, his back to the solid wood, then grasped Brun under his armpits and slung the sodden, bulky body over his left shoulder. Fredrick, exerting all of his energy, took a wide stance, but lost his balance and leaned into the mainmast. He recovered and inched his way forward against the gale force winds.

He struggled to stay upright as the ship rolled to the starboard. He balanced himself at the rail with his right hand, now so cold that he could barely feel it. He worked his way, one step at a time, grasping the bull rope as a support and a guide in the blinding rain and rolling deck. He hunkered down against the wild wind and stinging sleet. Still the rescued man did not stir, did not regain consciousness. He was dead weight.

When Fredrick released the hatch, he fell into the wheelhouse with a crash. Captain Mandville turned toward him, but maintained his grip on the ship's wheel. A sailor, Perkins who had the watch approached Fredrick and the Second Mate who lay lifeless on the deck. Fredrick had to shout to be heard over the roaring of the storm.

"I found him face-down near the base of the mainmast, Captain, beside a pile of sails. Perkins, help me roll him on his side. He's been lying in sea water that covered the deck."

As the two men rolled the Second Mate, a river of red flowed from his open mouth. Fredrick dropped to his knees to examine the downed man more closely. Even in the dim light, Fredrick could see enough to report.

"He's white as a sheet, he is, and his lips are blue."

Fredrick put his ear to the victim's chest but realizing that he could hear nothing due to the noises of the storm, he placed his left hand to Clayton Brun's chest, but felt no rising and falling. Perkins did the same to confirm the findings.

"Try warming him with this blanket," the Captain shouted, and Perkins and Fredrick struggled to remove the victim's icy slicker and soaked shirt. As bare skin became visible, both men noticed that the right side of the chest had a caved-in appearance. Fredrick thought, still no breathing. He approached the Captain to discuss his findings.

"Looks like he might have slammed against something--a gust of wind knocked him into the mast, maybe?"

The Captain shouted above the din.

"A terrible blow, by the sounds of it." He turned toward Perkins. "Take the helm while I come over with the lantern."

"Aye, Captain." Perkins moved slowly toward the wheel.

As Captain Mandeville crossed the rolling deck, Fredrick returned to observe the body before him. From his experiences at sea, he held out little hope of Brun's recovery, and watched the captain's grim expression as he held the lantern to best advantage.

"As soon as we get free from this squall, we'll move him out of here." He turned to Perkins.

"When you are relieved, go to O'Murphy, the carpenter and tell him that Mr. Brun has died, and to prepare him a coffin. He should have enough wood. In fact, tell him to stand-by in case any of the passengers have suffered a similar fate. God knows, I hope not, but we are in very rough seas, and it's not over yet."

…

At last, the seas calmed and dawn came spreading deep red across the eastern horizon like the path of an artist's broad brush of red paint across canvas. Bloody red, Fredrick thought and remembered the teachings of Uncle Emile on their first voyage together. "Red sky in morning, sailors take warning…" Reviewing the calamities of the past night, the warning red sky seemed to be coming after the fact, or at least he hoped so.

When Captain Mandville took an accounting of his crew and

passengers just after first light, a second casualty came to his attention.

"Ah, Van de Mere, the carpenter has yet another task-- though a small project in comparison to Mr. Brun's requirements. A wee one was thrown to the deck, hits its head during the squall and has died just within this hour."

Fredrick removed his hat upon receiving this news and turned in the direction of the starboard rail. Standing forlornly away from the group of passengers, a young couple huddled together with two children, one a babe in arms and the other, a young boy who was tugging on his mother's coat.

"I will go now to inform O'Murphy that his work is not yet complete. Where is the child's body?" The Captain pointed toward a small, still bundle next to the hatch.

On his way to the carpenter, he passed by the lifeless toddler who, he recalled, just days before had energy to run up and down the ship's deck from one parent to the other.

Below, he found the carpenter, Morton O'Murphy lying in his bunk, but not asleep.

"O'Murphy, I've returned with news from steerage. A tiny child was badly injured at the height of last night's squall, no doubt. Captain says build a small box about 20 inches long with many holes in the sides to enable quick sinking. The parents are undone and need not watch that little casket float for any length of time. It needs a quick sinking."

"Ah, Van de Mere," the short, scrawny, red-haired Irishman rubbed his eyes with the back of his shirtsleeve and got off his bunk. "And we was lucky, we was that only two boxes I'm buildin'. Two year ago--a worst of times--I built as many as sixteen of them boxes when some in steerage died from fever, children too. Used every scrap of lumber aboard...I've heard tell of ten, twenty, maybe thirty from steerage dyin' from somethin', the smallpox, congestion of the lungs, scarlet fever, dysentery. I heard tell of such illness aboard that passengers were refused permission to land. Then what to do?"

"My second voyage from Bordeaux to America-to Brooklyn-my Uncle Emile, Captain Van de Mere took on passengers. Uncle Emile and the port's medical officer blocked the gangway and each passenger coming aboard was examined then and there. Three were turned away--refused passage due to illness. Uncle told me--nothing worse than having his passengers refused entry when they got to America..."

"No, nothing worse--other than this..." and O'Murphy gestured toward the large coffin that would soon be put to use. Then, without another word, he turned to begin construction of the second box.

...

The long mess table supported two coffins made of rough boards, the larger and longer structure holding the body of the Clayton Brun, the Second Mate, and the tiny coffin, by comparison, bearing the body of the two-year-old boy, Pierre Arlay.

Fredrick stood with the crew as the Bosun ordered the sailors to remove head covers. The cock-bill hung limply atop the gallant yards as tall, billowing white clouds drifted peacefully in the west. The ship sat motionless, the engines subdued, the sails out of trim in deference to the impending burial at sea.

Fredrick looked about him. Passengers gathered against the port side rails of the main deck. Captain Mandville stepped forward and stopped at the far end of the table that held the two coffins. He knew that in the absence of a priest or clergyman, the ship's captain officiated in the service. The rising sun felt warm on his skin and he gratefully accepted a modicum of comfort from the warmth, a pleasant contrast to last night's icy blasts of freezing rain and stinging sleet. He appreciated the relief that it brought.

"I am the resurrection and the life..." the Captain intoned. Fredrick became lost in memories of other burials at sea, almost too much for a young cabin boy of nine years to absorb, he thought.

"The Lord giveth and the Lord taketh away. Blessed be the Name of the Lord..."

Next, the Bosun signaled four of the crew to upend the mess table, plunging the large coffin into the ocean with a deep splash. Then, the tiny coffin followed.

"We therefore commit their bodies to the deep..."

Fredrick followed the gaze of the Captain, his crew and the passengers as the coffins floated away from the still ship. We're dead in the water, he thought, in the middle of the North Atlantic somewhere. Silence followed until the Bosun gave the order to dismiss and get underway.

Engines growled to life; the crew drew down the cock bill; and sailors and passengers returned their hats to their heads and began to move about. Off the port side, the coffins floated momentarily as the ship created a wake. Then, Fredrick noted, each coffin slowly sank into the deep, as was intended. He recited to himself.

"And we commit the bodies to the depths…amen."

…

As the three-masted steamship sailed into Upper New York Bay and approached the East River, the navigator put aside his spyglass and called out his final calculations to Captain Mandville, who shouted orders to the crew to drop the remaining sails. The 2700-ton ship chugged slowly into the docks at the Brooklyn Navy Yard as the crew manned the ropes and lowered the camels over the ship's port and starboard sides. As soon as the crew secured the *Pelican* in a berth, the captain surveyed the crews' work, climbed to the pilothouse, and joined his navigator. They talked as the Surgeon of the Yard accompanied by the Lieutenant of the Yard came aboard to take accounting with the First Mate of the immigrant passengers.

"Excellent soundings and calculations, Van de Mere. Where did you learn such skills at your age?"

For a moment, Fredrick was taken aback by the compliment from the stern, gruff captain who seldom smiled nor handed out compliments--to anyone. On this run from the Port of Bordeaux to Brooklyn, he had noted that the Captain ran a very tight ship in which he meted out discipline with an even hand, but where the ship's crew had good morale. This was his first voyage with Captain Mandville, and he knew that he and his cargo were in skilled hands. The sailors were well trained and the captain knew his business.

Fredrick smiled at such high praise, showing a row of straight white teeth beneath a carefully clipped brown mustache.

"Ah, Captain, I was a lucky lad, no doubt. You see, my uncle, Captain Emile Van de Mere took me to sea with him. I was his cabin boy. I was nine-years-old at the time. You see, my father, Capt. Van de Mere's brother succumbed to the fever in Charleston, South Carolina where I was born. Several years later, when my mother determined to marry a wealthy cotton farmer, she needed to find me a place to live."

"What, how did that come around?"

"The planter was much older than my mother and had grown kin of his own. Seems that he did not cotton to being burdened with another man's son to raise. At first, I was shocked and angry. But when Uncle Emile came to fetch me, and he told me about going to

51

sea with him, I was excited about that kind of adventure, and besides, I liked my uncle and his family. So soon I got over being angry and sick for home. As I got older, I came to understand that there was little else my mother could do other than re-marry. My father had no savings to speak of. How else could we have lived? She did what she had to do."

"So, Captain Van de Mere was your kin? Well, I'll be...I remember when word came that the *West Wind* went down. That was tragic. Where were you then?"

"I was in France. Uncle Emile treated me like his son. He never had a son, only a daughter. When I reached my fifteenth birthday, he determined that I needed an education and a trade. Just ten days before he was lost at sea, he took me to meet relatives of his wife, my Aunt Yevette. These kin were second cousins and all lived in the region of Bordeaux near the Garonne. They owned vineyards, took me in, taught me their language and I worked in the fields--planting, learning the soil, rootstock grafting, pruning, cultivating--all of that. It was an education and I think they were glad to a have another set of hands and a strong back. I learned the business and that's why I'm shipping these barrels of Sauvignon Blanc and Pino Noir to New York and Brooklyn. I am building a clientele, restaurants, hotels, and inns to buy our wine."

"Well, that's a story. You are a fortunate fellow--a wine merchant and a mighty good sailor, too."

The Captain began to stow the ship's log and he gathered up papers for the Harbor Master.

"Well, son, we need to get moving. I know you're ready to get off this ship. Where will you be staying until we set sail in five days coming? I need your contact in case plans change."

"I mentioned that Capt. Van de Mere had a daughter, my sweet cousin, Katherine. She had written to me after her mother passed just four months ago, and she was having a sorrowful time. Since she has no siblings, I am her only relative. Our correspondence has been scant, but I expect to stay with her in Brooklyn Heights. I wrote her address for you."

They were walking together toward the office of the Master of the Yard, when a slight, bespectacled figure moved slowly toward them, cane in hand.

"Ah, Captain Mandville! Master Fredrick! Welcome to Brooklyn."

Fredrick embraced his <u>old</u> friend, Ebenezer Elliot, then turned to the Captain and introduced them.

"Master Elliot is an old friend. When my uncle and I would make port here, Ebenezer always greeted us with hot tea and sweet biscuits made of oats and molasses--our regular welcome here."

He turned to Ebenezer.

"I was relating my circumstances of life with my uncle, now missing." He dropped his head and looked down at his boots. "I still miss him sorely."

"And I do as well, Fredrick. He was a saint of a man, he was. An honest, upright gentleman."

He looked up at the captain.

"Your crossing--how was it this time of year?" Ebenezer inquired. They walked slowly toward the port offices as they talked.

"Well, rough enough," the captain answered. "Four days out of Baltimore, we hit a big squall that endured the entire night. Had to work to keep from swamping--lots of pitch and roll. Worst of it was I lost my Second Mate. He'd been sailing with me for eleven years. Good man, good navigator, he was." He described the events of the storm and the subsequent deaths aboard and burial at sea.

"The big surprise was the blockade of the harbor at Baltimore, our first scheduled stop. A federal vessel warned us off at the mouth of the channel. Said there was unrest--riots, soldiers and civilians at the rail connection--Pratt Street at the Baltimore and Ohio and Wilmington Railroad stations. Told us that federal troops were in the midst of a hotbed of southern sympathizers who hate Lincoln."

"What's going on, Ebenezer? I have been following some of this rebellion through the French newspapers. It sounds serious. Let me hear the news."

"Yes, Fredrick, some people in Baltimore been throwing rocks, bricks, boards at the federal troops, and flaunting their new flag. Flying the colors of the South--right out in the streets. Protesting against the soldiers--mostly from Massachusetts who are trying to pass through on their way to Washington. Aiming to protect the capital from Virginians." He paused. "Virginia seceded from the union just last week--making nine states now siding with the South. Virginia's so close to the capitol that federal troops have been called in. When all this started, only old General Winfield Scott was head of the U.S. Army--and he's from Virginia! So, he and his assistant, Charles Stone--another southerner, scrambled up some troops--clerks and others to defend the capital…And if Maryland goes, Washington will be surrounded."

They entered Ebenezer's office and discussed the offloading plan, management and security of the ship's cargo. Captain Mandville removed himself to a far table to complete the required paperwork.

"Just got a wire in saying that the Norfolk Navy Yard is being evacuated. Things are getting worse..." Ebenezer paused and moved toward his safe.

"But of more importance to you, Fredrick..." and he bent to open the safe. Ebenezer lost no time in removing the beige envelope left by Katherine. He placed it in Fredrick's hands.

"Pray, examine the contents hastily, Fredrick. There is trouble in the wind, I fear."

At first, thinking that the envelope might be an invitation to stay at Katherine's house, he felt surprised at Ebenezer's assessment. He quickly ripped open the envelope to discover Katherine's letter. He started to read, and then abruptly sat down in a nearby chair, stunned by its contents. When he had finished, he looked at his old friend, then back at the letter, and ran his left hand through his sandy-colored hair.

"How much of this do you know about?"

"Enough that I am extremely relieved to see your face this day. I know that Barrister Plugge has removed Katherine from her family home, forbid her to return to the Brooklyn Female Academy, and has put her to work at a place she despises. She wanted not to give me details of where she is, nor the nature of the business she is forced to endure. I sensed her anguish and realize that she is in dire straits."

Fredrick related the contents of the letter.

"What is this place, the Red Lantern Inn? Where is it?"

"So that's where she abides. No wonder she is so upset! It is nothing better than a brothel. It is up from the waterfront on Mercer Street in Manhattan near Henry Street. Apparently, Plugge located his business in an area rife with men too long at sea. And now with regiments of the New York Militia called up, they frequent the area as well."

Ebenezer paused and looked into Fredrick's eyes.

"These are tumultuous times, my boy, tumultuous times." He turned toward the window that looked out onto the yard and the docks. Fredrick followed his gaze and saw soldiers swarming about, dressed in bright red knee breeches, white stockings, blue jackets, and red caps.

"Who are they, Ebenezer?"

"Those are our boys of the Fourteenth Regiment of the New York State Militia. Got called up to join the Union Army. Some of them are boarding the steamship, *Marion* tied up on Pier 5. And it just got back from transporting the Thirteenth New York Regiment to Annapolis last week. This place has been humming with activity. Sounds ominous, sending our soldiers off to fight. I don't like the look of it. Trouble's a'brewing in this country."

Captain Mandville approached and handed his completed papers to Ebenezer who took the opportunity to provide both men with more information about recent events in the country.

"You heard first-hand about the Baltimore riots. The federal government is setting up blockades of all southern ports. That surely will affect shipping to and from almost any port on the East Coast and the Gulf of Mexico. The newspapers are full of the latest news."

A discussion ensued among the three, then finally Captain Mandville turned to take his leave.

"I'll be bunking for five nights at the hotel on Fulton Street. Here's the address." He turned to Fredrick.

"Farewell, then--until Friday. And many thanks for standing in for the Second Mate. What a sad end he did meet." He paused, and then continued, "I am pleased to have had you aboard."

"Thank you, Captain."

Intent on supervising the offloading of the *Pelican,* the captain crossed over the threshold of Ebenezer's office, then turned and paused.

"Bad storms' are on the horizon in this country, all right."

With Captain Mandville gone, Fredrick turned to Ebenezer.

"I'm flummoxed by this horrid news from Katherine. Ebenezer, I need your help; I need your advice. We should move decisively and quickly."

The Red Lantern Inn

Manhattan, New York, April 1861

The manager of the Red Lantern Inn, Blanche de Brunt waved her plump, milky-white hands for emphasis, and when she spoke, her head, piled high with orange-red hair that was secured with a gold and pearl comb, bobbed about as she spoke. Her face was accentuated with bright red lips that clashed dangerously with her tresses, and her painted eyebrows rose and fell in sync with her voice volume's increases and decreases. Katherine thought that she looked the part of a marionette with her gaudy clothing and overwrought make-up, fresh from the stage of a Punch and Judy show.

"Katherine, Master Plugge was not pleased to come here yesterday and find you gone. He said he had important business to attend to and it involved you and your late mother's estate."

Katherine feigned a surprised expression.

"Business of my mother's estate? I wonder what it involves…"

"He did not discuss the matter with me." Her eyebrows raised as she spoke. "More important is the fact that you were not here when he came by. I was ill prepared for his appearance yesterday as he usually picks up the earnings on Friday mornings."

Katherine nodded, waiting.

"I did cover-up for you." She paused dramatically as if providing a cue for audience kudos. "I told him that I had sent you on an errand that involved your training here, to make several purchases for the inn. I'm not sure that he believed my story." She paused and looked directly at Katherine.

"Next he said, 'Under no circumstances is she to leave this building.' So, don't ask me about taking a buggy ride again." Her strident voice and her penciled eyebrows both had risen. "I like my job here and don't want to lose it."

She tossed her head to stress her point, making the long gold earrings that swung from each ear tinkle like tiny bells on Christmas Day.

"He told me that he will be back with papers. You'd better

be here because they are to be signed."

Her fingers, bejeweled and glittering with a ring on almost every digit drummed on the wooden table, then she stood abruptly.

"So, I need to work with you on something important. The Barrister Plugge informed me that he plans to bring an important, and wealthy client, a traveling man here on Friday evening and you are to entertain him. Not just with your singing and piano playing either. He had me keeping you back until he could bring a high-stepper who can pay well for your services."

Katherine involuntarily shrank back from the table at that pronouncement and felt an icy shiver run up her spine.

"When? Friday? That's in just two days!"

"Yes, and we have important preparations since this will be your first real customer. You must look voluptuous, so I'm to find you the perfect dress. And your hair--We'll rearrange your hair..." She cocked her head as she surveyed Katherine as if for the first time.

Suddenly, Katherine heard heavy footfalls on the wooden stairs leading to the main entrance from the street. Who could that be at this time of day? Deliveries come to the back door and into the kitchen, not in the front. Katherine and Blanche turned in unison as the Barrister stomped into the entry hall, shaking the rain off of his tall, black hat.

"Well, young lady. It's a good thing you're here this time. Where were you yesterday?"

Katherine sat up straight and took a deep breath.

"I went to the apothecary shop."

"Where?"

"On Wilson Street."

"Which one?"

"There are several. I don't remember which one..."

"What did you need from the apothecary?"

When she hesitated, he stared at her, frowning.

"I'm having headaches and I went for something to relieve them."

"Headaches!"

"Yes, Stepfather, headaches."

"What's wrong with you that you have headaches?" She could hear his voice rising with irritation. She fought back tears.

"I don't know."

Then she lost control and started to cry. A torrent of tears rolled down her cheeks.

"Well, say girl! What's the matter with you?"

"I wanted to get outside and take some air for a while. I am cooped up here--inside all the time."

She paused and like a bursting dam, her words flowed like a waterfall in the Catskills following a heavy rain.

"I miss my school friends. I want to return to school as Papa' had intended for me to do. And continue learning to play the piano." She took a shaky breath. "I don't want to be here!"

Sobbing, she laid her head in her folded arms on the tabletop. She heard a chair scrape the floor. The next thing she felt was someone grabbing her hair and jerking her head up, off of the table, and with her neck extended upward, she was staring into the red, sweaty face of her tormentor, the Barrister. She looked beyond him and saw the metal plates that decorated the ceiling of the dining room. Her neck hurt and her scalp was being stretched. She saw the sweat around his collar and smelled his sour breath. She was in agony. How she despised him…

"I have papers for you to sign. Here…" And he unfolded a sheath of papers, flattened them on the table, and then shoved them directly in front of her.

She felt his grip on her hair and scalp release and her head dropped forward, smacking the table top with a thud, and scattering the papers across the table. He gathered them again and shoved them toward her. She could barely see the papers and a place for signatures through her tears. Her head throbbed with pain.

"Sign here!" He thrust an inkwell and pen at her.

"What am I signing?"

When no answer came, she threw down the pen, spilling the ink from its container and it flowed, like the incoming tide across the table toward the gaudily ornamented manager.

"No! I will not sign papers against my will. I will not!"

She pushed herself away from the table and got to her feet, preparing to run.

"Get back here, you vixen! You will do as I say. Sign!"

Suddenly, she felt her body slammed onto the tabletop. She was face down and could feel his bulky body holding her in place. As he leaned into her, she felt his rigid appendage pressing into her buttocks. A horrible memory flashed into her aching head and battered brain.

She was back at her house in Brooklyn just hours following

her mother's burial…

. . .

The Barrister reached for her hands and put them between his own. Katherine was unaccustomed to touching and being touched. She instinctively pulled her hands back, away from him. He renewed his grip with his right hand and looked her in eyes.

"I told you that you would be taking your mother's place…" With that, his long-left arm reached around Katherine's waist and he pulled her to him.

The shock started in Katherine's head and zigzagged down her spine. She tried to pull away, but he held her firmly. He was so close she could smell his breath.

Suddenly, a red-hot log on the dying fire crumbled and scattered on the hearth in front of them. The room grew dimmer. She felt dizzy, and the bile rose in her throat. What was happening? What did he mean by, "You must take her place?"

They sat there like that, in front of the dying fire. She was trapped, unable to move. It seemed like hours to her. He pulled his silver flask from his vest and took a long drink. Then, with eyes gleaming in the low light of the spent fire, he pushed the flask toward her lips.

"Drink this. It will make things a lot easier." She struggled and gasped, and when he would not relent, she screamed.

"There's no one around. Don't make this difficult for me. I've been too long without. I need some relief. You can help me. It will be just in the eyes of God. Only the two of us need to know."

With that, he pushed the flask between her lips and tipped the flask up.

She gulped and sputtered as the burning liquid made its way into her mouth. Silently, he placed the flask between his knees and put his hand over her mouth, waiting for the inevitable swallow. Then, he pushed the flask into her mouth again, then again. Finally, she began to feel strange and she stopped struggling against him. She could see an expression on his face that was foreign to her. His eyes studied her and he pulled her face to his.

Suddenly, his lips pressed against hers, then she could feel his tongue in her mouth. He would not let up as his tongue explored her. She closed her eyes as she felt him pull open the fastenings of her black crepe dress. The room was whirling as she felt his rough hand on her exposed right breast. She struggled and gasped trying

59

to roll away.

"Let me go!"

Her former protector and benefactor pulled her toward him as he reached up under her rustling skirts. To her horror, she saw her pink pantaloons dropped around her ankles, covering her black-laced shoes. She jerked her head away and screamed.

"Stop! Why are you doing this? You are my stepfather!"

"Let me say that this is your initiation into that job in Manhattan."

"No, no no!" she screaked. "I'll go to the constable! You can't do this to me!"

"Who is going to believe a word you say? You're just a grieving young woman who is hysterical over the death of her mother. It will be your word against mine, and I will deny everything. There are no witnesses. You might end up in Belleview or the Women's Hospital for the insane. I have the power to admit you to such a place. I have the power..."

He grabbed her head in the crotch of his left arm and forced the flask to her lips again. The amber liquid was hot in her mouth and dribbled out of the corners. She swallowed to keep from choking. Her throat ached from screaming and burned from the liquor. He forced the flask again and she sputtered and coughed, but swallowed most of it.

With her body pressed tightly to him now, he removed his waistcoat. She could feel him reaching below, between her legs. She heard his heavy leather belt hit the wooden parlor floor, the metal buckle making a loud clatter.

She felt light-headed, dizzy from the shock of the physical assault and the alcohol. Her throat ached and her mouth burned. She continued to squirm away from him. When he used both hands to remove his heavy boots, she rolled away, untangling her pantaloons from her shoes as she dragged them across the polished floor. She struggled to pull up the bodice of her dress over her exposed breasts and staggered to the steps that led upstairs.

As she grasped the smooth wood banister, she wretched and vomited. The slimy gastric contents with a foul odor dripped from the second to the first step as she struggled to gain momentum.

As she mounted the third step, she could hear him fast approaching with one boot yet on, dragging his breeches. The effects of the forced alcohol were doing what her pursuer had intended, making her dizzy and uncoordinated. Terrified, she looked back and saw a sight that would be burned into her memory forever. She saw her barrister, esteemed church-going stepfather naked from the waist down, except for his right boot. Even in the dim light of the whale oil lamp mounted at the bottom of the stairway, she could make out an appendage that protruded from under his large belly, poking from between his thighs. She had no idea what it was, but its presence alarmed her and made her cringe in the horror of such a thing—-of such an exposure of male parts. She screamed loudly, but was frozen in fear. She wretched and vomited again, this time on her stepfather's barefoot and highly polished boot.

He grabbed her around the waist with one arm, and dragged her through the slimy vomitus, back into the parlor in front of the dying fire. This time, he said not a word as he threw her face-up on the settee, knocking over her tea beaker and it rolled under the nearby chair. As she kicked and screamed, he pulled her soiled dress over her head and used the hem to muffle her screams...

...

Katherine's head throbbed; her mouth was dry as she lay on the hard-wooden floor. Where am I? Her back ached. She heard a voice, a woman's voice.

"Katherine, can you hear me?"

She rolled her head to one side and opened her eyes. All she could see was cloth, a skirt and then a face came into focus. A worried Blanche de Brunt peered down at her. She had a wet rag in her hand and she placed it on her forehead.

"He's gone, Katherine. It's all right for now, but he said to tell you that he'd be back."

She slowly lifted her aching head. Where was Papa'? Where was Fredrick? Where was help...?

...

"We've got to prepare you for Friday evening, Katherine."

"Oh, Blanche, how can I continue? What should I do?"

"Well, child. You'll just have to pretend. Act as if you're happy. Flirt with this client; sing and play the piano but remember your job is to make him want to go upstairs with you. Like the other girls do with their men callers. It will be my job to get him to pay what the Barrister says is your price--how much it will cost him to gain your favors..."

Suddenly Katherine felt hot stomach contents in her mouth.

She dashed to the bedside chamber pot, lifted the lid, and vomited.

"This will never do, dear. You've got to get yourself together." She moved toward the window and away from the odoriferous pot and the retching remonstrator.

When Katherine recovered and returned to sit on the edge of her bed, Blanche continued.

"Some of the girls pretend that the client is somebody they loved--an old gentleman-friend--someone other than the client."

Katherine took in a breath that came in short staccato gasps followed by a lengthy silence. Finally, she spoke.

"What does Athena do, Blanche? I've seen her taking a pill before she comes down to the parlor in the evening."

"Athena takes something to calm her nerves, laudanum. Pricilla takes several shots of whiskey. Most girls have ways to do it, until they're used to it. It can be difficult at first."

Blanche held out a red dress to Katherine.

"Here. This is a beautiful dress. Let's see how it fits you."

Katherine stood slowly and unbuttoned her dress.

"Take off your petticoat since this dress has a lining. You don't need all that."

She felt awkward and exposed in only her corset and pantaloons. She could feel Blanche's eyes on her.

"Katherine," Blanche said slowly, "loosen your corset. It looks very tight."

She complied, exposing the bulge she'd been hiding under layers of clothing. Silence followed and she turned to look at Blanche whose hand was covering her mouth. Her painted eyebrows were arched higher than Katherine had ever seen them.

"Katherine, you're with child! Look at your belly! Oh, God…"

The room went out of focus. She felt dizzy and her left eye began twitching. She took several deep breaths and blinked. She staggered to her bed and sat down hard.

"I wondered why I was getting fat. I thought it was having regular meals here."

Blanche flopped back in the armchair beside the dresser.

"Oh, Katherine, this changes everything! You can't entertain Plugge's wealthy client. Good lord!" She paused.

"Now, you're really in trouble with the Barrister. Being 'that way,' you're of no value." Her eyebrows leaped upward and her voice now at a high range was strident.

Katherine gasped.

"With child." The only man who had ever penetrated her was her stepfather, back in January for an entire month--over and over almost every night--before he sent her to the brothel. The idea made her dizzy. *He* was the cause of her pregnancy.

Quickly, she slid off the edge of the bed and hung over the chamber pot of the second time in the past thirty minutes. Her head swam; her body ached.

"Oh, Blanche! What am I to do?"

"I've got to think what you should do…"

...

That evening, Katherine played the piano and sang as men of various descriptions gathered in the lounge near the bar at the Red Lantern Inn. Blanche had assisted her in recovering, and after she left her alone, she closed her eyes, practiced deep breathing, and recited her father's soothing words, "It's always darkest before the dawn," over and over until she felt calm enough to enter the lounge. As she stood behind the curtain, Blanche appeared with a shot of whisky for her.

"Here, this will take the edge off of things."

As she gulped down the burning liquid, Katherine realized that her portion of the entertainment was an important part of the business. The show must go on. Buoyed up by the effect of the alcohol, she smoothed her dress, pulled her shoulders back, and stepped with determination into the commotion of the bustling saloon.

Tonight, the place seemed to be busier than usual. Among some regulars, she noticed some younger men. Probably soldiers out of uniform, scheduled to leave to join the Union Army soon.

Whether it was the whisky or providing the music, she realized that something was having a calming effect. She actually felt better than she had all day today. When she ended her singing for a short respite, she heard applause amid the clinking of glasses intermingled with men's voices, the girls' laughter.

She slid slowly to the end of the piano bench and prepared to stand up for a stretch when she spotted Barrister Plugge standing beside the bar, hands on his hips, staring at her. Quickly, she swiveled about on the shiny bench and resumed playing with gusto. I cannot endure another encounter with that evil enslaver again today. I would rather play until my hands bleed or I fall facedown onto the keyboard with fatigue, than be forced to face him again.

Fifteen minutes passed and she paused again, this time to find something to sooth her parched lips. She was thirsty. Happily, Plugge had disappeared from her sight. During the applause, as she began to rise from the bench, a man stepped forward and began speaking to her. The audience returned to their conversations and drinking.

"It's always darkest before the dawn," he said quietly. She gasped and looked him over carefully. Who was he--dark mustache, eye patch over his left eye and gray hair. No one she recognized.

He moved closer, speaking in a low voice.

"Katie, it's me, Fredrick. Sit still, don't move. Play again and then come over slowly to my table in the right-hand corner…have a drink with my companions and me and we'll make a plan."

Katherine's heart pounded against the inside of her chest. Tears of joy sprang into her eyes. She gasped for breath. She gripped the edge of the piano bench to resist the almost overwhelming urge to rise from her seat and melt into Fredrick's arms. Instead, like the practiced actress she had been forced to become, she slowly turned back to the piano and played as never before, out of sheer joy. Fredrick had come at last.

…

At noon the next day, Thursday, Petrus Plugge returned to the Red lantern. He seated himself in front of the fireplace, legs splayed. There were no other people in the room.

"Well, Katherine, my girl. Are you ready to sign?"

She noted that he spoke in a quiet controlled voice. She took a deep breath. I guess he's trying a different approach this time. She steeled herself against whatever was coming next.

"You must understand by now that this job, our business venture is the chance of a life-time for you. Good money, a place to live; prestigious clients who have social connections." He paused and watched her. "Otherwise, here you are. No husband to support you, no work, no skills…" He paused for emphasis.

She waited, saying nothing.

"Well?"

"What are the papers, the ones I am to sign? What do they say? I suspect that I am giving up something. My freedom? Whatever is left of Mama's' possessions? What?"

"It's just saying that I am not responsible for you. That's all."

Katherine knew better. Ebenezer had made it clear--spilled the beans about the property being in her name.

"Why is that necessary? I am of age. I am over ten- years-old."

Plugge gathered up his spread-out legs and sat up straight. She watched him begin to breath more heavily and tug at his high-upstanding celluloid collar. She knew that he was losing patience with her. All he could do is threaten her.

"Do you know how close you are to being put out? Out of here? I have a mind to sign you into the Institute of Insane Females! Or to the House of Refuge on Randall's Island. You know I serve as a legal advisor to their board of directors. I could have you committed within the hour. You are troublesome. If you won't join me in this business and you refuse to sign these papers. I will have you locked up!"

He slammed his fist on the arm of his chair, and lowered his voice when three male customers entered through the front door.

Katherine felt relieved with this opportunity, and ushered them to a table, took their orders, and disappeared into the kitchen. She watched from the safety of the pantry, peering over the top of the half door as Plugge pulled his bulky body to his feet, and headed for the manager's office. Soon after, she noted that he had left. She saw Blanche open her office door and motioned for her to come in.

"He plans to return on Friday with his wealthy client at six o'clock. He said that you had best be ready to sign and to entertain his traveling gentleman."

Katherine smiled to herself and curtsied to Blanche who looked confused at her response.

"I'll be ready."

The next day, Blanche sat at her desk and listened as Katherine reviewed the inventory of wine and hard liquor, and studied the cook's list of food needed for the coming weekend. She counted the week's income as the manager observed and made entries into the Red Lantern's ledger. Then she watched as Blanche put the money into a cloth bag with a string closure as was customary in readiness for Plugge's pick-up in the morning on Friday. She observed as Blanche placed it in a strong box, and then put the box in the top drawer of a chest of drawers. She turned the key, locking the drawer.

Blanche switched her attention to Katherine.

"Well, Katherine, what are you going to do? What is it that the Barrister wants you to sign? You know, I can ignore your condition for just a month more, and then it will be obvious, especially to clients who you will entertain. Better decide what you need to do."

"Yes, I am racking my brain for solutions. I may contact a friend and ask to work for her, in her household. She married well and has children and a large house."

She thought the manager seemed relieved and satisfied with her answer, for now.

Whenever Blanche departed for the dressmaker or some other errand, she had left Katherine in-charge. As the manager rose to depart, she asked,

"What am I to do if the Barrister arrives early for his pickup--since he has the special client to deal with tomorrow?"

Blanche hesitated, but fished a key out of her skirt pocket. She reluctantly reached out toward her. The stones in Blanche's finger rings glinting as she dangled the metal object in front of her.

"Here's the key. I suppose almost anything is possible given his unexpected appearances during this past week. Just give him the bag."

As soon as the horse and carriage bearing Blanche pulled away, Katherine opened the top drawer and removed the paper money--greenbacks. She replaced them with sheets of paper the same size and weight. Next she removed the twenty gold pieces, replacing their weight with copper coins and small smooth river rocks, then tested the weight, river rocks and paper in her left hand, and the gold and greenbacks in the right. They seemed close in weight.

She knotted the string on the bogus bag and locked it back in the drawer. She slid the bag with the gold into her skirt pocket and headed to her room. If she got caught at this, the Barrister would have just cause to have her committed, but the risk was worth it. The least she could get from her harasser was a week's income from the inn.

Back in her room, she divided the gold and paper money into small bags and slid them into the skirt pocket of the dress she planned to wear that evening. Then, she packed her few personal items in a small carpetbag, lingering for several moments as she picked up a small familiar item.

Katherine turned a long-handled mirror over in her hands and ran her fingers over its surface. The back was made of bronze and had at its center a single embossed rose with leaves. The mirror on the opposite side was beveled and fit tightly into the frame. She found it easy to pack among her belongings since it was small-only eight inches long and half that wide.

The piece had been a gift from Papa' for her sixth birthday when he returned from a voyage to France. She remembered holding the mirror, staring first at her own reflection and then fingering the back with its metal embossment.

"It's for my beautiful Katie, my beautiful girl." Those words had burned into her brain. From then on, she knew that she was beautiful. Her Papa' had said so.

Now eight years later, she fingered it again. The brass needed polishing, but the mirror was intact. This was her most treasured possession. And after all she'd been through, she still had it. Dear Papa'…

. . .

That Thursday evening as twilight descended upon Brooklyn and the Red Lantern Inn, Katherine played and sang her last piece with gusto before sliding off the piano bench. Amid scattered applause, she glided among the male customers, greeting them, smiling and flirting, as she was expected to do. Finally, she sauntered over to a table of three men, Fredrick, the bewhiskered ship's first mate, Ricardo, and a young sailor named Sunshine, not old enough to grow his own beard.

A drink awaited her. Talking and laughing, she flirtatiously sat on Fredrick's lap. The three kept up a steady banter as she slipped one-by-one the small bags of gold out of her pocket and into Fredrick's tall, black boots.

After about thirty minutes, Sunshine announced, "I'm going to go to 'the head,' Boss." He left the table and disappeared behind a heavy dark curtain to find the men's latrine.

Minutes later, Katherine noisily took her leave of Fredrick and the first mate.

"See you boys, later…" and moved around to another group of gentlemen. She continued working the room for another thirty minutes. Then she slipped through a doorway that led to a corridor and the side steps to the second floor.

Quietly, she opened the wide window of her bedroom,

propped it with a book, and lowered her packed carpetbag on a rope. It landed with a soft thump. She could see a dark figure below and feel the tug on the rope. She pulled up the cord and untied a bundle that was attached.

Quickly, she undressed, got out of her corset and petticoats, hung her dress on a peg on the back of her door, and loosened the tie on the pack she'd just pulled into her room. She shook out the wrinkled clothing and laid them on her bed.

From those items she donned dark-colored knee breaches, black stockings, a loose, long-sleeved, dog-eared jacket and a pair of wire-rimmed glasses. She clipped her long hair back with a large barrette, donned a black-knit navy cap, and pulled on a pair of well-worn black boots that were a bit too large. She stretched the jacket sleeves to cover her hands, then descended the side stairs slowly, trying to walk quietly in her ill-fitting boots. She paused with each squeaking step, listening intently, but the noise in the main room was so loud that no one heard her making her descent.

As she eased out into the dark street, a soft whistle alerted her to start walking in the direction of the bay. She could hear a horse and buggy approaching. Sunshine sat beside the coachman. The carriage halted, the seaman alighted, and offered his hand in assistance.

Katherine gracefully climbed into the passenger seat and shrank back as far out of sight as possible. The rig pulled up in front of the inn's main entrance. She could see a guard, the Inn's watchman standing to the right of the door. He looked at each person, entering and leaving. Just as a number of clients were entering, Fredrick and Ricardo emerged during the confusion and climbed into the carriage with her and Sunshine.

Her heart was pounding at such a bold escape. The horse and carriage turned south on Broadway, headed toward the East River and Robert Fulton's steam-powered ferry bound for Brooklyn. For her, it meant freedom from her tormentor. It gave her hope, hope for her future.

The darkness was fading. The dawn had come.

News from Elias and Life on the Home Front

Borough of Oil City, Pennsylvania, 1861

Dear Folks,   Camp Curtain, Pennsylvania
                                        June 13, 1861

I want you to know that I am in good hands here with the Bucktails. My feet are durn sore from a long march, over 200 miles from Pittsburgh to the state capital, Harrisburg. Me and the men from Warren, who picked me up on the flatboat are camped together here sleeping in pup-tents. We were waiting for orders and today are told that our rifle regiment has been re-named. We're now the Kane Rifle Regiment of the Pennsylvania Reserve. But we still call ourselves the Bucktails, just so you know.

How goes Pa? Did he settle down after I left?

It is said that we will be moving out and marching toward the state line, south of here.

Has anyone spoken to Gala?

I miss you all.

Your loving son and brother,

Elias

...

Dear Folks,   October 10, 1861

At long last, I have come upon some paper for writing.

The weather is getting cold at night. We are at a place called Tennallytown, near Washington, living in tents. We marched the distance under the command now of Col. Kane for which we are all grateful. Do you know he is from up the river at Warren?

All of us from along the Allegheny keep each other in good company, although I miss home and that great waterway.

I am in hopes of receiving those heavy socks about which you wrote. I hope you can turn out a pair or two for me to wear under these boots. They might catch up with me here as so far we have no orders for movement.

My news is that our outfit is not under a 3-month service as we had been told. Now they tell us that we are in this fight for the duration.

I miss you all. Please send me more news of what's happening at home. I'm glad that Pa seems better since going to Grandpa's farm for a rest. Is Uncle Matthias planning to come to stay with you this winter? Is Luke minding the store?

I must close,
Your loving son and brother,
Elias

...

Dear Folks,   January 10, 1862

Finally, time to write. My unit was ordered in against the Rebs near a place called Dranesville, near the Potomac River. Saw my first artillery duel. It was frightening—the loud noise, smoke and men screaming. Colonel Kane ordered 20 of us to take over a brick house from which we poured hot fire upon the advancing Rebs, and our firing being too much for them, they withdrew. When the colonel commenced to follow them, they shot him in the face. He screamed out and I turned to see he was hit in his mouth. I was one of the first to get to his side. Me and another guy staunched the bleeding and helped him to his feet. He is tough. As soon as we bandaged him up, he went forward with us—after those Rebs, but they got away. We had two men killed and a score more wounded. We all helped each other and got them to a nearby hospital set up in a church. Do not know when we will see Colonel Kane again. Now we have Major Stone. Both of these men rode the flatboat with me to Pittsburg last April.

I am weary.
Your loving son and brother,
Elias

August 1862

"Luke! Luke!"

He heard Jesse before he saw him. Luke looked up from his sweeping the last of the clumps of dried mud from the corner of the doorway to see his friend running around the ruins of the iron furnace. Jesse leaped a dry gully and kept running right up to the three wooden steps that led into the Kahle's store. Jesse's face was flushed and his dark stringy hair tumbled over his ears. Luke could hear his panting, breathing hard.

"Luke, I overheard Reverend Dobbs who just arrived from up the creek talking to your Pa. Says the oilmen been drillin' during the last two months, and yesterday and their well came in at thirty-five barrels at the second sand. Said they want to ship it quick while the price is yet at sixty-five cents a gallon."

"Think he'll organize a pond freshet? Water's been a might low on Oil Creek."

"Recon so, that's his job. He said that oilmen have already paid to use the water stored-up in the ponds up the creek." Luke knew that the Presbyterian minister had been appointed as Superintendent of the pond freshet system for the Oil Creek valley.

"Seems as if he'll have to, especially if that driller wants to get his oil outa' here."

"When?"

"Don't know exactly when, but heard him say, 'Soon.' If they keep the usual schedule of Wednesday or Saturday, could be Saturday, comin.'"

"Better get this store ready for a bunch o' folks who come to watch, and be wanting things to buy." He picked up his broom and took a deep breath.

"Jesse, any letters for Ma and me in today's mail bag?"

Jesse shook his head, and shoulders slumping, turned to leave.

"Maybe tomorrow there will be word from Elias 'cause Captain Hannah is scheduled to tote empty barrels in here from Pittsburgh on the *Allegheny Belle No. 4*. He usually carries the mail up with him for Franklin and Oil City."

Since Elias' departure in late April 1861, Cornplanter had changed. The excitement of the new and growing oil commerce altered the sleepy village into a bustling, hustling spot on the Allegheny. Paddlewheel steamers and flatboat fleets lined the muddy landings of the north banks of the river for a half-mile to the south and stood ready to haul barrels of oil as well as boatloads of bulk shipments southward to Pittsburgh and beyond.

Cornplanter swelled with eager speculators ready to get in on the act, dreaming of making a quick fortune. Those lacking funds necessary for buying or leasing property came in search of lucrative jobs and the possibility of purchasing stock--even one sixteenth of a share--in a nearby well that speculators rumored would produce a major strike and barrels of oil. These recent arrivals pushed the population of 200 to 600 in a two-year period.

Spurred to action by the growing oil business, the Michigan Rock Oil Company, owners of a large portion of land on the west side of Oil Creek began development. The company had built warehouses and boat landing area on the river flats near other river landing operators, Abrams', Orr and Company and J. W. Hanna's. Michigan Rock Oil built two oil refineries that covered 500 acres bordering Main Street. A number of stores including a hardware store added to the development of five hotels.

The influx of humanity strained the village resources. Some of the newly arrived lived on barges tied up to the crowded river banks, while others survived in shoddy shacks wherever they could find space. Some residents opened their houses to accommodate those needing a room. Businesses dealing with leasing or purchasing oil land occupied recently constructed buildings. In 1862, a resident, W.R. Johns launched the first newspaper, *The Weekly Register*. This confluence of Oil Creek and the Allegheny River was considered by lumberman and river pilots as the largest and safest eddy on this waterway to the Gulf of Mexico. The place was rife with change.

In response to these changes, the movers and shakers of the settlement decided to change the name, Cornplanter to Oil City in reflection of the current importance of the settlement with the production and transportation of oil. The area was fast becoming referred to as "the Hub of Oildom." The newly dubbed Oil City applied for a charter as a borough and was granted it in late 1861.

Elias' absence had created a vacuum and friendships had shifted after his departure. Jesse had taken on Elias' role of keeping an eye on Luke. The two had become closer in the past five months and Jesse understood Luke's painful pining for his older brother because he missed Elias, too.

...

Three days later, Luke and Jesse positioned themselves among a throng of noisy neighbors. The long line of excited onlookers stretched north on the east bank of Oil Creek as far as the boys could see. Luke and Jesse chose a spot several hundred yards upstream of the footbridge.

The day was overcast and gave relief from the sun's hot rays to observers as well as to the skilled river men who waited upstream for the agreed-upon time of the release of all dams at once. Expectantly, they stood at the ready, looking for the optimal water wave that signaled them to let loose of the moorings, and plunge their boats loaded with oil into the rushing water that would raise the creek's level two to three feet. River pilots and crude skinners worked with experienced eyes, and knew when to unleash their guipers loaded with twenty-five to fifty barrels of oil, or French Creekers that held 1000 to 1200 barrels.

When the price of oil was high, barrels were used for shipping to decrease the loss of the load. Barrels could be retrieved from the water if the boat capsized and the barrels remained intact. When prices were low, oil was shipped from the creek-side wells into bulk boats and vessels with wooden tanks aboard. Even the slightest motion of the water endangered these loads that could capsize and dump their greasy cargo into the creek.

Shippers paid the expense of pond freshets, $200 to $300 to upstream millers for the storage and use of their water. At times, from 200 to 800 small vessels jammed the creek. The volume of pond freshet traffic varied depending on the well productions, the current price of crude, and the navigation conditions of Oil Creek and the Allegheny River from Oil City to Pittsburgh.

The 130-mile river-run was fraught with dangerous sandbars, small islands, sunken snags, rugged rocks and shallow water at notorious locations such as the infamous Scrubgrass Ripple. If not impeded by such hazards, downriver trips took about thirty to thirty-five hours. Although conditions aboard the riverboats varied, on most river steamers at night, male passengers slept fully clothed on mattresses arranged on the cabin deck. These travelers were required to rise early so that galley crew could set up the breakfast dining tables that were later used for evening poker games.

Luke had heard John Obadiah refer to his river trip, telling Molly that the busiest man on the steamer was the bartender, but the most important person was the clerk who handled the mail and money for some of the most prosperous oilmen on Oil Creek. The entire process of moving crude oil from well to market required skilled river men, expert pilots who knew the waters.

The first efforts in transporting crude to buyers was by pond freshet. This timed release of many upstream dams at once was patterned after the practice of lumbermen, and during periods of low rainfall, it provided a means of overcoming the lack of creek water necessary to propel lumber, and now oil, to the Allegheny River.

The raucous event created an atmosphere of expectation and revelry among all present, a great percentage of Oil City's population. This included Luke who was caught-up in the excitement.

Luke wanted a good view of this tumultuous and precarious delivery of oil borne down the creek on a wild water wave to the boat landings. When he looked down the creek to the south, he could see the masts of the steamers, Captain Gorden's *Echo* and Captain Kelly's *Leclaire* that were tied up at the Oil City landings, awaiting the oil that would be transferred from these smaller creek boats, if they survived the trip, into the holds of their steamers. If these boats did not capsize or dump their loads into the turbulent torrents of the artificially elevated depths of Oil Creek, the second leg of the trip from Oil City to Pittsburgh would cost $.25 to $3.00 per barrel depending on the weather, the conditions of the creek and river, and the market.

"Look'a there Luke! Looks like everybody and his brother are here to watch!"

Luke followed Jesse's gaze and surveyed the banks of Oil Creek. Both east and west shores were lined with children, women, and men of the village of about 600 people. When he turned toward the river, he saw the landing flats congested with onlookers instead of wagons and horses that were a common sight. Today, they were at rest, their previous tasks completed.

With low water in the creek, teams of two horses had dragged upstream guipers loaded with empty barrels. They slogged up the center of the waterway over the rocky, uneven creek bottom with their cargo. Today, those same boats now laden with full barrels would come down-stream delivering crude oil bound for Pittsburgh and beyond.

Luke listened to voices on his left.

"What time the reverend set to let loose those dams, ya think?"

"I donna know fer sher, but I heared it's gonna happen at high noon, this time."

"Well, sun's overhead now, so must be about time."

Just then Luke heard a rushing, rumbling noise coming from up the creek. Jesse lifted him on his shoulders to improve their view. Suddenly they heard the crowd farther upstream begin to shout.

"What's ya see, Luke?"

"A big rise o' water with a bunch o' boats all crammed together behind a barge that has turned sideways 'cross the creek.

Barrels being dumped into the creek while men are trying to use their poles to push off the west bank and right the stuck raft."

"Should be good skimmin' and dippin' this time with all that oil bein' spilled into the creek. Good thing we got us that barrel and a skimmin' board."

"Gotta get to that place under the bridge 'fore other folks do. Good spot for collecting oil off the surface. Yah, make us some money again this week."

Jesse lowered his young friend to the ground so that they could run alongside and see the colliding crafts and hear the blaspheming crude skinners attempt to manage their valuable loads. Just a few yards north, a scow-shaped guiper with twenty some barrels aboard hit a snag along the east bank.

Mouth agape, Luke watched while two on-coming boats crashed into the stalled vessel, throwing the operator into the oily water along with a row of oil-filled barrels that rolled from the smashed boat's portside and tumbled into the raging high waters of the careening creek. The barrels washed along with the swift current until one of them hit a large river rock and split in half like a cracked hen's egg exposing a yellow yolk, but instead, a barrel spewed olive-green oil across the surging surface. The boatman dragged himself back aboard his damaged vessel while several onlookers waded in to push his boat off the impediment and back into the fray.

More watercraft bearing unstable cargo washed uncontrollably toward the Allegheny River amid broken barrels, floating debris, and spilled oil that floated on the surface of the churning water. Barrels were smashed like so much kindling for a bonfire. The bobbing boats were crushed like eggshells by larger intact vessels as they approached the junction of Oil Creek and the Allegheny River.

As Jesse and Luke raced along the creek, they approached the footbridge, made their way through the crowd, and crossed to the west bank, then headed for the landings. The spectators on the landing flats at the confluence pressed toward the creek amid barking dogs and shouting children who ran toward the flotilla of cursing men whose dinghies were caught up in the mass of floating debris. More boats surged into the convergence of the creek and the river, crashing into the previously wrecked watercraft.

"Look! That's William Hasson, Luke! He's the gent who owns the land that we hunt on--up yonder on that ridge." Jesse flung out his right arm in a gesture toward the hills to the east.

"Pa says Mr. Hasson and his partner, Peter Graff bought 1000 acres--own this half of Oil City we're standing on. I've been to his hardware store."

"Well, Luke, just last January when Cornplanter got big enough, folks voted to make it a borough and Mr. Hasson is one of the leaders, a burgess. He's a big man around here."

The boys watched as the oil spattered, muscular young gentleman, wearing a knobby necktie, stand-up collar, and a suit, his face smeared with crude, dropped his rafting pole and rolled up his trouser legs to the height of his knee-high boots. With the agility of a cat, he leaped from his beached boat into the murky mud of the landing. He smiled as he examined the intact load of his boat, then walked toward John Obadiah who was in charge of the cargo bound for Pittsburgh.

"Well, Mr. Kahle, that's my last trip down the creek for a while."

John Obadiah looked up from his ledger.

"That so?"

"I'm wanted in the army--Company I, 142nd Regiment. I leave in two-day's time."

The two men walked to Hasson's oil-loaded vessel. The shipping manager took note of Hasson's cargo, then handed the oilman a receipt.

"You know, I'm not the only one leaving the oil field. I hear that at least twenty or so are coming off the farms up the creek. Being recruited for a unit down in Franklin, the 63rd Regiment, Company I by Colonel Sandy Hays, the veteran of the Mexican War. That will leave many a producer scrambling to find help."

Hasson turned toward John Obadiah and extended his hand in a gesture of finality.

"I'm sorry to be leaving, but our country needs me. Got to get this rebellion stopped."

Then, as the boys watched, Hasson turned his back on the beat-up boats, broken barrels, and rubble-filled creek, and walked away.

Jesse slung his arm across Luke's shoulders as they headed toward the skimming tools they had stowed earlier under the footbridge that spanned the oily creek. Hearing Hasson's declaration about joining the army made Luke think about Elias.

"Wonder where he is now…"

"Don't know…"

Luke walked alongside his older friend in silence. Amid the stench of crude oil, the chaos and clatter created by the excitement of the pond freshet, he thought about the future.

"Maybe skimming oil, I can sometime buy part of a share in one of these wells for Elias and me. But Pa won't have it. Says I should know enough to stay away from the river and I'm lucky to be alive."

With that they arrived under the bridge. Jesse reclaimed their empty bucket that held a skimming board, an oar stem and two long-handled iron dippers.

"Let's get dippin' while it's not crowded under here. At least we're in the shade."

He rolled up his pant legs well over top of his boots, and stepped into the eddy that was covered with the greasy crude. Taking the board in both hands, Jesse skimmed the water's surface, guiding the floating oil toward Luke who stood ready.

Luke dragged the dipper across the drifting oil that Jesse had amassed with his board. He continued skimming off the crude, emptying his catch into the wooden bucket behind him.

"Looks like a pretty big spill. Should be a good day. A good day to scoop up this stuff."

He produced a small glass bottle from his pocket and ladled some crude into it. He held it aloft, thrust it into a shaft of sunlight. Illuminated, the oil appeared a light amber.

"Look, Jess. Looks like liquid gold."

Jesse stopped working the board and laughed. "That's what folks say, Luke. 'Liquid gold!'"

"Yah, does…maybe some time, we can do like some of these other folks and get an oil boat, and gather us 'liquid gold' faster."

"Yah, and pull the boat sideway against the stream. That's how to collect it quicker and without wadin' around, getting your clothes all greased up. Look! It's like thin molasses except not sweet. Can't eat it on corn bread." Their laughter was followed by Jesse's encouragement.

"Let's see if we can get us a full barrel today. Think Mr. Vandergrift's man down at the landings will run it through his still again, for us? Got to get the water out before we can sell it."

"Yah, think so. Keep scooping, Luke. Some dippers get five to ten barrels a day. Maybe we can get us two barrels full this afternoon."

They skimmed and scooped for another hour without

stopping. Finally, Luke waded into the oily stream to cool off.

Just then, the sound of a particular pedestrian gait on the overhead bridge alerted both oil gleaners simultaneously. Jesse froze in place and put his forefinger over his pursed lips, waving to Luke to move farther under the bridge. Luke had already covered his mouth with his left hand. The two stood silently, looking up at the underside of the wooden structure that spanned the creek. They listened intently. They knew those footsteps belonged to John Obadiah.

Suddenly, they heard a loud thumping and dirt and grit rained down from above.

"Allison Luther! I know you're down there. How many times I got to tell you to stay away from the river?"

Luke looked at Jesse and rolled his eyes upward and made a face.

"Yah, Pa, I'm down here scooping."

"I'm not acarin' what you're doin' down there. Get out from there now!"

"But Pa, you said not to go near the river. This here's the creek."

"Well, today it ain't no creek. Got turned into a roarin' river, and you know it! And don't you talk back to me! Already lost one son to who-knows-where, and I don't intend to lose another!"

That said, John Obadiah leaned over the bridge rail and peered down, trying to locate Luke. Instead he saw Jesse.

"He's OK, Mr. Kahle. I'm with him. We're working together to earn some money from this big oil spill."

"Don't care what you're doin.' Luke has got to get up here now, or he's gonna get a thrashin.'"

Luke shrugged and laid down his scooper. Jesse patted Luke on the shoulder.

"Better do what your Pa says. See you later and let you know how much we got."

By the time Luke emerged from under the bridge on the east side of the creek, some neighbors had stopped to listen. They stood at the east entrance of the bridge and stared hard at John Obadiah who stood in the center of the bridge. When Luke climbed up the east bank, several nodded to him and made way for him to pass, but did not budge from their location that was now between Luke and his father.

He felt grateful for their presence that seemed to have a calming effect on his surly father. John Obadiah's temper tantrums and explosiveness had become common knowledge in this small community. Folks had defended Elias from being stabbed months before, and they remained on alert for future abusive behavior from John Obadiah. As he looked back over his shoulder, he was relieved to see that his father was not following him. Instead, he hobbled across the bridge to the west side of the creek and returned to work at the landings.

Silently with shoulders slumped, Luke headed for his house. He wondered how many neighbors were aware of John Obadiah's increasingly frequent bouts of drinking. Just last week, he had shouted and cursed at Luke for something. He could not remember what infraction had occurred, but he vividly recalled his father's out-of-control, drunken behavior. Molly told her husband that she and Luke were going for a walk until he calmed down. She had concealed the half empty bottle of homebrew in the folds so her skirt, and once out the door had placed it in a chink, out of sight, in the cabin's exterior chimney.

Today's public dressing-down was just one more of his father's distressing diatribes. Although he had had some understanding of Elias' reason to leave months ago, he was now learning first-hand some of what his brother had endured.

Like Elias' experience, Luke's dreams were being crushed as well. Dreams of earning some money, money of his own that he could use to buy a portion of a share in one of the wells. Even the smallest slice of a share, $1/16^{th}$ was available to anyone with the money, even an eleven-year-old with dreams of the future. When will Elias ever return…

Luke and the Ice Gorge

December 7, 1862

On Friday after a dinner of venison stew and corn cakes, Luke opened the front door.

"Put on your coat, Luke. It's getting colder by the minute. I can feel it even in the house."

Luke closed the door and retrieved his coat from the nail in the kitchen wall.

"Ma, it's really snowing out there. Looks like the slush on the steps is beginning to freeze. Where's the broom?"

Armed with his tools, he tried the broom, but discovered that the dropping temperatures had quickly frozen the afternoon's melting snow on the front steps. It was so hard that he abandoned the broom for a shovel, and began pounding the ice with the shovel's blade. The ice chopped away, he turned toward the woodpile and picked up three logs to revive the dying fire. Standing quietly and listening to the soft sound of the snowfall, he could feel the increasing cold quietly penetrate his deerskin boots and homemade woolen socks. He wiggled his toes for warmth.

He wondered if Elias' stockings that his mother had knitted and mailed six weeks ago had gotten to him. He shivered and tried to picture his brother putting on his new, warm footwear in some cold, far-off place. Then he turned to carry the logs to the hearth and stoked the fire to ensure the burning of the cold, damp wood.

"The price of crude in Pittsburgh has come to thirty-one or two cents a gallon while oil is being' stored in our warehouses at the landings."

John Obadiah was addressing his younger brother, known to Luke as Uncle Matt. Twenty-eight-year-old Andrew Matthias Kahle had arrived several weeks ago from the family farm in Pitch Pine, twenty-seven miles to the southeast. Just as last winter, once the crops were harvested on the farm, Uncle Matt had come to live with them in Oil City for the winter months. He brought Topsy, Luke's grandfather's horse to town in the winter. Not only was Topsy a means of transportation for the family, but they knew that the presence of the horse was another deterrent to Luke's sadness of missing Elias.

Uncle Matt slept in Elias' bed and kept things more harmonious within a household that was now less subject to John Obadiah's episodic, explosive, frightening behavior. Luke was aware that his mother seemed happier, less nervous, and he felt somewhat sheltered from his father's wrathful ranting. Beside those advantages, Luke's life had improved in another way. His uncle made it possible for Luke to learn about oil.

Uncle Matt had a job up Oil Creek on the Hamilton McClintock Farm, assisting the operators with whatever tasks they had for him. In March 1862, the farm had eight flowing wells and fifty-six that were not producing--dry wells or dusters. The flats on both sides of Oil Creek and the hills were pockmarked with abandoned wells, piles of palings from the diggings, and greasy, abandoned equipment. The once-green meadow grass and low scrubby brush lay trampled and blackened with oil. The hills were barren, denuded by oil strikes. The coveted oil had shot up eighty-feet into the air by the pressure of releasing gas, and splattered everything around it. The suffocating spray killed every living blade of grass, wild flower, tree and bush in the area. All was black with grease.

Luke listened as Uncle Matt talked with John Obadiah...

"Those flowing wells are putting out oil at about 500 feet deep, 235 barrels a day. Seems like a good investment of those gents who leased that land--cost them about $3000 a well. As long as the price of crude holds, they got plenty of work to keep me busy, so I'll be staying on for a while longer."

Luke was happy to hear that news from his uncle. The part that he enjoyed most was being allowed on occasion to accompany Uncle Matt to that worksite, even for a short time. Finally, he had some first-hand knowledge, his own observations on the drilling of wells, and that helped to satisfy his curiosity...

The 350-acre McClintock Farm, three miles north of Oil City, spanned both sides of Oil Creek in Cornplanter Township. According to people living nearby, it was on this section of the creek that for fifty years, inhabitants of the area gathered oil to sell. Crude flowed up with underground streams and floated on that section of the creek where early settlers collected it in barrels and sold it down the river, long before the wells on this farm had been dug in 1861.

According to the owner of the farm, as well as pioneers to the area, Seneca Indians had found the floating, greasy crude useful.

On one visit recently, Old Mac, a relative of Hamilton McClintock had told Luke about the Seneca's and the Six Nation tribes who had gathered every year on the land that was now the thriving oil field.

"I got my story from what was written in a letter to his government by the early explorer, French Commander, Montcalm. He wrote about the grand finale, the celebration at the end of the tribes' meetings. They would set fire to the oil that was floating on the surface of Oil Creek."

"Set it on fire-the whole creek?"

"Yes, must have been a mighty wild experience, fearful, if you ask me. All that burning crude on a wide surface of a flowing creek."

"Wish I could have seen that. Wonder if it caught some trees on fire."

"Maybe a wonder if it didn't."

"My Pa said they only lit one of the pits, not the whole creek."

Luke could hardly wait to inform his father about this version of Indian lore.

Old Mac had pointed to a huge boulder on the creek's west bank.

"It's said that that is a 'paint rock.' Those early Seneca's mixed red clay with oil that was war-paint--put it on their bodies, especially their faces. On that red rock, right here in front of us. And other boulders like that along the Allegheny, too."

Luke was fascinated by the tales and looked forward to his times with his uncle and his visits to the McClintock Farm. Being with people who would answer his questions and discuss his ideas fueled Luke to dream of the future.

Apparently, Old Mac enjoyed Luke's interest in the burgeoning oil business and when time allowed during his visits, he had provided the young visitor opportunities to learn. One clear day in October, the retired farmer had walked him around several of the eight producing wells on the flat.

"This here one is called the 'Watson' and is named after the gent who drilled the well."

"But it's on your family's farm. Why is he drilling it here?"

"'Cause he's paying us to use my land. We agreed on that.

It's called a 'lease.' When he sells some of his oil, he pays me a certain amount of money from the sale--that's for using my land."

Luke nodded his understanding. "Do all the wells have names?"

"Sure enough, they do. Some men name their wells with their sur names, like Jonathan Watson did, and others use names of somebody, like their wives or whatever. This was just one of Watson's wells."

Old Mac turned and moved slowly toward a flat area near the creek.

"Now, you see, after Drake struck the first oil along the creek, Mr. Watson saw an opportunity and moved fast. He figured that there was more oil to be had along the creek flats. You know what he did?"

Luke nodded to the negative.

"Just a few days after Drake's strike, he got on his horse--he was a good horseman--and quick, before most folks caught on to the importance of Drake's oil and learned how their land had increased in value, he rode to all the farms that had land along the creek and offered them money, just to use their land. A bunch of Scotch-Irish and German farmers couldn't believe their luck. You see, the land along Oil Creek was kind of worthless for farming. And here came neighbor Watson. These folks all knew each other--and wanted to pay them to use their land. Of course, he paid them only a small portion for it compared to what the land was worth just a month or so later. Most of those farmers jumped at the chance to make some money--farming's a tough job--so they signed leases, allowing Watson on their land. Watson's a businessman, and he knew what he was doing. Now we call it American capitalism. Folks like Watson got rewarded for his imagination and resourcefulness. Lot of that going on around here in this oil country."

"Did Mr. Watson make a lot of money from his leases?"

"He sure did. A lot of money and it keeps coming."

They walked near the Watson Well where Luke saw a tall derrick, blackened with oil, an engine, a pile of empty wooden barrels, and a large tank with a trough. Dark green oil was pouring into the greasy black receptacle from underneath the derrick. Grass and bushes near the well were dark with oil, and the pumping rods squeaked as they moved.

"How deep is that well, Mr. Mac? "

"All these are about 500 feet--goes down to the second layer of sand, called 'the second sand.' See these piles of stones and sand? That's what come out of the well during the digging."

Luke looked around and saw pile upon pile of rocks and dirt scattered across the field amid stumps of trees laid waste in order to drill at various locations. On the other side of the creek, he could see the Turnpike that passed through the McClintock Farm. With Topsy pulling them in the wagon, he and Uncle Matt had traveled that rough road from Oil City to the McCormick Farm.

"Watson's well was the third well to strike oil along the creek. Came in after several months of kicking down that well."

"Did he use a spring pole? My Pa told me about digging that way."

"Sure did. Hard work, for certain."

"How did Mr. Watson know where to start digging?"

"Good question. See over yonder." He pointed farther north along the creek.

"Another gent dug a well there, and it's a dry hole--no oil-- even after a lot of work and expense, $3000." He paused. "These acres got fifty-six nonproducing wells here so far."

Luke's eyes widened. "Why?"

"Well, not sure. Some folks depend on hydro-geology by using a divining stick--some call it a dowser--to decide where to drill."

"What's that?"

"You see, you take the natural fork of a peach tree or a hazel tree and cut the limbs equal. Then you strip off the leaves, so it looks like this." He bent over and used his finger to draw an outline of the divining rod in the loose dirt.

"So, then you take hold of both limbs, palms up and backs of your hands down toward the ground. You hold it out away from your body and start walking forward over the land where you're thinking about drilling. If the fork ends turn toward the ground, some folks believe that there is oil under there--that's 'the spot'--at least that's what some folks believe."

Luke looked at his mentor and shrugged.

"How's it work--to do that?"

"Dunna know. Folks been using that method of finding water for centuries before all this oil excitement. Just has worked for years, for finding water. And besides, doesn't cost much of anything."

"So that's the way to find oil..."

"Well, there are other methods. Take spiritualism, so

84

example. Several wells 'a been successful when the speculator's hired someone who claims to contact spirits that tell them where the oil can be found."

"What?" Luke's stopped walking and his mouth dropped open as he thought about it.

"Well, that's what some folks believe in."

Luke wondered if Elias knew some of the things Old Mr. Mac was telling him--especially about the creek lighting and the spirits.

He missed Elias…

. . .

Just then, Uncle Matt's voice pulled him back to the present.

"You're saying that 40,000 barrels of crude been brought out by freshets and are awaiting pickup from the warehouses there at the landing?"

"Yup, just sittin' there waitin' for a flood, or the river to rise enough to get the streamers in. The rates for haulin' are high just now and we got a bigger than usual number of the oil fleet just sittin' at the landin's, waitin' to take advantage of the water risin.'"

"What's a gallon worth now? Last I heard, it was going for seventh-five cents earlier in the week. Told me that up at the McClintock wells that was the price when bought at the well."

"You see, Mathias, that's just it. Like I said, the price of crude in Pittsburgh has dropped to thirty-two cents a gallon. There are some worried drillers and producers--tired of waitin' for the conditions to improve. And to complicate matters, the boats that brought oil out'a the last freshet--they're sittin' at the landin's for a half-mile down the river, loaded with crude and ready to go."

"With the temperature dropping as it is tonight, bet the river freezes. That sure won't be good for the river fleet, all moored along the landings."

"It'll bring things to a further standstill, Matt, that's fer sure…"

. . .

Late the next afternoon, Saturday, with darkness approaching, Luke stomped the heavy snow off of his boots, and sat on the wide boards of the cabin floor to remove them. He opened the cabin door, took a boot in each hand and banged them together to remove the remaining frozen clumps that clung to the tops. He dropped them near the hearth to dry.

"Where's your Pa and Uncle Matt, Luke?" Molly stood at the stove.

"Pa's still working and Uncle Matt is down at the landings helping the boaters. Told me to skedaddle on home since it getting colder and colder."

"Helping the boaters--the fleet?"

"Yeah, Pa says since the temperature's dropping fast, that the river ice will form quick. Slush on the creek is freezing too. Probably going to block up the river with ice and push hard on all those boats and rafts tied up there."

"Come over here by the hearth and get yourself warm. Is it still snowing?"

"Coming down so hard that I couldn't see the landings, once I crossed over the bridge. Snow's clear over top of my boots. Look."

Molly eyed his soggy boots and took a quick look through the open door, then quickly closed it.

"Heavens, looks like a real blizzard. Good thing Uncle Matt is down there with your Pa."

"Uncle Matt said he'd see to it that Pa gets home. They'll be awhile, so many boats all crammed together. Trying to keep them from wrecking in case the ice jams and shifts. And most loaded with crude-barrels and bulk."

About an hour later, Luke heard voices and thumping sounds on the steps. He jumped to his feet and opened the door. The falling snow formed a curtain of white as Matthias and Jesse emerged through the blizzard, supporting John Obadiah on both sides. The trio was covered in snow, and his father sagged, near exhaustion from the effort of trying to stay up on his one leg. Luke flung the door open wide for them to enter while Matthias and Jesse got John Obadiah out of his snow-covered coat. Then Molly, who stood ready with a quilt that she'd hung near the hearth, wrapped her husband in the warmed cover. Matthias lowered him onto a cot near the fire.

"Jesse, can you stay here tonight, and go home in the morning?"

"Thanks, Mrs. Kahle. But my Mother would worry and wonder at my whereabouts." He turned to leave.

As Jesse plunged off of the stoop and into the storm, Matthias removed his coat and leaned out the door to shake off the snow.

"Yes, it was a long afternoon. It's not over yet."

...

A few hours after sunup on Sunday, Luke ate a hardy breakfast of cooked oats and honey with his uncle and his mother. John Obadiah had not stirred and they left him alone in the next room. Although no one discussed his absence, Luke knew that his father had imbibed in a good bit of homebrew last evening. His nonappearance at the breakfast table as well as the landings was expected, since he and most workers did not labor on Sunday. In fact, within their cabin, an unspoken consensus of relief supported his father's sleeping late. The silence in place of his angry ranting was a welcome respite for all.

Luke stepped off of the cabin's top step and into snow that came well above his knee-high boots. Overnight, the world had transformed from the dark, muddy river banks and leafless, listless trees to a frozen winter wonderland of swirling white that covered fences, trees and all of Oil City's buildings that were in sight.

"Look how deep it is, Uncle Matt!"

Taking long strides as they waded their way toward the bridge, Matthias and Luke created a path from the cabin where wood smoke drifted up from the stone chimney. They had progressed about fifty yards toward the creek when they stopped for a breath.

"Looks like the river did freeze up last night, but so much snow, it's hard to say."

As they plowed through soft snowdrifts to the downhill slope toward Oil Creek and were easing their way on to the footbridge, Jesse appeared a distance away near the riverboat landings. He cupped his mittened hands and put them on either side of his mouth.

"Be careful, and don't get too close to the creek. Some workers here told me there could be an ice gorge on the creek."

They waved to Jesse.

"Must have formed overnight."

"What's an ice-gorge, Uncle Matt?"

"It happens when blocks of ice settle in the shallows of the creek, then freeze all the way through to the very bottom-called 'ground ice.'"

He pointed up the creek.

"Look upstream. See there, Luke, where it's made a dam. Look how the water's backed up behind that jam of ground ice."

He followed his uncle's gloved hand as he gestured toward the north.

"That water's gotta be ten feet deep, maybe more."

"Dangerous situation…all that water backed up Oil Creek like that."

"Yes. Best we get off this bridge."

"Where's Jesse?"

"Over yonder on the flats with some workers."

Luke turned toward the flats.

Abruptly, loud cracking sounds split through the quiet morning, and echoed off the nearby ridge.

Without a word, Mathias grabbed Luke's arm and jerked him off of the east end of the wooden crossing.

"Gotta get out'a here, Luke--fast!"

Suddenly, there was a roar of rushing water. Uncle and nephew struggled through deep snow, moving up and away from the ice-clogged creek. Advantaged by his long legs, Matthias could maneuver faster than Luke, so he felt himself being dragged. Matthias located their previous trail through the snow and moved quickly toward the cabin. Luke regained his balance and turned toward the creek.

Just then, he heard a loud crash. He turned to see the dammed ice give way suddenly. A huge pile of broken ice, like a floating island, ground its way toward the river. Blocks of frozen water laying on the banks were being swept along as if pushed by a giant broom. He stood, transfixed, only a few yards away, as the huge pile of ice swept toward the confluence of the creek and river. Like a giant auger boring through wood, the icy water forced open a narrow channel, rapidly ramming chunks of frozen creek water downstream into the Allegheny and toward the moored boats and warehoused oil.

Mesmerized, Luke watched as the huge volume of dammed-up water, now released, forced its way downstream, just clearing the bottom of the footbridge where they had stood only minutes before. Surging onward, the mass of jagged ice and water flowed under the river ice, lifting it up, causing a huge gorge. Suddenly a second flow of ice from the creek slammed into the river's ice gorge. He could feel the ground shake under his feet. He moved closer to his uncle and shivered.

The massive weight of ice and water crashed against the first of the moored boats along the shore. The ropes that held the boats strained, then snapped like thin thread, pushing one boat upon another until like a row of dominoes, one-by-one the vessels were crushing against one another. Wood fractured as the doomed crafts slammed together under the strength of the rushing current of dammed-up fury, one huge mass of ice forced into the river, pushing wood, hemp, oil and iron from the crushed boats and broken barrels with it.

One after another as the ice-mass and frigid water flowed downstream, additional boats' reinforced tethers snapped, making a cracking sound as increasing numbers of adjacent crafts folded-- crushed and splintered from the pressure of the gorge.

The deafening cacophony was audible for miles, filling the snowy streets of Oil City and echoing from shore to shore along the Allegheny. Within seconds, heads popped out of doorways, people without overcoats ran outside to learn the origin of the sounds.

Suddenly the valley was quiet. Luke could see clots of oil bobbing among the broken pieces of ice only yards from where they stood. He and Matthias said nothing for several minutes, stunned by the sudden but brief show of power that wreaked havoc upon property that was strewn up and down the riverbank.

From behind him, Luke heard a familiar voice calling. He turned to see his mother waving at him from the stoop of the cabin. Matthias also turned toward his sister-in-law.

"Best we get back up there. Molly must be frightened at that those sounds."

The two made their way quickly along the path they had laid just minutes before. By the time they arrived at the cabin, John Obadiah stood on the top step of the stoop, wrapped in a blanket and leaning on his crutches.

"Did ya' see it happen? The crush of ice? How many boats involved, could ya' tell?"

"Looks as if they may have lost the entire fleet and a lot of oil."

"If that's so, it destroyed some 200 boats and 60,000 barrels of crude. That's what was on the books yesterday, 60,000 barrels just sittin' there, waitin' for the river to rise." He shook his head and looked toward Luke who was surveying the devastation from the distance of the cabin.

"Like I've said in the past. Investin' in oil is real risky, real risky."

Matt took a deep breath and exhaled.

"Phuee, I am shaking so hard. Never saw such a spectacle. Wonder if anyone was hurt or killed when that thing let loose."

He stood then turned quickly to Luke.

"Luke, let's you and me go hitch up Topsy to the sledge. See if we can help anybody at the landings. We can keep an eye out for loose barrels before they all float down to Pittsburgh."

Luke jumped at that invitation. "Can I take the reins this time, Uncle Matt?"

Luke loved Topsy. Caring for the sleek brown horse was like a salve over a wound for him. It helped to ease the pain of separation from Elias, a separation that seemed never-ending.

Together, they trudged through the snow to Topsy's stable.

John Obadiah in the Conflagration

December 12, 1863

The late afternoon sun sank, stretching shadows of the river birches on to the Vandergrift landing where Luke stood coiling a length of boat line and securing its end. Since his twelfth birthday, he had worked here after school and on Saturdays. Now with his first part-time job--a real job, he realized that Sunday was a day of rest and only a few people were on hand in the rare case of a riverboat arriving from Pittsburgh. Up and down Oil Creek, even the oil drillers and the teamsters ceased their work on the Sabbath. On all other days, the steamboat and oil landings were bustling with activity.

Crude oil came and went onto the landing flats that stretched a half-mile downstream on the north bank of the Allegheny River. Shipments were stored in the vast warehouses that bordered the landings, and after arriving passengers had disembarked, barrels were loaded into waiting steamers.

The Vandergrift Landing, established by Captain J.J. Vandergrift was one of the first and largest shippers in the business. The company purchased vast amounts of crude from up the creek, and prepared sizeable shipments of oil for the 135-mile trip down the river. The landings were a hectic place and job opportunities abounded for boys like Luke who were ambitious enough to do the work.

He liked this job for its steady pay, but just now, he was hungry and ready to end his workday. He heard footsteps behind him and turned to see Jesse.

"Ready to go get your Pa'?"

"Yeah, it's quitting time for me. Better get moving before its pitch dark."

The friends walked past the boat landings that covered the Allegheny's north bank. As they approached the area where John Obadiah worked, they heard loud voices and saw a group of workers gathered in a circle.

"Wonder what's going on? Where's your Pa?"

As they drew closer, they saw John Obadiah. He stood with

his back against a wooden rail and had his crutches at his side.

"Yah, I told her to get off the landin'. No place for an Indian squaw with half-breed young 'un."

"Well, it's said that 'half-breed' is your grandchild. You driving off your own kin?"

John Obadiah's arms were crossed in front of him as he leaned on the landing rail.

"Well, who says so? That ain't true…just a rumor."

Luke watched the man who was confronting his father. Was Amos the person who had told John Obadiah about the near drowning incident that had infuriated his father several years ago and caused Elias to leave home?

Suddenly, Gala's dog, Mohwa trotted to the edge of the knot of bystanders, his nose to the ground. He stopped behind John Obadiah, took a sniff of his boots, then moved on to smell his crutches. After a few moments, he lifted his hind leg, and sent a volume of yellow fluid streaming down the wooden supports and onto the base of his crutches. The urine puddled into the mud. Several men smiled. John Obadiah cursed at the dog that departed before the recipient of his insult could reach him. Mohwa continued tracking Gala. His black nose to the ground, he ran down the landing flats to where his mistress waited.

"The whole borough of Oil City knows it, by Jove. Only one who don't believe it is you! That baby's got blue eyes and blonde hair, even favors Elias and you know it--saw it for yourself."

"You son of a polecat! I'm gonna get you--you been the one spreadin' the rumors."

Luke watched in horror as his father grabbed his crutches and swung one at his confronter.

"Be careful, Amos. He has a knife and knows how to use it!"

Even in the dying light of day, Luke could see the familiar red, sweaty face with its twisted expression of hate that had become all too familiar this past year. He could see his father's hands shaking. Had he been drinking here at work? He hoped not. Luke dreaded his bouts of binging. He had witnessed the confrontations at the cabin that were kept within their family by Uncle Matt, Molly, and him. John Obadiah's episodes of drunkenness and irrational behavior had been increasing in frequency and ferocity. Uncle Matt's interventions in dealing with his brother's drinking and resultant abusive behavior were required more often as of late. Now in this situation, Luke felt helpless and embarrassed.

He was grateful that each day, Jesse had been walking with him over the frozen ground to get his crippled father home from work, especially now that there was snow and ice to complicate the travel. That assistance was keeping John Obadiah in a job and the family in money. As it was, his mother had gone to Pitch Pine to see about his ailing grandfather. Now, he and Uncle Matt, who was working up the creek most days were managing things for the two weeks of Molly's absence. So, Jesse's assistance was more important than ever.

Sixteen-year-old lanky Jesse stepped forward and faced Luke's furious father.

"Mr. Kahle, Luke and I are here to see you home."

Jesse turned toward Amos. The group of men stepped back. The circle widened.

"Hell, no! I don't need no one tendin' to me. Get out'a here!" Then he swung his crutch, hitting Jesse on the shoulder. The blow knocked his would-be-helper off balance, and Jesse fell backwards. One of the bystanders caught him.

"Better let him cool down, or you'll get hurt. He's ferocious when he gets aggravated. I've seen it."

"Luke, go see if Matthias is back yet from the McClintock Farm."

Frightened, Luke started in a run toward the bridge across Oil Creek. It was times like this that he missed Elias the most, and now his mother was gone too. Arriving at the cabin, he found it dark and the hearth, cold. He gathered wood and laid a fire, not lighting it, but saving it for when his father would arrive. To him, it seemed like hours until he heard footfalls on the steps outside.

Instead of Matthias, Jesse hustled into Luke's cabin.

"I tried to stay with him, but he yelled and hollered at me and swung his crutches at my head again. So after that happened several times, I decided to come up here and stay with you."

"It's cold in here. Let's light the fire. No telling how late Uncle Matt may be."

The boys stood facing the growing fire, the yellow flames dancing upward, warming their hands. Famished, Luke found some cornbread from breakfast and they sat in silence while they ate.

Not knowing what else they should do, they waited for Matthias. It was dark by the time he traveled the two-and-a-half miles down the creek, and stabled Topsy.

Hearing the bad news of John Obadiah's poor public

treatment of Gala, apparent drinking on the job, and nasty, assaultive behavior on the landing, Matthias hastily ate the remainders of the cornbread and the three quickly filed out of the cabin.

It was about 7:15. The night air was cold and still. Luke could see some stars between the clouds as the three descended the slope toward the footbridge.

Suddenly, a heavy explosion shook the ground and the buildings nearby. All three stopped--dead in their tracks, and stared hard into the void of darkness, trying to ascertain the origin of the blast.

"Sounds like someone shooting a well, but not here in town."

Suddenly, only 20 yards away, a sheet of bright flame shot up from the mouth of the creek. Yellow blazes and black smoke billowed into the sky. Streams of flaming oil spread across the water and leaped 100 feet into the air, spewing heavy, black smoke that soon covered the expanse of the river.

Instinctively, they backed up several feet.

A second thunderous blast flung jets of flaming oil over nearby vessels at the up-river end of the wharf and they ignited instantaneously. Those blazing boats laden with oil exploded and then broke loose, covering the river with the burning debris. One flaming vessel, not firmly grounded, careened toward the south shore. Then a river current carried the burning boat in an almost direct line, back to the Oil City riverbanks. There it crashed into a line of tethered oil boats that exploded one-by-one. The entire river seemed to be on fire. Gradually, they began sinking into the dark waters of the Allegheny.

Thick, black clouds of smoke from the incinerated petroleum hung over the scene, and yellow, leaping flames cast an eerie, but pink tinge on the underside of the black mass. Flashing explosions like rockets emitted smoke and created exceedingly spectacular showers as over-heated barrels of oil blew up and spewed burning crude in all directions. As the lit oil hit the water, it crackled and snapped, displaying yards of burning oil that leaped fifteen to twenty feet into the air, spreading sparkling spangles, like a naval battle at sea.

"Look! Must'a started on that barge that's been stuck on a sandbar."

"Yeah, been there since the last freshet--along with some others--all loaded with oil."

Neighbors were streaming from their houses. One man ran

94

past them with a white dinner napkin yet tucked under his chin. Others left their uneaten food as they plunged into the cold and gathered along the riverbank, talking excitedly.

"This could spread to more boats. Musta' burned thirty to forty of 'em."

"Could catch-on to the buildings."

"Light the whole town afire!"

"Could be a catastrophe!"

Just then, a second nearby barge ignited, shooting streams of fire, like flamethrowers, down the entire length of the larger vessel. People shirked and dogs barked. The suffocating, heavy black smoke billowed over the wary watchers.

"That there is the barge with bulk oil. Just today, we been all day loading bulk oil into barrels from there. Look! There's the boat with the empty barrels. It's gonna go next!"

Suddenly, silhouetted against the yellow flames that licked like golden tongues into the black sky, a group of figures moved toward the boats nearest the burning barge, and threw out cables to them. The crowd rushed across the bridge and ran forward to help. They pulled on the hawser-laid cables, slowly dragging the threatened vessels to the shore and out of danger.

During the next hour, the horrified citizens watched the blazing barge, its load lessened by the fire's consumption of crude, break loose of the sand bar and commenced a dangerous drift toward the north shore of the Allegheny.

"Look at that! The barge is gonna' set fire to the rest of the boats—scores of 'em. Could burn up the entire fleet."

As the stunned crowd watched, flames shot across the waters as more crude dumped into the Allegheny River. Additional hot and expanding oil-filled barrels, exploded like pyrotechnics on the Fourth of July as they floated into the main channel, flames billowing skyward. Heavy black smoke hung over the area like a shroud and left some of the onlookers coughing and choking.

"Wonder if this is what the preacher is talking about when he preaches about Hell?" A pair of spectators moved nearer to Luke who stood staring at the catastrophe that was unfolding before their eyes. For some time, none of the three spoke.

Finally, after initial impact of the resounding shock and horrendous excitement of the exploding boats and burning oil, John Obadiah's rescuers' attention returned to their mission.

"Matthias, think we can find John Obadiah in this mess?"

That said, they hurried across the bridge and moved through the crowd.

"Let's split up, then meet back at the bridge in about twenty minutes. Keep an eye on that floating barge. Whatever you do, run if the fire starts to spread. I'll go toward the mouth of the creek. Luke, you and Jesse head west toward the moored boats. See if John Obadiah's over that way."

Luke and Jesse ran to the spot where they had witnessed the confrontation with the landing workers and John Obadiah's assault on Jesse. All around them, people rushed about, trying to move some of their crafts to save them from the drifting, flaming raft.

The boys kept searching the area, concentrating first on the moored boats and then the warehouses.

After twenty minutes, they returned to the bridge by the light from the nearby fires. Matthias stood waiting for them. He had something in his hand. As they drew closer, Luke could make out a crutch, a single crutch.

"Found this at the edge of the creek. Would have been close to the first exploding oil boat."

They looked at each other in the semi-darkness, the burning barge behind them, the continuing conflagration creating swaying shadows as they talked.

"Think he might be somewhere along that shore, near the mouth of the creek? Just watching the fire?"

"Would have been too hot to stay there for long. Besides, I did look there."

"Can't get far with only one crutch, either."

"Wonder if he was there when the barge blew up. The explosion shook houses and buildings--even the ground. Could have knocked him unconscious."

"But no sign of him. I looked hard."

Luke covered his mouth at a thought that made him shiver, despite the heated air around them.

"Could the blast have knocked him into the creek, ya think?"

Luke saw Jesse and his uncle turn toward each other. "Well, that's an idea. T'was a huge explosion. Guess that might be."

"Well, no one else around here has crutches that I know of. Has to be his."

Suddenly a breathless neighbor ran up to a group of on-lookers standing nearby.

"They got control of the first burning boat with some chains.

Took chains to do it. No using rope in this heat. Used the chains to tie the barge to a tree on the island out there in the river so it can't go anywhere else."

"Who did that?"

"Three gents, Mr. Titus, Knightlinger, and W.L. Lay."

"They sure are heroes--savin' the fleet!"

"Well, that ain't all. While you been standin' here, Mr. Phillips and John Vanausdel took the ferry chains in a skiff, and towed the second burning boat, the big barge--the one t'was hauling the bulk crude--pulled it into the middle of the Allegheny. But not before some of the moored boats caught fire from it. They joined up with the other men in boats and floated the fire monster to the head of Moran's Island. Just now came back from there and are trying to save the boats that got lit by the flames from the big raft. Boats of the fleet are so packed together, if one or two goes up in flames, the rest could follow."

"Yeah, and the wind's rising, too. Don't want all those oil barrels and warehouses to catch fire, either."

"Do they want more help?"

"Sure wouldn't hurt."

Several men broke away from the gaggle of fire-watchers and headed toward the moorings.

Having heard the latest news, Luke, Jesse and Matthias moved away from the crowd. For the next hour, they covered the area of the landings, the mouth of the creek, and the banks of Oil Creek from the Allegheny to the footbridge. They talked with those workers fighting the fires and men who were moving boats out of harm's way. Jesse approached Amos who had been antagonizing John Obadiah a few hours earlier, but he nor anyone else Luke asked had seen his father since the incident.

Several hours later, they called off the search until daybreak and returned to the cabin. Luke felt confused. That night, he lay awake thinking about the events of the day. He was worried about his father's disappearance. What would his mother say? Would she be disappointed in him? Had he caused the problem? Should he have stayed with his father instead of Jesse? What could he have done to persuade him to come home? He felt lonely and miserable. He missed is mother, but even more, he missed Elias.

. . .

The next day, Matthias, Luke and Jesse talked with the

Sheriff, S.A. Thomas about John Obadiah's disappearance.

They answered his questions and the sheriff wrote down the information they provided. Then he took off his hat and leaned back in his chair. His eyes were inflamed and his face puffy.

"Sounds as if you did your best to find him. Last night was an inferno. Worst fire ever for this place. Looking at it in daylight, it's a wonder the town didn't go up in flames." He paused for a moment. "Considering all that happened last night and the fact that John Obadiah might 'a been drinking makes me wonder if he fell into the river or the creek--lost his balance--since you found one of his crutches. Both those blasts were mighty strong and close to shore, too."

He paused and shifted his weight in his chair.

"You know that fire went on down the river. Found out this morning when Len Davis came up here from Franklin with a passenger in his hack, said was the only way to get here 'cause of the fire. Told me one of those burning barges floated on down the river, passed under the bridge that crosses the Allegheny at Franklin--the suspension bridge--and burned it up. Even down there, the floating crude was afire and burned as it passed under. Said they could see the flashes of light up our way. You know up here, the clouds reflected the fire from below and turned red then pink. Actually, was quite beautiful if it had not been so destructive and threatening."

"Did they figure out how the whole thing got started?"

"There were four men on the first barge that was loaded with crude and it exploded. They said that one of their mates who was badly burned in the face and hand, caused it. Said they all suspected that the boat was leaking oil. So, this gent, the one in charge, decided to take a look using a lit lantern that he lowered into the hold through the hatch. That's when that first explosion rocked the area. The other three men were blown off the barge and into the river at the mouth of the creek, but they survived."

Matthias nodded.

"Sure caused a horrible situation that looked like the regions of Pluto! You say no one was killed?"

Sheriff Thomas turned toward Matthias.

"But now your report on the fact that John Obadiah is missing makes me to pause and reconsider. We'll be retrieving chains and other equipment from the area and also from Moran's Island. I'll tell those involved to watch for any signs of him. That other crutch should float since it's wood. 'Course it could have been consumed along with the floating, flaming crude. Meantime, take another look where you found the one crutch. Maybe he was knocked unconscious from the blast and overlooked during the mayhem that ensued."

He stood as a sign that the meeting was over and shook hands with each of them.

"I am sorry for such a situation."

...

February 1, 1864
Bristow Station, Virginia

Dear Mother and Luke,

With great sorrow, I read your letter of some months ago. What a terrible end for our poor father. He was a troubled soul, no doubt. Mother, I am grateful for you explaining to me and Luke the sad change in him following his accident that took his leg. It helped me to understand him better.

I miss you and Luke even more so, knowing the frightful surroundings of his disappearance. I am sorry not to be with you in such a time. Thanks be to God that Uncle Matthias was with Luke, in your absence. How is Grandfather getting along now?

We are in winter quarters for a few months, located between Washington and Richmond. It has been frightful cold here, living in tents, and I am ever grateful for the wool socks from home.

I am wondering if this War of Rebellion will ever come to an end. I get comfort from the men with whom I fight because we fight for each other. Despite losses, we remain a solid team. Our leadership has changed several times on account of illness and officers being wounded or killed. It is a bitter battle. Yet, I am proud to serve with the men from up the Allegheny.

I love you and miss you sorely.

Your loving son and brother,

Elis   ...

Dear Mother and Luke,   April 25, 1864

I write with good news at last. Yesterday, we learned that our Bucktails unit will be mustered out in the next five weeks, our time in service having expired. No sure date has been given us as yet, but I will write upon learning of my release time.

We break camp in a few days. It is rumored that we will engage the enemy somewhere near here, but we have not been told of our orders as of yet.

I dream of returning to you as soon as these last few weeks are over.

Your loving son and brother, Elias

Katherine Hires A Muscleman

Return to America, April 1864

As the early morning sunlight filtered through the dissipating fog, nineteen-year-old Katherine stood alone, as straight as a ramrod at the ship's rail, her chin tilted slightly upward, like a wary, wild wolf scenting the wind. The gentle April breeze riffled the surface of the sparkling Bordeaux Harbor and tugged on the pheasant feather clipped to her brown hat, and, with gloved hand, she reached up to ensure its anchor. She deeply breathed the salty, familiarly pungent sea air, then exhaled slowly through her slightly pursed lips, a cultivated, calming habit that had served her well during the petulant periods of the past three years.

Her bright blue eyes followed the flight of the squawking sea birds as they hovered overhead, held aloft by the wind over a widening wedge of water between the diminishing dock in the busy, crowded French harbor and the stern of her departing sailing ship. Now, it was gathering speed seaward and out of the Gironde Estuary. She wondered at the birds' graceful swooping and diving deep into the white foaming froth of ship's wake, fishing for food. Fascinated, she watched their movements, hoping that she too could carry out her mission with equal success, finesse and grace.

As tears formed, she waved her final farewell to cousin Fredrick whose image became smaller as the distance between them grew. He stood on the disappearing dock among the waterfront workers who had loaded the casks of Pinot Noir and Sauvignon Blanc from their family's vineyards.

As she stood at the ship's rail, she thought of her life during the past three years. French culture and her mother's family had been a whole new world to her, but the most foreign and fascinating were the fragilities and the complexities of the viticulture of the vineyards…

…

Her family's land consisted of gravely quartz soil that facilitated drainage, so vital to the successful growth of the grape vines. That downriver soil had been washed there by the north-flowing Garonne River that descended from the Pyrenees. Fifteen miles north of Bordeaux, it joined the Dordogne River to form the Estuary of Gironde. Conditions in the area were near perfect for vineyards.

For several generations, her mother's family, the Gereaus had farmed a number of acres in the Medoc on the west bank of the Garonne. The wine trade had been the mainstay of this family in recent years. Her father, the late Captain Emile Van de Mere had transported their wine and that of their neighbors from Bordeaux to ports on the East Coast of North America. When Fredrick came aboard as the *West Wind's* cabin boy, the Captain determined that Fredrick should develop skills and knowledge about the growing of the vines and production of the wine that they carried. By accident rather than by design, she had returned to her French roots as well, and become involved in the family business of exporting wine.

Since her arrival in France, Katherine's curiosity of her family history had deepened, and she'd come to appreciate her French heritage. However, three years earlier, she had felt fearful regarding how her sudden arrival would be viewed by her mother's people whom she had never known. The inevitable meeting of these total strangers had concerned her during her voyage from Brooklyn to Bordeaux with Fredrick in April 1861, and she had voiced her anxiety to her beloved cousin.

"Fredrick, what will these people think of me--a homeless, abused fifteen-year-old, and obviously with child? I look a disgrace! I'm dressed in the only skirt and blouse that I could fit into my get-away carpet bag--no corset, hoops or crinolines. I'll arrive with only a man's knee breeches, a dog-eared jacket and a pair of boy's ill-fitting, scuffed boots, and bearing my one prized possession, the hand-mirror given to me by Papa.' Oh, good grief!"

Concerned, Fredrick had reassured her that she would be a welcome addition to this family.

"Think of it, Katie. I wasn't even directly related to them, only through the marriage of your Mama,' Aunt Yvette to Uncle Emile, and they took me in and treated me like one of them. They are good people. They will do well by you."

To her relief, Fredrick's prediction proved to be true. Her newly introduced family of fifteen people of all ages, one to eighty-one, had warmly welcomed her. Most of them had worked, or were working in their family vineyards. At that crucial first meeting, everyone seemed to be excitedly talking at once.

Katherine had concentrated, trying to understand their

discussion as much as her limited French would allow. She determined that the dominant theme of the chaotic conversation was about how much she resembled her late mother, their direct relative.

"Look at her eyes--just like Yvette, bright blue!"

"Her nose is the same as her Mama'—-straight--perfect."

After the excitement had subsided, her Aunt Gisele, her mother's youngest sister had talked quietly with Katherine about her stressful situation. Slowly in English mixed with her limited French, Katherine described her terrible treatment at the hands of Barrister Petrus Plugge. Blonde-haired Gisele listened intently, her fists clenched, her jaw set as Katherine spoke. On several occasions, she held her breath then exhaled loudly as she listened to her niece's terrifying tale.

For Katherine, their conversation brought great relief for the first time in months. Landing in this supportive family had begun the process of healing, much needed salving of the wound laid wide by the violent treatment of the greedy, treacherous Barrister who was akin to the wolf tending the hen house. He had savaged her body and her mind. But after three years of kindness and tutelage, she was recuperating.

Her gradual recovery she credited not only to her relatives, but to another insightful individual, a laborer at the vineyard. She remembered her first impression of him. She had begun her training in the vineyards.

His name was Jacques Guyot and on first sight, Katherine was afraid of him. What caught her attention was the black patch that covered his left eye. A wiry, but muscular figure, Jacques appeared shorter than most of the other workers since his frame bent forward and caused his neck to jut out from his barrel-shaped chest. A long white scar crossed his leathery face from his left ear to where it disappeared under the black eye patch. Although she wondered about his injury, she realized that she really did not want to know or to see the results. She had stayed her distance from this formidable figure.

"Katie," Fredrick said as she approached him one morning on a hot, sunny day in mid-May, "Today, Jacques will teach you how to prune vines. Here is a knife for you, probably belonged to your great grandfather, who knows. It's very sharp, so carry it this way in the sheath. Jacques is a good teacher and will show you how to use it safely. He is working about eight rows back in this vineyard," and he pointed the way for her.

Feeling intimidated by Fredrick's assignment, she hesitated a moment and then reluctantly turned in the direction of Jacques' location, passing row after row of vines. She thought about how, over the past three weeks, she had gratefully accepted the tutelage of her various family members on some aspect or other about the vineyards. Now, she realized that she was enjoying the camaraderie of working with them, and even the odors of the vineyard had become familiar to her. The aroma of nearby blossoms blended with the odor of soil permeated with grapes from previous harvests and she found it to be pleasant and now familiar. Somehow, it made her feel hopeful. She felt useful and was gaining skills never contemplated previously.

However, Fredrick's assigning her to work with Jacques set her on edge. She steeled herself for the challenge. He had a reputation of not welcoming strangers, and to him, she was a just that. Besides, Jacques was one of the few workers who was not family--apparently not kin to the Gereus. She knew little about him except that he was a veteran of the French Foreign Legion and had returned to this area after having been injured.

"Bon jour, Jacques!" Katherine greeted him brightly.

Unsmiling, he bowed slightly and tipped his broad-brimmed straw hat.

"Good morning, Mademoiselle Van de Mere," he said in English with a distinct accent that she could not place. He was dressed in his usual deep red, long-sleeved shirt that was already wet with sweat that descended from his broad back to the top of his black breeches. A gray rope anchored his worn pants and supported a knife sheath that housed the hook-shaped vine-cutting implement that looked like the one Fredrick had given her just minutes earlier. The open-toed, leather sandals that he wore in any weather--hot, cold, rainy or dry were dark with dust.

"So, you speak English, Monsieur Guyto? Since I am yet struggling with French, I am relieved to know that you can instruct me in English. The knife looks very sharp, and I want to make no mistakes."

Jacques gave her a hard look.

"So, you know nothing of this--this knife?"

She shook her head and was silent. The sun seemed to burn hotter as they stood there in silence. Finally she broke the stillness.

"Please teach me. I understand you are an expert with the knife."

"Yes. I will show you." He turned abruptly and moved into the shade of a vine, then beckoned Katherine to follow.

"This is a very ancient knife that has cut the vines for hundreds of years." That said, Jacques demonstrated for Katherine step-by-step the subtleties of pruning and splicing the vines.

The sun was high overhead and the morning breeze had disappeared when Katherine heard the familiar clanging of the distant noontime bell, the signal to the workers for rest and food. She and Jacques stopped their work and followed the path at the edge of the vineyard toward the house. She felt hot and tired but remained silent on the matter.

Suddenly, Jacques stopped in the shade of a tree and turned toward her. To her surprise, he looked straight at her, into her eyes.

"You are very good with the knife--a natural, Mademoiselle Katherine." For the first time in four hours with Jacques, he was conversant, other than the language of instruction.

"I want you to know that I am aware of your reversal of fortune. Fredrick has told me." He paused and shifted his weight. "He has also informed me of plans that the two of you are creating that involves the wine trade in America. I know that there is trouble--a war in America and for you alone, it could be dangerous. But business must go on despite that." Here he paused again, took a deep breath and continued. "He and I have discussed your safety in this work, and the need for you to be able to protect yourself during travel and business transactions. He asked me to teach you ways to defend yourself. I said, 'No, not until I work in the vineyards with you--to see your abilities and endurance.' So, today, we are doing that and now I am willing to provide you with some training--more skills for you and not working with the vines this time. I think you will learn quickly and have ability." He smiled at her, revealing a row of straight, white upper teeth that was interrupted by several empty slots--like a picket fence missing some boards.

Although she was surprised at his disclosure of his conversations with Fredrick, she was pleased. She now realized that Jacques had been evaluating her manual dexterity and readiness to learn. She smiled.

"So, I passed the test, did I?"

"So, you did. After discovering your situation, I agree with Fredrick. I will teach you how to use several weapons for your protection. That includes training you in moves of your body as well--getting out of a lock or hold, such as your stepfather may have used on you. Since he is yet alive and moving about, you need to be ready for him, should you encounter him in your travels in America."

Katherine looked at Jacques and was no longer afraid, but proud to be his friend.

She smiled, remembering...

...

Now with deliberateness and a sense of purpose, Katherine grasped the wet wooden ship's rail in a silent salute to France, and turned resolutely to face the open sea--the way west and back to America and into her future.

Since the *Moselle* was heavy with cargo, much of it scores of barrels of Bordeaux-region wine that had been loaded aboard under Fredrick's and her supervision, the ship sailed with only a small number of passengers. Relieved at learning that there were few other voyagers aboard, she was counting on the week's journey to give her time to sort things out. She did not want unnecessary or insouciant interactions with fellow passengers to interfere with her contemplations, nor did she want to be subject to prying people and querying questions. She realized that her unescorted traveling was unusual, and possibly subject to censure.

Jacques and Fredrick agreed that she needed to assume an alias--another surname in order to facilitate her traveling alone, as well as to avoid detection by her former stepfather. After all, they had reasoned, she had absconded with an entire week's earnings from the Red Lantern Inn. But of greater concern for the entire family was the Barrister's possible reaction if he were to discover that he had fathered a son. He might pursue the relationship, perhaps for reasons of inheritance. The Brooklyn house remained in her name, as her father had arranged years earlier. Claiming a son whose mother owned the property might be to the Barrister's advantage, especially through some legal maneuvering of which, they all realized, he was capable.

A greater threat of Petrus Plugg's possible discovery of his paternity was the child's having his life interrupted by this callus, evil man. Since little Pierre was being absorbed into the extended Gereau family, being raised by Suzette and her husband along with their three children, a disruption would be devastating for the child--for their entire family. In order to avoid detection during her present and necessary travel in her native country, a new surname had been created. She was traveling as Madame Antoine G. Garrone, a married woman with dual citizenship. To satisfy questions of any authorities, she had the proper papers to support her new identity.

She needed time to think and to plan, since so much had changed for her, following her clandestine departure from Brooklyn three years earlier. In fact, her nation had changed as well, and she needed to understand the vicissitudes created by the deep division and civil conflict among the American public over the slavery issue.

The London Times had agonizing accounts of the war that was dividing her country and dragging on forever. The horrifying stories of bloody battles and depressing damage to the bodies and souls of those suffering soldiers on both sides caused her concern about re-entering the war-ravaged areas by herself.

She reviewed one of the particular points in the worrisome war, the July 1863 Battle at Gettysburg, the farthest north that the seditious Confederate forces had pushed. Reports of 51,000 soldiers dead was simply beyond her comprehension. The disruption of life in the areas of fighting had been a long and debated topic among her French family, who were concerned about the disruptions of their wine trade. Fredrick kept a close eye on the news, and once the newspapers described the fighting as having receded south to the forests of Virginia and the hills of Tennessee, he finally determined it safe enough for her solo travel into the northern areas of country. He and her family were depending upon her to help build their business.

"I can do it."

She knew she could, that she could hold up her end of the bargain.   …

The wooden planked warehouse owned by the Baltimore Port Authority smelled musty and was poorly lit, even in broad daylight. The stark contrast between the sunny morning in early May 1864 and the inner sanctum and dank surroundings inside the cavernous portside storage building jolted Katherine. The only lighting she could discover flowed from within the high ceilinged structure. Shafts of sunlight penetrated from a row of windows mounted close to the cobwebbed beams supporting the roof. A soft cooing sound emanated from above, and she looked up to see a fine feather drifting downward, lazily, rising and falling with the slightest change in the air currents.

She stood, hands on her hips, surveying the wooden wine containers that port workers had transported from the hold of the

Moselle across the docks to their current location, this dark, dank building.

The Harbor Master's representative, a stout, red-faced fellow with wire-rimmed spectacles and pen in hand stared at her when he arrived, huffing and puffing. His job was to inventory and log her shipment from Bordeaux.

"Madame Garonne, I presume?" He studied her, like a hungry pelican spying a fish, then handed her a telegram. As she shoved the hastily folded message into her left-hand skirt pocket, she guessed that he thought it unusual for an unaccompanied female to be responsible for such a large and expensive inventory that he was recording in his leather-bound ledger.

She smiled at his departing back, amused at his apparent consternation of her gender and appearance in such an environment as this--rough dock workers, dark warehouses and the lack of anything remotely feminine.

Finally feeling relieved at the successful transport of her first cargo from France, she marveled that no barrels were damaged nor rolled off the docks and into the salty sea. Best of all, the shipment numbers were accurate and matched the exiting records from Bordeaux.

She slowly slid the creased telegram from its place of safety, smoothed it out, and moved into a shaft of sunlight to read it.

"Welcome home STOP Fredrick states I am to stay in touch with you STOP Send me address in Baltimore STOP Ebenezer"

Her eyes filled with tears when she recalled her last meeting with Ebenezer, her old family friend whose concern and compassion, together with Fredrick's ingenuity had extricated her from the sordid snares of the Red Lantern Inn and its despicable owner. She dabbed the tears and chided herself for having such sentimentality at this juncture, not the time or place for such emotion, alone in this dingy dungeon of a waterfront warehouse. Jacques had schooled her well. She imagined that she could hear his voice.

"Be ever alert to your surroundings, Katie. Don't let down your vigilance."

She slowly surveyed the vast wooden structure and shivered. Alone now that the Harbor Master's man had waddled away, she squinted in the dim light to read the markings that she and Fredrick had placed on each wooden barrel. Now her task lay in organizing and arranging the shipping of specific wine casks to each customer-

-hotels here in Baltimore and Washington. She knew she would need help with this, and she decided to return to the docks and hire an assistant. A strong man was required for the job at hand.

A shuffling sound from behind a stack of inventory startled her and broke the silence of the large enclosure. She felt a jolt of energy run through her body and she froze in place. Rats, maybe. Fredrick had warned her about such inhabitants of waterfront storage areas. She stared into the dimly lit area, but could see nothing moving.

Suddenly, a silhouette of a figure stealthily inching from behind the last row of barrels caught her eye. Spontaneously, she gasped in surprise. She could feel her muscles tense, and she moved her feet into a wider stance for fight or flight. When the figure continued to move toward her, she automatically stepped backwards toward the exit.

Instinctively, she felt for her pistol secured in the right-hand skirt pocket and then reached to ensure the location of her boot knife. Now at this moment, she realized that the hours of Jacques' training would pay off. She gripped the Stocking Model 1850 pistol and pressed back the hammer, ready for action.

"Who are you and what are you doing among my inventory?" she demanded in a clear, audible voice.

The figure stopped and stared at her through the gloom.

"That's right! Stay where you are. Do not come any closer!"

"Sorry, Madam, to startle you. I needed a place to rest, away from everything, so I found a space behind those barrels."

The voice was deep and the words carried a distinct accent that she recognized.

"Well, those are my barrels and I am responsible for them, so move on and find another resting place."

Now she could see the speaker, this intruder, as he moved into the path of sunlight that streamed through one of the high windows. The shaft of sunshine reflected dust particles floating languidly around the intruder and illuminated a handsome, rugged face, light brown hair, and dark eyebrows that accented uncommonly piercing dark eyes.

"What's that accent I hear? Are you German?"

"Ya—Württemberg. That's where I'm from--from Germany. My parents brought me to Syracuse when I was eleven years old. They own a gymnasium business. And you? You are French?"

_____

He smiled exposing a row of straight white teeth. Then he took a step closer and the shaft of sunlight revealed more of the man. He was tall, almost six feet and muscular with budging arms that filled the sleeves of his shirt, and legs as thick as tree trunks. Never had she seen such a person. She thought he looked close to her own age.

She took a step backward as she kept him in her sight. The fingers of her right hand pressed the smooth contour of the loaded pistol's wooden grip. The weapon remained obscured in her skirt pocket.

"Yes, French. I am French. I am shipping wine from my own vineyards."

When he took another step forward, she saw blood on his right leg that had saturated his once white stocking, turning it dark red.

"And you? What happened to you? You're injured. Stay where you are. Don't come any closer."

He was so near now that the metallic odor of blood filled her nostrils.

"I caught my leg when I jumped a fence back there." He gestured with his right hand toward the docks.

"Why were you jumping a fence? Was someone pursuing you?"

He hesitated before answering, and looked directly at her.

"Well, ya." He sounded reluctant to say more.

"Who?"

"Soldiers." His loud voice echoed in the half-empty warehouse. The only other sound was the seagulls' squawking as they hovered around the nearby docks searching for food.

"Soldiers? What soldiers?"

"Union."

"Why are they after you?" She squinted at him in the dim light.

"They want me in the army."

"I see." She frowned and then she turned her attention to the more urgent issue--his bloody leg.

"You have quite a wound."

"Ya. Can't get it to stop bleeding. That's why I was resting back there. Had to get off that leg."

Slowly, like a huge cat, he moved another step closer, but Katherine did not feel threatened. He was not menacing, but looked as if he needed help. Besides, she had the hidden pistol in her grip.

"Looks like you need a doctor. What's your name?"

"Benedict. People call me, 'Ben.' I don't know any doctors here. I can't look for one because I don't want to get caught by those Union men." He hesitated. "Maybe you can help me?"

"Maybe." She paused. "My name is Katherine. I used to live in Brooklyn." She let loose of her tight hold on the pistol, and reached her right hand toward Ben.

His grip was warm and firm, and he looked into her eyes. She felt a jolt of energy flow through her body and she shivered.

"Well, Ben-from-Syracuse, maybe you can help me, too. I need someone to assist with organizing and moving these wine casks for shipment to my clients."

"Ya, I could use some greenbacks." He looked down toward the blood oozing from the wound on his leg.

Katherine followed his gaze and made a decision. "First your leg has got to heal some. You can't go on like this…"

Suddenly, the sound of footfalls came from out on the docks and both Katherine and Ben turned in that direction.

"Soldiers!" Ben looked alarmed. "They're back!"

As the sounds became louder, men's voices were audible.

"Check this warehouse, men. He has to be here somewhere."

"I've got to go--to hide again." He limped toward his former hiding place, but before he managed to reach the back row of the barrels, four uniformed soldiers stomped over the threshold of the warehouse entrance.

Katherine glanced toward them and then turned toward her exposed, recently hired help.

"Now call out the markings on the barrels in the second row so that I can record them for the shipment to the first Washington hotel," she spoke loudly in French.

Ben took his queue and moved away from the threatening soldiers. He disappeared among the rows of wine barrels.

She turned toward the approaching men and smiled. "Bon joures, misères."

They stopped at a distance from her and gapped with surprised expressions, not unlike that of the Harbor Master's man some minutes earlier. One of the soldiers who she thought must be in charge, stepped forward, removing his hat and nodding toward her.

"Good day, madam. Pardon our intrusion. We are looking

for someone--a young man who seeks to avoid us."

She stared at them saying nothing.

"Have you seen anyone in this warehouse--a man?" The leader spoke in a demanding voice that was louder than necessary since his approach brought him within five feet of where she stood. When she failed to respond, he turned to his troops.

"What language is she speaking?"

They stared at her, this beautiful woman in a dim, gloomy warehouse who must have seemed to them, she thought with amusement, like a cat in a strange garret--out of place. Two shook their heads in negative reply and the third, a short dark man spoke.

"Sounds like French--maybe."

Their leader turned back to face her.

"Do...you...speak...English?" he demanded slowly, emphasizing each word.

"Un petite--a little."

A shuffling sound emanated from Ben's location.

"Who is with you--back there?"

"My hired man who comes with me." She gestured as she spoke.

"Come out of there!" The soldier shouted toward Ben's location. Nothing happened.

"He does not understand the English, you see." She smiled broadly. "He is from the Port of Bordeaux--only a worker for me." She sought to divert him.

"Oh, mister." She paused to cough. "A question please. Do you know of a doctor nearby? I am feeling ill since my long voyage. There was illness aboard and I am in need of medical assistance--if you please."

"Illness you say?" He looked alarmed and moved quickly away from her and toward his three waiting companions. She coughed again, failing to cover her mouth as she did so.

"We're wasting our time here. Take a look around the other end of this place--let's get on with it!"

In unison, the three soldiers turned their backs on Katherine and scattered, searching in the opposite direction. Their leader addressed her.

"Thank you, madam. Sorry for the interruption. You had best speak to the Harbor Master regarding a doctor." He moved toward the warehouse entrance.

She watched as all four of the uniformed authorities

completed their search and then tramped noisily back over the wooden docks and away from her.

She moved toward Ben and found him sitting on the floor, leaning against a barrel. His face was pale.

He looked up at her.

"Well done--my thanks."

"Now we'll tend to your wound. We're rid of them. You will come with me and we'll get you some help."

She looked down as Ben peered up at her, his new employer. She thought that he looked relieved. He smiled weakly as she helped him to his feet.

Surprisingly, she felt attracted to this handsome, muscular, but injured man, and a shiver shook her body. She wondered what Jacques would think of this encounter with a total stranger--this striking stranger. Was she being cautious enough, as her mentor had counseled? She shook off the thought of any adverse outcome, took a deep breath, and exhaled slowly.

Suddenly, she realized she felt pleasure in the company of a man. This moment was a turning point for her in the long, lonesome journey back to her country.

Benedict Hagan's Early Life

Syracuse, New York, July 1852

The sound of approaching footfalls sent the lithe, sun-tanned youth into action. Instinctively, Benedict slid deftly, without a splash, into his favorite hiding place out of the sight of everyone. The cold canal water felt good against his sun-scorched skin as he clung to the partially submerged bull rope at the stern of the barge. Hitching a ride on a commercial barge appealed to the sense of adventure of the eleven-year-old.

His family had easily blended with the earlier immigrating German and Irish who had worked on the Grand Erie Canal, an inspiration supported by New York Governor Dewitt Clinton. The project that had been proposed decades earlier was commenced in 1817. Referred to by opponents as "Clinton's Big Ditch," the Herculean labor was completed and open to traffic in 1825. The 363-mile-long manmade waterway turned out to be a major success that carried 33,000 commercial shipments at its peak, breathing new life into the communities along its banks from Albany to Buffalo, and transforming New York City into the major shipping port of the nation. So, anyone catching a ride in the heavy barge traffic had many options, as did young, handsome Benedict Hagan.

Slipping surreptitiously into the murky, cool waters of "The Erie" provided the tow-headed lad with an opportunity to cool off from the constant rays of the overhead July sun. He heard voices of a few boarding passengers and wondered if the small pile of clothing he had shed earlier would be detected by these new arrivals.

"Syracuse-next stop" called the barge's ticket taker in a voice loud enough for even he to hear from his position at the far end of the barge where he clung to the heavy rope used to secure the boat during docking. He had no ticket so each time the flatboat took on additional passengers, he slid into the water to remain unnoticed by anyone, most especially the captain or his hoggee who handled the horses. The distance of their current location from Syracuse was more than Benedict knew he could handle if he were put off and had to walk. His last morsel of food was twelve hours earlier when under cover of darkness, he had pillaged a passenger's travel bag and found only beef jerky and an apple.

The water, which at first had provided him relief from the sun's hot rays, now had wrinkled his fingers and made them mottled and white, and he shivered with cold. He knew he needed to quickly get back on the barge, undetected.

Minutes later, he heard the captain give a loud command to the two huge brown horses that pulled the 200-ton barge along the towpath on the north side of the refurbished seventy-foot-wide canal. They were underway again and any noise of his emerging from the water would be masked by the sounds of labored locomotion, conversing passengers, and clomping draft horses. He quietly pulled himself onto the ledge behind a bench holding several passengers, and lying on his back, he basked in the sun, unnoticed by anyone.

Benedict closed his eyes, and had drifted off for a nap when the clatter of nails on the wooden deck awakened him with a start. His eyes fluttered open and he came to full alert when a large shaggy dog's head and two brown front paws came into view, right above him. The critter's bared teeth and snarling alerted the animal's owner who arose from her seat and crossed the deck to see what the cunning canine had discovered. He heard the rustle of skirts, and the owner's high-pitched voice came nearer.

"Luscious, come here! What are you doing?"

Before the stowaway could slide from his perch back into the water, a ruffled red bonnet and flushed face appeared overhead.

"Well, look-a-here!" she exclaimed in a loud voice. "Look what Luscious found!"

Benedict, clad only in his wet, gray-tinged, knee-length under-drawers stared back at the now smiling face framed in a floppy sun hat. He remembered that his belongings were to the left of the bonneted face and he calculated that Syracuse was only a mile or so farther. He needed those clothes, especially the boots that he had worn from Wurttemberg to America. They still fit, although now a year later, they had begun to rub on the sides of both feet, turning his little toes red from the pressure. He acted quickly.

"Oh, hello, madam." He spoke in a nonchalant manner. He placed his right index finger over his pursed lips in an effort to silence this excited explorer.

"Please don't' tell Captain Lewis you found me resting here." He continued conspiratorially. "It's my job to lookout for anyone who tries to board without permission."

The woman's blue eyes widened and her jaw dropped.

He continued.

"I got so hot that I took the opportunity to cool off. Please hand me the clothes to your left."

The sunbonnet turned, ducked out of his sight, then reappeared with a pair of scuffed Brogans worn down at the heels and his shirt and britches in her out-stretched hands.

"Of course." She now employed a low voice. He was relieved that Luscious had grown quiet and was out of sight.

He went on talking as he pulled on his shirt.

"You see, I must get off at our next stop to pick up an order of fresh fruit for you passengers."

The woman nodded appreciatively and backed away as he stood to pull up and button the fly of his knee britches. The boots were last and he pulled them on just in time to hear the captain's command to the team pulling the barge.

"Whoa, boys, whoa!"

As soon as the flat boat approached the shore, Benedict stood, then crouched, estimating the distance, and finally sprang for dry land with a powerful leap like a newly hatched frog on a warm spring morning. His daring departure up the south side of the canal alerted Luscious who began his vicious barking while running to the starboard rail, and then stood on his hind legs whining loudly.

Benedict clambered crazily up the bank of the stone-lined canal, and ran wildly toward a clutch of passengers, tickets in hand who were preparing to board the barge. He turned to see Captain Lewis standing wide-legged on the starboard deck, shaking his clenched fist high in the air.

"There goes that little scallywag! I knew he was on here somewhere!"

He had escaped again.

...

Thirty minutes later with both parents at work in his mother's athletic training facility and his father finding jobs as a carpenter when time allowed, Benedict opened the apartment's small ice box and found a slice of beef, then retrieved a chunk of white bread from the breadbox near the stove. He assumed these were his portions of yesterday's dinner. He was ravenous, and glad that his mother was not present to witness his actual time of arrival.

He could eat in peace.

Just as he washed down the remainder of the bread with milk from his tin cup, the door swung open and his parents burst into the room.

"Oh, Benedict where have you been? We have looked all over for you and have been very worried!"

He stood quickly to address them in German.

"I went to the camp meeting with Jerome and his Ma. You know. They're always wanting you to go…" He looked directly at his muscular, dark-haired father who taught boxing, wrestling and weightlifting.

Benedict had heard him complain about "those pesky religious women," yet swept up by the region's religious fervor of the Second Great Awakening, that had a continuing impact years after its origin in 1790. The deeply rooted movement, like a holy cleansing conflagration, produced persistent converts who kept calling around, knocking on their door. He knew his father wanted nothing to do with these avid advocates of the American Bible Society, such as Mrs. Abercrombie, who came too frequently to express her concerns for the necessity of "saving their poor sorry souls." Teaching men the skills of fighting—boxing and wrestling was anathema to their Christian beliefs of non-violence, and from their viewpoint, the condition of one's soul who taught such desecration was certain to be in perpetual peril.

"Well, Mrs. Abercrombie just insisted that I go with them— her and Jerome—to share a meal—'breaking bread together,' she called it and I didn't want to insult her, so I went."

"Where were you last night? You didn't come home. We were worried."

"Well, Ma, the food was so good. I got so full, and the singing went on and on. It got real late, and Jerome and his Ma just kept on singing, and I guess I fell asleep. Once, I woke up in the dark, but didn't know the way back…and I was warm enough 'cause someone had throwed a blanket over me, so I went back to sleep 'til first light. Then, I jumped up and ran home and went to bed. Just woke up a little while ago."

The errant son examined the stern faces of his perplexed parents. He knew his father would not approach Mrs. Abercrombie for fear of a long-lasting lecture about the condition of his "unsaved soul." He was sure of his safety there and his mother was still hesitant to speak to her neighbors because of her difficulty with understanding English.

He was on solid ground with his story, this time.

November 1856

Benedict swept out the gym after the last client had departed. As well, he had to clear out the space that his father used for building cabinets when he was fortunate enough to get an order. His parents expected, demanded that he cleanup at the end of each busy workday.

Benedict leaned on his broad broom and with his right hand, he dug into his knee breeches' pocket. He produced a glittering gold piece and a silver pocket-watch complete with an intricate gold chain. Funny how these people, well off enough to take boxing lessons, did not miss some of their belongings--like the items in his hands, a shiny gold coin and an expensive-looking time piece. Did they own so much that they did not miss a few of their possessions that he had picked from their clothes left hanging while they took instruction from his father?

He figured that he added to his collection about once a week, never stealing from the same person twice and yet no one had complained to either parent about their missing items. Good for him, bad for them. After all, he got paid nothing for the work he did. "Family business. You are part of the family, so you work. Work is good for you, Benedict. Make you strong…" He had heard Joseph Hagan say that since he was old enough to understand. Working around the gymnasium did have its advantages other than providing an easy way to pilfer items of value.

For years, Benedict had watched the boxing lessons that were offered by his father and one assistant. After his end-of-day cleanup and alone in the wide spaces of the gym, he would don a pair of gloves and punch and jab, mimicking the moves he had observed earlier. Occasionally, his father would take time before dinner to spar with Benedict and correct his technique. As a result, his acquired fighting skill, reaction time and physical strength were unusual for his age. He took pride in this and it gave him confidence and status among his peers. However, his dexterity and strength had unforeseen consequences.

Now he was no longer in school. He had rationalized that expulsion with little hesitation, as he had explained to his distraught parents.

"The schoolmaster had put me out for punching that punk, Lancaster Bointon. That punk took a swing at me first. It was just that no one had seen that. I just finished the fight and I got punished. That guy did not even get into trouble--only I got punished."

He looked around in the dim light of oncoming evening.

"Well, I didn't like sitting in there all day, anyway." He shrugged and picked up the broom just as the sun sank slowly in the western sky, making the silent shadows loom long, and the Fall air, cool. Unbeknownst to Benedict, his secret stash of stolen spoils was in jeopardy.

...

Two weeks later, Gretta Hagan followed her life-long pattern of annual pre-Christmas house cleaning, instilled in her by a strict German upbringing, and Benedict returned home to find both parents pondering his treasure trove covertly compiled from his productive pillaging. They sat at the dining table with his special box between them, his stolen items spread out in rows on the tabletop. His parents turned in unison when they heard him enter. His father stood, pushing his chair back so abruptly that he upset it, and the wooden seat fell to the hard, recently scrubbed floor with a loud crash.

He stopped in his tracks at the scene before him and prepared to run back out the door. As his male parent stooped to scoop up the fallen furniture, he looked at Benedict.

"Son, take a seat at the table. Your mother and I have some questions, serious questions."

Realizing that evidence of his thievery was spread out for all to see, he knew he was caught. The discussion that was sure to follow would not in his favor, and his mind scrambled for a defense, but for once, none came.

"Where did these things come from?" His father spoke to him in German. He could feel his mother's eyes on him. He stared down at his dirty fists and would not meet the intense gaze of either parent.

"Oh, here and there…"

"This looks like Ward Bulfinch's pocket watch. I've seen him with it. He is one of our best customers." His mother paused and leaned forward in an attempt to meet his eyes.

"You're stealing from our clients, Benedict." Her voice was

pitched an octave higher.

"We will lose our clients! Do you know what will happen when these people quit our gym?" Her eyes filled with tears, her fists were clinched.

"We will have no 6-Kreuzer—no money to buy food. No money for the rent. The landlord will put us out on the street!" She covered her face with her hands and sobbed.

"Benedict, you have gone too far this time. Bad enough was your thieving those books from that minister's library, volumes with steel engravings. But tearing out the sketches and throwing the books away! And for that you got thirty days in the Onondaga County jail. I thought you learned your lesson. But now you've been at it again, but this time it is different, much different."

"Your stealing could bring us down—ruin our business—the only means we have to keep us going." His father's voice sounded steady and loud. The volume hurt his ears, but he knew better not to cover them. Previous experience with his father had taught him that.

Benedict remained sullenly silent and stared at the parallel leaves of the dining table. His eyes defocused and he momentarily withdrew from the serious scene.

"Gretta," Joseph looked at his wife as she blew her nose and wiped the tears from her face. "Get some pen and paper. Benedict here needs to list every item on this table, and you write that down. He will give us the name of each person who owns it, and you write that name beside each thing. We must return these belongings to their rightful owners."

"But Joe that will get Benedict in big trouble. Someone might report him to the constable—the sheriff. They could arrest him again and put him back in jail…" and she began crying again.

"Gretta, this boy must learn his lesson, take the consequences of his bad behavior. We cannot afford to lose our customers."

"Benedict, what do you have to say about this?"

He shifted in his chair. The seat was hard and without a cushion.

"I don't know where those things came from."

With that, Joseph Hagan jumped to his feet and moved swiftly toward Benedict who knew that he was helpless before his formidable father, this pillar of power. He was afraid of him. He could feel perspiration forming on his upper lip. He felt like a sly red fox that got caught in the henhouse with feathers sticking out from his teeth. The odds against him were overwhelming and seemed insurmountable. He had to talk and talk fast.

"Well, nobody missed the stuff, did they? Why do we have to tell them that we have their things? You could tell them that you found them somewhere at the gym."

Parental patience had expired, was exhausted. His father shook his head sadly.

"We gave up everything in Wurttemberg and moved here to give you a better future—for you it was." His voice grew louder now.

"To escape the political unrest and to keep you from being subject of a king. To get you away from the revolution and chance of bloody wars—and that's all you can say?" Now his father was shouting and his mother wept aloud and without restraint.

"I will take this up with the authorities. We cannot have you continue stealing and living under this roof. I will not allow it!"

Benedict's life was about to change.

...

He awakened to the sound of loud coughing and the murmur of voices. Before he opened his eyes, he heard shuffling footsteps that seemed to be coming toward him. In the dim light of daybreak, he could make out the shapes of several silent silhouetted figures standing quietly beside him, staring at him. Without moving, he stared back, trying to focus on the closest figure. His hands and feet felt cold and when he wiggled his toes, he realized that his boots had remained in place throughout the night. In fact, he was fully clothed just as he was when he left Syracuse.

"Who are you?" A voice came almost over his head, and he sat up quickly, sending the speaker several steps backwards.

"I'm Ben—Benedict Hagan. Who are you?"

"My name is John—John Weimer. I'm the senior man here—of this area."

He stepped back as Benedict got up off of the low-slung bunk with a thin straw mattress. Benedict noticed with relief that his greeter was his own height, no taller.

"These here are Henry—we call him Hank, and Pete, and this here is Clark."

"What are you in for?" John asked.

Benedict eyed them carefully, weighing his possible

responses.

"In here for....?"

"Yah, what have ya done to be put in the Refuge—the House of Refuge?"

"That where I am?" He could feel the group moving closer to him, so he stretched and yawned, and they fell back a step or two.

"Oh, I got in trouble for taking some stuff that didn't belong to me. Just borrowing it, ya know."

The greeters stood silently.

"So, where am I?"

"The Western House of Refuge in Rochester near the Genesee River. If you're thinkin' of leavin,' ya got to know how to climb over this here twenty-two-foot wall that's around us."

"Ya!" They turned to Pete and they all laughed.

Benedict looked around at his welcoming committee. They were dressed in dark colored knee breeches and long-sleeved shirts, some of which were tattered at the cuffs. The boys were not very tall, except for John.

"Just how old are you boys?" Benedict eyed them.

John Weimer spoke for the group.

"Sidney here is twelve—he thinks. No Pa, no Ma, so he's not sure."

Benedict saw one of the figures step forward, take a deep breath, stretching his scrawny fame to full height-about four feet and ten inches, as Benedict estimated.

"Ya, I am old enough to steal a pistol and three knives, before I got took in..."

"And Pete." John pointed to a sullen-looking lad to his left who had not moved nor looked at the newcomer. He just stared straight ahead at the wall.

"He's fifteen—in for hangin' 'round in the streets at night 'til the neighbors took him to the constable since he had nowhere to be."

In the increasing daylight, Benedict could see Pete shift his weight and turn toward the group.

"Ey, well, me Pa died a year ago last month, and me Ma stays where she works—no room for me, though. So, I took to taking a loaf from the baker, and a few coins where I could put my hands on them. Neighbors gave me eats sometimes."

John turned toward his left, and pointed to a dirty looking, thin figure with a sad expression on his face.

"I didn't take nothin'. Just borrowed a silver dollar from a farmer who gave me some work, and I been here over a year for that…"

"How old are you, 'dollar-stealer? What's your name?" Benedict turned to look more closely in the dim light.

"Clark—Clark Little and I'm thirteen." He smiled hesitantly with the group's attention on him.

"Where are you coming from, Benedict?"

"Syracuse—actually, from Germany."

"Me too." John said. "Came here with my Ma and uncle."

"Me folks came from Ireland—across the sea—sent me out to work the fields as soon as I was old enough. Then me mother died of the fever. I stole a pair of breeches and a shirt 'cause mine was wore out." Benedict followed the voice to the corner of the cramped room where a blue-eyed, red-headed child sat quietly on the edge of a narrow bunk.

"What's your name?"

"Henry—folks call me Hank." Another under-fed inmate, Benedict thought. Am I going to get enough to eat?

Suddenly a bell clanged, startling Benedict.

"What's that for?"

"It's the wake-up. We got up early 'cause we heard you come in after the lamp was out. So now we have fifteen minutes to make our beds, get dressed, then thirty minutes for breakfast—then work 'til noon. Get an hour for dinner-so work lasts for seven to eight hours a day. Some schooling, but I'm usually too tired to care about that."

"Work. What kind of work?"

"Shoe-makin' and building' chair-seats mostly. Some of us do tailoring."

"You mean making clothes?"

"Ya, but I like the shoemaking the best. It's hard work. Got to get the stitching just right or the shoes rub sores on the feet."

Benedict followed John as he reached his unmade cot and began straightening the covers. "Our group is younger, boys like Sidney, and it's easier work than what goes on with the girls and older inmates."

"Girls! There are girls here too?" He felt surprised at this news.

"Ya, the girls wash and cook, make clothes and stuff for beds for all of us. The older boys in the North, they make frames, like for chairs and seats, do some work with wire, and build rattraps."

Benedict heard the bell ring again.

"That's the breakfast bell."

"Guess I go with you now?"

"Ya, until they decide which division for you—North or South. North Division is older guys with more serious trouble. You were with us last night 'cause we had an empty bunk. They sent that guy out to work for a farmer. It's called indenturing—kind of like slavery, I think, for you don't know how long you're gonna be there—like being in here. No date for when you can leave, no matter how good you behave. Just work, work, work…" John paused.

"Come on Benedict, I'll show you where we eat—see what they have to offer this morning—usually the same stuff, no choices. Got this gruel that we call 'slop' but at least it's food."

…

Benedict shifted from one foot to the other as he stood outside the office of Superintendent John Ketcham. Finally, the door was flung open and a short, stout, smiling figure of Howard Dash, Manager beckoned him with the swoop of his left arm, then marched him into a spacious room with high ceilings and tall, narrow windows. The place reeked of whale oil lamps that provided a modicum of illumination for the stony-faced men who sat on both sides of a shiny wooden table. He was not invited to sit, but left standing in front of them.

"Mr. Benedict Hagan, this Admission Committee has reviewed your record and come to a decision as to your placement here at the Western House of Refuge. You and other inmates are indeed fortunate that the State of New York and the City of Rochester as well, have made possible such desirable accommodations and industrial system as here in Rochester. This institution has set both moral and intellectual standards so as to prepare inmates to be productive members of society, as was set forth by the founding members of the Society for the Prevention of Pauperism and Crime in 1818.

"We have determined that you will be placed in the North Division where you are expected to excel at work as well as academics. North Division is of course under my supervision and direction." He glanced toward the upturned visages aligned with the table's edges, then continued.

"So there are no misunderstandings regarding our system of

rewards and punishments, I will list them now with these dedicated men as witnesses."

As Benedict tried shifting his weight toward his heels to relieve persistent foot pain, he faced these decision makers who seemed determined to bring him into tow like his parents had tried to do. Would he get another pair of better fitting shoes from this high-minded group? His attention was on his sore feet and his growling stomach, but the lecturer droned on.

"The five-grade system is divided thus: the highest group is the Class of Honor; then the next is Class One, made up of those who attend to their schedules, are peaceful, truth-telling inmates, who if they refrain from obscene language, and do not attempt to escape for a three-month period... Level Two are striving to be free of vicious behavior. Class Three includes those with nasty behavior, but not severe enough for Class Four who are head-strong, break the rules, and generally malcontents—vicious and have attempted to escape."

Now he looked straight at Benedict, who by this time had rocked forward slightly and onto his toes.

"The rewards and punishments are also in gradations:

Class of Honor and Class One wear badges that set them above the lower classes—a distinction. They have special privileges. Punishments, however, are meted out as follows from higher to lower." He now read from a paper.

"Depravation of play hours; will work the maximum number of hours; will go to bed with no supper at dusk; bread and water for food; solitary confinement in unlighted... corporeal punishment delivered with deliberateness and not with anger."

At the mention of no supper at night, and only bread and water by day, Benedict switched his attention from his feet to his aching stomach. They took away your food. What? At the next remark from the powerful Dash, he cringed.

"Of course, we will start you out with the Badge of Distinction so that you will stand out to all of the others in your group and surely strive to keep this honor."

...

When the dinner bell rang at noon, Benedict dropped his tool used for carving leather, and headed to his bunk in the North sleeping room. His coat was too warm now, and he planned to secure it in the small chest that was at the foot of his bunk. As he stowed his coat and turned to leave for dinner, he encountered a sullen looking inmate with a pockmarked face and a sweaty brow. He was taller than Benedict.

"Well look at the new guy. He's got a Dingy Badge! What a dandy-candy!"

Benedict saw the fist coming, but too late to duck the blow that glanced off of his left jaw and knocked him into the bunk next to his. Gathering himself up, he regained his posture and prepared himself to lower the scum-bum who had surprised him. He struck back with a vicious right to the abdomen that sent the attacker backwards, landing on his backside and sliding into the corridor. The fellow lay there with his eyes rolled back in his head, like a big frog sunning on a lily pad on a hot August afternoon in the cool waters of the Erie Canal.

Benedict looked around and saw that no one had witnessed the short and vicious fight, so he stepped around the unconscious lout and walked toward the dining area without a backward glance.

So much for the Badge of Distinction, he thought. It was nothing more than an invitation—a setup to test the "new man." He realized that this was only the beginning. He was ready, prepared for whatever came his way. With little control over his immediate future, he felt no hesitation to use his well-honed fighting skills for his survival.

...

Since the officials at the Refuge had not set a date for the end of his indenture to Captain H. D. Boysen, master of the vessel, *Humboldt*, Benedict was determined to take matters into his own hands. Although he was not sure of his exact birthday—sometime in the Fall of 1841 his mother had said—but according to his calculations, he was now nineteen-years-old, and he felt deserving of his freedom, to have a life of his own.

He was tired of the long days and nights of work that was rewarded by the ship's food—hardly fit for animals let alone humans. The hardtack biscuits, fish, soup, beans or soggy, sour potatoes were tiresome. Aboard the *Humboldt*, the drinking water, fetched from the River Elbe in central Europe was stored in wooden barrels so burned on the inside that the water was black. At first, he had closed his eyes when he drank it. But worse than that was water for consumption that was available when the water stored in wooden barrels gave out. Then the water supply saved in metal barrels became a necessity. Those iron containers emitted rust-red liquid that was objectionable, but necessary to maintain life aboard ships for weeks at sea. Now he hated all of this—the water, the food, the work. He was ready for a major change, a better life.

As in the Refuge, on the *Humboldt,* he had fought his way into a position with the crew where initial challenges had been quelled by this fast footwork and flying fists. His final nemesis had been the Chief Boswains Mate whose openly hostile behavior toward him had been diminished by Captain' Boysen's intervention. That had made life bearable for the past twenty-seven months aboard this ocean-going ship of 789 tons, German-built in 1853.

December 1860

Finally, the *Humboldt* approached the docks across the sparkling water of Mobile Bay, Alabama and prepared to dock. After he and other crew offloaded the cargo of coffee, spices, iron and textiles, the Captain announced twelve hours of liberty for half of the crew which included Benedict. All were paid in full, except him. He received only a portion due him to guarantee his return to the *Humboldt.* Captain Boysen assigned the deckhand called Lloyd, ten years older than Benedict, to accompany him ashore and to ensure his reappearance at the end of their liberty.

After several hours of freedom, Benedict bought Lloyd another tankard of ale as they sat at the bar of a waterfront tavern. Lloyd had told him for the third time about his woman who was waiting for him in Brooklyn. He listened patiently, realizing that it was only a matter of Lloyd draining this last amount, and he would be too overtaken by alcohol to walk or even care if his young shipmate disappeared. He would give his guardian the slip just as soon as Lloyd slumped over.

"She sounds like quite the woman, Lloyd. What is her name again?"

"Suss..anna," Lloyd slurred.

"Let's raise a glass of ale to Suzanna!"

Then he raised his glass and clinked it with Lloyd's. His drinking companion took another deep draft of ale, and looked at him with unfocused eyes and a crooked smile.

"Yes, here's to my Suss...anna..."

He watched as Lloyd lowered first his drink, and then his

head to the surface of the wooden bar. Benedict slid from his seat and took a long look at Lloyd with his beaker of ale in one hand, and his head, padded by his seaman's wool cap, resting on the bar, sound asleep.

...

A ship's shrill whistle split the air announcing the end of liberty for the fero-bank players. Benedict collected his considerable winnings, jumped from his wooden box-seat in the dimly lit shack, and headed for the door. He moved down the pier at a rapid clip, knowing that the loot made him vulnerable. Suddenly, he felt a man on either side of him, crushing against him while they felt his pockets for the money. He moved swiftly.

While he pushed one away, he kicked the larger one in the gut. Losing his wind, his attacker careened into the wooden rail of the pier. Benedict turned and punched the younger gambler in his crooked nose, sending him sprawling over the rough boards. He picked up the limp body and dropped him from the pier. When he did not hear the expected splash, he realized that the tide was out. Now the only sound from that direction was groaning.

The big guy regained his feet and silently approached Benedict from behind. As Benedict was staring toward the location of his first victim, he felt a tight chokehold and painful pressure on his neck. He could not breathe. He struggled to pull his knife from its sheath. With a quick sideways move, he drove then twisted the seven-inch blade into his attacker's ribcage. Then everything went black.

When he came to, the sky was dark, and the moon was low on the eastern horizon. The only sounds were the waves pounding the nearby rocks and pier supports below as the tide flowed in. He got up, looked around to see his attacker's body lying lifeless. Assured that his winnings were intact, he ran through the dark, down the long wooden walk. At the end of the pier, he slowed and the metallic odor of blood filled his nostrils. He felt something sticky that soaked his shirt. As he came into the flickering light of a streetlamp, he passed several men who turned and stared. One of them shouted, and Benedict broke into a run, clutching his takings from the faro game as he fled.

...

The Yellow Dog Saloon was packed with men. Benedict

stood at the bar listening to the polyglot of languages discussing the possibility of war and what it would mean for this large port city. With emotions running high, boisterous sailors, French speakers, German and Italian immigrants, an assortment of characters crowded into the small New Orleans establishment. Benedict silently consumed his ale when one particularly loud voice rose above the din. Curious, he turned slightly to his left to identify the speaker. A gent named Baldy realized that he now had the attention of many of the salon's occupants.

A stocky, muscular man, eyes flashing, fists clenched as he addressed his audience, Baldy stood with legs spread as if ready for immediate action. Benedict saw that the speaker's face was red from the stuffy, over-heated saloon or the excessive consumption of alcohol, he knew not which. He listened while the braggart announced that he could best anyone present with his elite boxing skills.

"No Northerner can beat me!"

Benedict took note with increasing interest. Among the crowd there was murmuring, but no one took on the fighter's challenge. Benedict felt for his gun, a six-shooter that he packed since leaving the ship. He considered being armed for his own defense was especially important since he had no friends in the area--no one.

He pushed through the sweaty onlookers to get a closer look at the challenger, sizing him up.

"I am from the North, from New York--Syracuse, New York. You want to fight? Then I'm your man!"

The crowd moved away from him, giving his challenger full view. Baldy looked Benedict up and down.

"You're a damned Dutchman who could not defeat a 'Southern gentleman,' such as I!"

The two bristled and stared at each other as they maneuvered into a fighting stance. The crowd moved away from them; the circle enlarged as chairs were pushed aside. The space was inadequate. Baldy scowled at Benedict and sneered, "The fight is on then, Dutchman! See you outside!"

The crowd scrambled to the exit of the saloon and the two combatants arrived in the middle of the busy street. Someone in the crowd advised that fighting in front of the saloon would soon have the pugilists arrested and the excited crowd, growing as it went removed to the outskirts of the port city.

Quickly, the two went at it, bare fists pounding. When Benedict landed a square punch to his opponent's left eye, Baldy cursed and screamed, turning the fight into an anger- infused brawl. They rolled to the ground, fists flying and feet kicking. Benedict bested the Southerner, pinning him facedown to the ground. His knee was in his opponent's back. Baldy could not move.

He had won. He released his opponent.

On his feet again, Baldy suddenly drew a revolver and held it to Benedict's temple then pulled the trigger. When the gun misfired, he fumbled to re-cock his weapon. Benedict drew his revolver and shot his opponent in the chest. Bleeding, Baldy fell to the ground.

"My God, I am shot!" Then he went silent, his body limp.

The speechless crowd saw that Benedict's actions were justified. A pall fell over the once excited audience. Baldy lay lifeless.

As Benedict replaced his revolver in its holster, the bystanders quietly gathered to look at the dead man, the Confederate challenger. One in the group gathered-up Baldy's belongings and several men bore the dead fighter's body back to the city. Benedict turned himself in to authorities. Since the focus of everyone in New Orleans was on the possibility of war and not this local skirmish, justice was dispensed quickly.

The next morning, Benedict reported to his hastily scheduled arraignment in the parish courthouse. Upon hearing the facts of the matter in the killing, and listening to the testimony of willing witnesses, the judge passed sentence then and there. The magistrate ordered the Dutchman from Syracuse to serve in the Confederate army.

Within twenty-four hours, Benedict made his escape and headed out of the city.

Benedict Hagan on the Run

April 1863

By the time Benedict had seen his last customer to the exit of his New York City gymnasium, the lamplighter had come and gone leaving his street dimly lit. The air was heavy with an early spring rain. He began sweeping the gymnasium floor when he heard a sudden, sharp knock. He unlocked and opened the heavy wooden door to find Jasper, one of his cronies, shaking rainwater from his hat as he spoke.

"You ready? We have a meeting tonight--remember?"

"Ya, I know. Just finishing up here."

The two had recently formed The Banded Brotherhood of Bounty Jumpers, a growing group from the neighborhood--drinking comrades who met on a regular basis. Over the past six months, The Brothers had discussed ways to earn easy money, and were spurred on when the United States Congress passed legislation for a draft, The Civil War Military Draft Act on March 3, 1863. The intent of the new law was to swell the numbers of soldiers in the Union Army.

The Confederate officials had passed a similar law. Both acts allowed for a draftee to pay another man to serve in his place. That substitute-soldier could be paid a bounty of up to $300 for joining the Union Army. But the bounty for the Confederate cause was only $50.00 to $100. As well as collecting the government bounty, the draftee would pay the man going in his place. Members of the Banded Brotherhood of Bounty Jumpers agreed that the government had handed them a means to acquire quick money.

Benedict, Jasper and nine others had concurred on a plan. The process concocted by The Brothers required that each member would enlist in either army in place of a draftee, collect the bounty and then escape the military authorities when they abandoned their enlistment assignments. Before they left New York, they pooled a pot of ten greenbacks each, a reward for the first man to return from his initial bogus enlistment.

The Brothers considered bounty jumping was good money for the risk. The hazards varied from being sentenced to prison to public execution, sometimes in the presence of army soldiers. But to many, such as the impetuous and invincible young Benedict, the gamble was worth the take.

He enlisted several times in New York City and deserted when the troops moved toward the frontlines. The last enlistment was for a gentleman in Leeds, Massachusetts. The bonus had started at $300; the man who hired him paid him $200; then the city and state added their payments. On that one enlistment, Benedict had cleared nearly a $1000. This time he stayed with his company, the 35th Massachusetts Regiment as it moved into Virginia then toward the Rapidan River. When his unit maneuvered to cross the water and move closer to the battle line, he deserted--got "lost." Once away from his organization, he started running along the railroad tracks by night and sleeping in the woods by day until he could jump a northbound train under cover of darkness.

The timing had been tricky on that one. By the time he dropped off outside of Washington, he had consumed all of his rations and was famished. To make matters more difficult, now a year after he had begun his career as a jumper, the Federals seemed to have improved their AWOL notices and tracking methods. They had spotted him within a day of his arrival in the area and kept him on the run from Washington to Baltimore.

In addition, bounty-jumping had become more competitive since, in December 1863, the Confederacy had stopped the practice of allowing a draftee to pay someone else to serve in his place. That left the scores of men of his ilk only the federal units to pick from. For him, that meant staying around Maryland and Washington. As it was, the federal troops were looking for him now, maybe on several counts.

"Bounty-jumping worked for a time, but I'm not stupid," he said aloud. "Darn near caught me this time. I might be doing time right now--or worse--hanging."

Yes, the last episode was too close, even for Benedict Hagan...

...

Katherine watched while Dr. Sidney Bryant, his grey hair disheveled, his shoulders hunched, and his hands shaking, completed dressing Benedict's wound. The aged medical doctor turned slowly away from Benedict and addressed Katherine.

"You tell your man, here, that he's lucky that his wound is relatively shallow. This bandage should slow the bleeding. If there is puss in a few days, that will be unfortunate but expected with such a tear of tissue. As you saw, I did remove several pieces of debris--looks like wood."

He adjusted his wire-rimmed spectacles, and lowered himself to a quilt-padded chair.

"So, madam, will you be seeing about him, since he is your hired man?"

Katherine smiled.

"Oui, doctor, I will tend to him. You see, we have arrived only within a day from Bordeaux. He has no one else, and speaks only French and German. Do you understand?"

He nodded and his assistant moved forward to accept the charge for services. Katherine paid for the care, then received instructions on changing the dressing.

"He will need a good drink of whisky when you change the dressing. Change it in two days' time. It will be painful for at least a week or so. If the wound does emit bloody, thin puss, return here and I will pack it with an astringent. Or if it requires bromine to be injected at the edges of the wound, he will need anesthesia." He stood to assist them out the door.

"It would be a tragedy for such a fine-looking fella to lose his leg. Got enough of those young soldier's coming back from the battles, missing limbs. Pity." He shook his head and grimaced at the thought.

With the help of the old physician's young protégé on his right, Benedict hobbled out on to the street with Katherine on his left. She looked about the busy street, and was relieved that there were no soldiers in sight. They climbed into the waiting carriage.

. . .

Katherine was gone. Benedict felt at a loss. For a second morning, he awakened to realize the she had departed...

"Washington, first, then a place called, 'Corry,'" she'd told him. "Somewhere in Pennsylvania to meet up with the Pinot Noire that shipped from Bordeaux a fortnight ago."

They had walked to the B&O Station, two blocks from the rooms she had rented--Benedict's shelter. At that moment of her departure, he wanted to reach out and grab her by the waist and kiss her, kiss her hard so that she would remember him. But he had had so little experience with genteel, refined women that he had hesitated. The moment was gone, and she turned to board the train.

133

Then she had stopped, turned, and gazed up at him and smiled. The best he could do was reach for her hand and put it to his lips.

"Thank you, Benedict. You have been a real help to me."

He had felt a pang of separation that surprised him, the tough, independent fighter as he saw himself. Her smile was staying with him; the memory lingered...

How had such fortune befallen upon him, to meet this particular beauty...her blue eyes had pierced his soul. Yet, no words about their feelings had been spoken. She stayed in her room, he in his except when she came to care for his wound or bring him food. About a week before she left, his leg had healed enough for him to bear weight. He had accompanied her while she arranged the shipments to each customer. He was impressed with her forthright, determined approach to things.

She had handled the business of the wine transactions with confidence, letting no railroad clerk's condescending remarks discourage her. He admired her acumen as she negotiated shipping rates and rail accommodations for her product. She hired a stevedore and then he and this new man moved barrels as she directed. She was shrewd, formidable and knew her rights and her business, but at the same time conducted herself with grace. A rare beauty with a certain magnetism that could not be ignored. He had to admit that for the first time in his life, he was enamored...

For several minutes, he lay on his back staring at the wood plank ceiling. Then, with a return to the present, May 29, 1864, he rolled off of his narrow bed, and looked at himself in the mirror. His brown beard made him look different, older than the Benedict Hagan the Union soldiers were seeking. Three weeks earlier when he had met Katherine, he had had no facial hair, nor place to hide after he had ripped a jagged tear in his leg. If it had not been for Katherine's quick thinking and willingness to take a chance on him, he might be looking out from between bars of Old Capitol Prison in Washington or worse. Instead, his wound had healed and he had no pain when walking.

Thick, pink tissue had replaced in the jagged, torn flesh on the inside area of his right knee. Fascinated, he traced the irregular pattern with his finger.

She was the first person who had treated him with respect, without his having to prove himself with his fists. On one recent evening, they had shared a beaker of wine, a sample of one of her products, a pinot noir. As the light faded and evening wore on, they talked, talked at length. Mostly, he realized now, she had said little about herself, and he had led with a few stories about his exploits.

"Bounty-jumping had been good money until I injured my knee." Lucky he'd run into Katherine and he said so.

Through the dim light of the oil lamp, he saw that she was smiling, but he was not sure of her reaction to his revelations. He pictured her again. She was his first real friend in years...

"Maybe I'll see her again somewhere, sometime."

The thought made him feel hopeful. He pulled on his britches, and turned to locate his boots. He needed coffee and some food.

Outside, birds were chirping as in a chorus while Benedict was finishing his breakfast of hot coffee and brown bread. Now that his hunger was satisfied, he felt filled with energy. He moved toward the door, opened it just far enough to look both directions, then made a quick exit. He headed south toward the B&O Station. He sauntered two blocks when he heard shouting behind him.

"Halt! Stop--you, yes, you!" He could hear heavy footfalls getting closer, but he did not look back. He picked up his pace, trying not to break into a run, then slipped deftly into an alley on his left. Once out of sight of his pursuers, he took off in a run......

...

Benedict smelled the acrid odor of gunpowder that lingered in the river valley that lay east of Kennesaw Mountain. In the July heat and humidity, he could see the dark silhouette of the 691–foot-high Kennesaw Mountain that only a week earlier had been the site of ferocious fighting that went on for five days. In terms of attrition, the Rebels had won the battle: 3000 Yankees to 1000 Rebel soldiers killed. Despite the loss of troops, the Yankees pushed the Rebels toward Atlanta by outflanking them.

As Benedict's eyes traced the outline of the mountain, he could hear rifle fire to the south. He sat on a rock that was partially submerged in the languid current, and contemplated his situation. Here he was, camped at the edge of the Chattahoochee River, the last geographical obstacle protecting this key city in the south, deep in Confederate territory. He, the strongman, the acrobats and other performers were here to entertain troops, and anyone else who happened along and had the price of admission. It was an adventure at which he could make some money.

He unlaced and pulled off his latest acquisitions, his military boots that he had liberated from a body weeks ago near Chattanooga, Tennessee. The dead chap was clad in a blue Yankee uniform. His eyes were yet open and his mouth agape, as if he had been surprised. Benedict could not bear to look any further to discover other sordid details. That dead soldier could have been him. He pushed the gruesome image from his mind and threw a small smooth stone toward the beaver lodge. It skipped three times before sinking below the surface.

"Got those boots before someone else did…"

As he devised a plan, he felt the cool water relieve his cramped feet, too long inside those boots. Now he had the means to make a change, leave this traveling gymnastic company that, to Benedict, seemed bent on staying right up near the frontlines. The gymnasts were immigrants, like him, new to America and scrambling for a way to make a living. The risk of being caught-up in the fighting did not seem to concern them. In the short time he had been with them, the troupe had been on battlefields of Kentucky, Tennessee, and now Georgia. The carnage of the battlefields had been enough to satisfy his curiosity and his wanderlust. It was time to make a decision…

The sound of voices brought him back to the present. He could hear shouting from downstream. He stood up and saw several men up to their chests in the river. Just then, one of them waded toward the riverbank, and got out. He could see that the man was naked. Soldiers off duty and getting a bath, no doubt. He decided to follow suit, and quickly pulled off his britches. He looked down at the scar on his right leg.

"Katherine. The scar reminds me of her."

He arose from the rock and plunged in, enjoying the feel of the cool current and imagined that she was with him, here in the water. He imagined her blue eyes and her bare breasts…he lingered, floating on the surface, the sun bathing his face, his chest.

Then after a few moments, his vigor renewed, he plunged into an eddy, a quiet pool out of the main current. The cold water provided relief to his hot body. He ducked his head under the surface and ran his fingers through his hair. He remained submerged until he could feel goose bumps on his arms. He pulled himself on to the sunbaked rock whose hot surface began to warm him.

With conviction, he tossed a small stone into the center of the river. The time had come for him to slip off into the night away from the traveling troubadours and the morbid scenes of the battlefields.

He had heard trains heading north last night, so the tracks must be cleared and repaired by now. Since Atlanta, with the original name of "Terminus" was a major railroad hub, and the end of the line for four major rail routes, hitching a ride north from this location should be fairly easy, he reconned. Now these railroads were a target for federal forces whose strategy included gaining control of the trains in and out of this railroad center. They were the supply lines for the Confederate Army.

Relaxing, Benedict lay on the large rock, resting-up for his departure right after the troupe performed for General Howard's soldiers, whom were camped on this side of the river. Someone had told him that the troops were awaiting the arrival of federal pontoons since the bridge at Pace's Ferry crossing had been destroyed by the retreating Rebels--burned. Federal troops were moving southward on several fronts and might push onward to the southwest and into Alabama. Who knew? He had no desire to follow them any closer to Mobile where he had fought and killed the two faro card players who tried to rob him. Even though that had happened two years ago, he might be wanted by the law. That determined his plan.

"As soon as it's dark, I'll head for the tracks and go north. The oil country is up north," he said to himself. "Maybe I will meet up with Katherine again. I can only hope…"

In Oil Country, Katherine Meets an Actor

Franklin, Pennsylvania, July 1864

Katherine's left eyelid began twitching, tears ran down her cheeks, and her hand shook so violently that the wire from Ebenezer fluttered to the wood floor. She sat down hard on the edge of her narrow cot and stared at the fallen paper that documented the terrible turn in her life.

On this hot, humid afternoon in July, she received the telegram that sent her into a cold, clammy sweat. Despite Franklin's relentless heat and high humidity of her hotel room, she felt goose bumps on her forearms and the hair rising at the nape of her neck. The news was not good, in fact, when she learned what had happened, she was devastated, and felt desperate and deserted.

"In another week, I won't be unable to pay for my room or meals. Just when my life was turning around."

Katherine had been feeling excited and proud of arranging her first successful sales and she had plans for more. She hoped to travel as soon as she could to several other towns in the booming oil fields. Oil City and Titusville were in her sites. But two weeks later when her cousin failed to wire her again as planned, she became concerned.

"Ebenezer, not heard from Fredrick STOP Did the June 28 shipment arrive at your location STOP Have you been in contact STOP Where is he STOP. Katherine"

Ebenezer wired her saying that federal authorities enforcing the blockade of southern ports had boarded Fredrick's ship on the high seas, arrested him on account of "travel papers listing birthplace Charleston, South Carolina-Rebel territory." Authorities confiscated the cargo and Fredrick was imprisoned somewhere in the North.

Now, Katherine felt stranded and alone. She would extract a promise from Ebenezer that he would learn what had happened to Fredrick, where he was being held and let her know. Meanwhile, she should consider the cargo lost.

Franklin's *Venango Spectator* reported that confiscated

cargo from the blockade usually was sold at auction and the sailors on the arresting vessel would split the proceeds. Now, aware of that action by the Federals, Katherine felt angry but sorrowful at the same time. Someone else is drinking our wine, the lifeblood--survival for my French family and me.

Shaken, Katherine assessed her situation. Now, she was unable to fulfill her new wine contracts and had no income, nor means to leave this oil area. The worst part of it lay with determining where she should or could go, if she did have the money. Not back to France to the vineyards of her village--to what purpose. Certainly not travel to Brooklyn to claim her rightful property and to face her stepfather. She worried that by now he had somehow heard about the birth of the baby. This concern surfaced again and again in her mind.

"That would be awful."

The sound of her own voice in the quiet, stuffy room startled her. Staring at the dusty, wide boards of the floor, she struggled to regain her mental balance from the news of this latest event. A disaster--not of her making--nothing she had done caused this calamity. Her eyes defocused and she reviewed events and her decisions of the past several months, since her arrival in Baltimore.

"I got to Baltimore with no damage to the wine casks. I met Benedict who was trustworthy. He fell into my lap. We got the wine orders sorted and shipped.

Making arrangements for shipment had been easier than she had imagined, perhaps because she had him at her side. She did not appear as an unaccompanied female to the officials of the B&O Railroad. That railroad line, she realized was having its problems.

The B&O had remained under attack for months since Confederate forces disrupted schedules and destroyed supplies. Apparently, Cousin Fredrick had been unaware of these lesser-known military actions, otherwise, she yet might be in France.

The Baltimore newspapers noted that Rebel raids were so unpredictable and damaging that the B&O's President John Garrett had taken his complaints, a year earlier, to the Secretary of War Edwin Stanton in Washington. The perpetrators, a group of Confederate raiders were an independent unit whose leader was Captain John McNeill. A native of western Virginia, he had formed his company of over 200 men from merged Virginia cavalry and infantry units that became known as McNeill's Rangers. Union officers referred to these partisans as "Bushwhackers." In southern

Pennsylvania, the Rangers had succeeded in destroying train engines, and burning carpenter and machine shops. Not only had they disrupted rail schedules, and captured train mail, but they had liberated over 100 prisoners of war who were being transported to a federal prison.

As well, in northern Virginia and southern Maryland, a second military organization, Mosby's Raiders had tangled with Union troops but nevertheless succeeded in cutting telegraph wires and burning canal boats near Washington. By late April 1864, the Confederate independent military organizations were delivering more damaging and frequent blows. These attacks required dispatching greater numbers of Union forces to subdue the assaults.

She had heard discussions about the problem and even more details from Benedict. She was concerned about the effect of these raids and the impact on the railroad service, and subsequently, on her cargo deliveries.

Despite her current dilemma here in Franklin, she smiled at the thought of any of those scrawny-looking railroad workers facing her muscleman with a booming, commanding voice during the negotiations and arrangements for the transport of her merchandise. She had been glad to have had him accompanying her, for moral support, and besides she liked him. She had to admit that she felt attracted to his good looks, his piercing blue eyes and most of all she liked the way that he carried his muscled body, despite his injury, with strength and agility--like a cautious cougar, carefully planting each step with perfect balance.

She shook away his memory and re-focused on her current problem over which she had no control. Her shoulders slumped and she found it difficult to breathe. To get some relief, Katherine opened the window of her hotel room and took a deep breath. Then she collapsed again on her bed.

"It's always darkest before the dawn...." After taking several minutes for feelings of self-pity, she marshaled her forces, stood up, inhaled and exhaled slowly, and with her handkerchief, dabbed around her eyes. She reached for the bottom storage of a chest of drawers, opened it, and produced a small silver flask hidden in the folds of her extra set of pantaloons.

She stared at the initial engraved into the front of the metal flask: "K." Fredrick had given this gift to her just prior to her departure from Bordeaux. She remembered his saying, "The 'K' is a sure thing, Katie. Your surname may change once, twice--who knows how many times, but the 'K' is good forever."

Dear Fredrick. Her eyes filled with tears at his memory. It transported her back to France as she remembered one major crisis...

...

Katherine felt someone take her hand, and she turned her head to see Fredrick lift her hand to his lips and kiss her fingers. She felt as if she were underwater and she dozed until the next contraction seized her. The great pain slammed through her body, and she screamed out, by now her voice, hoarse.

"Damned be to that horrible man who raped me. He should burn in Hell!" She felt a new determination, a major change within her--no longer the victim, but now, the avenger.

"Push, Katherine!" Madame Duprey ordered. "Push child! And yes, damn him!"

Katherine gathered her strength from her pent-up anger against her stepfather. She screamed obscenities against him, grunting, panting and pushing over and over as the midwife coached her through the birthing of a baby she did not want, had not asked for.

"I will kill him! I hate him! I will kill him, that fiendish stepfather!"

With a strong, determined push, she bore down as hard as she could, eager to rid herself of this curse.

She heard Aunt Gisele declare, "It's done, Katie! He's born. Now you go to sleep."

She heard a squall of the newborn before she drifted off to the soft sound of varied voices, one who was Fredrick. He was at her side, her hand in his...

...

Now here in Franklin, she needed relief from the anxiety caused by her current dilemma. She removed the stopper of the flask, lifted it to her lips, squeezed her eyes shut and drank two swallows. The burning liquid rushed down her throat and into her stomach. She could feel its hot course all the way. In seconds, she forgot her smarting tongue and stinging throat.

This last wave of news washed over her like the surging surf at an Atlantic Beach before a storm. Surely, she deserved respite from the shattering report of Fredrick's imprisonment--imprisoned somewhere in the North by the Federal authorities.

As she clutched the flask, she realized that this item was one of three possessions that she actually owned, besides her clothing. Her hand-mirror, the flask and her Mama's wristlet made from a converted pocket watch. That item was a gift to her mother from her dear Pa-pa.' It was a gift at the end of his last voyage home to Brooklyn.

She sank into the only chair in her room, a wooden rocker with a faded-green seat-pad and stared out of the open window framed by white lace curtains.

Outside on the streets of Franklin, the sounds of oil pump engines provided a background for voices shouting commands to horses, and the footfalls of pedestrians walking on the wooden-plank sidewalks, an escape from the ever-present mud. Loud cursing of someone who sank up to his knees in ruts of oily green-black muck that passed for streets, rang out like the staccato notes of a music score. The gentle breeze of hot air carried the mixed stench of horse excrement and crude oil, both ever-present, but exaggerated by the heat of the day.

She watched as the sun sank slowly and shadows slipped silently across the dark derricks that studded backyards and barnyards, rose up from former flower gardens and pockmarked the rich bottomland created at the curve in French Creek a half-mile above its junction with the Allegheny River.

Before disappearing behind a river ridge, the setting sun illuminated the dark green leaves at the very tops of the elm trees growing along Elk Street near the United States Hotel. The rugged ridges that lay parallel to the river cast shadows that lengthened as the sun dropped, then disappeared into the west.

A century earlier, this confluence of the Allegheny River and French Creek was among the disputed territories of two powerful nations, France and England. Border disputes ignited into open conflict in the 1740s.

In November 1753, the Governor of the Colony of Virginia, Robert Dinwiddie commissioned George Washington to carry out a British directive. This mission required travel into the wilderness of the Allegheny and Ohio River basins. Washington, a twenty-one-year-old officer in the Army of Virginia was directed to deliver a letter of warning to the French Commandant located somewhere on those rivers. Dinwiddie's letter remonstrated against French plans to expand their fortification at the present site of Franklin.

On December 4, 1753, Washington arrived at Franklin. In carrying out his directive, Washington assessed the position, location and strength of French forces, as well as learning the amount of assistance and communications the French were receiving from Canada. In the spring of 1754, troops under Washington's command encountered French soldiers in the contested territory. They exchanged fire, igniting the French and Indian War, 1754-1763, a contentious conflict between the colonies of France and England in North America.

With the eventual defeat and withdrawal of the French from the region and the effects of treaties with local Indian tribes, settlers traveled into Northwestern Pennsylvania. With the few resources available, they managed to eke out an existence until 1859, the year when everything changed.

In August 1859 near Titusville, twenty miles North of Franklin, Colonel Edwin L. Drake drilled the first oil well that produced saleable crude oil. A newly formed, Connecticut-based Seneca Oil Company hired Drake as their agent. With a reputation for perseverance and honesty, Drake was hired by the oil company for another reason. As a former railroad employee, he had a free rail pass for the 400-mile journey to Titusville, Pennsylvania.

Drake arrived, a stranger to the area, but with dedication and a strong belief in his mission. After fits and starts to the project, the colonel and his right-hand man, "Uncle Billy" Smith, a former salt-well driller developed a method to obtain oil from the land. They struck oil at a depth of sixty-nine and one-half feet and demonstrated its successful extraction. This promise of new commerce set off a firestorm of enthusiasm. Fortune-seekers swarmed into the area searching for quick and easy wealth.

The tiny town of Franklin felt the impact of this onslaught that brought strangers flocking in from many parts of the country. Every stagecoach that slogged into Franklin disgorged outlanders whose travel brought about demands for services. They arrived with hardy appetites, inquiries about accommodations, and some, an unquenchable thirst for hard liquor, local brews or imported wine.

The sudden horde of hardy comers required hotels and restaurants to schedule meals in three to four seatings. The existing resources were strained to well beyond their limits. To support this sudden influx of humanity to this sleepy, remote area required a change of pace for its citizens. As well, it created a major market for equipment, lodging, clothing, food, liquor, and good French wine.

Katherine had recognized this opportunity and contacted Fredrick. He agreed to expand sales of wine from the family business into this area that was teaming with thirsty fortune seekers who had money to burn.

Franklin was her first stop in the oil region. Here she had contracted for wine sales with two hotel managers and immediately wired Fredrick. He assured her that he would set sail from Bordeaux to Brooklyn within a fortnight. The wine shipment from New York to Franklin was to arrive by rail...

Katherine shivered at how the winds of war had adversely affected her plans and could only wonder at the sudden reversal of fortune.

She took a deep breath, stood in front of the wall mirror and straightened her voluminous silk skirt. With her back to the wall-hung mirror, she held aloft her Papa's long-ago gift and inspected her back. Satisfied that her hair was in place and her dress hung properly from her shoulders, she descended the stairs to give the manager of the United States Hotel the bad news about her present predicament and their wine contract, now null and void--her first independently negotiated wine sale.

...

July wore on while Katherine awaited news of Fredrick's location and release. Finally, when no news came, she decided to accept an offer of employment from the hotel's manager. Little money was to change hands in this agreement since she would get room and board in exchange for her services, playing the piano and singing. Her only cash would come from tips and was dependent on the kindness of strangers, diners and those at the hotel bar.

Since being hired as an entertainer in the salon and dining room of the hotel, she felt some relief at now having an income, as modest and uncertain as it was, but grateful for any employment. At least, this position offered by Mathis George, the hotel manager came with one meal a day and a room. True, the new tiny, second floor location was tightly tucked under a back staircase, one floor above the toilet used by the kitchen crew.

Transferring to her new quarters had been quick and easy since she had only a few belongings, and Barnswell Buchanan had helped her. She felt fortunate at this point to have him as a new friend, a bartender, and to have an income source and a roof over

144

her head in this bustling community overrun by job and fortune-seekers.

Employment opportunities for males sprang from the new, booming oil industry, and men of all descriptions flooded the area. A few veterans were returning from the war and sought jobs. Others were lonely immigrants new to the country. Yet some were fortune-seekers including miners returning from the California gold fields. Then there were the locals, area farmers, weary of worrying about the weather and late frost blighting their wheat, oats and potato crops. They, like the others were now eager to cash in on the wild oil boom.

All of the five hotels in Franklin were packed full. Often two or three strangers shared to a room, and frequently, two shared a bed, positioned head-to-toe. Sleeping space was at a premium for those who could afford the price. Townspeople rented out spare rooms and haylofts, woodsheds and chicken coops. A few wayfarers slept in bobbing boats tethered to the river docks. Lease workers might hole-up in a tiny space, a doghouse near an oil derrick and sleep there. Many found solace and companionship at the long shiny bar of the United States Hotel.

At a distance from the bar, Katherine eyed the customers, drawing her conclusions based on her growing experience. A few of the imbibers appeared to be charming and well-bred, but not so with others who drank to excess, became bothersome, boisterous, or braggadocious at the bar. Six-foot-tall Barnswell, Katherine's friend would quit serving them until the hotel's security man would escort them off of the property.

Friday and Saturday evenings attracted oilrig workers, attic hands and greasers with dirty hands, encrusted fingernails and oil-streaked faces, along with red necks who reeked of horseflesh and human sweat. All of them were caked with mud, but their priorities were topped with a good stiff drink, almost always before a much-needed bath. Many could use a good hot scrub that would improve the environment for all, Katherine mused.

She thought of a Friday night regular, a local loud-mouthed tail sawyer whose muscular physic, imposing height and sandy-colored hair made him memorable, but undesirable. She noted that after a few drinks at the bar, he would lock his eyes on her during her break from entertaining. Barnswell would give her a hard stare as if to warn her off, and she would adroitly move away from the tipsy backwoodsman.

———

At the hotel, she had encountered too many men, like the sawyer, who were rough around the edges in manner, as well as dress, similar to dock workers in Baltimore and Bordeaux. Both places, the docks and the oil fields attracted strong, adaptable men who could tackle manual labor, long hours, and inclement weather. Every evening, the bar was packed with toolies, drillers, rig builders and rafters, all pressing toward the source of libations served by Barnswell and his assistants.

From Katherine's observations, these laborers had something more in common than muddy boots and smelling of stench of the barns and the pungent odors of the oil fields. They used tobacco--snuffed it, dipped it, cheeked it, and chewed it--spitting with abandon anywhere in the mud-clogged streets and elsewhere. Few smoked. The posted notices in the oil fields were clear: "SMOKERS WILL BE SHOT."

To accommodate these tobacco users, hotels had brass spittoons at various locations to encourage these spitters to use them, instead of leaving their uncultured marks on the dusty floors of their rooms, or in globs of slippery spittle on the wide wooden boards of the bar or the lobby.

The worst, she thought, were the smokers, many of whom worked in close contact with flammable oil. Talk around there was of smokers putting themselves and others in peril. At the bar in the hotel, stories of oil field fires were part of daily lore among concerned citizens and wary newcomers alike.

One gloomy, late afternoon during a constant downpour that created almost impassible roads, men with their wagons and horses slogged slowly into town from the wells. Since bar business was unhurried, Barnswell Buchanan told about one of the area's most famous fires. Katherine and everyone at the bar were quiet with attention riveted on the animated yet sensitive storyteller.

"In 1861--the same day as the fall of Fort Sumter--one of Henry Rouse's wells near the Buchanan farm--that's my family's farm--up north on Oil Creek--came in big--shootin' up a geyser of oil. It was a real spouter! But the worst thing happened. It caught fire. Flames shot seventy feet into the air leapin' across to a second well, then to oil stored in large wooden barrels nearby. Lit up the whole sky. Next, our barn full of grain and oil blew-up. That barn belonged to my uncle. It was awful to see. Burnin' boards flyin' through the air, smoke that made folks cough, their eyes smart and itch. I lived not far from there, then. Our house was not burned but

146

you could feel the awful heat from the flames.

"The explosions were so loud that some folks thought the blasts were artillery barrages--that the War of Rebellion had broke out right here as well as down in South Carolina. They were so bad that the ground shook. Smoke everywhere, people coughin' and heavin,' and the stench...it smelled like burnin' oil and burnt flesh. Eighteen men includin' Henry died--burned to death. Henry survived, all burned, for several hours.

"That brave man dictated his last will and testament, givin' his kin, friends and neighbors--so many people--some of his money. He helped all them people while he lay there dyin'. He was a nice man, and everybody loved Henry. Later, they named the place of that fire after him--Rouseville."

Barnswell stopped, wiped a tear from the corner of his eye.

"I still have bad dreams about that fire, sometimes. One reason I moved down here--to get away from the place of that terrible fire, in the shadow of that well that killed Henry and all those other people." He cast his eyes down and shook his head sadly.

The story reminded Katherine that Fredrick had told her about the fear of fire at sea, how her father had schooled him about that hazard. Now, here she was in oil country where fires were common and equally deadly, but on land, not sea.

Among this crowd of tobacco users, Katherine detected accents of all lilts, Ireland, Germany, the Confederacy, New York, and the twang of the local mountain men. They worked Katherine's imagination as to their places of origin--all migrated here to over-crowded Oildom. On the other hand, Katherine had learned from Barnswell about a better class of men who came here.

Early one evening before she was due to entertain, she sat at the end of the bar, and talked with Barnswell when he was not busy. He said the place was flooded with speculators eager to invest or to lease land for drilling, that they had money--plenty of it.

"That there is John Hanna, one of them land agents who bought some of the first stock in the Franklin Oil and Mining Company. Him along with Arnold Plumer who used to be a Congressman, and some local fellas' are makin' money from their investments. Like Gabe--Gabriel Smith, a Franklin lad who piloted boats on the Allegheny before Drake struck oil. He had investments in the *Monitor 2* and some other boats, but the oil excitement got him movin' in that direction--buyin' and sellin' oil and diggin' wells around here."

"See that tall gent--just walked in--with the moustache and big black, western-lookin' hat? That's California Sam."

"California Sam?"

"Samuel Crawford. Got that name 'cause one day, folks said, when he heard about the gold strike in California, he just hung-up his plow in his barn--had a place near Emlenton down river--and headed south to Panama. Trekked through the jungle from Atlantic side to the Pacific, without getting' sick or killed, then caught him a boat goin' north to California. Went diggin' for gold there and later in Idaho. Folks said he came back with near $5000 in gold--after four years. Now he's into oil, sort of a liquid gold, I guess you could say. And he's got property and wells below us here on the Allegheny and an oil business, the Big Bend Oil Company. Oops, got to go and fix him a drink."

As barman, Barnswell knew his customers, and to Katherine, he continued to quietly point out these wealthy men who gradually changed her opinion regarding the type of customers who drank at the bar and were seated in the dining room. Not so bad as she had thought. But by the appearance of their dirt-caked boots, mud did not discriminate between oilrig workers or stockholders and lease owners. The knee-high and thigh-high boots of worker and wealthy alike were caked with the black oily stuff that was made more odoriferous by horse droppings. For sure, the oil boom was attracting all sorts of people who brought change to Franklin, like it or not.

Folks here said that Franklin, its population of 936 had grown in the past three years, almost doubling in size. Since then, oil had been pumped out of almost anywhere in and near Franklin, along French Creek where it joined the Allegheny, near the old Fort Venango, in front yards or a neighbor's garden. As far as the eye could see, oil derricks spread across the waterway flats and up the sides of the river hills.

To Katherine, it was an eerie scene that resembled a forest. It looked like a forest of tall, wooden structures, greasy-black with oil, surrounded by machinery that was sunk into the ever-present mud. Most trees had been killed and the wood used for derricks, out-buildings, plank roads or wooden sidewalks. The forests were devastated, denuded by the activity of greasy well-drilling, mud-slogged wagons, excited men, and over-worked horses.

For Franklin's inhabitants, the destruction moved some to tears because anywhere near an oil well, the shrubbery, flowers and

148

grass had been trodden down and a forest of dead trees, wooden oil derricks, now transformed the landscape. Some residents were distraught over this destruction until their oil shares paid, or the well they had dug in their side-yards struck it big and the green gooey crude sprayed greenbacks right into their bank accounts. Then they celebrated with gusto at the local restaurants, and some came to the hotel where Katherine sized them up.

As she entered the dining area, she smiled at Barnswell who winked at her, and then she made her way through the men around the bar. The tall, portly oil speculator from New York with whom she had made acquaintance several days before had returned and nodded to her. She gave him a quick curtsy and a broad smile, and glided toward the square grand piano that dominated a corner of the room near the tall windows that looked onto Elk Street. She brushed past a spreading potted plant and seated herself at the keyboard. She felt relief that a cool evening breeze wafted through the open window.

Katherine noted that despite the booming oil explorations, the diners appeared to be more subdued than last night's crowd. The place even smelled better--more of lamp oil and food cooking than horse dung and greasy crude.

Wondering how she could lighten the prevailing mood, she decided to play some music that might cheer up the customers who may have been reacting to the recent news of the sanguinary war that ground on and on. Even in this remote region, citizens and oil workers heard about the war.

To Katherine, the statistics were horrible: a total of 520,000 Union and Confederate soldiers lay dead; hundreds were wounded. The all-out effort of the Union was at a standstill. Now in the summer of 1864, 200,000 Confederate forces and 650,000 Union soldiers clashed on battlefields. The Confederates, despite heavy causalities held Richmond. Half of Grant's army was destroyed. Union troops had captured Mobile Bay, but the Confederates held Charleston, South Carolina and Wilmington, North Carolina. The Union blockade had tightened. Federal and Confederate troops made the front pages of the *New York Times,* and the *Washington Star,* as well as the local news, *The Titusville Gazette* and *The Venango Spectator*. The newspaper articles may have contributed to the customers' gloom and demure demeanor.

The other pervading issue at that moment was the tumbling value of oil. She wondered if the price had dropped because of the market glut created by their very success--productive wells and the seemingly endless flows of Pennsylvania petroleum. She could not discern which topic was creating an unusually hushed audience, the plummeting price of a barrel of crude, or the dire data of dead and wounded, not until she talked with some of them would she know. She compared the interest in Oildom news with that public's attention to the conflict. She thought announcements of wells striking it big, often overshadowed the attention to the wearisome war. Tonight, for whatever reason, Katherine did not hear much laughter or talking. During her short break, only subdued murmurings and the clinking of silverware and glasses were discernable.

As she re-seated herself at the keyboard, she too felt anxious and feared for her own future since she'd lost contact with Fredrick. Where was he? Not lost at sea like her father, thank goodness, but locked up in a federal prison somewhere. The very thought caused her to gasp aloud for breath. At least, Ebenezer knew that he had been taken by the federal authorizes--but where.

"It's always darkest before the dawn..." she whispered to herself. She forced the worries out of her mind, and turned to her job, to entertain the clientele. I need to select something that will pull all of us out of the doldrums.

Instead of "Weeping, Sad and Lonely," a popular 1863 ballad, Katherine launched into several songs that were also familiar to people, "Turkey in the Straw," and "When Johnny Comes Marching Home Again." She smiled out at the audience and swayed as she played. When she began an old sea shanty that her father had taught her: "Yo, ho, and up she rises," she noticed that some diners looked in her direction and several in the bar area, turned around to face her. As she sang, a few in the audience were singing with her. Several men standing nearby tapped their feet to the music, glasses held high, beaming.

Smiling broadly, Katherine looked toward the cheerful audience and sang with gusto. She tossed her head and winked at men who saluted her with their drinks. It was working and she felt satisfied that her entertainment was raising spirits and probably promoting more business for the hotel, and job security for her in her uncertain situation.

As she followed those songs with several other familiar tunes, out of the corner of her eye, she noticed someone standing beside her, on her left. She glanced over and saw the profile of a tall, well-dressed gentleman, not the ilk of a laborer, but that of a real gentleman--dark suit with a white shirt, shiny brown boots and a black bowtie topped his celluloid collar. He was standing close enough that she noticed with relief that he did not reek of tobacco, nor were his boots caked with mud. Since she was nearing the end of her four-hour stint at the piano, she concluded with a closure to her playing, and nodded toward the scattered applause. Then she turned toward the gentleman as the audience resumed conversing, drinking and dining.

"Bonsoir, misère," and waited for him to state his business. When he said nothing, she rose slowly and extended her hand to him. He took her hand, put it to his lips, and bowed to her. A shock of pleasure soared through her body as she stared at him.

"I have enjoyed your musical talents, Miss Katherine. You have lifted my heart this evening from the dire news of the day. May I ask the pleasure of having a drink with you?"

She lowered her eyelids to half closed and raised her carefully shaped eyebrows and gave him the well-schooled expression of pleasure that she had cultivated during her training at the hands of the bejeweled Blanche de Brunt at the Red Lantern Inn.

"Why, I would be delighted, Mister..." and she paused to let him introduce himself.

"John Wilkes Booth, at your service, Ms. Katherine," and he escorted her to a small round table near the window.

She tried not to show her amazement and excitement at the introduction. At this point, she presented herself as a sophisticated woman of New York who had been schooled in France. However, in a move to appeal to his ego, she tilted her head to the right and smiled.

"*The* John Wilkes Booth, the actor?"

"The same," came the response. "I am here on business, and am currently doing little acting. Just came in from New York City." He paused. "I understand that you are a fluent French speaker and have traveled considerably."

"Yes, I do speak French. And I understand that you travel a great deal with your profession, as well." Booth smiled at the recognition and her focus on him.

"What brings you to this tiny town when you could be on the stage in New York?" She smiled and shifted her position, giving him a good look at her glossy hair and slender neck.

"I have an interest in the oil business--the exploration for oil in Pennsylvania that has created great excitement among investors like me. I have traveled to Franklin, walked the fields around here, and determined that there is a real future in the efforts of extracting and shipping oil. It's all the talk of the business world."

As they continued to converse, Katherine was taking in the mannerisms of the brown-eyed, well-groomed speaker whose dark eyes locked on hers and whose voice infused her interest. His charismatic demeanor, good looks, eloquent speech, and graceful hand movements caught Katherine off guard, and she found herself mesmerized by his presence. Admiring his manly physic, she felt a pleasant shock of adrenalin shoot through her.

From what a different world he had come, compared to the miserable situation from which she had escaped only several years earlier. The boorish face of Petrus Plugge forced its way into her consciousness. She mentally pushed away the disturbing image, and refocused her attention on the magnetic pull of Booth and what he was saying.

"In fact, while in New York, I purchased the written score of a recently published song that you might play here since a good number of patrons have invested in the oil business. It's called 'Oil on the Brain' and would be an addition to your repertoire. I will bring the sheet music for you to play tomorrow. When is a good time that we can try it out. When do you practice?" He paused and looked into her eyes. "Perhaps later, we could dine together."

They made a plan to meet the next day, and Katherine went to her room feeling light-headed and not quite believing that she was establishing a relationship with the popular Shakespearian actor, John Wilkes Booth. That night, she drifted off to sleep without the help of alcohol, but with pleasurable feelings of sexual attraction to Booth.

...

Katherine arrived at the hotel's kitchen in time to find Barnswell wiping his egg-smeared plate with a torn chunk of dark brown bread baked in the wee hours of the morning by William Wetzel, the hotel's German-born baker immigrated from Heizelbeck.

Brown bread was not William's specialty upon which he hung his excellent reputation. According to Barnswell, he turned out cinnamon chukka on a regular basis and apple pies in the fall as soon as the Northern Spies had ripened on his trees. His favorite, Barnswell had confided to her were William's cinnamon rolls with white creamy icing.

As she approached Barnswell, he reached for his beaker of milk. She noticed that a pan of those delicious pastries sat directly in front of him and half of the small pan's contents was missing. He licked icing from his fingers.

He looked up as she came near where he was seated, and waved the sticky hand, motioning for her to join him at the long wooden table. She chose a nearby chair that was across from him and sat down, her taffeta skirt making a swishing sound. She had learned that the hotel help as well as the clientele had to eat in shifts to keep everything moving as smoothly as possible. At this time of morning, however, most of the oil workers had eaten and departed for their work places so action in the dining room and kitchen had slowed.

"Well, Katherine, I noticed that you met the esteemed actor last evening. How did you like him?"

As usual, she noted, Barnswell did not miss anything that occurred in his domain, and her meeting Booth was no exception. He had witnessed it all. She took advantage of his observations.

"Does he stay here at the hotel often? Is he staying here now?" She peered across the table to watch her friend's expression.

"Well, when he first arrived here several months ago, he stayed here. In fact, the hotel was so crowded that it seemed he would end up sleepin' in the third-floor hallway. The manager was knocked-over by such an elegant and well-known arrival--really impressed--so he made an arrangement with a couple of gentlemen who did have a room."

"What sort of arrangement?"

"These guys, Harry Smith and Al Smiley are regulars here--been stayin' here for several months--so the manager asked them to make room for John Booth, and they did, for about a forte-night, the four of them, Joe Simonds from Boston came in with Booth and shared their double room with the newcomers."

"Did rooming together work out?"

"It did 'cause John started payin' for drinks and their billiards games. Yeh, Booth is real generous. He and Smiley got to be good friends, in fact. When Sarah's rooms came available, he and Joe moved to her place."

"Who is Sarah?"

"Sarah Webber owns a boardin' house on Buffalo Street. Now when he's in Franklin he mostly stays there. Comes to the bar here some evenings. What did you think of him?"

"Well, he said he liked my piano playing and singing. That was the start of our conversation. He mentioned about my speaking French--seemed to be impressed." She took a breath and hesitated, remembering her immediate attraction to Booth. "Then he told me about his interest in the extraction of oil, as he called it. Said he has a well or two near here. Is that true? I wondered what he is doing in this place instead of acting on the stage in New York or some other big city. I wager he was the only man in the room without mud-caked boots last night."

Barnswell laughed and took another cinnamon roll from the pan in front of him.

"Want one?"

She turned her coffee cup right-side up, and a waiter served steaming coffee as she retrieved the coveted pastry.

"So, what'd he have to say?" His blue eyes twinkled.

"Something about having some music I might like--has to do with oil. He brought it with him from New York--just out on the market." She paused and took a sip of her hot drink. "Barnswell, I was so shocked to see him standing there beside me that I'm not sure what we talked about. What I do remember is that he said he'd be pleased to have dinner with me sometime."

Barnswell sat up straight in his chair and looked her square-in-the-face--his pupils were dilated.

"Katherine, every woman in this town will be jealous of you. So many have set their hats for him. One followed him down Liberty Street and made sure she tipped her hoop skirt just so--like how far she would tilt it to get his attention. I watched that performance. He didn't seem to be effected. He is so well-liked by everyone--charmin' with a sort of magnetism--that he probably wanted to keep it that way--bein' in good graces with the town folks."

She smiled remembering how his good looks and dark eyes had captivated her from the start of their conversation. She felt even more flattered at last night's attention, hearing Barnswell's discussion about the local women and their attraction to the actor.

Just then, a familiar figure walked past the dining area and she recognized him.

"Oh, Barnswell, there he is already. He's early! I've got to go." Quickly, she pushed away her partially uneaten breakfast, stood, smoothed her skirt, took a deep breath, and headed toward the piano where John Wilkes had already seated himself.

Katherine felt her heart pounding in her chest as a jolt of energy traveled from her spine to her shoulders.

Maybe things were not so bad after all.

Stranded or Rescued?

Two days later, Katherine and Booth were returning from a carriage ride to view the Wilhelmina Well on the Fuller Farm in Cranberry Township. The well was owned by his enterprise, The Dramatic Oil Company whose over-seer was Thomas Mears, who had the reputation of a hard-hitting gambler.

"The Wilhelmina is a good producer. We hit oil at 800 feet after drilling through twenty feet of second-sand in February and it's been putting out 26 barrels a day. Tom's been a good manager, so far, and we've been selling shares at a steady pace. We named that well after Tom's wife. She's in Cleveland and I know Tom misses her, so I agreed to his naming it for her--since he is managing our company's business. After all, I have no wife--yet," and Katherine felt his sideways glance at her. She turned toward him and smiled. He reached for her hand as he grasped the reins with his other hand. She tilted her head to the side and smiled up at him. Their eyes met and held until he broke it off to mind the horses.

As they drove down the street toward her hotel, she noticed that people turned to stare at them in their sleek, white carriage drawn by a glossy black horse. Some waved and Booth doffed his hat to them. She thought him elegant--a standout among the lackluster locals and ordinary outsiders with his well-fitting dark pants, tightly-tailored black coat, and immaculately shined cavalry boots. A wide-brimmed black hat that he sported at a roguish angle topped his impressive figure. She thought that he looked like an exotic water bird that had just landed on the mud flats of some meandering river.

Besides being proud to be seen with him, she was feeling something deep within that was foreign to her, but excitingly pleasurable. She ached to be touched by him and wanted to stay with him, to never leave. She could feel heat rising on her neck and a wet tightness in her crotch. An undeniable desire to move closer to him on the buggy seat flooded over her, so she inched sideways and leaned lightly against his shoulder as they drew near her hotel.

Here we are in broad daylight with townspeople staring at us, she thought. Let them look. After all, I have no parent monitoring my behavior, no nosy neighbors eager to criticize me. I am my own independent agent, free to do what I please. Let them gawk. Perhaps they are staring at the future wife of John Wilkes Booth. She imagined herself arriving with him in New York City amid admiring crowds who were greeting them.

Suddenly, the dilemma of her being stranded here in oil country seemed less a problem. In fact, she found herself enjoying things. She sensed that she and Booth made a good match--her lustrous dark tresses, hourglass figure, and Paris-made gown, and his elegant demeanor, dashing build, and dapper dress. They made a handsome couple, and she knew it--her striking stature and his commanding presence.

The area near the front door of the hotel was crowded with more newcomers who had alighted from the grubby, dust-covered stagecoach that was stopped at the edge of the muddy street as near to the board sidewalk as possible. Strangers, mostly men with bed rolls strapped to their backs and carpet bags in their hands, stood in small groups, appearing to Katherine as if they were trying to get their bearings in a new environment. Some wore wide-brimmed straw hats, others dark head coverings that shaded their eyes from the afternoon sun.

As Booth jumped from the carriage, she slid on the smooth leather buggy seat toward her dashing driver, and he all but lifted her to the sidewalk. His arms were strong and his grip on her waist, firm. The murmuring voices of the newly-arrived quieted as they watched the two, some with open mouths as the dashing young actor took her hand to his lips, and bowed deeply. She looked into his eyes, then glanced around to see who was watching them.

"How wonderful to have been in your company this day, Miss Katherine."

As they entered the hotel and approached the front desk, Mathis, hotel's manager called her name, and she stopped to speak with him.

"I have a telegram for you, Miss Katherine. It's on my desk. Please wait a moment." He turned toward his office.

"Katherine, I must excuse myself to return the horse and carriage to Mr. Brigham, the liveryman. Please have dinner with me this evening after your performance."

He bowed again as he kissed her hand then turned quickly to exit the front door. Her eyes followed him.

Just as her handsome companion disappeared over the transom, the manager returned and handed her a telegram. She opened it quickly, her hands shaking. The words from Ebenezer were welcome, but yet shocking.

"Fredrick in prison at Fort McHenry Baltimore Harbor STOP Short visit with him STOP Looks thin weary but surviving STOP Worried about you STOP Many prisoners ill with fever STOP Needs released STOP Told me to appeal to Barrister Plugge for help STOP Ebenezer"

Inhaling in short, shallow breaths and eyes filled with tears, she sank slowly into a nearby chair. Whether she felt relief at knowing Fredrick's existence and whereabouts, or shock at learning that her stepfather would be involved with Fredrick's rescue, the news brutally shattered the pleasant bubble of haze and excitement of being with Booth. Like Cinderella after the ball, she was left with a pumpkin for a coach and rags for a ball-gown. Whichever it was, she wasn't sure, but her body shook, her left eyelid began to twitch and her breathing came in gasps. She stood shakily, retrieved her handkerchief from her skirt pocket then using it to cover her nose and mouth, she slowly mounted the wide stairway toward her second-floor room, grasping the smooth wooden banister as she went.

...

An hour later, partially recovered from the latest bad news, Katherine entered the hotel's kitchen. Since she was having dinner with Booth after her work was completed, she requested a generous slice of William Wetzel's brown bread and a wedge of local cheese to carry to her room. Once back, she opened the bottom dresser drawer, retrieved her silver flask, and took a mouthful of whiskey. She lay back on the bed and closed her eyes as the alcohol traveled from her mouth to her stomach and she felt the almost immediate relief that this distillate would bring her--without disappointment. Whiskey always delivered.

What was Fredrick thinking to involve her stepfather? He must be in dire straits to consider such a thing. He knew the risk, the danger to her of alerting the despot to the fact that she might be located. She shivered at the memory of three years earlier when his red sweaty face glared at her and he grabbed her hair, jerking her head up from the table. "Sign the papers!" She sat up quickly, opened her eyes, and slowed her breathing.

Another swallow of whiskey followed, then another until the once half-full flask was empty. She felt her head spin, but the relief she experienced was pure oblivion. She lay down again and closed her eyes, enjoying the blithe feelings of free-fall. No threatening stepfather...Fredrick will be freed...I will stay with John Wilkes Booth forever...

...

Sometime later, she awoke with a start to the chirping of birds settling down before sunset. The odor of meat cooking wafted up from the kitchen. She heard voices outside at the front of the hotel. She lay there staring at the ceiling, wondering at the time. She remembered that she should be preparing for her evening's entertainment in the dining room. She slowly arose, took a bite of cheese and a piece of bread to ease the burning in her stomach.

As she selected her outfit, she was relieved to hear the clock of the nearby Presbyterian Church chiming out the hour, six bells. She had just enough time dress and arrange her hair before she had to appear at the piano.

...

Several minutes before she was due to conclude her entertainment, Katherine spotted Booth at the bar, a drink in his hand. As she closed her program, he came forward, applauding. As she stood to join him, he bowed and took her hand to escort her to a table he had reserved for them. The dining room was crowded and prospective diners waited in the lobby and stood at the bar. No waiting for a table when she was with Booth.

She tried not to stare at his meticulous and distinctive style of dress as other diners were doing, but could not help but notice the change in this evening's attire from earlier in the day. As opposed to his black clothing that he wore when touring the oil fields, he had dressed in entirely different garb for this evening.

She admired his burgundy broadcloth jacket with a collar and labels to match, a suede waistcoat, and beige pants. She smiled at him over the large menu she was holding while trying not to stare at his costume. The silver buttons on his bright blue vest reflected the candlelight as they ordered their food.

"I hope that the telegram brought you good news this afternoon."

She took a deep breath and tried to organize an answer that would be unemotional, but accurate.

"In one way it was very good news. My cousin Fredrick who handles the wine shipments to me, is alive. How well he is remains

159

questionable. Our good family friend, Ebenezer traveled to Baltimore to visit him. Fredrick has been in prison for the past month with no release date."

Booth lay down his menu and sat up straighter.

"In prison. Why?"

Just then the waiter approached. Katherine said nothing and placed her order with the busy restaurant worker. Booth did the same.

As soon as the waiter had turned his back to leave their table, Katherine told Booth what had happened to Fredrick, how it had impacted their wine trade, the reason for her having to provide entertainment at the hotel.

"You understand, I am resentful of the Federals for arresting my cousin, and for no good reason. He has spent most of his time in France, ten years--since early 1854-- went there just before Pa-pa's ship sank."

"Your Papa's ship sank?"

Katherine explained to Booth about her father being a ship's captain and his apparent demise.

"They never recovered his body?"

"No. And of course I sometimes wonder if he is still alive somewhere. Anyhow, I guess I'm stranded here--at least for a while."

Booth reached across the table and took her hand.

"So, you were living in France with your cousin?"

"Yes, I was fortunate to spend time there learning the wine trade from him and my family near Bordeaux."

"Now I understand how you have come to speak French..."

Their discussion was curtailed by the arrival of the appetizer.

"Later, we can discuss the matter of your being stranded here--somewhere else where we won't be interrupted."

He smiled at her as he lifted his wine glass in a salute to her. She followed suit. Their eyes met and held as each took the first taste of wine.

At the conclusion of dinner, Booth led her to a secluded area of the lobby that was mostly deserted due to the late hour. It was almost midnight. As they settled themselves, drink in hand, near an open window, the clock on the church tower struck the twelve bells of midnight. Katherine shivered more from her realization and excitement of being with Booth than from the lightly cooled breeze that wafted through the open casement. He positioned himself in a chair perpendicular to the couch where she sat, pushing her voluminous skirt down with her hands.

He leaned forward, speaking in a low tone.

"I am not a fan of the Yankees and Mr. Lincoln's war on our southern brothers. Of course, I am not in a place where I dare speak plainly about my political leanings--not good for my standing in the theater, nor for making friends and doing business in this northern territory. Do you understand?" He gently placed several fingers under her chin and tilted her head back. Their eyes locked. Then, he withdrew his hand and traced her jaw with his index finger, down her neck to the cleavage of her breasts. He paused there, then moved his hand.

She nodded and took a sip of her whisky. Then he continued. "The Colored have their place and usefulness in our society, and I do not of approve of Lincoln's Emancipation Proclamation--not something we should be fighting about. What damage and suffering it is causing in the southern states." He shifted his weight and sat forward in his seat. "I do not fight because I promised my mother I would refrain from doing so." He paused. "I hope my bluntness does not offend you, my dear."

She nodded, but was stunned by his intense conversation. She remained silent.

He looked around for anyone who might overhear their conversation, and seeing no one, he continued.

"I am trying to assist the cause by providing some of my earnings from the theater which is about $20,000 a year as well as some of the profits from the oil venture to patriots of the South." He paused and gave her a long look.

"Most recently, I invested money, $1000, only a fraction of an interest in a lease held by the Boston Oil Company. It's in an unexplored, woodsy area farther up the Allegheny. It's called Pithole. Said to have promise of oil extraction--but in rugged land, hard to get there. You go either on foot or by horseback, and there are rattlesnakes and huge boulders near the creek, Pithole Creek."

She was astounded at his forthrightness with her. She thought this gentleman had everything--money, good looks, talent, and a following of admirers. She wondered why he was enmeshing himself in a cause that seemed to be waning. With news of Sherman marching on Atlanta and the fighting in Mississippi, both places in the Deep South seemed dire for the South. It sounded to her as if the Rebels were falling back.

As if in answer to her thoughts, he continued.

"You may be wondering why I am telling you these things. I have reason." He paused and took her hand.

"I now know that your cousin in a prisoner in a Yankee prison. Perhaps, I can assist you with his release." He gave her a hard look as she gasped.

"You could help free Fredrick?"

"I am working with others whose aim it is to get the release of southern prisoners of war. Fort McHenry is among our targets. We have plans, but I am not sure of the timing. It will require gold, leverage and luck to ensure our success."

Katherine's heart pounded at the thought of Fredrick's release by some other means than through her stepfather, if it were not too late. She wondered whether Ebenezer had contacted her nemesis for assistance in freeing Fredrick. She felt the urge to jump up and send a wire to him, but instead, she drained her glass of the whiskey that had its usual calming effect.

"Let me get us another drink."

Booth excused himself and went to the bar, leaving her to ponder his words and political stance. She leaned back on the horsehair settee, stifled a yawn, and momentarily closed her eyes. She heard, emanating from the dining room, the clinking of glasses and silverware, and the murmuring of late diners. Outside, the sounds of relentlessly present engines of nearby oil wells broke the silence of the night. Could Booth really help get Fredrick freed from Fort McHenry?

She opened her eyes when she heard approaching footsteps. Booth's. He placed two drinks on the table near them, and this time, sat beside her on the settee. She noted the increased closeness between them, smiled at him and waited.

He turned toward her, and in a low voice.

"I have been thinking. Perhaps we can help each other. I help get Fredrick freed, and you assist me with a small project."

He moved forward to the edge of the seat, turned toward her, and looked her straight into the eyes.

"What do you think? Can we come to some agreement?"

"Well, I would be forever grateful if you can help Fredrick." She pulled away from him. "But what is the other side of the bargain?"

"I need a courier, someone to deliver certain valuable items. It would involve travel, about a week or ten-day's time from this location. Your fluency in French is a definite asset."

She took a sip of her drink, smooth whisky and it burned her mouth as she swallowed. She could feel the pleasurable relief that flooded over her. She put the glass to her lips again. She waited for additional information, but it was not forthcoming.

"Where would I be taking these items? How would I travel? By coach or carriage?"

"Train is the means by which you would proceed to Montreal, Canada."

"Montreal...I have never been there. How far is it from here? Where would I catch the train?" She paused. "You know I have little money..."

"So you are considering it--working with me?" He smiled. "I want you to think seriously about it--contemplate this agreement for a day or so and let me know. There is also payment in gold for you."

"If it means freeing my cousin. I fear for his life. My friend said that the prison conditions are poor and the fever is raging among the prisoners held there."

"Yes, he is correct. That is one of the main reasons for working to liberate those southerners held prisoners of war. Diseases and infestations of rats, and food of poor quality are taking a toll on these poor wretches. We must act to get them out of these hell-holes."

In the light of the oil lamp, she saw his knuckles grow white as he clenched his fist nearest her, and that was when she saw 'J. W. B.' tattooed on his wrist. She turned to look at him. The pupils were dilated, making his dark eyes even more attractive to her. He lifted his glass of brandy, took a long swig, then turned back to her and spoke in a low voice.

"No one here knows how much I hate Lincoln and his regime, his war with the southern states, and his entrapment of so many young prisoners of war. You, Katherine are the only one in whom I have confided. Do we have an agreement of silence regarding that?"

He reached out and grasped both of her hands in his then tightened his grip on her. She stared back and was powerless as he took her in his arms and kissed her. She was left breathless and bedazzled by his possessive manner. When she leaned away, he drew her into his arms, wrapping them around her, pulling her into him. As they lay on the couch, he pressed her into his body so that

163

she could feel his enlarged organ arising from his crotch. Her impulse was to pull away but the memories of Plugge's attack three years earlier faded, squelched by her overwhelming arousal with Booth. This time it was different. She wanted him.

He seized her long hair and smothered her with an extended, sensuous kiss, his tongue exploring the inside of her mouth. She felt her private parts swell and she showed no resistance to him feeling her breasts. She was helpless in his arms. She was smitten…

…

With daylight came the realization of what had transpired the night before. Or at least what she could recall. As she remembered their bargain, she dressed quickly, took out a pen and paper, and composed a telegram to Ebenezer. She must stop his appeal to Petrus Plugge. Now she had another means of freeing Fredrick. As she entered the hotel's kitchen for a cup of coffee, she encountered Barnswell just beginning his breakfast. He looked up and raised his coffee cup as a greeting.

"Come join me, Katherine."

He stood as she pulled up a chair across from him.

"Heard you and Mr. Booth had dinner together last night." He looked at her as if awaiting an accounting. His blue eyes seemed to twinkle.

"Yes, we did. He is quite a gentleman and businessman-- impressive."

"You like him, then?"

"Well, yes, I do. Why do you ask?" She pushed her coffee cup toward the arriving waiter who approached, bearing a coffee pot.

"Well, most folks here just about worship Booth, especially the ladies. But there was one time some folks didn't take to him. It was a secret for a while, but word got out about him being attacked down on Catfish Street. It was when he first arrived here and was bunkin' with Alf Smiley. The two of them went slummin' one night followin' several billiards games and some drinks. Walked to this dance hall, Sim Marshall's place on this side of the bridge over the Allegheny. Just wanted to watch people dancin'. Most of them were girlfriends of rafters off the lumber or oil fleets and deck hands from several steamboats that had pulled in for the night.

"You've seen Booth all dandied-up in those colorful and expensive clothes he sometimes wears. Well, that night, he must have looked out of place. When a fight broke out, Smiley and Booth moved in closer to watch the action. This bunch of roughnecks spotted him and Smiley standin' there watchin' the fight, and about six or seven of them bullies decided that they were a couple of dandies who needed a lesson from some of the locals. They got into a fistfight, bloodied their noses, then one of them big guys picked Booth up and literally threw him out the door of that place. Booth and Smiley were embarrassed and the beatin's they took, came limpin' back in the dark, and kept it shushed up until someone else who was there that night told it 'round town. Their friends ragged them and laughed about it. It was all in good humor, and Booth took it well."

"Barnswell, you have some stories. That's one on Booth."

"Katherine, I'm here to tell you to be cautious 'cause Booth has some sympathies toward the Rebels, but mostly keeps it under his hat 'round here. I hear there is a nest of Southern Sympathizers--Republicans, some in Meadville, but mostly up the Allegheny in Oil City, and Booth visits some of them. No trouble from any of it that I've heard. I got friends up there, too."

"These town folks here have sons and fathers in the Union army. Like James Shaw from Cooperstown joined-up two years ago--Company I 42nd Regiment--a goodly number from here went with them. Shaw had been a carpenter here, a good worker, I heard, and he lost his arm at Gettysburg." Barnswell shook his head slowly. "Don't know for sure what he's doin' since he got discharged."

"Another who signed on with the Pennsylvania Volunteers, William Richards, a captain. Got captured and spent four months in Libby and Salisbury Prisons. He got freed in a prisoner exchange and they promoted him to colonel. His cousin was at the bar last night and told me they just heard--got a letter--that he's been wounded in June at Kennesaw Mountain, down in Georgia."

"Oh, and one more comes to mind. John Rockwell. He came here from New York. His Pa was a Revolutionary War soldier. So he joins up, and was captured at Gettysburg. Still in prison somewhere his wife says."

He paused and gave her a hard look. "So ya see, Katherine why Franklin folks don't take to someone sidin' with the Southerners who started it all. Things can get mighty heated 'round here when that topic comes up--the topic of this never-endin'-darn war."

Katherine looked down at her hands, then raised her head to

look at Barnswell.

"Thanks for the warning. I will pay close attention to what he says about politics. He's been showing me his Wilhelmina Well and taking me by some of the sites down near the creek and the river like the old fort, Machault. Not anything left of it. It's really beautiful where there are no oil wells, but the rest of the area is quite devastated from the oil and extraction activity. Impressive."

She remembered one thing clearly from last night. Booth was placing a great deal of confidence in her and had extracted a promise of silence about his political leanings. She, on the other hand, expected him to keep quiet about their intimacy that she hoped would continue. However, she valued her job, and did not want to lose it for any reason. He had put his trust in her. He knew she could also expose his intentions of liberating southern prisoners of war. Those were their secrets. She had given her word, and by consensus he, his.

She sipped her coffee.

"When does the telegrapher come to work? I need to send off a wire this morning."

"Oh, he comes early, about dawn since so many people are buyin' stock in companies, and sendin' wires for business purposes. You can see him now. He's been here, had his vittles and left for the telegraph office."

As she finished her scrambled eggs and ham, she felt in her pocket for the telegram she would send to Ebenezer.

When she finished eating, she excused herself as Barnswell dug into a pan of icing-covered cinnamon rolls. She left for the telegraph office by way of the hotel lobby, where Mathis flagged her down.

"Miss Katherine, a wire just arrived for you. Let me get it from the office," and he disappeared for a moment.

A minute later, she held the telegram in her hands. She sat on a nearby chair to read it.

"Plugge agreed to provide legal help STOP Only in trade for information about you STOP Said he knows about birth of child STOP Forced me to show him telegram records between us STOP Otherwise refused to help STOP Sorry be on alert STOP. Ebenezer"

She stared at the telegram. She felt dazed at this news. She had had no time to stop Ebenezer from contacting Petrus Plugge. She needed a drink, but her flask was in her room. As her left eyelid began twitching, the muscles on the back of her neck tensed and ached. How did he know about the birth of the baby? How?

Her ears rang and her head began to throb with pain. She closed her eyes and a scene she had blocked out of her memory suddenly sprang to life. She was with Blanche de Brunt in a small room…it was her room at the Red Lantern Inn. "Katherine, you're with child! Look at your belly! Oh God…" So it was Blanche who told her secret. Then a second memory of Blanche flooded in. "I like my job here at the Inn and don't want to lose it…"

Now she did need a plan. Life was becoming very complicated, faster than she had imagined. She moved to a seat in the lobby near an open window, and found the cool morning air refreshing. She sat quietly, breathing deeply as she allowed her eyes to defocus. She was lost in a jumble of threats and promises. She sat as still as a hunted rabbit in the deep grass, not moving a muscle in fear of giving away her position.

What and when were her next moves?

The Deal

Early August 1864

Katherine walked slowly from the hotel lobby. Her mind swam from the rapidity of change in her situation. A clear focus eluded her. Things were murky, obtuse and lacked order. She felt as if she were in a fog.

Then, as she ascended the stairs to her room, she remembered as a small child awakening earlier than usual to the realization that her father had returned from an Atlantic voyage…

Still clad in her nightgown and bare-footed, she had rushed downstairs to find him seated by the kitchen hearth, a metal mug in his hand. When she approached the bay window near her Papa', she could see nothing outside, only a white world.

"What is that Papa'? Where is everything? Where did it go?"

He had laughed as she climbed onto his lap and they talked about fog. She remembered that he had reassured her that it would go away soon, that either the wind or the sun would get rid of it…

It was a comforting memory, and she felt calmer, and released her cramped fingers from her tight right fist. The anguish and confusion would go away--sometime. She just had to make a plan, and things would clear-up for her.

She sat in her room's only chair with its faded-blue cover and tangled tan tassels attached to the seat's edge, and closed her eyes. She listed the facts that now confronted her. First, her stepfather now knew her location and that she had birthed his child. Second, Booth had made an offer for help in freeing Fredrick. Third, Booth's offer was an agreement, and he required something from her in return. What was it? Then she remembered. Booth needed someone to deliver items to some people in Canada, to Montreal. But how far away was Montreal, and how many trips did he expect of her before Fredrick's release for Fort McHenry?

She took a deep breath and exhaled slowly. Remembering that he said he would pay her in gold to cover travel expenses and for compensation came as a huge relief. That was a major benefit. She needed money. As well, the traveling would be to her advantage since she needed to relocate anyway. If Petrus Plugge sent someone to look for her here in Franklin, the travel to Montreal surely would confound his search. But move from the United States Hotel to where? Without a steady income, her stay anywhere else would be temporary, until Booth's payment money ran out. Then what?

The other issue was the trap that her stepfather had laid for her. Could she and Ebenezer trust Plugge to do what he said, to give legal assistance to free her cousin? She hoped that his word was good, but who knew? Only time would tell.

To turn down Booth's offer seemed disloyal, a betrayal of Fredrick. And she loved her cousin. They had been raised together as siblings. He had helped her when she had been in a disastrous dilemma. He sat with her during the long labor and painful process of birthing a baby she did not want, and listened to her ranting and castigations against her rapist, and then provided her with a way to make a living in the wine trade.

Now Fredrick was in dire straits. He needed to be out of that prison. She could not fail him by turning down an opportunity, in case Plugge would not come through.

She jumped to her feet and began to pace in her small room. Should she admit to Booth that Plugge might help Fredrick? Booth might not bother to hold up his end of the bargain, to request assistance from his contacts, thinking that Plugge's help would be sufficient. Hmmm… Then where would she be? If both Plugge and Booth dropped their efforts, Fredrick would be stuck in Fort McHenry forever, or maybe until the end of the war, but who knew when that would happen.

She stopped walking and sat down on her bed. She wanted to trust Booth, but she sensed a risk of telling him too much. She decided that she would not reveal the possibility of Plugge's legal assistance. She needed to keep that to herself.

The situation and decision-making made her head ache and her neck muscles tense. She felt compelled to seek relief, so she opened the bottom drawer, withdrew her silver flask and lifted it to her lips.

…

A half-hour earlier than she was scheduled to start entertaining in the dining room, Katherine arrived at the bar. She was determined to talk with Barnswell before he got busy with the customers who were returning from the oil fields.

"Good afternoon, Katherine." He came to where she sat at

the far end of the bar.

"Barnswell, do you have a moment? I have a favor to ask."

He looked at her quizzically. "Are you looking for more stories about our actor?" Then he winked.

She smiled. "Well, no--nothing to do with him…"

"Continue. What can I do for you, my friend."

"Thank you. That is exactly why I am asking you. Because you are my friend."

He smiled, exposing slightly overlapping front teeth under his neatly trimmed, brown mustache.

She reached out to touch his hand.

"Barnswell, there may be someone inquiring about me in the near future. You know more about me than anyone else, except maybe the manager, Mathis and he knows only about my wine selling. So you know more than he does."

"Who will be asking?"

She withdrew her hand, and gestured as she spoke.

"That's a good question. My stepfather or someone representing him. For several years, he has been trying to convince—-force--me to sign some papers. They have to do with giving up my ownership of property in the area of New York City. You see my late father, my dear Pa-pa,' when I was an infant, placed my name on the deed for the house and land where I lived all my life. It was, until my stepfather had forced me--after my Ma-ma' had died and was buried--to leave that house and go to work for him."

Barnswell shifted his weight, frowned and nodded.

"That was when I learned about my owning that property. But, you see, it is not my step-father's to sell. He is trying to force me to turn it over to him. I just learned from a telegram that he now knows where I am, so I am forced to relocate." Her eyes filled with tears.

He looked concerned, and stared at Katherine.

"You will leave us, Miss Katherine?"

"At least until he gives up trying to find me…"

"Where will you go?"

"I don't know--yet. I am deciding."

"I see."

"And I shan't tell you where I'll be so you can honestly say you don't know where I went."

Barnswell looked crestfallen.

"But I will let you know later, so we can stay in touch."

"Oh, I will be glad to do whatever will assist you."

"If someone comes asking, just say you knew little about me or my whereabouts. My stepfather's name is Petrus Plugge."

"I will do as you say."

She reached out to take hold of his hand.

"Thank you, Barnswell. You are a true friend."

Then she turned to cross the room to the piano. When she sat down at the keyboard, she spotted an envelope with her name on it. The note was attached to the sheet music given her by Booth.

"Dinner this evening? I will be at the bar. JWB"

Katherine could feel the jolt of energy surge through her body and her heart pounded. Booth's dark eyes, handsome face and muscular body flashed into her mind. She gasped aloud. The heat of a blush rose from her neck and flooded over her face like a wild river running high over its banks. She looked up from the note, and saw that no one had noticed her reaction.

Tonight was the night to give him her answer about accepting his deal, their verbal agreement would be made solid. The timing was right. She could not hesitate. She was glad that she had spoken to Barnswell, just at the right time.

...

At forty-miles-per-hour, the Atlantic & Great Western Railroad train with four broad-gauge passenger cars attached chugged its way along the east bank of French Creek in a northwesterly direction toward Meadville. Katherine was seated next to the window on the left side of the car with Booth seated on the aisle. The window was partly open and the morning air seemed refreshing to her. The landscape was changing gradually.

She watched with interest as they passed fewer and fewer old greasy, black oil derricks interspersed with new clean wooden structures that formed a pattern like a black and white checker board, until she could spot only a solitary derrick here and there. Instead of streets clogged with mud-mired horses and cursing drivers, the road that meandered near the railroad track appeared dry and dusty with only an occasional solitary horse and buggy. Farther along, trees in full leaf surrounded by tall standing grass and colorful wild flowers prevailed. It seemed like a miracle, only a few miles away from the oil fields.

Booth stirred in his seat and took her hand. She turned her attention toward her handsome traveling companion. He pressed her

171

fingers to his lips, then leaned closer to her so that he spoke into her ear.

"I am grateful that we have come to an agreement. This next step is important since you will be making acquaintance with one of my most supportive collaborators who is strategically located where several railroads serve, making travel from there less complicated and time consuming."

She nodded and looked around them to see if anyone were close enough to hear their conversation. She turned back and looked straight into his dark eyes.

He squeezed her hand and moved his mouth close to the right side of her face.

"The time has come to decide on how to change your name. Have you thought about that?"

"Yes, I have. How does 'Elizabeth Louise Granger,' for short, 'Betsy' sound?"

"Good. You've decided to alter all three names. That should work well. Were there other options?"

"Well, I thought of taking a French name, 'La Conte,' but decided that I needed something that would not standout to anyone."

"I agree. You chose well." He smiled at her and continued. "When we arrive in Meadville, Betsy Louise Granger is your name--from then on. No one need know anything else. I have been thinking of a background for you. You are the widow of a soldier--depends on circumstances whether he was a Yankee or a Confederate who was killed on the battlefield. How's that sound to you? You can emulate an accent of the south when needed, can you not?"

She turned close to his ear and whispered in a southern drawl.

"Well, I do declare! It's Mr. Booth, is it not?"

…

The sizable depot and covered waiting area of the Meadville railroad station came into view and the shrill blast of the train's whistle announced their arrival. Passengers all around them started to gather their belongings in preparation to depart the coach. Steam hissed from the engine as the train slowly approached a crowd of people standing along a spacious wooden platform.

As Katherine and Booth stepped into the crowd, she turned to him.

"Even the air smells better here. No more oily smell, and it is fresher. I think I will like this place."

He gripped their travel bags and she took his arm as they made their way toward a waiting carriage.

"We have a reservation for two nights at the McHenry House, a most pleasant accommodation. The best in Meadville."

Katherine stopped in her tracks, and he had to turn quickly when she disappeared from his side.

"Betsy, are you coming?"

She stood staring at him.

"What's the name of our hotel?"

He moved to her side. "The McHenry House."

"The same name as the prison in the Baltimore Harbor. My cousin, Fredrick..." Her eyes filled with tears.

He seemed surprised at the coincidence.

"I am sorry. I should have warned you." He took her hand and they continued to walk. "How careless of me."

Katherine thought he seemed somewhat downcast and distracted as they approached the hotel. She said nothing, but wondered if his business ventures in the oil fields were not playing out as he had hoped. If not, what was the source of the gold she was to transport for him? When would he get information on freeing Fredrick from his imprisonment? Had she cast her lot to her advantage?

"Welcome to the McHenry House, Mr. Booth. It's good to see that you have come to Meadville again."

Katherine sat nearby the registration desk while Booth spoke to the desk clerk. She thought this lobby well-appointed with its carved wooden banisters, creamy-white ceiling, and exquisite glittering chandeliers... much fancier and more attractive than the United States Hotel in Franklin.

When Booth nodded to her, she stood and approached the desk. She glanced at the guest log the clerk was completing: "John Wilkes Booth and his lady."

She felt relief at the anonymity. She involuntarily shivered and could feel goose bumps rising on her forearms as they made their way to their suite of rooms.

Late August, 1864

Katherine emerged from the Meadville telegraph office and

headed toward the house two blocks away where she rented a room from Mrs. Wilson, a young war widow. Sarah Wilson's late husband had been wounded at the Battle of Gettysburg in July 1863, then died from infection a month later. She wore black for two-and-a-half years, as was the custom to honor the memory of her 20-year-old husband, Thomas.

To Katherine, she was pleasant but they spoke little since Sarah's tailoring business kept her occupied. She sewed during the day to have the best light. A constant stream of customers came and went from her parlor that she had set up as a workplace. It had a side-room complete with a curtain that served as a fitting area where she would measure clients, or pin the partially sewn garment to assure its proper fit.

Katherine's room was on the opposite side of the large two-story house, and had its own separate side-entrance. Her rental agreement was on a weekly basis and seemed perfect to meet her needs for geographical flexibility and personal privacy.

Sarah seemed withdrawn and disinterested in the affairs of her only renter. For this, Katherine was grateful, and she had little reason to share or hide any personal information. She had told her landlady that she too was a widow of a war casualty. She kept her own business to herself. She was relieved and thankful. No need for covering-up or spinning yarns to satisfy the curious.

It was she who was curious, not regarding Sarah, but curious to learn whether anyone in Franklin was inquiring of her whereabouts. Three weeks after she and Booth had traveled to Meadville, she had decided to contact Barnswell.

"Want to inform you, I am fine STOP Anyone inquiring of me STOP Respond to Betsy at American Telegraph Company, Meadville STOP Keep location quiet STOP Katherine."

...

The late afternoon was pleasant and cool, as the result of a sudden downpour an hour earlier. Rainwater stood in puddles on the street, the water made muddy by the passing wagons and heavy horses that strained to pull the mud-clogged wheels of the carriages through the now sundrenched streets. Water dripped off of the leaves of overhanging trees and from yellow lilies and white daisies that grew close to the walkway where Katherine lifted her skirts to avoid contact with the wet soil.

She arrived at the telegraph office just as the clerk was

closing his books and preparing to lock up for the night. He smiled his recognition of her from her earlier visit that day.

"I am glad to see you, miss. Not five minutes ago, I received a wire for you." He handed her the paper.

She departed and headed for a small bench at the edge of the city park. She wiped off the wet surface with her handkerchief, sat down and opened the telegram.

"Good to hear from you STOP Five days hence two men asked about you STOP Offered me reward money STOP I gave no information STOP Kept after me STOP Mathias had them escorted from property STOP Holding a telegram for you STOP What to do STOP"

Her hand shook and she looked quickly up and down the street to see town's people going about their daily lives. She was relieved to see no one was looking at her or even in her direction. She gathered her skirts along with the telegram and headed to her place by a less direct route, longer and circuitous. Now she had to be on the alert. Five days ago? They could be here in Meadville now.

The next day, she had the forwarded telegraph message in her hands. "Plugge here Aug 20 STOP On his way to Baltimore & Fredrick STOP Will contact you in several weeks to let you know STOP You lie low STOP Ebenezer"

A prearranged knock on the side door brought Katherine to her feet. Sarah's customers used the front entrance and this rapping had a prescribed rhythm as agreed upon by her, Booth and his Meadville contact. She tucked the telegram under the bed cover and moved to answer the knock. She passed by a window. The sun was low in the western sky, but she could make out a large horse tethered to the hitching post at the side of the street.

She answered the door and was face-to-face with Rufus Stoops, a tall, lanky Kentuckian who farmed land outside of Meadville to the west. When he saw her, he removed his broad-brimmed black hat with his right hand, the left appeared crippled.

"Can I have a word with you?"

She recognized his slow southern accent and gracious manners, both of which he had displayed when Booth had introduced them three weeks earlier. She stepped aside and he moved into the entranceway.

He looked around before he began speaking. It was the end of the landlady's workday, and they could hear Sarah preparing dinner amid clanking pans, clinking silverware and clattering dinner plates. She was in the large kitchen on the other side of the house. Katherine nodded to him.

Rufus spoke in a quiet voice, just above a whisper.

"Got news from JWB. He says you are to meet him in Montreal on October 19. I will have a package and details for you the day before you leave. Just want you to have time to plan."

He smiled and handed her a pile of folded greenbacks.

"For your travel expenses." He turned to leave. "If you need to speak to me, I come into town most Wednesday afternoons, do some buyin' and have a drink at the McHenry House. Leave in time to get home before dark."

With that, he slipped quietly out the door. She could hear him talking to his horse as he mounted and rode off into the fading sunset.

By early September, Katherine had heard nothing more from Booth and with each passing day, her anxiety grew. They had an agreement, a deal, and she had future orders that upheld her part of their bargain. However, he had provided no information about the Rebels' plans to release prisoners from Federal prisons--his end of the agreement. How long must she wait to hear about plans for the release of prisoners from Fort McHenry? The long period of silence was weighing her down. The lack of contact with him made her question her decision to trust him. Why was she not hearing from him? A curtain of doubt enfolded her like a blanket of fog.

To add to her consternation, there was no news from Ebenezer. She knew the reason for his silence. There was no news, yet, about Plugge's legal efforts to gain Fredrick's freedom from prison. The silence from both possible sources of information was gnawing away at her. Besides, being idle for days on end, no job, no piano to play, gave her time to consider her position--too much time. Finally she could tolerate the unknowing no longer. She needed relief--information about Fredrick or at least some words of hope about his condition or future release.

...

About 4:00 on the next Wednesday afternoon, a sunny day, Katherine dressed in one of her finest outfits, arranged her hair in an attractive manner, and armed with her parasol, walked to the garden-like town green. She positioned herself on a bench surrounded on three sides by roses bushes that were in full bloom. She enjoyed their odoriferous presence as well as their beautiful colors of reds and

176

yellows. The peaceful park soothed her nerves and provided her a sense of order and the confidence that she could spot Rufus Stoops.

From this lookout, she could observe patrons coming or going from the McHenry House. After fifteen minutes of surveillance, she was rewarded by the appearance of a particular horse, a chestnut colored mare and its broad-shouldered rider who was wearing a black Stetson. She watched as Rufus Stoops dismounted in front of the hotel's hitching post, tethered his horse, and sauntered to the entrance. That was the queue she needed.

She waited from her vantage point for about five minutes. When Stoops did not reappear, she assumed that he had ordered a drink and was planning to stay at the McHenry House bar for a while. She casually made her move from the bench and sauntered toward the hotel.

Once inside, she located the dining area and asked for a table. Their being few customers, she had her choice of locations.

"The one in the corner, please."

With her back against the wall, she could observe patrons at the long, wooden bar as well as the sparsely occupied dining room. She spotted Stoops' profile as he sat alone at the bar, a drink in front of him. She watched to see if he were joined by anyone entering the area, but he appeared to be alone.

She signaled the waiter and ordered herself a whiskey.

"Please buy the same for the gentleman at the bar. That's Mr. Stoops, is it not?"

Several minutes later, the waiter had done as directed, and when Stoops turned to discover his benefactor, she raised her glass in a salute to him. As soon as he paid his bar tab, he approached her.

"What a pleasure to see you again, Miss Betsy. May I join you?"

She smiled and nodded her consent and he pulled up a chair. As he did so, she watched him survey the area to see if anyone were close enough to overhear whatever conversation ensued from this encounter.

"I felt a need to talk with you, Rufus." She looked away from him momentarily in order to maintain her composure. She need not expose her weakness to this pillar of strength who risked his life in supporting the Confederacy.

She looked directly at him.

"Did Mr. Booth tell you that we struck an agreement regarding my willingness to act as a courier?"

When he shook his head slowly, she continued in a subdued voice.

"He assured me that plans were being made that involved the release of prisoners of war from Federal incarceration. He promised to inform me of any such schemes. You see I have a relative, a cousin who is very dear to me, who is imprisoned at Fort McHenry at Baltimore. He was snatched off of a merchant vessel on the high seas by the Federals who were enforcing the blockade of southern ports."

She went on to explain the details of their wine trade and what she considered a tragic mistake of her cousin's arrest.

"You see, I am planning to hold up my end of our agreement, but I have heard little from Mr. Booth since he departed Meadville some weeks ago, only one message through you. Can you help me?"

Rufus Stoops gave her a hard stare, then leaned back in his chair.

"You are correct in assuming that I had no knowledge of the bargain between you and Booth. He simply told me that you had agreed to assist by acting as a courier."

Katherine took a sip of her whiskey and was silent.

"What is it that you want to know?"

"Are there plans to free prisoners from Federal prisons?"

"Well, yes, but it is highly secret."

"Since I will be carrying messages of this sort--at great risk to myself--how much may I be told? After all, I am now one of you."

For a few seconds, Stoops stared into a space over her head.

"Yes, what you say is true. Except that you are not one of the planners or the freedom fighters. You only have the responsibility of providing a line of communications between our groups."

"Without which, you all would be handicapped, and perhaps fail at your purpose."

"That is true. But providing you with details of plans could put our projects at risk if you were taken into custody. If you know little about details, you would have nothing to tell arresting authorities."

She shifted in her seat, then drained her glass. This was not going well for her. She needed another strategy.

"Do you understand my position? Booth appears to be shirking his end of our bargain. He gives me no hope of my cousin's rescue, yet you and 'The Cause' has me committed to a run to

Montreal weeks from now. What of that?"

"Let's have another drink before this place gets busy with diners." He flagged the waiter and submitted an order.

They sat in silence until they were served and the waiter, gone.

"I am uncomfortable with Booth's silence."

"Yes, I understand."

"Am I to be only a bit player, only a pawn, due to my being a woman?"

"I am not aware that your being a woman is the problem. The levels of secrecy among our enclaves have more to do with the need to know details of raids or attacks behind the lines."

"But I am not asking for details of the raids. Only if and when they are planned."

When Stoops stayed silent, she went on.

"If Booth fails to uphold his end of the deal, I may need to reconsider mine." She gave him a long stare.

"Your contribution to our cause is too great to lose you for such a default on Booth's part. Let me inquire of my colleagues and get back in touch with you. Can we meet here again in a fortnight?"

She nodded her consent to his plan, drained her glass of the remaining whiskey, got to her feet and left the hotel.

The next day, heat and humidity folded in upon the citizens of Meadville, and Katherine in her rented room was no different. It was stifling. Nor did her anxiety about her current situation abate. The high heat and devilish dampness seemed to agitate her even more. Her doubts weighed heavily on her furrowed, sweaty brow.

She had growing misgivings about Booth and his Confederate cause. And then there was Fredrick. Was his prison cell as hot as her room at the Widow Wilson's house? She opened the only window in her room, removed her dress, and loosened her corset before pulling a chair toward the slightly cooler in-coming air. Yesterday's newspaper served as a fan. She poured some water from a pitcher sitting on the dresser to her left. Her thoughts kept nagging at her.

Would Booth back out of their agreement without notice? If so, she would be stranded again, alone with no job and no money. But she wanted to trust him. After all, he had mentioned marriage only several weeks ago and they had a bargain and he was paying her, too. She chided herself for her lack of trust.

On the other hand, he had not contacted her with any

information about a raid on Fort McHenry. Two weeks' wait hung like a heavy wooden ox yoke on her shoulders. It was proving to be a long time when she had little to occupy her. She needed relief from the exhausting heat, high humidity and gnawing nervousness.

…

Two weeks later, Katherine sat at the same table in a near-empty dining room and waited while she sipped a whisky. She heard voices at the hotel's entrance as someone alighted from a carriage and entered the lobby. She looked at the wristlet. It was almost 4:30, later than Rufus Stoops' arrival two weeks earlier. She looked up to see a man dressed in black travel garb walk gracefully into the dining room. He seemed to be coming toward her, and when he removed his hat, she recognized John Wilkes Booth.

In a dramatic movement, he swept a deep bow, flung back his travel cape and put her hand to his lips.

"Betsy. I have returned."

Minutes later, Katherine took another sip of Pinot Noir, and noted that it was not as fine as that produced in the area along the Gironde Estuary and wondered about its source. A pang of missing her home and family in France swept over her. She shook off the lonely feeling and smiled at Booth. The light from the table's single candle cast his shadow on the wall behind him and it bobbed about as he gestured. Between courses and the waiter's presence, he related his strategies in the oil business, one of the reasons for his traveling to the area.

"Things are going well at the Wilhelmina. Tom and I figure we can sink another well in another location. Remember I told you about how I had trekked over a new area at Pithole that's got many speculators talking? This time, I bought a lease on one of the farms there."

She listened to him describe his travel, but grew anxious to broach the discussion of her choice.

She looked around at other diners before she directed her key question in a low voice.

"Is there any news about freeing prisoners?"

Booth appeared taken aback with her change of subject, and shifted in his seat.

"Well, yes and no. There is a plan that is closer to us than you might expect, but nothing specific about Fort McHenry, yet."

"Well, tell me what is planned. I am anxious about my

cousin. Several weeks ago, I did talk with Mr. Stoops since I had no word from you. I expected him to meet me this afternoon." She smiled. "Your arrival was a wonderful surprise."

"Yes, he contacted me. I am on my way to Montreal. Betsy, these are exciting times for the Confederates." He looked around, then leaned closer to her.

"Several raids to liberate prisoners are planned and the money to carry them out has been gathered. Families of the South are donating to support the cause."

He ceased the discussion as the waiter approached with the check.

"I will explain later."

When they were alone again, he pulled her toward him and looked into her eyes.

"You will accompany me to my room upstairs..."

She looked into his eyes and felt the familiar magnetic pull of his fine features and powerful physique. Although he seemed to have forgotten their agreement, she was falling for him all over again. Her doubts about him vanished.

...

Katherine stood on the plank platform of the Meadville Railroad Station feeling more hopeful. As the Atlantic and Great Western railcars disappeared into the haze of early morning, headed northeastward toward Corry and a railroad junction with the Philadelphia and Erie Railroad, she held close the secrets told her by Booth.

She felt ambivalent about the fact that she now had information about the network and its key players. Maybe her ignorance of such had been to her advantage. Too late now.

"I can't undo something, so I'll just have to live with it."

Booth had confided that messages she would be carrying concerned plans for raids on federal facilities that he referred to as the "western front."

"You will be carrying blue prints--layouts of federal prisons that hold our poor soldiers who are suffering. At Johnson's Island in Sandusky Bay they say that prisoners are stacked three-high with two men in each bunk. It is damp and cold there and they have scant clothing nor bedding."

He had shaken his head, and then continued to divulge additional information.

The money to finance these raids was in the hands of a Southern Congressman, who had been placed in Toronto by the Confederate government. He and a Confederate general, who recently had been ordered to Canada by President Davis were given the power to approve written plans that she would be transporting to them. The intent of the raids included freeing Confederate prisoners of war as well as to create disturbances in cities along the lake front. The commando assaults were to be launched from Canada and the waters of the Great Lakes. The strategy was designed to divert Federal troops away from the Richmond area and draw them to the Canadian border and Lake Erie, spreading the Federal forces and weakening their front lines at the point of current conflict.

She realized that knowing such plans put her in jeopardy were she ever questioned by authorities, but she told herself that was not likely, since she lived a quiet existence and had few acquaintances. Booth had taken the opportunity to divulge information to her. But by hindsight, she felt as if he had planned it, to draw her further into his scheme and to expand her involvement.

Now, she moved to begin her growing duties to include surveillance and gathering information for the Confederate Secret Service who circulated through the area. Her contact as before was Rufus Stoops.

At Booth's direction, she purchased several local newspapers, entered the dining room at the McHenry House, and was seated in the midst of the dining room, instead of at her favorite table against the wall near the bar. From this new vantage point, she was privy to conversations of diners at six nearby locations. Again, she chided herself at becoming more embroiled in the Southern Cause. Was she sinking into radical quicksand? At least, she had extracted more than information from Booth. He had given her some money to carry out her current mission, and had made a promise for more. She opened the *Meadville Daily Reporter* and practiced listening to diners' conversations.

. . .

On September 21st, Katherine located a news article about the Rebel raid to which Booth had alluded. He had given her just enough information that she knew of the existence of a plan. When she read the article, she realized that he had told her the truth.

That afternoon, a Wednesday, she sat at her usual corner table and waited for Rufus Stoops to arrive at the McHenry House

182

bar. He spotted her when he entered and sauntered over. She invited him to join her. He did not look happy.

"I saw the news notice about the raid on Johnson's island." She continued in a low voice, "What happened? You can tell me now since it is over and done."

"Well, Captain Cole got arrested before the raid got underway. I'm afraid he's in a peck o' trouble. Too bad. It was a good plan." He talked quietly making sure that no one could overhear their discussion.

She was curious.

"I know some of the story, about Cole and the Mount Hope Oil Company of Pennsylvania. Did he sell stock in the company as revenue to fund the raid?"

"Think so." He paused and took a sip of the whiskey in front of him. "He did get ten or so of our boys into the 128th of the Ohio Infantry. They guard the prisons includin' the one on Johnson's Island. Plans were for a group of Rebs led by Captain John Beall to seize the *Philo Parsons*, a steamship that ran on Lake Erie and to anchor it outside of Sandusky Bay."

"Did they get control of the ship?"

"Yea, they did and were waitin' to hear from Cole who was onboard the Federal gunboat, *Michigan.* It was close-by. Before Cole could drug the gunboat's officers--they were havin' a dinner party--authorities from Johnson's Island came aboard and arrested him for spyin'. Wrecked the whole plot."

Katherine's mouth dropped open at the failure of the scheme.

"Oh, goodness...what do you think will happen to all of those men--Cole, Beall and all?"

"Can't say at the is point. Beall and others got away, but it doesn't look good for Cole..." He bowed his head for a few seconds, and his shoulders sagged.

"Do you think the network has been exposed? How far, how many people?" Katherine was beginning to panic.

"I hope not. If I get word--warnin'--I'll let you know." He finished his whiskey. "Gotta get goin'--sun's sinkin'." He walked toward the exit, and disappeared from her view.

She stared into her whiskey glass, feeling very alone and vulnerable.

Just then, two men, strangers to Katherine, took the table next to her. She pulled out an evening newspaper and pretended to read, despite the fading light. ____

"Well, Jethro, I say we telegraph the barrister and tell him we can't find hide nor hair of that gal."

"Yea,' I agree. Besides I'm tired of being on the road. It's been a month now. Let him find someone else to do it. I'm ready to get back to the big city. This oil area is crowded--can't get a decent place to stay--neither in Franklin or Oil City. This place ain't so bad--and it don't stink of oil."

Katherine could feel the hair rising on the back of her neck. She was so close that she could reach out and touch either of them. She neither moved nor spoke until they finished their drinks. She watched them head for the stairs leading to the hotel's rooms.

Tomorrow, she would track them to see whether they left the area or were just considering the move. She felt as if things were piling up again. Now she also had the federal detectives to watch for, in case the Confederates secret communication network been discovered.

When she returned to her room, she pulled open the lower dresser drawer and unwrapped the silver flask. She took what she considered to be a well-deserved, long swig of whiskey.

Dangerous Conspiracy

October 1864

As the train approached the Montreal station, Katherine gathered her belongings and prepared to leave the train. She automatically felt for her pistol, deep in her right skirt pocket and touched the handle of the knife strapped to her right leg. The package that Rufus Stoops had entrusted to her, she'd sequestered into the left side seam of her voluminous black crepe dress.

Since Stoops had suggested that she travel as a widow in mourning, the black veil hid her face and the matching broad-brimmed hat topped off her disguise. She had surveyed herself in the mirror and deemed her disguise authentic. She had taken advantage of the traditions of mourning by speaking to no one except the conductor during the entire two-day journey.

As she descended from the coach, she felt cooler air than at the last stop and noticed that the waiting area was more crowded with passengers and people meeting the train than in Meadville or Franklin. She looked about her and followed the directions given her by Stoops. She had memorized them so that she could seem to anyone watching, that she might be a citizen of this city, and not a courier carrying materials to an enclave of rebels.

Stoop's briefing her was turning out to be helpful. She now had a clearer understanding of the situation. Southerners who had escaped by running the Union blockade were now nested in one particular hotel in Montreal, the St. Lawrence Hall, owned by a man named Henry Hogan. Stoops had described the refuge as "the unofficial headquarters of Confederate agents and others."

He had described for Katherine the group of about twenty-five or so men who were smugglers, Confederate Secret Service, draft dodgers, blockade-runners, and federal detectives. Stoops listed several prominent men such as former Mississippi congressman, Jacob Thompson who had served in President Buchanan's administration as Secretary of the Interior. Another was considered one of the most radical of Rebels, Kentuckian George Sanders. She noted that Booth's earlier divulgences were consistent with Stoops' descriptions.

185

"Keep an eye open for them. John Wilkes is brave to mix it up with that bunch. Now don't get me wrong. Montreal makes a good place for refugee Rebels. It's a friendly city toward us. But me, been there once, but I'd rather be a distant link in the effort to assist the Southern cause, closer to home."

She remembered that he had paused to take another drink of the bourbon he had poured for each of them. He had given her a long look, and she wondered how old he was, her age? And why was he part of this conspiracy? It seemed to her that his knowledge and experience was extensive for someone so young. He had appeared to be readying himself to confide in her. She had remained silent and sipped her drink.

"In fact, I cain't say a word about my feelin's toward this war around my aunt. This is her farm here where I'm stayin'. Helpin' out until my uncle and cousins get back from the fightin'. Livin' here all their lives, they are real Yankees. Just my aunt comes from Kentucky, but she sides with the rest of her family, not with my ma' who lives near Louisville. We just don't speak of it."

She shook off the memory and became alert to her surroundings. She progressed to the north end of the train station and encountered a long line of horse-driven carriages. She paused, her back to a broad pillar, as she surveyed the crowd around her for anyone who might be following her. She could feel her heart pounding as she realized the dangers of her mission, her first trip to carry messages to the enemies of the federal government. She took a deep breath and exhaled slowly. She waited and when no one approached her, she relaxed a little and looked behind her. She was relieved that no one who appeared to following her.

Feeling more confident, she focused on the animals and carriages pulled up in a row along the street that lay parallel to the north side of the station. Spotting a brown horse with a small red ribbon tied to its halter, she walked slowly toward it. A dark-skinned man of slight build was sitting up straight as a poker in the driver's seat. He tipped his hat to Katherine when she approached and patted the horse's nose.

"Name's Rebecca."

"Then your name's Samuel."

He smiled, revealing a gap in the upper row of white, straight teeth, and climbed down to assist her into the carriage that had black side-curtains and a lap blanket. Once inside, she closed the curtains and placed the wool cover over her knees. She felt protected, hidden in this carriage and with Samuel whose calm presence soothed her. That helped her relax from her continuous vigilance during her journey.

"They told me to bring you direct to the St. Lawrence, that you would be tired after that long train ride. That so, miss?"

She smiled at his question and answered in the affirmative, then closed her eyes and swayed with the movements of the carriage, as Samuel and Rebecca brought her the last section of her travel. Feeling safe now, her mind drifted to her upcoming reunion with Booth. She smiled at the thought and imaged her excitement of looking into his dark eyes and handsome face.

Katherine roused from her musings as Samuel stopped at a side entrance of the St. Lawrence Hall. With agility belying his age, he hopped down to unload her bag from the carriage, and assist her into the building. She followed him to a room close to the side entrance. He quickly helped her inside and placed her bag on a chair.

"You need me for a ride, let me know. Ask at the desk. They know where to find me."

"Thank you, Samuel."

With a smile and a tip of his hat, he was gone, like a ray of sunshine disappearing behind a dark cloud. She had felt relaxed with him, a good beginning for her time here among strangers, all strangers except for Booth.

…

She awakened from a nap to hear a din of voices somewhere in the hotel. It reminded her of the bar and dining room sounds at the United States Hotel, a chorus of voices like the rising, rushing in-coming tide at the beach near Brooklyn. Feeling rested after her long journey, Katherine was standing at the wall mirror arranging her hair when she noticed a small object on the floor near the room's entrance, apparently slipped under the door while she was napping. She recognized the handwriting on it as Booth's. "Betsy."

Her hands trembled as she opened it to find several high-value greenbacks folded inside a note.

"Hope you had a good journey. Dine with me this evening at Dolly's Chop House. Come to my room 150 at 7:00. JWB"

She smiled and laid his note on the dresser below the mirror. She consulted her wristlet to realize that it was 5:00 P.M., plenty of time to dress for dinner. She checked her favorite garment that she had shaken-out before she napped. Most of the wrinkles were smoothed out. She aimed to look her best for her dinner meeting with Booth.

Now the voices sounded louder. She decided to explore the place and see what the ruckus was all about. She changed out of her mourning garb, slid into the green taffeta gown and glided into the hotel's spacious reception area to find it crowded with men whose voices were raised as they tried to make themselves heard above the clamor. The air was heavy with cigar smoke and men talked excitedly, hands gesturing and episodes of loud laughter, about something, but what? Small groups of nearby revelers were toasting, drinks in hand.

She made her way along a wood-lined sidewall toward a young boy in a blue uniform. He looked like one of the hotel's employees. She spoke to him in French.

"What is happening? Do you know?"

"Have you not heard, miss? The hotel staff just received notice from the Montreal authorities that some Confederates attacked a town across the border in the United States, in Vermont." He took a breath and leaned toward her to be better heard when she cupped her hand around her left ear as if to improve her hearing.

"Then the soldiers ran for the border. They say that some of them are now near here, in Canada. No one knows for sure what happened—what they did. Some say that they killed people and robbed banks." His blue eyes danced with excitement.

She thanked him, and withdrew, standing with her back close to the smooth wood paneling, taking a long view of the excited crowd. She could hear the gentleman standing closest to her, his back to her. He had a commanding southern drawl, and wore an old-fashioned hairpiece. His dark mane fell back over his ears and was pulled into a queue at the nape of his neck.

"I'd like to see their faces when they learn how much our boys stole from them. Payback for how the damn Yankees treated, plundered our soldiers in the Shenandoah Valley. And to think that all of our raiders had broken out of Yankee prisons—those Hell-holes—and met together up here. They are the cream of our Southern manhood, Dr. Blackburn."

Luke Blackburn took his cigar from his mouth.

"Agreed, Senator Westcott. Any of those boys who could survive prison camp, then escape and make their way up here have to be a hardy lot, all right." Shifting his weight, he moved closer to Westcott.

"Now for my plan to rid ourselves of Mr. L. Send him that tainted shirt. I tell you, I got a formula for that poison. Would be one more nail in the Yankee coffin..." He returned the cigar to his mouth.

"I see Montrose Pallen workin' his way over here."

She watched for anyone moving toward the twosome who stood next to her, then spotted a short, stocky man in a black suit whose dark hat glistened with rainwater. He forged his way in their direction through the throng.

"What a day, gentleman!"

"Yes, Dr. Pallen. Quite a day! What news have you? Any reaction from the American consulate?"

"Just came from there. They are callin' the raid an international incident, a fracture of Canada's neutrality. Don't know where this will go."

"Recon the authorities will be askin' some questions?"

"Well, I hear that George Sanders is arrangin' for the defense of our Raiders. Good thing. That sly ole Kentuckian will take care of their legal problems, if it comes to that."

"Certainly a possibility, I guess."

Pallen removed his hat.

"What I'm hopin' is that the Federals will find a need to send some of their troops to the northern border-to protect it. Would thin out their forces that fought around Fort Harrison area. That's just south of Richmond, ya know."

The small group got quiet and Dr. Pallen looked down toward his feet. Then he raised his head.

"How much you think the boys got out of those banks over at St. Albans?"

Just then, Katherine saw movement to her left near the registration desk. She recognized John Wilkes Booth, left arm held high and waving while shaking hands of congratulations with by-standers and hotel staff.

Suddenly, he began wildly scattering silver coins about to bellboys, clerks and newspaper vendors nearest him. He seemed jubilant. She watched in fascination, wondering if he would show-up for their dinner engagement, or would be overwrought with celebration of the success of this affair. Still following Rufus Stoop's instructions, she kept her distance from Booth and tried to remain obscure.

...

At 7:00 P.M., Katherine made her way to room 150 and rapped on the door. When Booth failed to answer, she turned to leave and almost collided with him in the corridor.

"Let's drink to the Confederate Raiders!" He clutched a whiskey bottle in his left hand while he turned her about with his right. They entered his room together.

"What a day! What a raid on those Yankees! It's said that our boys took about $208,000 from those three Yankee banks!" His speech was slurred and he weaved about looking for a glass to pour a drink.

"Enough to replenish the Confederate treasury so the fight can go on! We'll show them--damned Yankees, damned Lincoln and his Emancipation Proclamation!"

He looked down at Katherine.

"I hope the 'Redcoats' will soon be on the march across the border to attack Federal forces in the rear!"

Suddenly, he abandoned the bottle and hugged her with both arms. He staggered, sending the two of them forward and they tumbled onto his bed. She could smell the odor of liquor on his breath as he kissed her. The stench of cigar smoke permeated his clothing. She had not seen him inebriated like this, in this condition, but Barnswell had told her stories of his heavy drinking while he was in Franklin. Now she knew the stories to be true.

Without warning, he rolled her away and sat up.

"I'll bet you're famished, Katherine--oops--Betsy. Long journey to get up here? Did Rufus give you helpful information?" His speech slowed and slurred.

"Where is the package he sent with you?" His voice trailed off as he lay back down on the bed pillow and closed his eyes. In a moment, he was asleep, mouth agape.

She stood staring at her unconscious lover, the great actor. Suddenly, she felt lonely, her handsome idol drunk and disheveled, and not able to function enough to take her to dinner as promised. She had not eaten since breakfast, and she was famished. She quickly exited the room that reeked of cigar smoke and stale whisky and wondered what to do next.

Then she thought of Samuel.

...

The next morning in a small park across the street from the hotel, Katherine sat on a wooden park bench and watched the red maple leaves float languidly from several trees that lined the walkway. They formed a carpet of scarlet wherever they rested. She admired the colors of the late-blooming flowers that grew to her right. She had Samuel to thank for this respite.

Last night on the way to dinner, he had suggested that she explore the park. She discovered what he had described to her. Bright colored goldfish swam in a large circular pond complete with water lilies.

The blue sky, warm sunlight and beautiful surroundings lifted Katherine's flagging spirits as she pondered her immediate future. Did she have further orders for her job? What of her relationship with Booth? Would it continue?

Several hours earlier, Booth had failed to join her for coffee and a pastry at the hotel's dining room. She took matters into her own hands and checked the train schedule. Certainly, she had no function here. With such a hubbub and goings on caused by the excitement of the raid on St. Albans, and Booth sleeping off drink, she was sure that his intentions of introducing her to ranking Confederate officers at this Canadian outpost was improbable. Some of these important men had been sent here by President Davis.

She remembered Rufus mentioning Commissioner Jacob Thompson, the ranking officer in the Confederacy in Canada. Although Thompson, a former Mississippi congressman had his office in Toronto, she wondered if he had been at last night's celebration. Rufus had told her that Thompson wielded considerable power since he controlled the outlay of money for planning subterfuge war against the Federals, for funding the Confederate Secret Service, and for freeing prisoners of war. She'd overheard someone in last night's crowd say that Thompson controlled the purse strings for some million dollars.

In the wake of the excitement of the St. Albans raid, it looked as if an appointment, as Booth had planned, with anyone of importance was impossible. Her mission accomplished. She knew it was time for her to leave Montreal.

Thirty minutes later, she walked into the front entrance of the St. Lawrence to find Booth in deep conversation with two men. When he saw her, he excused himself and motioned her to follow him. They ended up in his room.

"Betsy, where have you been? I have been looking

everywhere."

"Where were you last evening for dinner? Are you trying to starve me to death?"

He ignored her remark.

"You need to leave here within the next twenty-four hours. Word has come down that the authorities are planning to question some of my fellow Confederates about yesterday's raid, and they are starting here at the St. Lawrence. The Canadian police have a number of our brave soldiers in custody and are charging them with endangering the neutrality treaty. No need for you to get caught up in these inquiries."

She looked straight into his eyes. "What do you suggest? Is tomorrow morning soon enough?"

He nodded. "I will see you off with Samuel at 7:00 AM. Here is your train ticket."

"Where is my payment in gold that you promised?"

He unlocked a wooden box that he retrieved from his traveling trunk, and counted out a wad of greenbacks.

"This isn't gold which is easier for someone to steal. Paper is lighter and less noticeable when sequestered in your costume." He took her hand.

"Please forgive last night's behavior. I overdrank in my exuberance of the excitement of our victory against the Yankees." He paused. "Come with me to dine?"

When she hesitated, he took her in his arms, and held her close. "Betsy, please. This may be our last time to meet for a while. I have much business here and elsewhere that requires my attention…But, right now, you are mine."

…

In the fading light of a cold mid-November day, Katherine clutched a newspaper that some traveler had abandoned at the Meadville Train Station where she had stationed herself to observe the last train of the afternoon as it disgorged its passengers from Cleveland. Since Booth had reinforced his instructions, she continued her surveillance of in-coming and departing passengers on the Atlantic and Great Western. Anything or person who appeared suspicious—federal agents, railroad detectives, soldiers in uniform—she was to report to Rufus Stoops.

The wind picked up as she made her way to the telegraph office. She re-wrapped her travel cloak more securely against the rising wind and fine rain that had continued all this gloomy day. As she entered, the clerk with whom she was now familiar shook his head indicating that she had no wire today. She nodded and turned to leave, walking toward the McHenry House where she settled into the seat at the table she reserved on a regular basis. She was famished.

She imbibed in a glass of pinot noir as she waited for her dinner order to arrive. She took a deep breath and reflected on her situation. Since their meeting in Montreal on October 20, Booth had not contacted her, despite his promising her information about a possible prison break at Fort McHenry. Poor Fredrick, how was he fairing? Was he ill? Just yesterday, she had wired Ebenezer in the Brooklyn Navy Yard hoping to learn news about her cousin. This waiting seemed interminable. Would this war never end?

As she unrolled the newspaper from the railroad station, she was surprised to see that it was the *New York Herald* and not the usual Erie or Cleveland paper. Her interest grew. She had not read the *Herald* for several weeks, as it was not readily available in Meadville.

First, she scanned the arriving diners and seeing no one of interest, she began to read the front-page dated November 26, 1864. Immediately, an article caught her eye: "Vast Rebel Conspiracy." She leaned forward to read in the dim light. The article described New York City being thrown into confusion by fires across the city.

"The original plan of the Marauders was to have simultaneously fired the hotels at the lower and upper part of the city, while the Fire Department and Police had their attention distracted to these remote portions of New York, to fire the hotels and other public buildings in the central points."

She took another sip of her wine and looked up to see the server approaching with the plate of food she had ordered. Lowering the newspaper to her lap, she smiled as he placed the steaming dish in front of her. When he turned away from her, she relinquished her reading material, almost forgetting about the food.

"Rebels?" Confederates? She took a bite of her dinner and read on. Confederate agents—dozens of them, "Importations from Richmond and Canada..." arrived in the city carrying carpet bags concealing phosphorus and turpentine. The St. James, Gramercy Park, La Farge and other hotels had been set afire by lighting bedding soaked in the chemicals. She stopped chewing as she read. So, the Confederate raid had spread from Lake Erie and St. Albans,

Vermont to New York City? A surge of hope and optimism rushed through her body. Was Fort McHenry next? Was Baltimore in their sites? She lay the paper aside and continued her dinner with more enthusiasm. She drained her wine glass and ordered another. She felt like celebrating.

The next morning, when Katherine awakened, she realized that the room was cold from an apparent sudden drop in temperature during the night. The rain and wind had abated leaving clear skies, and the sun had no clouds to mute its warmth. She renewed the dying fire in her room's potbellied stove and set a kettle of water to boil.

As she was sipping her morning coffee, she realized that she had not read the other news in the *Herald*, only the article about the Rebel raid and follow-on fires. She located the paper and continued where she had left off the night before. When she came to the theatrical news, Katherine's hand began to shake.

Her John Wilkes had performed at the Winter Gardens with his older brothers: "The Three Sons of the Great Booth together on the same stage performing Julius Caesar."

Her eyes filled with tears and she dabbed at them to clear her vision so that she could continue to read the account of the performance. Respectively, Edwin and Junius had played Brutus and Cassius and John Wilkes, Mark Antony. The critic described John Wilkes as dressed in an above-the-knee, embellished tunic that displayed his muscular legs and fine physique. He was said to be the handsomest of the three, appearing clean-shaven for the accurate portrayal of his character. Comments praising his brothers' performances to the packed house, overshadowed the critic's comments about his execution of his role. That comment did not surprise Katherine. Once in his overdrinking, John Wilkes had raged to her about Edwin's persistent popularity for his acting, as well as their continuing disagreements regarding politics and the war. She pushed that painful image from her consciousness.

She tried to imagine John Wilkes without his well-groomed, dark mustache, and she smiled. She put down the newspaper, leaned back in her chair and, closing her eyes, lapsed into memories of her times with him. She felt warm and loved for those moments. However, like a lurking lion, the drunk and disheveled vision of him in Montreal caused her alarm, and her eyes flew wide-open. The nagging thought that kept invading her conscious mind confronted her squarely.

Could she trust him in his promises to get Fredrick freed?

Was it a coincidence that he was in New York City the very date of the Rebel Raid? How involved was he with the Conspirators along the northern border and in Canada? Was he only helping to furtively finance their attacks or intensely embroiled with the planning and execution? Worse yet, could she be implicated and tied to the conspirators because of her relationship and entanglement with him? She noted that these southerners were being arrested at each of their attacks on northern cities and fortifications. In their subsequent interrogations, how much were those Southern prisoners telling their Union captors?

She involuntarily shivered at the thought of somehow being incriminated and decided to contact Rufus Stoops.

...

A week later, over several drinks in the McHenry House dining room, Rufus Stoops quelled her fears. He agreed with her that the raids had moved toward the east and that attacking a city the size of New York City was a sign of growing strength for the Confederates.

"I cannot divulge details as you know, but it does look as if the attacks are moving in the direction of Baltimore." Stoops shifted his position and looked directly at Katherine. "'Caution' is the word, however, Miss Katherine, and vigilance. I can tell you that the powers in Montreal have authorized more funds for another attack on a northern city soon, but that's all I can say for now."

"What has happened to those arrested in New York?"

"The New York authorities are considering this incident as revenge for the Union operations in the Shenandoah Valley under General Sheridan. The destruction there was terrible. We need to fight back."

"But what will happen to the Raiders that got caught?"

"At this point, we don't know…but what I do know is that your courier services will be needed again in the near future, that I can tell you."

"Where, back to Canada?" She took a deep breath and waited for an answer.

"Most probably." Stoops looked toward the window, and Katherine knew that their time was running out. She could see the long shadow of a tree just outside the dining room lengthening as the sun sank in the west.

"Gotta go." Stoops got up, and put on his hat as he left the hotel.

...

Two weeks later, Katherine read in the *Erie Times* of an attempted attack by the Confederate Raiders on the Lakeshore Railroad near Dunkirk. They had been interrupted in an attempt to derail and rob a train. Two of the commandos were now in custody, their fate unknown.

Stoops had told her the truth. At least she could trust him.

Several weeks later, when he approached her with the news that Booth would meet her in Montreal, she sewed the Rebel packet of information for the Confederate conclave into the seam of her skirt, and packed her bag.

January 1865

Katherine stepped swiftly from the train at Montreal's station, and scanned behind her at intervals as she wormed her way through the milling crowd. Some people appeared to be arriving passengers, some departing and all dressed in heavy coats, boots and all manner of warm head coverings. Icy winds cut through Kathrine's reversible travel cape, one side, black, the other, a dark green plaid. The shock to her body from the cold wintry blast reminded her that her prior trip to this clime was more pleasant. She shivered involuntarily from head to toe.

Some things had not changed since her last time to meet Booth and transport messages. The winds of war continued to rip the fabric of America asunder like a scythe taken to winter wheat. How much longer will this awful conflict go on, she wondered as she worked her way toward the crowd that consisted mostly of men. A few well-dressed women with children mingled among the waiting passengers.

Bearded men in dark coats; young, scruffy-looking boys who could be escaped Confederate soldiers; and British troops, immaculately clad in scarlet uniforms swarmed around her. Despite the din of shuffling feet, the loud hissing of blackened steam locomotives, and buzz of voices, she could distinguish southern accents coming from passersby. On the previous trip to rendezvous with her lover-turned-recruiter, she had observed a similar looking group, but differently dressed, since that journey was in autumn, and the heavy, warm clothing was missing.

She forced herself to attention now. Where was that man who had followed her from the train? She didn't want to turn to look, so she ducked behind a large pillar that supported the station's roof to take stock of her situation. She pulled her small ivory-handled mirror from her carpetbag, took a partial step from the shelter of the pillar, and made the pretense of straightening her brown fur hat.

The mirror's reflection revealed a man who was standing along a wall and not moving with the crowd. He was the same traveler who had been seated four rows behind her on the daycoach since the last stop in New York State. Now, she felt sure that he was following her. She took a deep breath, exhaling slowly and decided to enact her well-rehearsed contingency plan.

Familiar with the station from the previous courier assignment to Montreal, she slipped quickly into the nearby public toilet as she returned the mirror to her bag. Fortunately, the lady's powder room was deserted except for one young woman who was busy caring for a small girl, and she did not look toward her.

In the privacy afforded by the ladies' powder stall, Katherine deftly reversed her travel cloak to its plaid side, exchanged her fur hat for a broad-brimmed felt chapeau with an attached long white wig, and placed the metal-framed spectacles on the end of her nose.

As she slowly emerged from the toilet closet, she took a deep breath and hunched her shoulders forward, and with head down, shuffled out of the rest room and into the flow of the people who were headed toward the north exit. Booth's acting training and disguise techniques were paying off, but on this journey, she felt her movements were more constricted, like a tightening noose, especially since recent rumors were swirling about various circles that the Confederacy was a lost cause.

Were Federal authorities working more diligently to shut down communications between the Confederate government at Richmond and the outpost of the Confederacy in Canada? Was the man on the train a Federal detective or her protection assigned by the Confederate Secret Service? Or even worse, was he a private detective set on her track by her dastardly, politically connected stepfather? Perhaps he had not yet given up, despite the conversation she had overheard at the McHenry House in Meadville.

Ebenezer had informed her that in New York, Plugge had placed a price on her head. She felt a shiver go through her body at the thought of being apprehended by whomever was following her. She was determined to shake them off her path.

She exited the station and hobbled across the frozen ruts of a side street, her bag swinging as she negotiated the uneven snow and icy patches underneath her feet. She stopped at the corner of a building, then turned to see if anyone followed. When she determined that the man on the train was nowhere in sight, she proceeded carefully, keeping her old woman posture. What she did not need was to slip and fall, drawing attention to herself.

Now a block from the station, she rounded a corner of a bank building to see her familiar transportation awaiting her, a splashed up black buggy with a roof and dark side curtains. She recognized Samuel, his head clad in a fur hat that partially covered his ears. Rebecca, the chestnut mare was draped with a blanket for protection against the icy winds that were blowing off the St. Lawrence River. The faithful horse stood patiently at the front of the wagon.

As Katherine approached through the crowd, she deftly signed the secret hand signal that brought Samuel into action. Smiling broadly, he returned the sign, hopped down from his perch, took her bag and assisted her into the carriage. She felt relieved to find the passenger seat empty. Being alone during her entry to General Edwin Lee's headquarters would provide a time to review her next steps.

"Samuel, so good that you are here to meet me." She spoke in her French accented English. "No time to talk. We need to hurry as I picked up a tail at the last stop, and he was tracking me at this station. I believe I've lost him, but let's get moving, just in case."

"Yes, Miss Betsy. I thought as much when you came so disguised--a clever cover, I think."

As she pulled the carriage curtains closed, the Negro driver climbed gracefully to his seat and they were off, bumping roughly over the frozen ruts. As property of one of the first Confederates assigned to the Canadian outpost, Samuel had worked to buy his own freedom and now had papers to prove it. Although he could choose to return to the States, she understood that he elected to stay in Montreal and take advantage of his position of liveryman and driver for the Canadian contingent of Confederate Secret Service agents stationed here. As Samuel had once told her, the war was far away, and his income, secure--at least for the time being, she recalled as she turned her focus to her current responsibilities.

The first task during the short ride was to change her attire, and look presentable. Her veil covering her face, the travel cloak reversed, and spectacles along with the broad-brimmed hat were secured in her bag. She felt for the large envelop with the wax seal that had remained safe, deep in the left pocket of her wool dress, obscured by the folds in the voluminous navy-blue skirt. Thinking intensely about this mission, she inhaled deeply and blew air out slowly between pursed lips.

This delivery mission was almost accomplished. Upon her arrival at the hotel, she was mandated to personally hand this dispatch to General Edwin Lee, whom she had never met.

She was more than ready to bring closure to this long trip. She admitted to herself that being tracked did un-nerve her somewhat. She knew that if the Federals halted her, their publicly searching and touching her would be considered an outrage by anyone, men or women, who might witness such an invasion. Besides, if she were apprehended in the Provence of Quebec, she might be able to claim her French citizenship since her mother was born in France and she had relatives there. She thought that French representatives who were on duty in Montreal might come to her aid. But just the idea of enduring such an ordeal was unsavory, and besides that, she would be revealed, unable to continue in her courier duties, a financial crisis for her at this time. One hundred dollars in gold covered her expenses and kept her comfortable between assignments.

The fact that she was paid so well spoke to the faith that Booth and the group of Rebels in the area had in her as a reliable, canny courier with the essential tools of the trade: fluent in French, physically attractive, youthful and able, with the innate ability to reason, think on her feet and act quickly. She prided herself on these skills and her unflawed record of several successful missions for the Southern cause.

However, she had to be honest with herself regarding the reason she had taken such a risky position with a regime about which she had limited knowledge. After all, she'd been living in France for three years, and when she'd arrived in Baltimore, she'd known little about the reasons for war. It was meeting Booth in Franklin and the development of their romantic relationship that had enticed her to take this courier position. But she had wanted to help Fredrick, as much as anything.

In his last letter to her, Booth had laid out a plan to meet her again in Montreal. She was carrying important papers for the Confedcrate contingency. As well, he wrote that he had information on plans for attacks on two federal prisons that held soldiers from the south. He did not specify, but she had high hopes that Ft. McHenry was in their focus. Rufus had hinted about the papers he was transferring to her, the reason for her trip.

"Betsy, the Confederate Secret Service needs the layout of one of the prisons that holds some of our highest-ranking military. It's a facility that is near to here, on Lake Erie, and the local boys have passed the sketches of the buildings along to me. Now, it's up to you to deliver the plans to the group in Montreal. Your contact there is General Edwin Lee. It's said that he is a relative of Robert E. Lee. Don't know. What I do know is that Edwin Lee and his wife are newly arrived in Montreal and that he has a great deal of power." Katherine was lost in thought and the sound of Samuel's voice caused her to jump.

"Madame, we have arrived at the St. Lawrence Hall. I will assist you with your bag."

She was jolted back to reality. With Samuel's help, she agilely alighted from the carriage, slipped quickly through the side entrance of the hotel, and bi-passed the main lobby and registration desk. As they skirted the dining area, she could detect the odor of beef cooking, and her mouth watered. She had not eaten for six hours.

…

Katherine sat at the window watching large flakes of snow stick onto a bare tree branch when a sharp-coded-rap at the door brought her to her feet. She slipped out of her travel cloak and smoothed her dress as she checked her hair in the mirror. She slid open the small cover from the peephole expecting to see Booth. Instead, a woman was looking directly at her door. She returned the coded knock, and then slowly opened the door.

A man with a white moustache and piercing blue eyes stood beside a woman. Of average height, he was clad in a dark jacket with white standup collar, black breeches and black knee-high boots that gleamed from recent polishing, civilian clothing, not what Katherine had expected of an army general during wartime. He bowed slightly then nodded to her.

"May we enter?"

Katherine stepped aside and more widely opened the entrance. The couple swept quickly into her room and closed the door behind them.

"I am General Edwin Lee and this is my wife. Since we have

recently arrived in Montreal, we have not met you."

"I am Betsy Granger, your courier."

Mrs. Lee smiled, exhibiting a row of crooked teeth, but her demeanor was engaging. She seemed pleasant Katherine thought. A diminutive woman, she rose only to her husband's shoulder.

Katherine pulled out a chair and motioned to them. The three sat at a small cloth-covered table that held a lamp with dark green-fringed trimming around the bottom of the shade.

"How was your journey?"

"The number of Federal agents seems to have increased since my last trip here. This time, they accompanied the railroad conductor when he was checking train tickets, giving riders a good, hard look."

"Did they require passengers to produce papers?"

"Only when we crossed the frontier at Buffalo. Be aware that I did not journey from Washington where, I understand, travel is more closely controlled." Katherine paused for a moment.

"Not only was there a greater presence of Federal men onboard this time, but there are more detectives at train stations. I am unsure as to whether they are railroad detectives or of some other source. I can spot them because of their boots-black to below the knee with a strap across the instep."

General Lee who appeared to be listening intently, broke his eye contact with Katherine, and looked down toward the floor. "Miss Betsy, your information is very revealing to me, to us." He paused and cleared his throat. "Just this morning, we received news, terrible news, from my close associate in Toronto, Jacob Thompson. His courier, one of our bravest, Lt. Samuel Davis was stopped in Ohio." He glanced at his wife who was dabbing her eyes with a handkerchief.

"He was on his way back to Richmond from meeting with Mr. Thompson. Despite Davis' rather ingenious arrangement to hide secret dispatches--sewed into the lining of his coat--the messages were recovered by federal authorities."

Katherine shivered and her left eye began to twitch. She felt the growing weight upon her shoulders to have increased tenfold. She took a deep breath before speaking.

"What will happen to Lt. Davis now?"

General Lee sighed.

"He was taken from Newark where he was apprehended to Cincinnati. Mr. Thompson believes that he will face immediate court martial. There is reason to think that Lt. Davis will serve as an example to other brave Rebels who support our noble cause. He future does appear dour."

Sobbing, Mrs. Davis turned away from their small group of three to blew her nose. She turned back to her husband and Katherine.

"He is so young to face such dire circumstances."

The general shifted in his seat and focused on Katherine again.

"Were you followed at any point?"

"At my last change of trains, I noticed a man seated several rows behind me. When I arose to move about a bit, I could feel his eyes on me. Then, when we approached the Montreal station, he positioned himself just behind my seat, followed me off the train, and then paralleled my changes of direction through the crowd. Only by entering the ladies' public toilet and donning a disguise did I shake him away."

That said, Katherine retrieved the small package from deep in her skirt pocket folds and handed it to Lee.

"From the contingent in area 6."

Lee fingered the package, nodded to his wife, then they arose as one unit to take their leave.

"Thank you."

Mrs. Lee paused before the door was opened.

"We have arranged to dine in our suite early this evening. Betsy, will you please join us?"

Katherine paused only a moment to remember the time of Booth's scheduled arrival. He should be here now, at any minute.

"Yes, I am pleased to accept your invitation."

The agreed upon time set, the Lees departed. Katherine sat on the bed and breathed a sigh of relief. Things were not going well for the Confederates. The capture of a Rebel courier alarmed her.

…

Mrs. Lee cleared away the dishes from the dinner table and placed them in a wooden container provided by the hotel's kitchen. Her husband lifted them to the door where they expected the kitchen help to pick them up.

They moved to the sitting room and with a glass of brandy, General Lee continued their dinner conversation.

"The condition in the prisons is dire, I fear. We had friends and neighbors back home who got letters from their kin." He looked at his wife. "Sue and her neighbors started the Mite Society that tried to help some of our brave men."

Mrs. Lee explained.

"We formed the Mite Society to gather up things they begged for--socks, boots, food, jackets--it is heart breakin' to learn of such poverty among them. I sold butter to raise my mite. One prisoner, Henry Gibson was locked up for more than a year at Fort Delaware wrote of needin' food, boots, socks and pants. Terrible cold in those horrible Yankee prisons. Those poor creatures."

Katherine listened as Mrs. Lee wiped a tear from the corner of her eye, then continued, her accent of the south seeming out of place in the French-speaking city of Montreal.

"I packed up one box some months ago with a good ham, and cakes and rusk that I had baked in my oven. That was for a prisoner at Johnson's Island Prison. I just worry so about those poor men, locked up like that."

Katherine thought of stories she had heard about prison camps in the south that housed northern soldiers. They sounded similar--just as dreadful. Her cousin, Fredrick remained in Fort McHenry yet, as far as she knew. But now, she had a more immediate concern.

Booth had not arrived this afternoon as planned, and she wondered what had gone wrong. He was to bring her news about the possibility of Fredrick's rescue. She took a deep breath and pushed his failure to appear out of her mind.

"You mentioned earlier that you have not been here in Montreal for long. How did you travel? By train?" Katherine asked.

"Mercy, no! We ran the blockade out of Wilmington." Mrs. Lee's eyes were bright. "Never thought I'd be doin' anything like that. It was frightenin'. The Federal gun boats had wrecked a steamer, the *Stormy Petrel* that was loaded with guns and ammunition for the Confederate army--drove it ashore, the very day we left."

"We got aboard the *S.S. Virginia,* a stern-wheeler, but Captain Moore determined that sailing in the open sea was too dangerous on account of a big gale so we put in at Fort Fisher for a spell."

"Then at 3:00 in the mornin' after the moon had set--it was mighty dark--we set sail again. All day long a Federal ship followed us 'til 9:00 that night. It was such a close call that the captain changed course and sailed for Nassau instead of Bermuda. I was never so happy as I was when we saw the Great Abaco Lighthouse comin' into Nassau--beautiful place. From there we went to St. George for a couple of weeks. In December, the *Alpha* carried us to Nova Scotia."

Suddenly, there was a sharp knock at the door. Everyone stopped talking until the spent dinner dishes were retrieved. Then, a man approached with a telegram for General Lee. The general stood to receive the message. When he had read it, he addressed his wife.

"Looks as if Mr. Booth will not be joinin' us tomorrow as planned. He sends his regrets, but says he has urgent business in New York."

Mrs. Lee commented.

"Maybe his business has to do with his actin' career. He is such a splendid actor. I was thrilled to see him perform in Baltimore a few years back."

"Yes, I am surprised at this turn of events. He seems to have become increasingly passionate about our cause here." General Lee returned to his seat.

"Well, his private life has changed some too since his engagement to Senator Hale's daughter, Lucy. Too bad he got mixed up with an abolitionist. Land 'o Goshen! Can't imagine Hale as Booth's father-in-law." Mrs. Lee shook her head sadly.

Katherine felt as if she'd had a bucket of ice-cold water thrown in her face. She sat on the edge of her seat, her back straight, like ramrod, and her face expressionless--like stone, but her fists were clenched and she could feel her face flush, the heat rising from her neck to her temples. Then her left eyelid began to twitch and she felt dizzy. She looked toward her hosts, but the Lee's seemed not have noticed her reaction during their interchange over the telegram news.

Katherine faked a yawn and Mrs. Lee turned toward her.

"Oh, my dear, how I have gone on. No doubt you are tired since your long travel over the several past days."

"Yes, thank you for such a pleasant evening. I really must retire. Good night." She rose and General Lee showed her to the door.

Katherine rushed to her room, threw herself onto the bed and wept. Full realization that Booth had used her, duped her into helping his cause hit her like a ton of stones forming the river bank of the Gironde River at the Medoc.

All of her maneuverings had not helped Fredrick get released from Fort McHenry. He had dropped his end of their bargain, not just dropped it, he had deceived her, led her on to get what he wanted. Her shock and weeping turned into anger, and she pounded the bed with her fists and beat the pillow until the fine feathers flew into the air.

After a time, she sat up, wiped away her tears and took off her shoes. She noticed an envelope at the base of the door. She bent to retrieve it and discovered a message, a telegram inside. She blinked in an attempt to focus through her tears.

"Mrs. Granger do not return here. STOP Federal agents looking everywhere STOP Rufus."

"Oh, no!" Katherine flung the paper away for herself, as if it were on fire. "Oh, no! Oh no!" She fell prone onto her bed, her face buried in the pillow, and screamed until her anger turned to fear. A paralyzing thought, like an icy hand clutching her throat, shot into her mind and she sat bolt upright in the disheveled bed.

Getting caught could send her to prison. She had to get out this situation as soon as possible. She needed to dodge any authorities or detectives in making her way back into the United States. But where would she go?

Not back to Meadville, nor to Franklin. She was easily recognized there. What to do for money? Since Booth was not arriving here, she had to appeal to the Lee's for payment of her services. She rolled over and felt her left eyelid twitching with no letup.

Through her copious tears and swollen face, she groped in her travel bag for the silver flask, now her constant companion. Whiskey gave her relief, blotted out the pain, and was faithful to her in her times of need. Whiskey…

Her head swam with the reality of her foolishness, for facing the dangers of supporting the southern cause--Booth's passion.

Yes, the painful, burning truth is clear. Booth's passion is for the cause, not for her… At that moment, at that realization, she wanted to end the pain, to end it all…

Minutes later, the empty flask fell to the floor with a thud and roused her to semi-consciousness.

"It's always darkest before the dawn; it's always darkest… Oh, Pa-pa'! Where are you?" Her voice trailed off; hot tears flowed down her puffy face.

Then she slipped into an alcohol-induced stupor.

Preserving Anonymity

Early February 1865

"Madame Le Conte, lift your veil so that I can see your face."

Katherine tilted her head to the side as if she did not understand the command, then shrugged her shoulders and stared at the authoritative figure looming before her.

The United States boarder official, a Union soldier moved from behind his counter, staring at her. He towered above Katherine who was seated in a chair across from his station. She knew he was studying her.

Despite the several weeks it had taken to obtain new identification papers from the Confederate Secret Service, she remained angry and disillusioned about the dilemma created by her infatuation with John Wilkes Booth. All she had to do was envision her current quandary and the betrayal by him, and her eyes immediately filled to brimming.

Piled on to her current anxiety was the alarming news of the court martial of another courier working for the Southern cause. That stoked her fears for her own safety. Federal detectives were said to be everywhere in Montreal, swarming like a bunch of bees. She had been advised to leave as soon as possible. Due to the close provincial police surveillance at the St. Lawrence Hall, she felt it unwise to communicate with Ebenezer--to draw any attention to herself. She needed to leave--get away from these people--this Rebel cause. Clearly, Booth had placed her in grave danger.

With tears streaming down her cheeks, she stared up imploringly through her black veil at the tall, muscular Union soldier who had pulled her aside at the Province of Canada frontier near Buffalo, New York. He attempted to study her face, but her cover proved to be too opaque for him to observe to his satisfaction. Suddenly, her left eyelid began to spasm and she feared he could see the movement, an obvious sign of her nervousness. She lifted her handkerchief inside her veil to temporarily obscure the twitching with the pretense of dabbing tears away.

Her widow's weeds had carried her into the Provence of Quebec, but could they protect her on her return to the United States? She quietly took a deep breath, and slowly exhaled as the border official moved toward the front of the room, his face turned away from her.

He seated himself at a desk facing her, and continued reviewing her documents, looking at her off and on during the process. He tilted his head to the right, then the left, picked up a folder and shuffled some papers held within, scrutinizing her as if a different vantage point might prove to be more enlightening.

Although she was uncomfortable, Katherine refrained from shifting her weight in the hard-wooden chair that made her feel as if she were already a prisoner. She, as yet, had not spoken and maintained a stony countenance--like a sphinx.

Appearing exasperated, the soldier stood, roughly pushed back his chair, and ran his right hand through his thick brown hair. He picked up a sheath of papers and left the room, closing the door behind him, leaving her alone in the small, stark room with bleak white walls that seemed to enclose her--like a trap.

As if on cue, she leapt to her feet and seized the folder that her inquisitor had opened. On the top of a pile of documents was a bulletin with her name written in large letters: "WANTED/REWARD FOR INFORMATION: MARQUETTE KATHERINE DURO VAN DE MEER also known as Elizabeth Granger, born Brooklyn, New York, February 1845. Eyes: Blue; hair, brown. Last seen at Corry, Pennsylvania Railroad Station. Suspected of collaborating with…"

Just then, Katherine heard footsteps approaching the solid wooden door, and she quickly closed the folder, returned it to its original position on the desktop, and slid swiftly into her seat. The male agent entered the room, followed by an obese, bald gentleman who walked with a waddle--like a duck.

"This interpreter is a French speaker, so I have asked him to assist with my questioning."

Neither did she move, nor act as if she understood his words in English. When the interpreter introduced himself in French, she turned to him and nodded.

"You must remove your veil."

The heavy-soled boots of the government official clomped as he moved past the interpreter and closer to her, inspecting her face. He was now so near that she could smell cigar smoke emanating from his uniform. She suppressed a gag.

For the next twenty minutes, the border guard stated each question in English that the interpreter painstakingly translated into

French. Katherine, her red eyes and bloated face exposed, answered in French. It was a time-consuming exercise, and she hoped they would quickly tire of this interrogation. She had memorized all of the data on her Secret Service papers including a given birth place, birth date and her fictitious husband's name and their address in Montreal. Other details, she constructed as it became necessary. Now with the veil removed, she could clearly view her surroundings.

The blackened potbellied stove in the center of the room projected an exhaust pipe that reached an opening in the ceiling, and produced an odor of burning wood and prodigious warmth to the extent that Katherine could see beads of sweat stand-out on the French speaker's upper lip and forehead. By the time the basic identification questions were exhausted, he had removed his coat and vest and loosened his celluloid collar. The agent seemed not to notice the interpreter's discomfort and kept the questions coming.

Finally, he asked her why she was traveling into the United States. In response, she slowly repeated the fabricated facts of her constraining circumstances.

"My husband of twenty-two years has died and poor Pierre does not know his Pa-pa' is dead--dead and buried." With that she wailed and blew her nose profusely on her thoroughly soaked cloth handkerchief.

"You understand my situation. My son, my Pe-pe' is now my only hope. Without him, I am alone and without money. My sole support, my little Pierre. Without him, I will soon be destitute, destitute." She broke into a crescendo of sobs, her body shaking. "I have sent six telegrams but never delivered nor claimed by him— my son. I am so frightened."

She dabbed at her tears, and leaned forward in the uncomfortable chair and began swaying from side-to-side. Relieved to be able to shift her weight from its hard surface, she answered what was to be the last question from her inquisitor.

"His last known address? Is in a town called Franklin, Pennsylvania. Where is it? Do you know? I must purchase a railroad ticket to go there. I dare not make a mistake. My funds are near depletion." She focused her reddened eyes on the dour border agent.

Even with her last spate of theatrics, the soldier yet appeared skeptical and adamant. As she listened to the two men discussing the situation in English, her left eyelid began twitching. Her heart was racing, pounding against her chest wall so loudly that she wondered if they could hear it from where they stood.

They consulted the folder that she had peeked at earlier, then watched her closely while they talked.

"With all this here sabotage--Rebel activity up in these parts, we're working longer hours until they get us some more help. Today's my twelfth-day-straight on duty. This burning of New York City and that raid on the railroad just down the lake at Dunkirk a month or so ago has put everybody on edge."

The interpreter nodded his understanding.

"Well, it appears that one Johnny Reb is due to hang in a couple of weeks--that guy they caught in Ohio."

With that remark, Katherine's left eyelid increased its twitching, but she sat as still as a stone statue.

"Yep, sure does look like he'll swing." The border guard went on.

"Well, Mayor Fargo has a good point when he set up his own intelligence network here in Buffalo. But, we as Union soldiers have got to carefully screen these people who are traveling into the United States. Trouble is folks like this woman--doesn't quite match the description of this here Marquette Van de Meer or Elizabeth Granger person, but who knows. She's got papers that are proper and documented, so I have no choice but to let her go. Just my gut tells me otherwise. Oh, well." He shifted his weight. "None the less, I am going to talk with the Provost Marshall General."

He gathered up her documents from his desktop and reviewed each page again while keeping her under scrutiny. Finally, both men stood and left the room, taking her documents with them.

The room was quiet. She could hear noises from outside the building. Several blocks away, a train whistled and railcars banged together as they were coupled at the nearby railroad track. If only she could get out of here and onto the Atlantic and Great Western bound for the rail center at Corry where she had options for her next destination, wherever that was. She took a deep breath. As she blew quietly outward, she whispered.

"It's always darkest before the dawn..." She felt as if she were trapped up a tree like a cornered cat--no particular destination except out of the tree and free to roam.

Twenty minutes later, the pair returned. The translator addressed her and explained that she was free to leave, and the Union soldier handed over her documents. She felt like running, but walked in a casual manner out the door and into the late afternoon sun. She followed the signs and walked into the United States, leaving the frightful frontier, the officious officer and Niagara Gorge behind her.

Now safely across the border and at a railroad station, Katherine felt like a bird let out of a cage. Using the paper currency sequestered into the seam of her petticoat, she could travel anywhere, but where? She found a train schedule and discovered that the next train that was listed to depart was bound for Corry. As she walked toward the ticket window, her mind raced. Would that be a wise choice? Back into the oil country again…maybe a good place to blend into the excitement of the oil frenzy. Besides, she still had the bartender Barnswell Buchanan as her contact in Franklin. The oil area had so many newcomers, so many men, so many jobs.

Gradually moving forward in a long line of ticket purchasers, she finally stood in third position to purchase her ticket. Suddenly an incoming train spewed its arrivals along the length of the wooden platform. As scores of riders flowed across the sizeable station, she sorted through the crowd with her well-trained observation skills. She spied several men with black hats and heavy boots who could be detectives. She watched warily as one headed straight toward her, then suddenly made a forty-five-degree turn. She let out her breath slowly. The black hats disappeared from her view, and she relaxed.

As she turned toward the cashier's window, she realized that she was going to be next up. She positioned herself sideways to keep track of her place in the queue and to also watch the crowd.

Suddenly she spotted a group of colorfully costumed characters bearing signs. She squinted to read, "THE GREAT HERCULEST;" "GYMNAST;" and "STRONGMAN." Katherine stared in astonishment. Coming along behind the conspicuous contingent, she spied a familiar figure wearing a black top hat and a heavy fur coat. Benedict Hagan! It was Benedict as surely as she breathed.

In her excitement, she took one step toward him only to realize that to break from her disguise would place her in immediate jeopardy. She stopped short. Besides that, the next train to Corry after this one was scheduled for tomorrow morning. Perhaps she just imagined that she saw Benedict. The person she had identified might not really be he. She would have been risking too much if she had followed her impulses.

"Next!" She turned toward the ticket window and stepped up to the waiting agent and purchased a ticket to Corry.

When she completed the transaction, she scanned the milling crowd. The person she took for Benedict was nowhere in sight, nor were the sign bearers.

Moving toward Track Number Five, she felt concerned and conflicted. She had been duped by Booth, scrutinized at the frontier, and tempted to break her disguise--all within the last few days. With fear and feelings of ambivalence, she boarded the southbound train to Pennsylvania. Had she missed Benedict, or was that person she saw an image of her imagination? Was she headed in the right direction...if not, where should she be going? As Katherine slowly sank into a soft seat by the wide window, she whispered, "It's always darkest before the dawn."

Mid-March 1865

Heavy, wet snow clung onto Katherine's warm wool hat as she walked along snowy Spring Street toward the Titusville post office. Titusville, twenty-eight miles south of Corry in Crawford County sat near the northern border of Venango County, the heart of the oil excitement.

The tiny town of 243 citizens once made up of lumbermen and saw mill owners had blossomed in just five years into a teaming town of 6000 inhabitants. Now three banks were entrusted with large amounts of oil money, and thirteen hotels struggled to accommodate the throngs of rail passengers who flooded into oil country. Buildings made of brick and plank sidewalks conveyed the message of permanence compared to other settlements whose newest structures often were hastily constructed of rough lumber and clap board that reflected the mad rush fueled by the oil excitement.

Titusville stood apart from Oil City and Franklin which were also immersed in the new oil mining industry. Titusville had recently constructed an auditorium that hosted lectures, concerts and other entertainment. A new well-appointed reading room, replete with the latest newspapers and periodicals was a place of certain civic pride. In fact, Katherine had found solace within its walls.

Instead of remaining on constant alert in train stations and hotels while providing surveillance for the Rebels, she sat in comfort and pursued the periodicals in partial peace. Peace, however, was not what the news provided. She followed the stories of captured

Confederate conspirators, their trials, legal turmoil and consequences.

The Confederate soldier who had been a courier for Jacob Thompson was hanged on February 17 at Johnson's Island in Sandusky Harbor. Another captured Rebel, involved in the fiery attack in New York City and the Buffalo Raid near Dunkirk, Robert Cobb Kennedy was arrested in Detroit, charged as a spy among other violations and was awaiting trial. Others of Thompson's Raiders were being arrested as well, some having participated in a number of Thompson's schemes to weaken the Union. The news reminded her that she too, had a price on her head, and needed to continue vigilance for her own survival.

Snow blew into Katherine's face and clung to her eyelashes as she crossed the street and carefully negotiated the frozen snow-covered ruts of mud. This was the fourth day that she checked with the postmaster to see if her packet of mail had arrived from Franklin. Barnswell had dutifully collected and kept several letters, agreeing to forward them to her new location. Now the mail service delays seemed interminable to her, and she visited the post office every day after her work as a part-time bookkeeper at the T.L. Monroe Lumber Yard on Spring Street. Today, she determined would be different and the letters would be waiting for her.

As she rounded the corner of a three-story brick building, she collided with a man wearing a black patch over his left eye. The memory of Jacques with his missing eye, working alongside her in the vineyards of France flashed through her mind. She lost her balance on the slippery surface of the walkway, and the one-eyed stranger reached out his arm to steady her. She grabbed onto him and regained her balance.

"Oh, thank you." She smiled. Then she realized that he was wearing a military uniform, and carrying a rucksack on his back. Suddenly, she felt a jolt of fear--like a lightning strike. Immediately, she let loose of his arm and took a step backward. Memories of her interrogation at the Buffalo frontier flooded her. In a few seconds, her breathing slowed and she gathered her wits.

"You're a soldier!" She announced what was obvious to both of them.

"Yes, I just got off the train from Corry."

"Are you just returning from the war?"

He smiled and doffed his military cover.

"Yes, and you are the first person to speak to me since I

boarded the train two days ago."

"Well," she scrambled for words. "I mean it is an honor to meet you."

She smiled, her episode of near-paralyzing fear, subjugated. She brushed the snow from her eyelashes to get a better look at him.

"Do you live here in Titusville?"

"No, my family, Ma and my little brother live in Oil City, as far as I know. No letters to me--or that have got to me for the past couple a' months."

The wind was picking up and the snowfall increased to the point that it obscured the church tower a block away.

"Do you know of a hotel near here? No train down Oil Creek until tomorrow."

"Yes, the McCray House is over there." As she pointed toward the nearby building, she saw that it was hidden by the blinding, blowing snowfall.

"I am staying there, and heading that way, except for a stop at the post office."

He looked down at her.

"May I walk with you...? This blowing snow is making my limited sight worse than usual. My name is Elias--Elias Kahle."

"And I'm Katherine Le Conte."

They proceeded in silence with their heads bowed against the wild wind in the blinding blizzard, the snow swirling around them. When Katherine entered the post office, the postmaster recognized her from prior visits, despite her coat and hat having been turned white by the wild weather.

"Ah, Madame Le Conte. I have something for you today."

The balding man smiled and handed her a small bundle of mail tied with a brown cord. Her heart raced as she anticipated the contents of the collection of a month's personal news. Thanking him, she secured the bundle in her deep skirt pocket and turned to leave. Elias waited for her just outside the doorway, away from the wind. Together they walked to the hotel.

Alone in her room, Katherine spread the envelopes out on the bed and examined the script of each. Her heart pounded when she recognized Fredrick's handwriting. Hastily, she tore off the soiled covering, and began to read.

"Dearest Cousin, at long last I am freed. My sentence has been commuted by the efforts of Barrister Plugge. He first contacted me in September and traveled to Fort McHenry a fortnight later. I am most grateful to him and Ebenezer for their efforts. However, I am pained to realize that in contacting Plugge, I have caused you much consternation. I am sorry.

"Every day, I prayed for your safety, Katie. You were left in a desperate state with no support from the wine trade, nor from me. I am anguished over your situation and wonder where and how you are managing.

"I know not when this message might reach you, so I tell you my plans now--such as they are. The confinement has weakened me. Ebenezer, that kind soul has offered me a place in his household until I can regain my strength--however long that will take.

"Please contact Ebenezer so that I know where you are and that you are safe.

"Your loving cousin,
Fredrick
January 5, 1865
Baltimore"

Katherine laid that letter aside, and stared out the window at the twirling flakes of snow as they danced onto the windowsill. It is not just Plugge who is searching for her. From the border agent's bulletin, she had seen, it was also the Federals who wanted her. She would need to cautiously contact Fredrick.

Next, she read a telegraph message that Ebenezer had sent three weeks ago.

"Fredrick doing well STOP Confiscated wine now recovered and in storage here STOP Where are you STOP Contact me STOP Ebenezer"

Spontaneously, she jumped to her feet, raising her arms over her head.

"Thank goodness! Oh, thank goodness!" Her gown made a swishing sound as she danced about in her room. Since the money paid her by General Lee was almost depleted, and her current salary, meager, she felt released--like a burdensome boulder being raised from her shoulders. Now, she could get some contracts started for the sale of those casks of stored wine. Except for the price on her head, the future was looking rosy.

Several hours later, finally feeling more optimistic than she had since her dreary days in Montreal, Katherine decided to take her evening meal at the hotel. Having dressed and carefully surveyed herself in the mirror, she instinctively felt for her concealed weapons, then glided from her room, and slowly descended the curved, carpeted staircase to the first floor. Ever on alert, she paused every three to four steps to observe the guests who were gathering below near the bar and at the entrance of the dining room. Spotting no one who appeared to be a detective or an agent, she moved forward deliberately and was greeted by the headwaiter.

"One for dinner, Madame?"

She nodded and he led her toward a small table in the corner. As they walked in that direction, a voice called.

"Mrs. Le Conte." A shock surged though Katherine's body. She thought no one here could identify her. To her relief, Elias was standing immediately in front of her.

"Mrs. Le Conte! Will you join me for dinner?" He was readily recognizable with his black eye cover--like a signal flag at a railroad crossing. Clad in his military uniform, he looked quite handsome to her.

She smiled at his recognition of their earlier meeting and greeted him.

"Why I would love to have dinner with you."

The waiter turned, and she gestured toward the seat she wanted with her back against the wall and a view of the restaurant entrance. It placed her at right angles with Elias. Having helped her to her seat, the waiter gave her the dinner list and departed.

"How nice to see you again, Elias."

Elias seated himself and smiled.

"How fortunate for me that we meet again. Thank you for walking with me this afternoon." He paused. "This seems a pleasant place, if only for one night."

Katherine smiled. "For me as well. So lucky for me to have someone with whom to dine on such a frigid and snowy night as this." She paused. "Do you mind if I ask you a question?"

He nodded his consent and looked directly at her.

"Why are you wearing that eye patch? What happened?"

"I was with the 42nd Regiment. In May, we were engaged in a skirmish with the Rebs in Virginia. My company, the Bucktails--all men from up the Allegheny River--we were on a reconnaissance mission under Major Hartshorn to observe the numbers of enemy. Suddenly, they charged." He paused and ducked his head. "Before it was over, a score of us were injured with one killed. I got hit in the face when a canister exploded near where we were entrenched. Broke my leg too."

Katherine listened as the waiter served their food.

"Who took care of you? Did they have a doctor in your unit?"

"Yes, an army surgeon, and he patched me and others up in a hospital in a church nearby. About a week later, we all got moved to a larger hospital near Washington." He took a drink from his glass. "Thought I was going to get through the war without injury. You see our outfit had less than a month 'til our service time expired on June 11. If I hadn't been injured, would have been home in June, not in the middle of the winter. Took me a good while to heal and get to walking again--even walking is different since I have only one eye."

"Sounds as if you were lucky to get back alive."

"Yeah, so many didn't."

They sat in silence for some time, he lost in his memories; she observing the growing number of diners.

Suddenly, the door of the outside entrance opened with a whooshing sound and a man appeared. He stood there and seemed to be surveying the occupants of the dining room. His heavy, dark travel coat was covered with snow, and hung down to meet his black boots that had ice-encrusted buckles.

Katherine recognized the black strap that crossed over the instep. She felt her muscles tense, her heart race, and the hair on the back of her neck rise. A federal agent. The news articles about captured Rebel Raids and those who assisted them shot through her mind. What should she do?

"Elias, please take my hand and look toward me."

She slowly shifted in her seat, turning her back toward the predator. Producing a fancy folding fan from her left skirt pocket, she opened it slowly, and leaned in toward Elias. She talked quietly.

"Elias, I have reason to believe that the man who is standing in the doorway is looking for me."

Elias looked quizzical.

"Why?"

"Unfortunately, my evil stepfather has hired detectives to find me. It has to do with my property and he is trying to force me to sign papers to that effect--to give him my property."

She hoped that her explanation would suffice for the moment, until the agent departed.

"I see the gent. He just rebuffed the headwaiter who offered him a seat. Guess he's not here for dinner. Not even removing his coat."

"Elias, I must avoid this man." Elias watched him in silence for several minutes.

"Now, he is removing his coat and hat. The waiter is taking them in the cloak area."

"This is not good." She took a deep breath and exhaled slowly. She could feel the hair bristling on the back of her neck.

"He's coming this way. Just turn more toward me and let's talk."

As she did as Elias advised, she caught a glimpse of the agent, a stout figure with a swaggering gait. As he drew nearer, she opened her fan and leaned toward Elias while talking in a low voice as if engaged in an intimate conversation.

"I do declare, Cousin, I have never in my life seen snow such as you have here in the North." She raised her voice with its distinct southern accent so that the interloper could overhear their conversation. "It's a wonder we have made it this far in our journey to get you home safe and sound after your injuries."

Elias smiled and picked up the cue.

"I was surprised when Aunt Lucy agreed on your traveling with me from Virginia. It's a long way--been a long trip."

"I have heard about your side of the family ever since I was a wee one. The last thing I would have dreamed of was coming up here. And in a blizzard, too!"

The agent strolled slowly past, so close that Katherine could smell the pipe tobacco that permeated his black jacket. He continued through the dining area, and seated himself at the far end of the long, polished bar where he had a clear view of most of the dining room and its patrons. Her palms began to sweat as she silently contemplated her escape. Deciding that her movement would draw his attention, she remained where she was, like a rabbit in the underbrush.

Thirty minutes later their main course consumed, Elias looked about and reported to his dinner companion that the feared foreigner stayed at his perch with his eyes on the growing number of customers who were arriving for dinner or a drink at the bar. The swelling numbers in the area helped to hide Katherine and she was grateful for the influx that blocked the agent's direct line of sight to her.

"Elias, I must quickly take my leave, while this place is busy. What do you think?"

Just then, the outside entrance door was flung wide and a

great mass of cold air blew into the room. Five men, their tall black hats turned frosty white by the swirling snow entered as a unit and stomped the clumps of white from their boots and shook it from their damp head covers. Their commotion created a scene that was distracting the agent. As the arrivals talked loudly, they quickly moved in unison to the bar where they ordered and were served their drinks. After lighting up his cigar, an authoritative arrival spoke in a vociferous voice.

"Time to celebrate our agreement, gentlemen!"

"Hear! Hear!"

A cheer went up and all heads turned toward the celebrants who downed the contents of their respective glasses and moved to order more. Loud discussion continued.

"Now that you are stakeholders in the Pithole Oil Company, an enterprise that has been in business since June of '64. Within the year, we've hired the most experienced oilmen in the business, walking our leases and determining exactly where to put down--to drill. This new oil field has caught the excitement of folks all over this country, and you are the far-sighted men who are in on the beginning of this new oil boom. Congratulations!"

The speaker paused, tugged at his collar and continued in a loud voice.

"Since you are now major shareholders in the Pithole Oil Company, you deserve to hear a bit of oil history.

The speaker went on and Katherine lost count of the time, but kept focused on the agent at the bar. She thought he seemed distracted and was listening to the host of the oil investors.

"Overall," the presenter concluded, "things have improved--we've moved on from the early days."

A deep male voice from the group asked,

"What's happened to that Phillips Well Number Two? It still producing?"

Their host smiled broadly.

"I am here to tell you that the well in question has settled down to about 2500 to 3000 barrels a day to this date…"

Katherine and Elias had continued to sit, remaining silent during the men's discussion. Their loud voices were difficult to ignore, and most diners also focused on their discussion. It was difficult to ignore them, let alone to attempt a conversation at their tables. For Katherine, it gave her time to identify the opportunity to make her exit from the dining room, undetected. She noticed that

Elias was listening with undivided attention to the speaker's words. Just as she was about to speak to Elias, the men restarted their loud discussion.

"I read in the newspapers that transportation of all this oil has been a contentious problem since the get-go. Besides the pipelines and boats, is anything else planned?"

The presenter cleared his throat.

"At this point, all I can relate to you is what I've heard. A circle of my business associates, men with connections in Cleveland and New York say that the railroads are becoming increasingly interested in this oil region... Our Pithole Oil Company leases are located along Pithole Creek, and rail transportation will greatly enhance moving our Pennsylvania crude--to markets in Cleveland, Pittsburgh and New York."

Just then, Katherine saw the headwaiter signal the speaker, who took his queue and slowly concluded the speech for his audience.

"Investors! Welcome to the future of the Pithole Oil Company. While Pithole seems remote to you, and I agree that it is, I am convinced that recent oil strikes here are reviving the flagging market. The future of the petroleum industry is now and is booming!"

The speaker paused for a drink.

"The fledgling oil industry had made significant strides during the five years of its existence. Numerous oil wells located on thirty square miles of land produced an average of 1,500,000 barrels of oil."

"The over-production, a glut of crude caused the oil trade to plummet into the doldrums. Oil production was slashed to half of its former output by the spring of 1863, as a nation, more concerned about the Civil War than the birth of a peacetime industry focused on other priorities..."

Katherine saw that the black-booted federal agent was fixated on the braggadocious speculators and excited investors and their discussion.

Just as two waiters appeared with several steaming platers of food, men in the discussion group rose to adjust their chairs for dining. The view of the federal agent was blocked by the activity of staff serving additional dishes. As the waiters huddled and several other staff brought additional plates, she saw her opportunity. Together, she and Elias rose from their table, now obscured from the agent by the dining room staff and the busyness of serving the food, and slipped to the exit that led to the hotel's lobby. No one seemed to notice.

Hastily, they mounted the stairs toward their rooms. Outside of her door, she turned to Elias.

"Thank you, Elias. I enjoyed our meal together. I hope that we will meet again, perhaps under less stressful circumstances, for me. Have a safe journey to Oil City."

As she turned the knob to her room, Elias bid her goodnight. Seeing that no one had followed them, Katherine entered her room and breathed a sigh of relief. Preparing for bed, she removed her dress and corset, and she opened the dresser drawer to put away her underthings, her eyes came to rest on the silver flask. She retrieved it from under her extra pair of pantaloons, sat back and took a long drink.

She had evaded her pursuers again, at least for the time being.

Elias' Homecoming

March 1865

By the time Elias arrived at Shaeffer's Farm seven miles south of Titusville on Oil Creek, a bank of gray clouds obscured the rays of the noon sun and large flakes of snow fell on the detraining passengers. Grateful that the southbound train had departed Titusville in the morning, Elias managed to squeeze into one of the three overloaded passenger carriages. He contemplated the second half of his trip, a twelve-mile hike from Shaeffer's Farm to Oil City.

Hours later, Elias negotiated the snow-covered wagon ruts and outcropped boulders that seemed unrelenting, and might have created obstacles for even those who had the advantage of seeing with two eyes. The lack of depth perception proved to be a challenge on this snowy journey. He had to remain constantly vigilant. Now he heard sounds muffled by the falling snow.

As he topped the rise of hard-rutted road, the sounds grew louder and Elias could make out a team of horses, four abreast with a flatboat attached. The teamster was shouting, urging them on with their burden. In this cold snowy weather, these beasts, up to their bellies in icy water and floating ice were dragging some eighty to one hundred barrels of oil over streambeds of flat, slippery shale. Their bodies were encased in ice, like armor, and their tails dragged low, weighed down by clusters of icicles. He wondered how many trips they had endured and were yet to withstand on this cold day. As in war, these animals of the oil fields led short and often wretched lives.

By the six-mile mark near the Egbert Farm, he was aching at the point of the healed fracture in his thigh where a cannon shot had penetrated his femur. Leaning against a huge rock, he stretched his legs, downed the two stowed biscuits and drank from his canteen. Looking up into the gray clouds, he could see only an outline of the sun that had moved into the western sky. He knew that he needed to continue the pace set at Shaeffer's Farm to make Oil City by dark.

In late afternoon, he reached Rouseville where he decided to stop for a brief rest and some food. He needed to warm himself. Through the falling snow, he spied Bunville and Stenet's Store and a sign on the door offered a hot mug of beef bullion for a pittance. Seated at the counter for several minutes, he realized that his military jacket smelled like wet wool, his hair was stringy, and his feet were thoroughly soaked. The flush-faced, be-speckled clerk urged him to sit by the potbellied stove with his shoes off, to dry his socks and warm his feet. He thanked her, ate quickly and rose to leave.

"Better watch that crik as you go 'long the Turnpike. It's been risin' all day yesterday and was prit'neer flooded down near the old Buchanan Place."

With that warning, Elias began the last two miles of his tedious travel and periodically observed the creek level. Oil Creek was coming close to the top of the banks.

Now on either side of him in this Oil Creek Valley, he was amazed at the number of oil refineries with their huge storage tanks dotting the landscape, amid a forest of derricks and clusters of machine shacks. Open torches burned, producing smoke that lingered in the once verdant valley, now denuded by the burgeoning oil industry. The acres of oil property were blanketed with snow, but the wagon ruts among the blackened tanks, tall derricks and dingy buildings oozed with mud that stained nature's white cover like blood flowing from a wound onto a clean sheet. To Elias, it was a different world than he remembered. With this amount of growth and change along the creek valley, what should he expect in Oil City?

Finally, the snow abated and even in the fading daylight, Elias could see the altered landscapes of Oil City, transformed during his absence of four years. On the west bank of Oil Creek, Elias read a sign: "BOROUGH OF OIL CITY, EST. 1862, THE HUB OF OILDOM: POPULATION 3000." He recalled the sparse population and several crooked muddy streets of 1861, the start of the war. As he passed the first few residential buildings, he recognized little. The meager, humble structures of 1861 had mushroomed into an impressive array of new establishments and Main Street seemed wider than he remembered.

As he moved toward the bridge, he caught a view the landing flats. Memories of his working days there washed over him, and he paused to take in the scene. In his mind, he saw John Obadiah, red-faced and angry, swinging his crutches at him, and Jesse pouring water on his out-of-control Pa. He shivered and realized how cold and wet he felt. He picked up his pace.

Along Seneca Street, people, mostly men were going about their business of the late afternoon. They were wearing top hats, heavy coats and high boots as they waded through the snowy streets. He studied faces in hopes of seeing someone familiar, but recognized none. He was a stranger to them, and they to him.

Despite the fact that he was wearing his Union Army uniform, nobody looked his way, nor turned to stare. For one reason he decided, he was partially covered with snow. On the other hand, he realized that he was one of many troops whose time in service had expired and great numbers of former soldiers were flooding the streets of various villages and towns. Perhaps these veterans had become a common sight among the civilian population. Or were these non-soldiers even aware that the war was being fought, that scores of men had died and were never returning? He shrugged off the thought of nobody caring about the sacrifices of the fallen.

He turned his back to the west and scanned for the family cabin among so many unfamiliar houses. Finally, he spotted it. His homestead was one of the only recognizable buildings which now lay crammed tightly together near the river. He was surprised at how small and shabby a place it now appeared, dwarfed beneath two towering oaks. Those he remembered.

As he approached, he noticed that no smoke rose from the old stone chimney and fallen leaves covered the wooden steps that led to the tiny front stoop. A cold chill permeated his body when he saw that there was no light, nor sign of the house being occupied. Where were his mother and Luke?

He mounted the stairs slowly and arrived at a closed door. He tried the latch and peered inside. It was dark and cold. There were no signs of life--no sounds, no odor of cooking, nothing. The place was unoccupied.

Had they not received his telegram from Titusville? In the near dark, he spied an envelope tucked into the frame of the door. He pulled it out and saw that it was from the telegraph company-- probably his message sent several days ago.

Now he realized that his family had been unaware of his pending arrival. A jolt of fear and disappointment shot through him as he opened the envelope. He sat down on the stoop to read and confirm that it was the one he had sent.

He sat there in the dying light, the door to his house ajar, brushing snow from the telegram. Suddenly, sorrowful memories ran through him--cold, chilling memories like walking among his wounded and dead comrades on the Virginia battlefield. Then he pictured his father, his stubborn, handicapped parent whose vehemence had driven him out, away from those he loved--his mother, Luke, Gala, and his friend, Jesse--into harm's way, into the combat and chaos of war that had damaged his body and mind forever.

For several minutes, he stared at the wet, limp telegram in his hand. During the long months of his convalescence and tedious train travels, he had envisioned the reunion of hugging his mother and Luke, and looking into their happy faces and tear-filled eyes. That anticipation had spurred him on today, as he dodged the ruts, boulders and ice-covered holes of the cold, muddy trail from Shaeffer's Farm to Oil City.

Now fear and disappointment flowed through him like an uncontrolled current of icy water. Where were they? He was stunned and disappointed. This was not the homecoming he had envisioned.

At last, he realized how cold he was. His body was shaking and his feet and hands were numb. He turned toward the area where the firewood had been stored four years ago, and could see nothing but mounds of snow. He stepped off the stoop and moved forward. His memory steered him toward a tall rise several yards away. He brushed off a layer to discover neatly piled logs, split, and some dry enough to burn.

Minutes later, Elias sat before the hearth and a growing fire. The bright light from the flames infused him with hope--hope that he would somehow be reunited with his family. After stripping off his cold, clammy clothes then hanging them to dry, he watched the third log ignite. His back was cold, but his face, chest and arms began to warm. Wrapped in his mother's patch-quilt, he lay staring at the fire, then growing drowsy, he dozed off to sleep.

...

"Who are you? What are you doing here?"

A man's deep voice together with a nudge of a foot awakened Elias with a start. Sleepy and confused, he struggled to remember where he was. Turning toward the voice with his good eye, he found himself staring at a tall, lanky man whose face was indiscernible in the light of the dying fire. Not feeling a dire threat, he did not move but stared into the gloom, and said nothing. Finally, fully awake now, he voiced his own challenge.

"Well, who are you and why are you in my house in the

224

middle of the night?"

"What do you mean 'your' house? I am in charge of this house by permission of Mrs. Molly Kahle. I saw smoke comin' from the chimney and came to investigate."

"That's my mother you're talking about. Who are you?"

"I'm Jesse May and I'm lookin' after the cabin for Molly."

"Jesse! You've grown up since I was gone. I'm Elias! I'm home--back this night from the war."

"Elias?" Jesse seemed dumbstruck. He took a step backward. "You're really here! We feared that you were dead!"

With that, Jesse dropped down and embraced Elias who had risen to his knees during their conversation. Both men were weeping openly, releasing their hug to look at each other in the dim light. Then they clasped again.

Finally, Jesse, as if in shock sat back and just stared at Elias. Then he jumped to his feet.

"Let me get some firewood. It's cold in here."

With that, he opened the door, leaped off the stoop and returned quickly with an armload of logs. Elias retrieved his clothing now dried by the heat of the fire, while Jesse placed a kettle of water on the hanger above the flames.

Both had a myriad of questions. The two old friends talked late into the night.   ...

Elias awakened to a steady drumming on the roof of the cabin.

"That sounds like rain, Jess. That snow yesterday was mighty wet, so the temperature must be even higher now. Snow's turned to rain."

Elias opened the cabin door and looked out.

"Think I'll delay my plans to strike out to Pitch Pine to see Ma. and Luke. At least I know where they are. Maybe wait for a day or so--until the rain stops. The Turnpike along Oil Creek was bad enough. Frozen ruts are thawing--makes walking difficult, and now with rain on top of it, guess I'll rethink my plans."

"That's a good idea. Don't you need a couple of days to rest before startin' out again, Elias?"

March 16, 1865

"Elias! Wake up, Elias!" Loud knocking awakened Elias and

he quickly got to his feet and opened the door. In the early light of day, Jesse stood on the stoop. He was dripping with water and his hip-high boots glistened with mud. Behind him, Elias saw rain was coming down in sheets. Jesse talked fast.

"Look out here, Elias! The creek's over its banks! And it's come up to four-foot under the bridge. Folks are feared that the risin' water will knock out the bridge. Down on the flats, they're tyin' the oil barges together to make a boom--keep stuff from floatin' downriver. Hasson Flats is under water and basements are floodin.' Some folks are movin' to higher ground. Say it's been pourin' down like this all night. And snow's meltin' all along the creek and tributaries, Cherrytree Run, Pioneer Run, Shaeffer Run, Cherry Run."

Jesse stepped into the cabin.

"Hurry! Come on, Elias. I'm here to help you pack up what we can. They are warnin' it's not safe so close to the water."

Wide-awake now, Elias pulled on his clothes and the two friends began gathering up as much as they both could carry.

…

Elias led the way to the only spot on high ground that he could think of, an old hunting shack on the ridge east of town, well above Hasson Flats. It was the place where he and Gala would meet and were undisturbed.

Even after four years, the well-hidden shelter was still standing and was a welcome sight to Elias. He could remember how Gala looked back then, waiting here for him. He wondered about her. Four years was a long time.

Breathless from their rapid ascent, they dropped their supplies and blankets into the dry interior. Jesse got a stick to clear out downed leaves, arousing several mice that ran helter-skelter across the floor and out into the rain. It appeared that the place had remained unused for a long time.

Elias squatted beside Jesse as they looked down at the scene playing out before them.

"Look at where Haliday Run usually comes down off the ridge. It's over the banks. Looks like its flowing right down Main Street and into those buildings at the base of Hogback on the west side of town."

"Are those oil barrels, floating in Seneca Street, Jess?"

"Coming from the oil yards at Fisher Brothers. Looks like

that's under water--streets are gone."

"Look at the oil barges jammed against the creek bridge--that one's cross-wise and against the support."

They watched in fascinated horror as a jam of logs, driftwood, and parts of boats slammed into the barge that was against the bridge abutment.

"Jess, look upstream! Seems like oil tanks, boats and a derrick are tumbling into the creek. Looks to be moving fast--taking everything with it."

Elias stood up to get a better view.

"My belongings are safe here, Jess. Think we better go back down to see if we can help."

The downpour continued into early afternoon as Elias and Jesse slipped and slid down the steep mountainside. They witnessed the rapid current that looked like a waterfall, tearing heavy boilers from their foundations along the creek, and slamming oil tanks, machinery from wells, trees and lumber into other stalled wreckage. Black crude flowed on the surface of the flooded waters.

"Look, Elias! That's a house floatin' past us! And buildin's too. This is awful!"

"There's the sheriff and a rescue party. They're getting some people off their front porches and into a boat."

"Never have seen such as this." Jesse paused. "It's as if the flood-gates of heaven have opened up and the deluge on Noah is re-happenin'. That's what the preacher would say, I reckon."

Suddenly, debris from trees, bushes, wood from oil derricks and several small houses washed off their foundations swept by, stacking up near the bridge. The rising waters shifted the ominous pile, and with a loud crunching sound, half of the bridge gave way. The mountainous mass washed toward the open channel of the swollen Allegheny River.

Jesse rubbed his eyes in disbelief. "That's separatin' the east side and the west sides of town. No way to get across now."

The two friends stood near a group of survivors some yards from the water's edge and overheard their discussion.

"Sherriff told us that the river was arisin' six inches an hour. Said by 12 midnight, it was comin' up a foot an hour. No wonder the bridge split in half and washed into the Allegheny."

"The water's way up over the doors of the upper warehouses--Shirk and Company and Parker and Castle."

"Look. The Allegheny has gone off its channel and is

floodin' the landin' flats and flowin' direct into the oil yards-- water's come into the west of Oil City. Oh, my God!"

"The water from Haliday Creek is pushin' all them buildin's over-crushin' 'em. Looks like the end of the world here…"

"Look! There goes the other part of the bridge! Oh holy gosh…bein' pushed along by all those uprooted trees and downed derricks! Can you believe this?"

"Couple of hours ago, they had to go in and rescue my cousins from the fast risen' water. Took 'em off their porch roof. And just in time, too. That current pushed their place out into Oil Creek and it was gone, just collapsed--caught up by the debris at the bridge."

…

By the next morning, the rain had turned to snow, and the old hunting shack was frigid. Jesse built a fire on a flat area behind the shack, protected from the wind. Elias unwrapped several pieces of beef jerky and the cornbread he had salvaged from the family cabin. A pot of water sat on a burning timber. "Sort of like being back with the Bucktails."

Jesse stopped chewing his jerky and looked up at Elias. "Was this what it was like, Elias? Four years of this kind of livin'?"

"Not all the time, Jess. Just when we were on the move. Even then, the army made sure we had vittles to cook." Elias paused looking up into the cloudy sky, remembering.

"When we were on the move—marching. We'd be all played out by the end of the day, and the first thing on everybody's mind was 'what's to eat?' And just like an answer to praying, there would come the supply wagons, catching up to our outfit. We were so happy to see them. It didn't matter how tired we were, we'd get those wagons unloaded pronto. Each carried six barrels of salt pork, and four barrels of coffee, or ten barrels of sugar, like that. Other wagons pulled five days of forage for animals, the horses."

Elias looked at Jesse who was sitting very still, listening.

"Then they'd break open a barrel of pork. We'd all get a piece and roast it on the end of our bayonets over the fire. It smelled so good and was delicious."

Elias thought Jesse seemed lost in thought. Finally, he continued.

"That was one of the good memories from the war. Don't have many."

Jesse shifted his weight where he sat. They lapsed into silence for several minutes until Elias spoke.

"Here we're on our own. No way to get flour or salt or anything from the stores down there in that mess. Nothing's left." Elias gestured toward the devastation below them.

Jesse nodded his understanding, then the two sat with their backs to the fire and looked toward town. Immediately below them, families huddled with blankets, their homes washed away in the night. Some had bundles or a piece of furniture at their sides and others scarcely the clothing needed against the weather.

Jesse sighed.

"My job on the flats has washed away, I guess. Most of us are now out of jobs. I hope my parent's house on Haliday Run is up high enough that it didn't get dragged away."

As daylight advanced, the snow let up and the destruction of the flooding spread out before them. From Center Street at the Gibson House to near the site of the now missing bridge, many houses were juxta-positioned having moved from their foundations while pieces of furniture, water-soaked logs, assorted sizes of lumber, bloated horses, and turned-over wagons floated nearby. Buildings were underwater to the second floor and overturned boats and trees drifted in the now calmer waters.

Between Center Street and the river, one large Graff and Hasson iron tank lay on its side, emptied of its 8000 barrel-capacity of crude oil and thousands of barrels, both empty and full filled the flooded area. At the mouth of Oil Creek, the boom constructed of lashed-together oil barges prevented debris of every description from washing into the Allegheny at that point. Water, ten-feet-deep covered the first story of every building within sight. Near the river landing flats, a few submerged warehouses held fast because they stored iron tubes and heavy castings that functioned like anchors. Farther downstream, oil derricks at that distance looked like tiny toppled toys, their wells now flooded.

Across Oil Creek to the east, Elias could not locate his cabin, nor the two huge oaks that had stood over the area since he could remember. He felt as if his former life had been washed away-- erased for all time.

He put his arm around Jesse's shaking shoulders. Both men were sobbing.

"Gone, Elias. Everything is gone."

In the end, Jesse and Elias realized they could do little to prevent or assist in the disaster. The conditions were right. Over that past five years, acres of land on both sides of Oil Creek and its tributaries had been denuded during the process of extracting the crude from the ground. Precautions regarding drilling for oil had been thrown to the wind, and run-off from the downpours and from rapid snowmelt ran rampant, barreling downhill, unrestrained, taking everything with it, seeking its lowest point, the already swollen waterways of Oil Creek and the Allegheny River.

Cleanup from this most damaging flood in history of the Pennsylvania oil country took months. With one person drowned while trying to save a horse, the total monetary loss to just the oil industry alone was estimated at $5,000,000.

…

Trying to be heard over the wind, Jesse turned toward the east and called to Elias.

"Does the road go to the right up here, or should we go to the left?"

The two stood at the fork-in-the-road where all around them was nothing but snow, fields of white. Elias pulled some beef jerky from his pocket and offered some to Jesse.

"We go to the right along that field where the corn stubble is coming through." Elias pointed out the direction to the east and then he brushed the snow off of a log and sat down.

"Let's take a rest here. Pitch Pine is about another five miles. We just crossed over East Sandy Creek. That's about half way to the area where my folks settled after they emigrated from Germany. One town they named here from their German past is Fryburg, just a few miles north of Pitch Pine. Good place for Ma and Luke to go--to be with Ma's folks."

Jesse was preparing to join Elias on the log, when he stopped to stare in the direction of their destination.

"Elias, here comes a horse and sleigh toward us."

When the travelers got closer, Jesse squinted his eyes, staring at them. Suddenly, he shouted.

"Mathias! Mathias!" and waved wildly.

Elias jumped to his feet. "Jesse, is that my uncle? That Mathias?"

"Yes, I recognize Topsy. It's them!"

Mathias brought Topsy to a halt and jumped down from the sleigh.

"Jesse! What are you doing out here?" Then he looked at Jesse's companion with curiosity.

"Mathias, it's Elias! He's returned! He's returned!"

...

That evening after supper, the family settled in front of the blazing hearth in the family homestead at Pitch Pine. They celebrated their joyful reunion, and discussed the shocking news of the devastating flood in Oil City. Elias told Molly that their property was flooded and the only thing standing was the stone chimney of the cabin. They agreed that it would take a long time for the waters to recede and re-building of the town to proceed. Meanwhile, they would remain in Pitch Pine.

Finally, Elias brought up the subject of Gala. He addressed his inquiry to Molly.

"I've lost track of her here lately. She came by to see me right after John Obadiah disappeared, and said she was sorry for my loss. But I think she was really wanting to hear about you and where you were by then. She had a baby with her, a toddler. Cute little thing. I was wondering if it was hers, but hesitated to ask." She paused.

"Been rumors about her...and you. After you left and all."

"Rumors, what rumors?" Elias was leaning forward in his chair.

"Well, the day that John Obadiah upset some of the men working at the flats, Gala had come on to the landings from her canoe. She had a baby with her. Guess he told her to get out of there...with a baby and her dog. Workmen overheard him ordering her off, and so they decided to talk to him about it. The upshot was, I think they were looking for an excuse to confront him about the baby. Told your Pa that the baby favored you--blue eyes, blonde hair and all."

Elias was mute. He felt dizzy and confused.

Luke stood and began gesturing.

"That's when Jess and I went to help Pa get home, after work, and they were talkin' to him then--in front of Jess and me."

"John Obadiah was havin' none of their talk and said so. Swung his crutch at one of them--got everybody stirred up." Jesse frowned. "He was so angry by their words that he wouldn't let us assist him like we had been doin' every day when work was over"

"Yeah, he was mad, all right. I went lookin' for Uncle Matt

and Jess tried to stay with him, but he ran him off by swingin' his crutches at Jess."

"Yeah, I finally gave up tryin' to assist him, so Luke went to see if Mathias was back from up the creek at the McClintock Farm, to get him to help. When they got back to the cabin where I was, we went lookin' for John Obadiah. All we found was one crutch, down at the edge of the creek." Jessie paused.

"And that's where we lost track of him."

No one spoke for several minutes. Finally, Elias broke the silence.

"Well, does anyone know where Gala is now?"

Luke shrugged, and Jesse shook his head. "Don't know. Haven't seen her on the flats--last time was in September."

"Did you hear from her, Elias? After you left for the army?" Molly looked at Elias.

"Just once. It was while we were near Harrisburg, before our unit got ordered into Virginia. I wrote back, but it was a long time later on account of being on the move."

"I was thinking, Elias, that maybe she'll hear that you're back now, and come into town. But from what you've told us about that terrible flood, folks are going to be struggling to survive, rather than just talking." Molly stood and moved toward the kitchen.

Elias felt confused. Was the baby that Gala had with her-- theirs? Perhaps she was taking care of someone else's child. She had said nothing to him, either before he left or in her letter to him. He remembered how she looked at him just before he got on the raft with the Bucktails. She had promised to wait for him. Now he imaged her with a baby--their baby? Where is she now? That was an important question.

He had to know.

Regaining the Wine Trade

Early April 1865

Katherine arrived early at the Pomeroy House on Diamond Street for an appointment with the restaurant manager. Selecting a seat at a small marble-topped table in the corner of the room, she sat close to the highly polished wooden bar with her back to the deep crimson-colored wall and had an unobstructed view of the outside entrance.

Since that evening a month ago with Elias, she had identified no other federal agents or lurking detectives, but assumed that the danger lingered. She did not let down her guard. Constantly listening and watching, she remained vigilant.

Clandestinely gleaning news through travelers, she eaves-dropped on conversations of new arrivals including Confederate and Union veterans streaming steadily into oil country on the Oil Creek Railroad. That railway line served Shaeffer's Farm on Oil Creek, Titusville and then north to the junction of the Atlantic and Great Western and the Philadelphia and Erie Lines at Corry some twenty-eight miles north of Titusville.

Passengers arriving in Titusville carried news and divergent sentiments regarding the War of Rebellion and General Lee's surrender. The discussions among many hungry arrivals gathered at the local bars and restaurants recognized that "the cause was lost," as southern sympathizers put it, while the majority of diners expressed relief and gratification of the northern victory. The Union had survived.

Efforts to quell the hostilities on and off the battlefield had been unrelenting, and rightfully so, Katherine thought. The bloodshed and the horror needed to end. She had only to think of the ill-conceived confinement of Fredrick and the lasting damage to Elias that brought a bitter taste of the conflict straight to her. As well, she had direct involvement in the War of Rebellion.

Indeed, the danger of her being sought out as a Confederate conspirator seemed unrelenting. She surmised that the Federals would continue to chase down certain individuals such as she. Weight of her involvement with the Rebels hung heavy on her--and all because of her infatuation with Booth.

Every time she thought of her foolishness and his deception, she felt her rage rising. Her face flushed and a lingering lump settled in her gut. She felt sick. She took a deep breath and unclenched her tight fists. She forced her attention to focus on the activity around her.

This Friday afternoon, the first few patrons who trickled into the bar traveled from the nearby oil wells. As Katherine listened to conversations about what seemed to be a promising petroleum markets, she thought about wine, not oil. With people streaming into that Pithole area, she was anxious to establish new wine contracts and this certainly looked like an opportunity.

Sudden loud talking jarred her thoughts, and another nearby conversation seemed to be escalating into a shouting match. Voices were rising in volume and a chair clattered to the wooden floor. The ruckus appeared to be coming from two men who were drinking at the far end of the bar.

"You some kind of a southern sympathizer?"

"Watch what you're accusin' me of."

The bartender hurried toward the contentious two.

"All right, D.H., what's the problem?"

Katherine had heard of D.H. Peterson, known as One-Eyed-Pete, but until now had not encountered him. Instead of an answer from Pete, his challenger, dressed in hip-high, mud-smeared boots, dark-colored, dirty trousers and a red plaid shirt stepped up to the bar and was face-to-face with the bartender.

"So what's your problem, Bar-Tend?"

With that, wary patrons slowly slid off their bar seats, carrying their drinks to tables near Katherine. The two arguing men stood glaring at each other.

"That's Abbot Hood. He's a teamster and meaner than a rattler," she heard the man sitting nearby say in a low voice.

Hood, a tall, muscular man began to roll up his sleeves. Just then, a lean, agile-looking patron stepped into the room and moved forward to stop the escalating friction.

"That's an oil well driller. Worked on the Sherman Well and others down on Oil Creek. Name's Jeremiah Duff. He'll settle them," said one of the spectators who stood safely out of the fray.

Quick as a cat, Hood landed a punch on the side of One-Eyed-Pete's face and sent him crashing onto a nearby table where a couple was having a drink.

____

Shorter than either man, Duff seized the attacker by his leather belt and flannel shirt, and part-carried, part-dragged him to the hotel's outside entrance. The two crossed the plank sidewalk with Hood cursing loudly. At the edge of the rutted, muddy lake that passed for a Titusville street, Duff heaved the angry shouting horse handler into the muddy murk in front of them.

"That'll cool 'im off," Duff said to gawking by-standers. He watched Hood limp away from the hotel then he returned to the bar and his drink. Duff placed one muddy boot on the brass foot rail, and smiled as he accepted a gratuitous shot of whiskey from the bartender.

Katherine's location had provided her with a front-row seat to the well driller's extrication of the tough teamster. Duff had more strength than his appearance suggested. As well, he was quite matter-of-fact about his intervention. He sat calmly enjoying the whiskey.

As the bystanders dispersed, Katherine watched One-Eyed-Pete walk between several dining tables, squat and retrieve an object from under a nearby chair. Without a word, he picked up his glass eye, and limped out the side door of the dining room. Being witness to the retrieval of the eye made Katherine think again of Elias. She wondered how that was affecting his current challenge of recovering from the Oil City flood.

Just then, the hotel manager arrived at Duff's side and thanked him for quelling the altercation. Then he turned to Katherine and ushered her into his office.

…

As their meeting concluded with the signing of a contract for twelve casks of formerly confiscated pinot noir that Fredrick was shipping by rail to Titusville. Then the hotel manager introduced Katherine to Jeremiah Duff who had remained at the bar.

"This here little lady could use your help, Jeremy." Duff stared at Katherine and their eyes locked for a second. Katherine smiled and held out her right hand.

"I'm Katherine Le Conte," she said in her French accent.

"Pleased to meet ya.' I'm Jeremiah T. Duff. The 'T' stands for Theodosius, so that's why folks here call me 'Jeremy.'" He smiled broadly and offered her a seat.

The hotel manager continued.

"She's come all the way from the Baltimore docks with wine

on account of her family's business in France. It's good quality, and I have ordered more, seein' that this here oil business is pickin' up again. Now, she could use your help in just I' down to meet Boswell Graves who's been hired by Capt. Vandergrift to do—like my job here at the Pomeroy House."

Jeremiah nodded and Katherine listened with interest.

"Boswell's responsible for ordering the liquor, wine and food for that new hotel that's bein' built near Pithole Creek, The Metropolitan Hotel. In fact, Vandergrift is one of the biggest investors at Pithole. Guess you know that, Jeremy. He's got money from his oil barges that a' been haulin' crude out of Oil City and down to Pittsburgh. And it's not just a hotel he's beginnin'. It's a theater, billiard and concert saloon, and stables. He's got big plans and big money to match."

"Pithole! What kind of a name is that?" Katherine asked.

Jeremy sat back in his chair and grinned.

"You want to go to Pithole?" He gave her a hard stare with an expression of disbelief.

"It's a real work-in-progress. Not much there…" His soft brown eyes scanned her from head to toe with un-apologetic interest.

"Yes, I need to meet Mr. Graves and complete a contract. My cousin, Fredrick, my boss has been corresponding by wire with him," she lied. "I have the papers here for the wine they agreed that we are to import. I need Mr. Graves to sign their agreement. But, of course, he wants a sample of the pinot noir, so I'll be taking a cask with me to Pithole."

"Pithole is no place for a pretty lady in fancy clothes like you. And touting' a barrel o' wine, no less. Place is muddy, stinks of oil, horses." He paused and looked directly at her.

"It's beginning' to fill up with gamblers, fortune seekers, wildcatters, drillers like me, and soldiers comin' back since the war's over. You'll get your skirts muddy there for sure."

She took a deep breath, sat up straighter in her chair, and looked straight at Jeremy. She spoke with the French accent she had perfected since her return to America and had used to best advantage.

"Well, Messier Duff, I have no choice. Importing wine is our family business and Fredrick tells me to go and get more contracts here in the oil country. So, I am here."

She looked directly at Duff. She needed him to believe her.

With the federals searching for Rebel conspirators, getting out of Titusville and avoiding the throngs of travelers who came and went from this rail center was tantamount to her survival.

To her relief, Duff seemed to change his attitude upon learning about her mission to get to Pithole. He began treating her like the businesswoman that she was—like an equal not a woman to be used and possibly abused. While she wondered how he came about that attitude, she appreciated his respect for her. She felt as if she were making progress.

After a long discussion, she was reassured when Duff finally agreed to accompany her into the heart of the new oil discovery. She pretended to mull over his proposal for a few moments, knowing full well that she had little choice. He had bluntly told her that "no respectable woman would travel alone into that place." She knew that journeying unaccompanied into such a remote outpost amid the mad dash of men looking for easy money and fabulous fortune was risky. Katherine had heard talk about the location of the new oil strike and the hardships of travel into that area. Yes, it would be risky, but she could use him to get her there, into hiding until the war and its aftermath had receded.

Workers from Pithole traveled into Titusville on Fridays and during those evenings at the McCray House bar, she had heard their talk, long and loud, about the oil speculation, the rapid investments and building boom that were occurring almost overnight.

The frenzied, chaotic locale sounded ideal to Katherine—a place where she could avoid being sought out by blending into the crowded conditions and constant influx of hundreds of people, all new to the area. She had diverted her travel into the turmoil of Oildom to avoid detection by authorities. By the sounds of the current commerce of Pithole, she could manage wine contracts and shipments from that rather clandestine location. The wine trade made a prefect camouflage for her where she could remain until she was no long hunted. The turmoil of these tumultuous times provided her a cover, until her pursuers, both her stepfather and the Federal authorities lost interest in finding her. Cousin Fredrick's last wire to her had given her instructions to "disappear until things calm down STOP Last shipment to arrive on April 14 STOP."

She had to move quickly and sell these last barrels of confiscated wine that Fredrick had recovered from the federal authorities. He had shipped them by rail from Brooklyn to Titusville via Corry. When the casks arrived, she would have to move them, despite the danger of her being detected by agents seeking her. Meanwhile in this game of cat-and-mouse, she planned to stay out of sight and wait.

...

When Fredrick's shipment arrived two days later than expected, Katherine signed for the casks of wine and had them moved to temporary storage near the railyard.

Then she went in search of Jeremiah Duff. It was time for her to get out of Titusville.

The Pomeroy House seemed like the logical location to await his arrival, and she ordered a drink and returned to the same table of her previous occupancy, near the hotel manager's office. She sat, sipped her whiskey, and waited.

She intended to leave for Pithole at the first opportunity that Duff would present to her. This rail center with all of its arriving and departing passengers made her nervous. She was vulnerable to being identified and now she had no reason to stay.

Thirty minutes later, her patience was rewarded.

She spotted Duff, his angular frame and broad-brimmed hat caught her eye as he maneuvered with a group of men to cross the muddy street made more difficult by the last of the thawing snow and the spring rain that had dominated the day's weather. She watched as the oil workers knocked the mud from their thigh-high boots outside the bar's entrance. Through the open door, Jeremiah looked around and his eyes came to rest on Katherine who flicked her fan at him and smiled with a nod toward an empty chair at her table. He dipped his head in agreement, then bent to clean his boots.

Minutes later, he dropped his hat into the empty chair near her.

"Well, hello, Madame Katherine. What are you drinking? I see that your glass is nearing empty and I'm going to the bar. What can I get you?"

"A whiskey."

"Two whiskeys, Sam." Jeremiah strolled to the bar. In several minutes, he returned with their libations in hand, placed a glass in front of her. She noticed that he was missing a finger on his right hand--his middle finger. She wondered how that had happened, but said nothing. Taking a seat across from her, he picked up his glass, took a long drink, then sat back. He looked directly at her.

"So did your shipment come in?"

"Yes, this morning--first train today. That's the last of that allotment of wine until Fredrick gets back to me. I am relieved that it has arrived."

"So what's next for you then?"

"As I told you, Jeremiah, I plan to go to Pithole."

He ran his right hand through his sandy-colored hair and smiled broadly, revealing a flash of gold in his upper row of teeth.

"You still determined to go there?" He seemed amazed despite her previous proclamation the day they met.

"That's why I'm here--looking for you. Figured I'd see you here at the Pomeroy."

He nodded his understanding and lapsed into a thoughtful gaze out the nearby window.

"Well, let's discuss the trip--gotta make plans for getting' you down to that place this time of year. Mighty tough goin,' with this rain and mud and all."

As they finalized their plans, he scanned the customers at the crowded bar. She watched people enter the fast-filling dining room.

Jeremiah turned to look at Katherine.

"You got plans for dinner?"

When she nodded a negative response, he asked,

"Will you take your evening meal with me?"

"Yes, that would be nice. Actually, I am famished."

Just as Jeremiah rose from his chair and was assisting Katherine from her seat, a young boy who regularly sold newspapers on the street rushed into the bar area and hailed Sam who was waiting on a customer. The teenager, face flushed and chest heaving from exertion, called out.

"Sam, I just come from the telegraph office. The President, Mr. Lincoln has been shot! They killed him."

Sam stopped pouring a drink and turned toward the youngster who looked as if he had been crying.

"Shot last night and died today, they said."

A sudden hush fell over the patrons in the bar area. Jeremiah and Katherine stopped in their tracks. She heard a ripple of discussion among the diners. She stood looking at her companion's grim expression, and stony-face. Someone's crying broke the stunned silence and low voices were replaced by a murmuring that grew louder and louder. Some diners rose from their seats, silverware clattered to the floor and voices seemed to rise together. There was a shout.

"Well, who done it? Does anybody know?"

Other voices came from near where Katherine and Jeremiah stood.

"How did it happen, after this long horrible war?"

The previously stunned crowd erupted in wailing, shouting questions, all talking at once--a cacophony of voices.

Katherine sank back into her chair and Jeremiah stepped toward the messenger. The boy held out the telegram for him to read. A hush fell over the crowd as the oil driller read the dire news. He raised his head to the waiting patrons and announced in a loud voice.

"It says here that the shooter was that actor, John Wilkes Booth. And a search is on to find him and other of his conspirators..."

A roar went up from the crowd. Men gathered near Jeremiah to read the traumatizing telegram for themselves. People were on their feet, dinner forgotten in the excitement of the announcement.

Katherine's head swam first with the dreadful report of the President's murder, but far worse for her, the news that the assassin was Booth. Her memories of her affair and collaboration with him shot through her mind, through her body like a bolt of lightning. She gripped the edge of the small table, tipping it slightly and sending the empty glasses crashing to the hard wooden surface at her feet. Shards of broken glass covered one side of the floor near her chair. She attempted to stand, but wobbled momentarily. In the excitement and confusion, no one seemed to notice. She regained her balance, shakily retrieved her travel cloak that was draped over her chair, and slowly moved toward the outside entrance. She needed air.

Was she dreaming? John Wilkes Booth had murdered the President? Her head ached as she made her way up the wet plank sidewalk toward the McCray House. Memories of Booth flooded over her. She could hear his voice.

"Damned Lincoln and his Emancipation Proclamation!" She recalled Booth's drunken excitement in Montreal when news of the St. Albans raid was announced at St. Lawrence Hall. She actually had loved this man, a supporter of the Southern cause and a killer.

Suddenly, she wretched and vomited along the side of a building. She felt her corset constrain her in a vice-like grip. She leaned on the rough brick for support. After a few moments, she looked about and was relieved that no one was afoot. She thought that no one had seen her, nor witnessed her reaction--over reaction--to the vile news of the assassination. Her guilty feelings of her own duplicities of being involved with Booth--a traitor and now, a killer-

-cut through her with a fiery vengeance.

Her ears were ringing, and her head throbbed. Only a block more to go. She wretched again and vomited while she struggled for her handkerchief. She was sweating as she mopped the dribble from her cloak. Grateful for the solitude of her sickness, she estimated that she had only another 100 yards to the side entrance of her hotel. She could hear voices coming from the bar and dining area as she mounted the stairs to her second floor room.

Minutes later with corset removed, she lay face down on her bed. She was shaking and crying. How could she have been so ignorant as to have gotten involved with him. Amid her chastising thoughts of her guilt by association, she suddenly realized that anyone conspiring with Booth would likely be sought out and arrested.

"Now they will intensify their hunt for me..." The shock of that realization compounded her feelings of guilt and terror. Breaths came in short shallow gasps. Now she needed more than ever to disappear from this highly traveled town. Her fear of being found out rose to new heights. She was terrified.

In the semi-darkness of her room, she groped for her flask. She needed another drink to stop the pain, to lessen the fear that now griped her like an iron fist that would not let go. She and Jeremiah had a plan, and now it needed to accelerate--to get her quickly out of here and deep into a new and untethered environment.

The whiskey burned her raw throat, but it affected her as she intended. Whiskey never failed her.

...

Katherine's hands were shaking so violently that she laid the newspaper on the bed in order to read it. She gasped as she read about Secretary of War Stanton launching a sweeping national investigation regarding the President's murder that included rounding up anyone associated with the assassin. She shivered when she learned that most members of Booth's family, his business associates, and anyone else close to Booth were being rounded up for questioning. Letters to and from Booth had been confiscated and federal authorities were searching his brother, Edwin's trunk for clues.

She reached for her flask. Alcohol numbed her conscience and the burning fear that was reignited with each piece of news about the bold killing of the President of the United States.

Mid-April 1865

A cold Spring wind whipped through the crowd waiting on the rough-wooden platform of the Oil Creek Railroad. The wood-shingled roof of the tiny railroad station glistened with rain but failed to provide shelter for two-thirds of the bustling over-flow crowd. The deluge poured onto the heads of a mostly male crowd of would-be passengers, a good portion of whom were wearing some type of headgear--black top hats, straw hats with broad brims, or dark brown leather, Western-style hats that shed the water efficiently. The locals expected rain at this season on the Allegheny plateau in this particular location just fifty miles south of the Great Lakes, but many in this crowd were not locals.

They were strangers to these austere gray skies with roiling clouds and unpredictable rainfall fronted by whipping winds that blew their luck and fortunes about like so many tumbling autumn leaves descending from the towering white oaks in the city park in Titusville. These frenzied fortune-seekers were gainers and losers in the high stakes gamble of the 1860's oil rush playing out in the rugged terrain of Northwestern Pennsylvania.

From where she was wedged between her traveling companion and a hitching post, Katherine stood behind a short, stout fellow smelling of garlic and clutching a strap of his brown haversack slung over his shoulder, and coarsely clad farmers wearing thigh-high, mud-stained cowhide boots that bore the imprints of miles of muddy travel that encircled their legs like concentric rings of a downed pine. She had heard that some of these farmers, despite their homespun appearance were wealthy, having unexpectedly come into money when oil speculators offered them more cash than they had ever imagined in their wildest dreams. The frenzied bargaining ranged from an acre or two of their farmland to, in some cases, a start-up oil company that bought the oil rights to their entire farms. During such offers and transactions, these farmers were stunned and speechless by the time the deal was struck.

Now, they were owners of a goodly number of the company's shares of stock, as well as thousands of dollars in cash. When there was no bank for depositing, they stashed the loot somewhere on their property, in barns or chicken coops, or under mattresses. Katherine found their stories compelling.

As she surveyed the weary and the wet, she noticed how differently they were dressed from the passengers at the Montreal Railroad Station. No fur hats or coats here-only cloth that soaked up the water instead of shedding it. The headgear that did resemble fur were the coon-tail caps worn by locals and those venerated veterans of the well-known "Bucktails" military unit of the 42nd Regiment, Elias' outfit.

Katherine turned to look into the crowd immediately behind her: neatly dressed men in business suits stood next to bearded young woodsmen in home-woven shirts, clutching carpet-sacks and who smelled of wood smoke as they stood patiently in the stinging rain that struck their faces and dripped from their beards. She felt as if she were crammed into this crowd that reminded her of swarming bees at a honeycomb on the hillside in the wine country back in France. Certainly, this is not like the sunny vineyards of Bordeaux, she mused as she shifted her weight on to the left foot for relief of the pain caused by standing for the past hour.

She wondered if anyone in this diverse crowd were federal agents. Since Booth had owned oil property near Franklin, it seemed like a realistic possibility. She turned again to scan the people crammed together in this crowd, but it offered her little relief of her fear of being recognized and apprehended.

As the rain on the brim of her hat drained off, it soaked her exposed auburn hair, and she could feel a trickle of icy water dripping off the end of her straight, patrician nose and onto her black and green woolen cape. She turned to look at Jeremiah Duff, her previously reluctant travel companion and current protector, a veteran of the oil fields and driller of numerous wells along Oil Creek since 1862. To some extent, his presence reduced her anxiety.

Suddenly, a train's whistle blasted so loudly that she involuntarily jerked and was shaken her out of her musing. As if on cue, the hopeful passengers began to surge toward the boarding gate like an incoming wave at the seashore, a mass of rain-soaked bodies propelling toward the hissing, rumbling sounds that promised to convey them to their desired destinations and future fortunes.

The odor of wood smoke wafted over the eager travelers as someone announced that there was to be no train down Oil Creek today. At the surprise of the news, comments and curses rumbled through the restive crowd as they contemplated other means of conveyance. A hum of voices rose as potential passengers considered alternatives to train travel.

Jeremiah turned toward Katherine and repeated what he had told her when he originally described the hardships of this journey.

"Miss Katherine, I don't know about this train…whether it's comin' or not. This time of year, the roads, if you can call them that are just rutted seas of mud, so they don't run a wagon or a stage. They just get stuck. If we get us a horse, those part-Arabians that are stabled here will either get stuck up to their bellies in mud, or will fall to their knees every time we stop. Getting' them back up and movin' takes time and a lot of work. If we can't get the train, it's best to walk seven miles ourselves 'cause it's usually faster than by horseback. So, I say let's just wait and see if we can get a train…or maybe tomorrow, we'll have better luck."

"I think we had best wait for the train, Jeremiah. I can't carry a cask of wine through the mud--can't even roll it."

He laughed out loud at that, and she thought that he was imagining her pushing the barrel through the mud all of those seven soggy miles. When he turned and grinned, Jeremiah infused Katherine with reassurance, since she doubted that she could negotiate miles of muddy, slippery roads with much success, especially since she was wearing long skirts and a heavy travel cloak.

She had seen some women here on Pine Street in Titusville slogging through the mud with their long skirts that had become coated and heavy with sticky, clinging caked dirt. One of the services at the Pomeroy was a skirt-beater who worked at the side of the hotel, removed the mud by whacking it out of ladies' skirts.

She tried to imagine the thirteen miles of rain and muddy conditions from here to Pithole, which was a different route from the train stop at Shaeffer's Farm. She looked about her, and saw that the crowd had spread out some, giving everyone more space, more breathing room. She took a deep breath. Suddenly a voice rang out a message.

"Train!"

As if by command, the crowd became compact again as bodies surged toward the sounds of an approaching locomotive that was backing into the overrun station. The formerly patient passengers transformed into a stampeding, mindless mob as they swarmed the coaches, pushing, and shoving each other, courteous behavior lost in the chaos of entering "Oil Dorado" as it was known. The few women present were rudely pushed aside as men grabbed the coaches' handgrips, determined to get aboard no matter what.

Manners and sensibilities disappeared.

Katherine felt Jeremiah's iron grip on her right arm as he shoved his way toward the third coach that was fast filling with men whose dreams of making it big in oil had subjugated previous politeness. Now as she saw it, they had completely extinguished any remaining modicum of manners in this raucous new world of claim speculations, bets, deals, and dreams of riches beyond the imagination of many who had grubbed the land in lumbering or farming on the rocky, previously uncultivated soil of the Appalachian foothills.

With Jeremiah's hand planted firmly on the small of her back, she felt him propel her toward the crowded metal steps as she clung tightly to her cloth shoulder bag that contained the bare necessities of her return trip into the tumultuous territory of the oil fields. Switching tactics, he surged ahead now, literally dragging her behind him as they clambered up the stairs and into what seemed like the last square inches of standing room of the third dingy passenger car. As she pressed tightly into him, she could scarcely breath and the stench of sweaty men, stale tobacco and wet wool struck her sensitive nose. She suppressed a gag.

At the McCravy House, she'd heard travelers' tales of brutal competition for conveyance on the few trains that were on the Oil Creek run. Now she realized that those stories were not exaggerations. They were true.

Descent into Pithole

Late April 1865

A frayed brown leather strap dangled a foot above Katherine's head, and she grabbed it with her gloved hand to steady herself. The doors of the southbound Oil Creek Railroad slammed shut as the steam whistle shrieked, so close and loud that she flinched involuntarily. Near suffocation, the crammed-in crowd—like wet, wiggly fish in a barrel—squirmed about as they stood in their own twelve-square-inches of space.

Through a tiny view out of the window that was otherwise occluded by the hats of those lucky enough to be seated, she viewed men running toward the train. Too late to gain entry to the three passenger cars that were packed to the gills, two men jumped onto the side of the train car and clung to the rail-steps while they kicked off other desperate would-be train travelers who tried to climb over them and take their places.

Another small group of desperados broke out of the left-behind travelers, shoving others aside as they ran through the still-crowded platform and leaped onto the overfull baggage car. One scrambled to the roof where he clung, waiting for the train to move. In the baggage car, determined males clambered up and over bags, boxes and cargo until they were out of her sight. She imagined them huddled amidst the freight. The scene reminded her of Benedict, hiding among the barrels of her cargo in the Baltimore warehouse.

Where was Benedict now?

Suddenly the overloaded train gave a jerk forward, then stopped, pressing some of the standing passengers backward, then forward. No one fell down or even toppled into each other because there was no extra space among them, so tightly jammed as they were.

The engine's whistle screamed long and loud again as the train cars attached to it lurched into forward movement again. This time, the locomotive slowly gained speed and the clickity-clack of the train over the rails initiated a rhythm that seemed almost soothing to her, as she clung to the overhead strap with her left hand.

Since most of the standing passengers faced forward, her

view was predominantly the backs of men's heads, their faces obscured to her. These anonymous no-face figures came as a relief to her. Being one in a crowd of people with no identities gave her the feeling of anonymity, just what she wanted and needed, to be an unknown person amid a sea of humanity, lost to federal agents and private detectives. She felt a flood of relief from the tension in her neck muscles.

Jeremiah looked over his shoulder at her. He half-turned toward her while anchored to his overhead support.

"We are about to cross over Watson's Flats, the place where Edwin Drake drilled that first well. If you can see a bit out of the window, the derrick will be on the right side."

She dutifully ducked her head and stared through the soot-smudged window to view the famous oilrig and several small wooden buildings. She mused that such a humble looking endeavor could launch such a continuing wave of excitement—worldwide enthusiasm about a new industry.

As it rattled down the track laid adjacent to Oil Creek, the train seemed at times to weave, causing the standers to lean to the left or right before it straightened out again. As if in answer to her thoughts, Jeremiah looked back at Katherine.

"They say that the railroad laid these tracks in such a rush that they didn't really grade the roadbed. Just followed the general configuration of the land. When you walk near the tracks, you can see where they laid the rails around tree stumps and boulders—too much time and trouble to remove those obstacles. Makes for unexpected twists and bends. Better than walkin' though. The roads are deep in mud this time of year. 'Villainous' some say." He shrugged and turned away.

By this time, Katherine's strap-arm ached, so she switched holding the leather loop to her right hand. As she turned to her left now, she spotted clusters of blackened derricks instead of individual wellheads that she had seen farther north. As the engine steamed southward over the seven miles from Titusville to Shaeffer's Farm, the number of oilrigs became denser, some with their steam-driven engines pumping the wells, metal rods creaked as they moved the crude toward the surface. Their wooden derricks stood stark against the solemnly gray sky, like a blackened, dead forest, trees, their limbs and green leaves removed, sacrificed to the great need for lumber to build the derricks, to build new commerce that forever changed the local landscape and infused hope into the war-weary nation.

When the train slowed and then jerked to a halt, Katherine thought they had reached their destination at Schaeffer's Farm. Her feet were wet, cold and aching, but she did not complain to Jeremiah. After all, she had pushed her request to travel to Pithole and been forewarned about the rigors of the trip. Why would she complain. This was her plan to escape the wide sweep of the federal net to scoop up and scrutinize anyone who even knew Booth, let alone conspired with him.

The train door swung open and the iron steps lowered with a bang. Through the open door, she read a sign, "INDIAN ROCK OIL COMPANY."

"Miller Farm, Miller Farm. Exit here for Miller Farm!"

A number of passengers surrendered their coveted seats, grasped their travel bags and squeezed through the standing passengers to detrain. Jeremiah grabbed Katherine's arm and dragged her to immediately claim the now-available seats. She willingly slid into the one next to him. She forced a smile.

From the train's platform, a boy's voice cut through the din of de-training passengers.

"Booth still at large. Federal troops and dogs searching Virginia countryside. Get your news here!"

The voice faded as the train doors slammed shut and the engine's noise dominated. Katherine's left eye began to twitch and she hoped that no one noticed, especially Jeremiah. She was glad to be seated next to him, and not across from him for that reason.

"Good of you to get us a seat, Jeremiah. My feet thank you."

He laughed and took off his hat, holding it in his lap. The crowd thinned out and people shuffled about claiming additional space.

"So, you saw the sign for the Indian Rock Company?"
She nodded.
"Yes, it said New York."
"Representatives of that outfit swarmed in here and bought a tract of the Miller Farm, about three quarters of their farm, 375 acres. That's a big setup. Took a lot of capital. At the time there were a good number of wells already drilled and operating. Indian Rock sold stock and started drillin' more wells. Now said to be worth $75,000. Looks like it's goin' strong. Lots of activity."

They lapsed into silence, and she closed her eyes as she leaned back, grateful for the luxury of a seat. She could hear voices of those around her.

"And I mean he hit it big…"

"Went through the third sand and hit oil."

"Invested $5000 and got him a dry hole."

"Now that's a deal. Right now, I'll sell you 100 shares of that spouter!"

"That land a year ago wasn't worth nothin'."

"Do ya know what the prices air'a doin' yesterday? Hain't seen no newspaper since Titusville's weekly come out some days ago."

She was relieved that no one within her hearing rang seemed concerned about news from Washington and the manhunt for Booth and his conspirators.

…

Katherine felt a touch on her arm and opened her eyes to see Jeremiah leaning toward her.

"We're almost to Shaeffer's Farm, Miss Katherine, and we're gonna' have ta' move fast. We got an early enough start that we're strikin' out for Pithole just as soon as we get some vittles at the hotel--only one for miles. They say that place feeds over 400 hungry men a day, and it's always a mad scramble to find a seat, 'specially with a trainload of travelers such as this. So, here's how we're gonna tackle it. Ya' see, I been through here and know the ropes. The Johnny Newcomes don't know how it works, to get a table.

He turned toward her and spoke quietly.

"A guy named Josh, Josh Carpenter's gonna meet us and pack up our belongin's for the trek down into Pithole. So, you show him our things, our bags and that wine cask you're toten'. He'll take care of those. While you're doin' that, I go directly to the bar and buy us dinner tickets. Can't get into the dining room without 'em. Those new guys don't know that they'll get turned back at the dining room by Big Rufus, the caretaker who helps keep order. He'll send 'em back out to the bar to purchase tickets. You come find me. I'll be holdin' us some seats."

"Shaeffer Farm. Shaeffer Farm! End of the line!"

The flood of excited passengers pushed toward the car's exit, sweeping Katherine and Jeremiah with them. As they descended the metal steps, Jeremiah pointed to a man who was to be their transportation.

_____

249

"There's Josh. You go meet him. I'm headed to the bar--for the tickets."

Katherine followed the sweep of Jeremiah's hand and saw a young man wearing a broad-brimmed hat. He stood off to the side, out of the way of the crush. Clutching their scanty baggage, the frantic arrivals rushed away from the train, shoving and pushing, toward the hotel to register before all the beds were sold, or to grab a seat in the dining room.

She waded through the crowd toward Josh and saw that he wore thigh-high boots that were caked with brown mud. As she drew nearer, she could see that even his freckled face was road-spattered and there was dirt around his mouth and nose. He anchored an unlighted cigar between his teeth. He stepped forward with an out-stretched, grimy hand that Katherine knew well she had to grasp. It was going to be a long five-mile trek to Pithole.

Despite the cold, damp conditions, his grip was warm and firm. When he smiled, a small gap revealed itself, right in the front upper row of teeth. Josh lost no time on amenities and forged his way to the baggage car, gathering up the wine cask, then their bags. He disappeared around the side of the tiny train station and Katherine went in search of Jeremiah.

As she entered the small hotel, she witnessed a struggle. Just as Jeremiah had predicted, the Johnny Newcomes were being ordered away from the dining room entrance and told that they had to purchase tickets at the bar. She felt like a fish swimming upstream as she pushed forward toward the odor of food cooking. The rejected diners flooded past her toward the bar.

When she approached the tall muscular Rufus, he looked down at her, and pushed away several persistent people without entry tickets.

"Move away, gents! Let this little lady pass." His deep voice resonated through the din of hungry men to where Jeremiah had staked-out three places at a long table that was filling quickly with other travelers. Her companion rose to greet her.

"Josh's comin' to join us. You find our belongin's all right?" She nodded, then turned to see the third of their party enter the dining area. As he claimed his seat at the table, he removed his hat revealing matted, uncombed brown hair. He quickly stashed his head cover under his chair. Katherine could see that none of them, and most especially Josh had washed their hands. She hoped that all of the food could be had with silverware.

As they were being served a meat-and-potatoes meal, she scanned the diners. Surely neither a federal agent, nor private detective was in this hungry hoard of dingy diners. She really was disappearing into the crushing crowd of swarming strangers, a ceaseless throng.

...

The sun was shining and the budding leaves of low-lying vegetation glistened with rain water, as Katherine, Jeremiah and Josh immerged from their hardy dinner in the tiny, dimly lit hotel. She squinted, adjusting to the strong light and saw a young man waving toward them.

"Goin' to Oil City? Need a ride? Come with me. Gotta a boat here and gonna leave just as soon as she fills up."

A tall, lean lad dressed in gritty looking trousers that were rolled up to the tops of his knee-high mud-caked boots stood wide-legged in front of them.

"Just three dollars and a half for the twelve-mile run down Oil Creek to Oil City. My packet boat's right over there." He gestured with has left arm toward the nearby creek.

Katherine saw the bow of a blackened flat boat tethered to a tree. When the boatman realized that they were not interested, he turned to other potential customers.

Josh removed the cigar from his mouth.

"That's one way to get down to the Allegheny. Oily flatboat with no shelter wouldn't be my choice--sittin' for twelve long miles." He smiled at her, exposing the empty space of his missing upper incisor.

"I'd rather walk than sit cramped up like that."

"Speakin' of walkin. Let's get started, Josh."

As they arrived at the hotel's rear entrance, she saw a mule tied to a hitching post, drinking from an adjacent water trough.

"This here is Ellie. She's a real good critter who can deal with mud and rocks much better 'en most horses. Just be a minute or two 'til she's packed up and ready to go." Jeremiah handed Josh the cask of wine, and they lashed it into place. The travel bags were next.

While that task was being completed, Jeremiah turned to Katherine.

"Can ya' hike-up your skirts, like we discussed the other day, Miss Katherine?"

She nodded and began to roll up her skirt at the waist, raising the hemline to the tops of her knee-high boots. She had foreseen that the elevated hemline had the disadvantage of blocking the access to her handgun which always remained in the pocket of her skirt, so she had stashed it in the inside of her right boot. She was trekking off into unknown territory with two men she barely knew, but desperately needed to undertake this move. She was more afraid of the federal agents than Josh and Jeremiah. Despite the apparent risk of this travel, she put her trust in these mountain men.

Now what would her former French Foreign Legion trainer, Jacques think of that decision, she wondered.

"Yes, I can. There won't be any skirt-beaters along this route, to get the mud off, do you recon, Josh?"

All three of them laughed. Josh handed her a walking stick. "Git on up there, Ellie."

They were off into the sea of mud that engulfed the entire perimeter of the hotel. With the sun shining on the wet surface, Katherine thought the hotel looked like an island in a lake of mud. The roadhouse functioned as an oasis, accommodating the lucky men who had secured a bed, and the hungry, like her and her traveling companions, seats at the dining table.

The beginning of the trek appeared to be well traveled. Wagon wheel ruts had been cut deep into the soil, and the recent rain filled the depressions, leaving deep pools of water. The entire area was a sea of mud whose depths could not be estimated.

"Gotta go easy here. This darn mud is slippery, greasy-mixed with horse droppin's and crude. Trouble is, you can't tell how deep it's gonna be 'til you walk into it. So, follow me close 'til we get away from the hotel. Don't wanna get stuck in this stuff."

The going was labored for the first thirty minutes, and Jeremiah supported Katherine on her left and she used a walking stick to best advantage as they trudged forward. The stench of manure and crude oil finally diminished, but the sticky, clinging clay persisted until Josh led them to a wooded trail that ran east toward Pithole Creek.

"Lumbermen cut this trail to get timber up to the railroad, most recently. You'll soon see that it leads right close to Pithole."

As they walked, Katherine realized that she was enjoying the journey with its clear air made fresh by the recent rainfall. Now they tread on solid ground and for the most part was free of the mud and the mire of heavily used paths. The trees and bushes that bordered the now-fallow fields of Shaeffer's Farm had bright green, young leaves. Clumps of new spring grass and dandelions grew along the trail, but the trekkers could see distant oil derricks built with the lumber, locally harvested.

As they approached the forest, Josh called a halt. Since they had left the mud behind them, they scraped their boots on rocks and with sticks. Josh pointed out a boulder to the side of the trail, and they rested while he patted Ellie. He dug into a leather bag and passed apples to Jeremiah and Katherine. He fed Ellie one, as well.

Feeling lighter in weight, and warmed by the sunshine, the trio set off again. Jeremiah looked toward the sun.

"Looks like we're makin' good enough time to get in by dark, do ya think, Josh?"

"Think so. As long as Pithole Creek isn't over its banks, floodin' when we get to the bridge, we'll be on time."

"Flooded lately?"

"Comin' up to Shaeffer's Farm yesterday, it was beginnin' to rise again with all this rain."

The logging road led into a grove of towering hemlocks, white pines, oaks and blue spruce. The floor of the pathway was covered with downed needles and dead leaves, a welcome relief after the sticky mud and rain-filled ruts of several hours ago. Except for the occasional snort from Ellie and a gentle wind in the trees, they were enveloped in a blanket of silence and pleasant scent of pines and wet wood.

Katherine felt herself relaxing. This hike was a welcome relief from the business of scanning crowds and continuing anxiety of being apprehended by authorities. This trekking and change of environment were surprisingly pleasant.

At this point, the trail widened so that they could talk as they walked.

"So how did Pithole get such a name?"

Josh answered her question.

"There are different stories. The one I heard goes like this: Somebody's dog got too close to a steep ravine down on the creek and just passed out an' died. You see, there are holes like small caverns in the sides of the creek bed. They think that there's methane comin' up outa those holes and the gas overcomes animals and people too.

"Story about a hunter stoppin' near one of them holes. It was winter. He was huntin' out there with several fellas' when he noticed that snow had melted near a hole. They said he sat down at the edge of the crevice, feet a danglin' over the side when he passed out--fell backwards. His companions pulled him away from the gas and he revived."

"That methane is one of the reasons oil prospectors decided to drill out here near Pithole Creek. Where there's gas, there's a good chance that there's oil down there too." Jeremiah paused. "Other folks say that there's a hole that goes so deep that you can drop a stone into it and hear it bounce and rattle from ledge to ledge. The thing is, the sound just dies out. It's never been heard to hit the bottom of that hole."

"So, it seems as if the creek deserves the name--Pithole." Katherine agreed.

Now, the lumbermen's path began a gentle slope downward and the undergrowth grew thicker. Josh called for a rest stop and pulled out the water bag. They all had a drink and sat on a nearby log to rest. While Josh fed Ellie a handful of oats, Katherine decided to take the opportunity to move away to relieve herself. Jeremiah stopped her.

"Katherine, I think it may be too early for snakes, but let me check out an area for you. Don't want to snake-bite just trying to get some relief."

"Snakes! What kind of snakes are here?"

"Well, worst kind—rattler--hangs out in the timber round here. They have poison in their venom, and you don't want to surprise one. Since there's still a little snow left on the north side of the hills, they may not be out yet, but could be sunnin'--like on that stump over there. Let me break the bushes before you go back there."

Josh turned away from Ellie.

"T'other one is the copperhead. It doesn't give any warning like the rattle from the rattler. By the way, it's called a 'pigmy rattler' in these parts. Said to be shorter that those out west. Heard that from some guy working a rig out near Shaeffer's Farm. Just gotta watch were you step and where you put your hands around logs and rocks."

When Jeremiah called to Katherine, she followed his trail into the bushes.

"This patch of ground is safe. I'll wait on the other side of the tree for you."

As Katherine arranged her skirt and pantaloons, she was

looking down and her eyes rested on a plant. It grew so close to the ground that she might not had spied it under other conditions. Its light pink flowers were in direct contrast to its dark green leaves. She plucked a piece and brought it out with her.

"Jeremiah, what is this beautiful, tiny plant? It was blooming right next to a patch of snow. Must be hardy to grow like that."

"That's trailing arbutus. Haven't seen any since I started drillin' wells. Oil kills plants. Blooms early before the snow's gone."

She held the tiny flowers close to her nose. "They smell delightful! I'm going to wear this sprig. What a wonderful surprise, almost buried in the undergrowth."

Katherine poked the clipping of the flower into the buttonhole of her blouse.

"The Indians around here use arbutus for medicine. Make a concoction out of the whole plant for when they got pain--like the rheumatism and for kidney problems. Some of the white folks livin' 'round here use it too. My Granny says it works for her."

Katherine listened to Josh with interest as she inhaled deeply, enjoying the sweet smell of her newly discovered flowering mountain plant. Its flagrance was a respite from the continuous foul odor of crude oil that permeated the entire oil area. Her discovering the arbutus gave her a feeling of pleasure in the midst of her fear and anxiety. She was beginning to look at this trek into Pithole as a sort of exploration, an adventure.

As they hiked on, Jeremiah estimating their arrival time by the position of the sun. Although she was getting tired and she could feel some sore muscles, Katherine felt as if she were holding her own with these two mountain men.

. . .

Two hours later, the trail began to wind downward and the right side dropped off sharply.

"Watch your footing here. It gets tricky."

Katherine appreciated Josh's warning, and the mule slowed her pace as well. The wild flowers along the way by now had disappeared with the path turning rocky and rough. As they rounded a sharp bend, they heard the sounds of rushing water.

"That's the creek, dead ahead. Sure has plenty of volume since yesterday. Careful where you put your feet."

The steep trail required each traveler to squat, and use his hands to brace himself against a too fast decent and possible plunge headfirst into the roaring creek. Ellie moved at a crawl now, one foot, then the other carefully, testing before placing her full weight, then proceeded. With the cigar clenched between his teeth, Josh moved slowly, bracing himself with his hands on outcroppings of rock. Katherine thought she might have to slide sitting down to ease her way to the bottom. Now, she realized why Josh had dirty hands. Before this trip was over, she would as well.

Boulders littered the mountainside and spring flowers and ferns sprouted among the rocks. The roaring of the creek drowned out all other sound. Finally, they were at the bottom. The air felt cooler than up on the trail. What was it like, going up the other side? Now her legs were shaking and her heavy boots were more of a hindrance, rather than a help.

Josh signaled for them to rest on a fallen log where they could see the rushing water up close. Its power amazed Katherine. At the same time, the sound was soothing to her. The mist off of the rushing water felt good to her hot face. She was glad to rest here, in this spot.

"How far have we come, Josh?"

"We have come about four miles--only a couple more miles to go, Katherine."

"When we start up again," Jeremiah had to raise his voice to be heard, "there's a mill up ahead. Is that right, Josh?"

Josh nodded, gave the signal, and they began their slow ascent up the other side of the ravine. They moved slowly with Ellie and Josh in the lead, leaving the roar of the tumbling water behind them. Now, the trail steepened with a switchback at its most precipitous point.

Without warning, Ellie and Josh abruptly halted. Josh signaled Jeremiah and Katherine to stop and be silent. Above them, she saw something move among the boulder-strewn bushes. She heard a shuffling sound. Then accompanied with a loud snort, a bear cub emerged from behind a huge rock. Ellie let out a whinny and stomped nervously.

"Don't move." Jeremiah whispered into Katherine's ear. "Hopefully we're downwind from them. Must have a den up in those rocks. Bears are really unpredictable. You can't count on how they'll react."

They watched in silence, then heard a deep growl that made the hair rise on the back of Katherine's neck. The cub moved back out of their view. They waited not moving, but Ellie was restless and Josh again tried to calm her as the mother bear's shaggy head appeared from the cave. She moved slowly toward them, to the edge of the bluff. All three travelers froze in place.

A moment later, a scream from the cub emanated from inside the cave. Finally, with only a backward look, the mother bear lumbered toward the cub's squealing.

Immediately, Josh signaled them to move quickly up and away from the bears' den. When they emerged from the ravine, they stopped to rest.

"Guess those cubs were up and out exploring their new world. Glad we moved on through without any contact."

Katherine shivered despite the fact that she felt overheated from the steep climb. Encountering a wild animal was frightening to her and she was not sure that she could run in her boots. She'd heard stories about the bears in this part of the county and wanted no close contact with them. They were ferocious, and most especially when they had cubs to protect.

Hours later, climbing up from the depths of Pithole Creek, the small party emerged onto a grassy spot that looked to Katherine like the edge of a fallow farm field. First, a two-story building that came into view on their left. Several outbuildings and a barn clustered nearby.

"Whose place is that?"

"That's the Holmden homestead--Walter Holmden. His brother, Thomas has a spread just over the rise in front of us. They've been here for years and own all this area that we can see. Recently, they leased out most of it to these oilmen--wildcatters."

She could hear voices and her eyes followed the sounds. In the clearing straight ahead, she saw piles of harvested timbers with their bark stripped away. Discards from dead pines, oaks and hawthorns had been heaped on to burn-piles while slash from fallen trees lay wasted, awaiting destruction. An acrid haze hung over the area and the odor of burning wood mixed with the familiar stench of crude rose from the gradual slope laid bare and muddy. Through the miasma were the outlines of various-shaped, squatty buildings. Men, horses, wagons and idled sleds were scattered over the occupied acre that teemed with activity.

On the downside to the East, a line of huge wooden tanks, blackened by their dark oily content stood in stark contrast to the yet-green forest beyond. Next to this oil storage, a cluster of derricks, one black with oil and two others, not yet totally tainted with the product, lined up along Pithole Creek.

"That's the Frazier Well, Katherine, a wildcat well. The one that's made this area a target for speculators and visitors." Jeremiah pointed to the well.

Katherine smelled the crude and smoke from the downed trees burned her eyes. She spotted a large sign near the log piles. "WELCOME TO PITHOLE." She frowned and turned toward Josh and Jeremiah.

"'Welcome to Pithole?' This is Pithole? Does that mean that we've arrived?" When neither of her companions responded, she continued.

"Where is everything? Where's the hotel?" She was incredulous. "We walked all these miles to this?"

It appeared to her that this once peaceful place had been ripped asunder and ruthlessly ravaged in the recent scramble for oil and its promise of wealth. The once vibrant forest had a slash in its green continuity. A gapping gash belched out the smell of smoke and the stench of crude oil.

Jeremiah nodded.

"Yup, this here is Pithole."

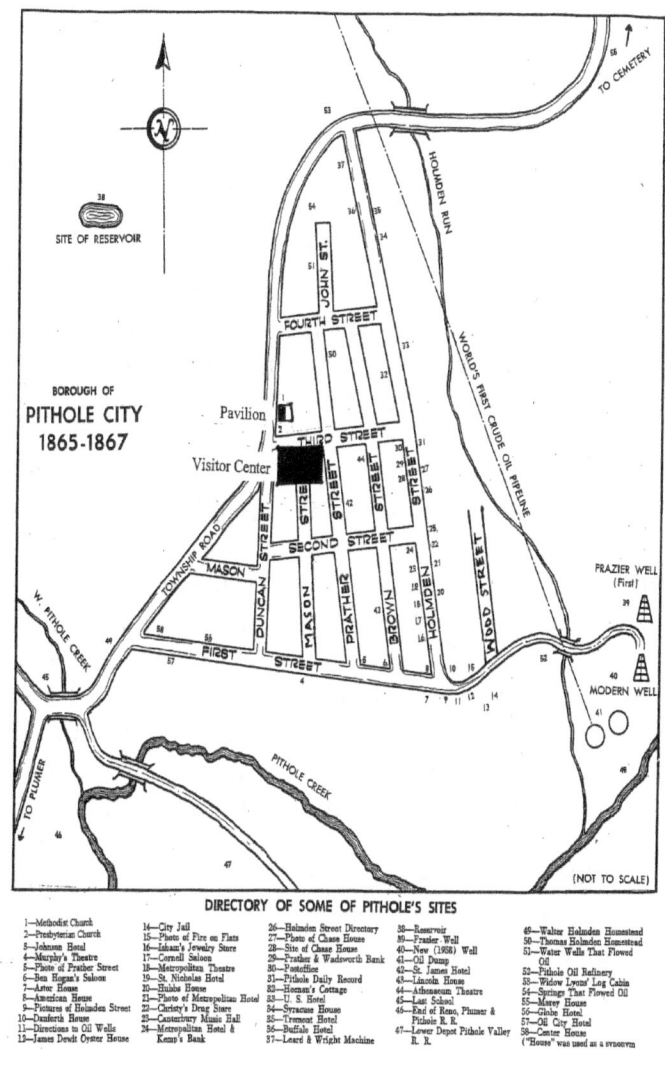

DIRECTORY OF SOME OF PITHOLE'S SITES

1—Methodist Church	14—City Jail	26—Holmden Street Directory	38—Reservoir
2—Presbyterian Church	15—Photo of Fire on Flats	27—Photo of Chase House	39—Frazier Well
3—Johnson Hotel	16—Isham's Jewelry Store	28—Site of Chase House	40—New (1958) Well
4—Murphy's Theatre	17—Cornell Saloon	29—Prather & Wadsworth Bank	41—Oil Dump
5—Photo of Prather Street	18—Metropolitan Theatre	30—Postoffice	42—St. James Hotel
6—Ben Hogan's Saloon	19—St. Nicholas Hotel	31—Pithole Daily Record	43—Lincoln House
7—Astor House	20—Hubbs House	32—Hoeman's Cottage	44—Athenaeum Theatre
8—American House	21—Photo of Metropolitan Hotel	33—U. S. Hotel	45—Last School
9—Pictures of Holmden Street	22—Christy's Drug Store	34—Syracuse House	46—End of Reno, Plumer &
10—Danforth House	23—Canterbury Music Hall	35—Tremont Hotel	Pithole R. R.
11—Directions to Oil Wells	24—Metropolitan Hotel &	36—Buffalo Hotel	47—Lower Depot Pithole Valley
12—James Dewit Oyster House	Kemp's Bank	37—Leard & Wright Machine	R. R.

49—Walter Holmden Homestead	52—Pithole Oil Refinery
50—Thomas Holmden Homestead	53—Widow Lyons' Log Cabin
51—Water Wells That Flowed	54—Springs That Flowed Oil
Oil	55—Mater House
	56—Globe Hotel
	57—Oil City Hotel
	58—Center House
	("House" was used as a synonym)

Courtesy of The Drake Well Museum
Pennsylvania Historical and Museum Commission

Raising Pithole

Pithole, Pennsylvania, Early May 1865

The morning sun illuminated the garden plot that lay some twenty yards from a squat log cabin. The smooth wood of the old hoe-handle felt cool on Katherine's fingers as she created a soft landing place for the seeds that had been laid out for her the night before. After carving several long rows one-inch-deep, she carefully dropped each seed three inches apart, covered them with soil, gently tamped down the dirt over them, then paused to stretch. Renting a room from Widow Lyon reminded her of her life in France, working the soil, tending the grapevines and having the luxury of being outdoors.

Besides that, she liked her landlady, a diminutive woman, dressed in homespun clothes, who had a quick, shy smile, and treated her renter with respect. That included not quizzing her about her circumstances, or at least not yet. If the landlady did wonder why she remained in this out-of-the-way, once lonely spot now teeming with oil exploration, she did not ask. Jeremiah and Josh told Mrs. Lyon that she was in the wine trade and here in the area on business. Apparently, that reason sufficed. If Widow Lyon have any suspicions about her, she had not expressed it, or at least not to her renter.

With living space at a crisis here, Katherine was fortunate that Josh had made arrangements for her to stay with his aunt, a task that Jeramiah had laid on him as part of the plan for her to travel to Pithole.

"Ya can't go into those parts without a place to stay, especially for a lady." Jeremiah had made that clear to Katherine while they were planning the trip. During their trek into Pithole, Josh had discussed the arrangement.

"Your sleepin' space will be the loft. Gotta climb a wooden ladder to get up there. She's gotta soft feather bed and wool blanket, good for cooler weather than we're havin' now."

To Katherine, the cabin sounded rustic as well as secluded. "Perfect," she had said to Josh.

"Aunt Gert can use assistance in managin' her garden and

berry bushes that she'll harvest as soon as things are 'ripe for pickin.'"

The cabin's interior smelled of wood smoke. The stone hearth along the north wall bore a large iron cooking pot and a brass kettle with a blackened bottom. The hard dirt floor had been swept clean and was partially covered by a heavy wool rug. A large oil-burning lantern sat on a small wooden table. The place felt comfortable and had a calming effect on the new renter. So far, this arrangement was working out.

Katherine felt more secure in this remote location. She needed to remain out-of-sight until Booth's murder of President Lincoln came to some conclusion and the search for his accomplices was spent and cancelled. Besides that, contrary to her expectations, no customers for wine, no hotels nor restaurants, except one existed here yet. On both counts, she needed to sit and wait things out.

Several days later, Katherine heard more voices than usual emanating from the busy area at the base of the hill.

The voices were so loud that she laid down her hoe and walked to the front of the cabin where she took in the view of the Frazer and Twin Wells. Men were encircling a horseman who was slowly riding into the midst of them. He raised his hat high, then brought it down with a swoop across his chest like a bow. As he dismounted, a loud cheer echoed from the wells to the forested hills.

Just then, Katherine saw someone hiking up the slope toward the cabin. When he got closer, she recognized Jeremiah.

"Jeremiah! What's going on down there?"

"General Avery has arrived. He's a Union officer, recently relieved of duty, and he's here to help with getting some of this stored oil outa' here." He paused and motioned her to join him on the steps of the cabin.

"You see, the deep March snow had made roads not passible. You remember how it snowed in Titusville? Well, then heavy rain--when Oil City flooded in March--hit this area too."

She nodded toward him.

"Then comes the April thaw and more rain. All the roads in the oil region were deep in mud--like when we came through Shaffer's Farm--mud up to over half a wagon wheel. Just a sea of mud. So, moving all that oil that was comin' from the Frazier and the Twins was bein' run into wood storage tanks. Couldn't get it out'a here. Then when the weather got better, didn't have enough teams to move it up to Titusville. No way to get it down to the

Allegheny. So, we been sittin' here on a dangerous situation. Could explode, catch fire--thousands of barrels stored there.

"Why is that general here?"

"Well, U.S. Petroleum went to advertising for men and teams to move their oil to market, and the general has come to help. You see, during the war, he commanded a cavalry brigade. So, when he heard about the call for help in movin' this oil, he called on his cavalry troops. Said his men can handle a mule or horse and they're headed for the oil country. Expectin' them to come in here during the next few days. The general traveled all the way from Appomattox, Virginia, the place where the war ended."

Jeremiah rose to leave.

"Well, thanks for that news, Jeremiah." She paused. "Where are all these men going to eat and sleep?"

"Good question. Think the folks at the Holmden place are gonna have a big crowd to feed. Think U.S. Petroleum will do something--especially about sleepin' all these teamsters."

Within a few days of the general's arrival in Pithole, fifty wagons loaded with oil from the Frazer Well were en route to Titusville. They followed fifty axmen who hacked a path through thirteen miles of forest, laying a temporary corduroy road of downed trees as they went. Finally, transportation of oil had improved, and the critical situation abated.

Added to that monumental effort, a traveler to Pithole, David Kirk, decided to build another road. Kirk had good reason to be concerned about transporting the petroleum he purchased from U.S. Petroleum, so he hired a crew of men to construct another road. They hacked their way southward to the Allegheny River where oil could be moved to market.

...

When Mrs. Lyons learned about the pending arrival of more men, she talked to Katherine about her interest in providing as many fresh farm-grown vegetables and fruit as she could muster for the Holmden's meal preparations.

"I'm a gonna get Josh to hitch-up Ellie and plow that open ground on the east side of the house over here."

For several days, Katherine and Josh worked to prepare the soil and then plant more crops. The weather cooperated and there was no rain. Since Mrs. Lyon had no steady income since her husband's death a decade before, she thought that Josh's aunt saw this as an opportunity to earn more cash. She felt sure that her rental payments were equally welcome.

The entire community witnessed the rapid influx of the war veteran-teamsters into this newly discovered oil field. Word came around that they brought with them a dire demand for ceaseless sustenance. Most were young men with vigorous appetites.

...

A week after General Avery had arrived, Katherine paused to look down the slope toward the two Holmden farmhouses, one belonging to Thomas and the farther one, to Walter. A line of men was already forming for the noon meal at Walter's place. The Holmdens had been providing a spread to newcomers in the area for several months. At first, the farm family had opened their homestead to feed a few hungry well-drillers, speculators and wildcat oilmen who were walking the land they had leased from Thomas Holmden. Those men worked for The United States Petroleum Company.

After the oil-strike at the Frazier Well in January 1865, the number of curious callers and hired hands increased, and the Holmdens extended their dining area to accommodate anywhere from fifty to one-hundred-fifty famished folks. Now that the numbers of diners swelled, the first rule of serving was that the oil workers and teamsters ate first, and the crowds of inquirers sat at later seatings, after the departure of the workmen to their work sites.

Frequently, the multitudes gathered two hours prior to the noon dinner begging for food. At the host's high-sign, hungry men pushed, shoved and engaged in horseplay while they struggled to grab a seat in the crowded dining room.

Those not lucky enough to find a place at a table among the workmen were relegated to a queue that led from the dining room doorway, through the sitting-room, to the front-door and out into the yard. They came like a swarm of locusts over ancient Egypt, stripping-bare the larders of the pantry as well as all things edible on the tables.

Emergency provisions had to be purchased at Plumer, four miles by horseback. Staples were toted thirteen miles by an ox-drawn wagon from Titusville to Pithole, requiring a team of drivers and a two-day journey over muddy, rough roads. Fresh foods in season grew in the Holmden garden and that of Widow Lyon.

Among the locals as well as the regular diners, the Holmden family had the reputation for being fair-minded regarding the cost of the meals they provided. Some people thought that they could have charged exorbitant prices for such a service, but that was not the case. Exacting a fair price for the food, the family cleared more money in one day than they would have seen in a lifetime.

The same was true of Widow Lyon. She soon would have an adequate income from selling her garden harvests. To further improve matters, her renter now helped out and actually enjoyed the labor--she had a willing worker.

From where she stood, Katherine watched the ferocious frenzy in the acre below her. In two days of clear-cutting, old forest growth was removed. She could see a workman using an adz, shaping all of the felled trees in just one day. The downed giants were cut into lumber, and used to build derricks the same day. Stumps were uprooted and the leavings burned in the fires that were continuous. The acrid odor of oil mixed with the smoke from the burn piles hung over the valley and beyond, making Katherine's eyes water and sting. Her vision was blurred.

Pushed back further by the building of the new road to the Allegheny River, the beautiful forest had been destroyed almost overnight, the stately pines and oaks devastated in the name of progress, she thought. Today, she noted that several men appeared to be measuring the area recently cleared of timber.

Suddenly, a loud footfall sounded behind her and she started and automatically assumed a position of flight or fight according to Jacques' training back in France.

"Hello, Miss Katherine. I hope I didn't scare you. Just stoppin' by to see what you and Auntie Gert want from town before we start out."

Katherine took a deep breath as she released her grip on the revolver in her skirt pocket. Since her arrival, few came to Gert Lyon's cabin except Josh and Jeremiah. She was relieved at that because the fewer people she encountered, the better. His unexpected appearance startled her.

"You're off to Plumer this morning?" She recovered from his sudden appearance.

"Yes, Ellie and I go over there two to three times a week. Pick up supplies for the Holmdens or the U.S. Petroleum gents sometimes. The main reason I go is to accompany new-comers from Plumer who are travelin' into this area. You know, they are strangers who don't know the way back in here--like to have someone with them who is familiar with the wagon ruts and trails. I have an agreement with several hotels in Plumer."

She smiled. "Josh, could you check at the post office there to see if I have any mail?"

Two weeks earlier, Katherine had sent a letter to Barnswell to let him know of her recent relocation to Pithole.

"And Josh, you remember what I told you about the detectives working for my step-father? Look at their boots for that black strap across the instep. It's a sure sign. Keep an eye open for me, please. And don't say anything to anybody about it."

Josh nodded and turned to Ellie.

"What are those men doing down there? Looks like they're measuring from what I can see."

"Guess you didn't hear about the sale."

"What sale, Josh?"

"Well, these two gents from Oil City, Col. A.P Duncan and George Prather come in here last week and bought the Holmden Farm. Just like that. For $25,000. Word is that they're goin' to make a town outa that area on the bluff, just on this side of the Frazier Well."

"So there really will be a town down there? That will be Pithole, right?"

"Don't know. Some folks are callin' it Holmdenville, and others, Pit Hole City, or just plain Pithole. That's what is bein' said."

He pointed out the streets for Katherine. "From the Frazier Well, that's First Street and intersectin' it is Holmden Street runnin' north. Then laid parallel to First is Second, Third, and Fourth, coming up the hill toward us." Katherine followed his gesturing. "Then lying parallel to Holden are Brown, Prather, Mason and Duncan. Looks like a good layout to me."

She nodded. "Thanks for the description, Josh."

She watched as Josh and Ellie descended the slope toward the activity below that was rapidly transforming the landscape.

…

As the sun cast long shadows on the greening pasture, Josh tied Ellie to a fencepost and readjusted the pack strapped to the mule's back. The four-mile trek from Plumer to the Holmden Farm took longer on the return, given the difference in weight of supplies and mail born by the animal. He gave her some grain and water.

At the Plumer Post Office, he had inquired about mail for Katherine. He collected one letter being held for her as well as all of the other mail and several newspapers for the Holmdens and the U.S. Petroleum Company.

Now, almost home, he watched Ellie finish her water, then he checked the pack strap again before starting out on the long trek downhill toward Pithole Creek. He started thinking about his aunt's renter.

Who was Katherine and why was she staying so long at Auntie's? The envelope was addressed to Katherine Granger. He thought her last name was Gerrone. Jeremiah had told him little about her, other than she was in the wine trade and planned to ship her product from France. At this point, there were neither hotels nor restaurants for miles around the development near the Frazer and Twin Wells, yet she had brought that heavy cask of wine with her from Titusville. She was beautiful, young, and spoke French, and she seemed out of place in the oil trade and farmlands of the area.

"She really jumped when I came up behind her this morning. Crouched like she was gonna' fight." He spoke to Ellie who flicked a fly off of her ear. "And that business about detectives and their black boots with the strap seems mighty strange. Maybe hidin' out from the step-father and those men he hired, I guess. Wonder why he's lookin' for her."

He scanned the trail ahead of them. "Good thing is that she's helpin' Auntie Gert get her garden planted." Josh decided he would tell Katherine that during his trip, he had seen no one who had that kind of boot.

He hiked on with Ellie, and soon the creek crossing came into sight. ...

Anxious to receive any mail, especially from Barnswell, Katherine watched for Josh to return as the sun sank low in the west. She sat on the cabin's front stoop, swatting at the mosquitoes that had just begun to whine in her ears. The valley below was cast in dancing shadows from the burning bonfires that were consuming tree branches and bark stripped from recently demolished trees.

Finally, a swaying yellow lantern light, like a blinking firefly on a hot evening came into view, and she could make out silhouettes of Josh and Ellie plodding slowly up the hillside toward her.

"Long trip, Josh?"

He nodded as he unburdened the last of the items from Ellie's pack. "Yup. Had a bigger load than usual since Walter Holmden needed several sacks of flour. Those dinner folks are eatin' them out of house and home." He paused. "Got one piece of mail for you and some for Auntie, too." He handed Katherine all of it, and turned to leave.

"Any news from Plumer?"

"Yeh, the Humbolt Refinery is takin' in more workers-- gonna' have up to 200 employees, they say. Seems as if they're getting' busy again with summer almost here." He patted Ellie. "Duncan and Prather's venture here is caught a lot of attention too. Sounds as if it took folks by surprise--plannin' a town and layin' out that area below like they have."

He yawned. "Oh, 'most forgot. The big news from the President's murder is that they caught that John Booth somewhere in Virginia, and he got killed--shot by one of the search party--about a week or ten days ago."

Katherine took in a sharp breath, and could feel her left eyelid begin to twitch. She was relieved that in this darkness, Josh could not see her reaction to his news.

Then, as if reading her mind, he went on.

"By the way, I didn't see any men with the boots you described, either. Nobody."

She suddenly felt tired and agitated. She had heard enough.

"Goodnight, Josh. And thanks."

As Josh and Ellie departed, she carried the mail into the cabin and sorted it. Besides her letter, she found a copy of *The National Republican News* that her landlady had requested. Then she located an envelope addressed to her that bore Barnswell's handwriting. Hands shaking from the news of Booth's death, she tore open the wrapper and slid the contents onto the kitchen table.

It was a telegram from Fredrick dated May 2.

"Arrived Bordeaux April 30. STOP Bad news from our family STOP Vines have succumbed to phylloxera during absence STOP No forthcoming shipments STOP Please come home STOP Will forward money as soon as possible. STOP Fredrick"

She placed her left palm on her forehead and stared at the paper laying on the table. Thinking that she had read it wrong, she turned up the oil lamp and studied the telegram. The enhanced illumination did nothing to improve the message. Unable to budge, she sat staring at the yellow telegram paper and her left eyelid continued to twitch. Her eyes filled with tears that ran down her cheeks and her nose began to drip. After some time, she started taking deep breaths, and exhaling slowly.

Finally, she gathered her strength and walked to the door. The night insects were chanting a message, and their loud noise filled the warm night. The odor of smoldering fires mingled with crude oil wafted up from the valley. She looked out into the inky darkness. She could not see the stars through the cloud cover, nor the moon. It was black all around, except for the circle of light shed by the illuminating oil lamp, and gas burning off of the Frazier Well below.

She tried to focus on her shifting situation--like a sailor trying to remain upright on a ship being tossed by a storm--being thrown this way then that way. She could not look forward to future wine shipments from France. She had no income. The Federal authorities had spread a wide net to bring in anyone who had dealings with John Wilkes Booth and she knew that she was included in their search. Barrister Plugge had detectives looking for her. And this place where she had chosen to hide held little promise, at least for the moment. She thought of her past arrangement in Franklin where she had room and board for her entertaining in the dining room. Even if she went back there, she would be out in the public, vulnerable to either federal authorities or her stepfather's detectives.

She sat down at the table bathed in a circle of lamplight. She was tired and tremulous with worry. With no immediate income, she had only enough money gained from the last wine sale to get her through another week or two. She did have the cask of pinot noir that she had brought from Titusville. If she could sell that to someone, that bit of income would help, then what? Even that money would not last forever.

"It's always darkest before, the dawn. It's always darkest before the dawn. Oh, dear Papa,' things would be so different if you were alive…"

Lured by the thought of her whiskey flask hidden with her spare underdrawers in the loft, she slowly rose. Then, she spotted the newspaper that had come with the mail from Plumer, and reached for it. Since Mrs. Lyon had "gone to bed with the chickens," as she put it to her, the newspaper was hers to peruse. Her hands shook as she read the headlines.

"Trial of the Conspirators…Testimony of Witnesses, Startling Revelations.

"Washington, May 12, 1865: The court is held in the upper room of the old penitentiary. Along the wall of the west side on raised seats were Doctor Mudd, David C. Harrold, Lewis Paine, Edward Spanghl of Fords' Theater, Michael O'Laughlin, Atzerot, and Samuel Arnold. Mrs. Surratt sat outside the palling. The counsel present were Thomas Ewing, son of the Ohio ex-Senator, Attorney Stone, Aiken and Clamnott. The court sit at a table at the north end...."

Suddenly, Katherine felt dizzy and nauseous. She got to her feet and hurried outside and off the small porch to a nearby bush and vomited. In the darkness of the night, she wretched twice before she felt in control enough to come back inside.

Most of those names set to testify she recognized from Booth's discussions. What would happen to them? It was clear to her that she could be there too, confused and confined to that courtroom.

As she read further, she came across a person that was unfamiliar to her. Booth had not mentioned a woman courier named Slater. It appeared that her name surfaced as a blockade runner who carried messages to Montreal. Like Katherine, Mrs. Slater wore a mask or veil and was a French speaker. Since she was not being interrogated, according to the article, Katherine surmised that she claimed French citizenship and had escaped to Canada. Maybe she too should have stayed in Montreal, rather than risk returning to the United States. But who knew of Booth's determination to murder the President and other administration officials?

How many women couriers had Booth and the rebels employed? So, she wasn't the only one. Had Booth led Mrs. Slater on as well, to gain her cooperation? She shivered.

Her vision defocused as she mulled over the facts. Finally, she re-read the names of the witnesses and accused, some of whom were sure to be hanged or go to prison. It was not over yet. She could still be one of them.

He had ensnared her and how many others yet to be identified and arrested? His extreme beliefs had affected an enlarging circle of people. His hatred has enflamed the entire nation. Now others would die for their collaboration with him and his conspiracy. How monstrous... She could feel her anger rising.

Finally, she closed her eyes and tried to envision her future. What would she do now? Where should she go? She felt as if the world were collapsing in on her.

She forced herself to focus. It felt as if she were climbing out of a deep, dark pit. She struggled for a scheme. Counting up her meager assets, she started listing: One cask of wine here in Pithole, six or seven stored in Titusville and the remainder of money, gold pieces, paid her by General Lee in February. She had heard big plans for this new city, Pithole. Perhaps she could start a business here. She knew that she was young and beautiful and could play the piano and sing. Her current dilemma was not fair. Life wasn't fair. She clenched her fists and squeezed her eyes shut.

Her anger began to give her strength, energy to look beyond her present perilous position. She thought of the thriving food service at the Holmden place--all those hungry workers who did have cash to spend. A restaurant here would do well with so many diners that you'd never run out of customers. She had learned how to manage business from Blanche de Brunt at the Red Lantern Inn. She could cook. Mama and Mrs. Marsh, their family's servant had taught her while she was young. But she couldn't do it alone.

She began to list her friends and discovered that she could count them on just one hand: Fredrick--in France; Jeremiah--worked in the oil fields; Barnswell--had job in Franklin, and maybe, Josh. He picked-up work where he could…

Her anger and frustration abating, she turned out the oil lamp, and crawled up the ladder to her bed. Maybe she could open a restaurant if she had someone else with some cash.

"It's always darkest before the dawn."

…

"No, Katherine. The Holmdens are teetotalers. And they don't want any of these workers drinkin' wine or anything else durin' the day--that's fer sure." Josh put one end of a long blade of grass in his mouth.

"I think you'll just have to wait a while before you can sell that keg that we toted down here from Shaeffer Farm."

"But, Josh, I need money now. I showed you the telegram from my cousin. It's finished--the wine importing from my family's vineyard. Done."

"Well, Auntie Gert said she would let you stay for a while longer. Until you can get back on your feet."

She tried to smile. "Think there's a chance I can get work over at the Holmden's place--helping with food?"

"I can check. Of course, I know Walter--know the whole family. That might be a possibility."

A week later, Katherine was lost in thought remembering her discussion with Josh as she scrubbed carrots and potatoes in the Holmden's kitchen.

In her total alarm and panic at the news of Booth's death, and seeing the names of his contacts on trial for their lives, she had forgotten several things that were key in her case. First, she recalled that when she traveled with Booth, he had not used her name on hotel ledgers, but had listed her as "his lady." So hopefully those records could not be used to implicate her, if the search were still on. Perhaps now that the trials were progressing, the federal authorities were satisfied with their wide-sweep of suspects and would call a halt to tracking down others, real or imagined.

Just then, Josh entered the kitchen with the weekly load of supplies from Titusville. He greeted her and playfully grabbed a clean carrot from the pile she had washed and crunched down hard on it.

"Josh, I've been thinking about that wine I have stored in Titusville. Could you help me get it down here? With all these plans for streets, and buildings going up almost overnight, seems like someone is going to open either a restaurant or one of these hotels is going to get constructed." She reached into the bushel basket at her feet, picked out four large potatoes and dropped them into a pan of scrub water.

"Problem is, I don't know where I could store those big containers here."

He took another bite of carrot and sat down at the table. "Hmmm. That is a big consideration. Getting' them here is one thing, but keepin' them until you can sell them is somethin' else."

"Yes, having some cash from a sale or two would give me some money to work with. By the way, I heard that Duncan and his partner are advertising lots for sale now."

"Katherine, you wantin' to buy some land--one of those lots?"

"I have been thinking about a number of things, but buying a lot would be timely, all right."

Josh was on his feet now, the remainder of his carrot left on the table.

"You serious?"

"Well, why not? This place is booming with oil and people

are swarming in from everywhere. I was thinking about a restaurant. Look how this place is flooded with hungry men. More places to eat are really needed."

She looked up from scrubbing potatoes and saw that Josh was waving his arms excitedly.

May 24, 1865

Josh pushed through the crushing crowd of some thousand excited buyers, potential renters, and bystanders toward the large map that was mounted on a makeshift sign-holder made of rough lumber. He needed to record the number of the lot he and Katherine had agreed on.

A crier hired by Duncan and Prather stood on a stump halfway up the slope, elevating him above most of those who were pressing closer to witness the auctioning of the first 500 lots carved out to form the new town.

Each piece of ground was up for grabs and measured 33 by 100 feet, with several larger at 33 by 165 feet. Josh and Katherine had determined to pool their resources, not to buy a lot, but to rent one, just as soon as it had been purchased by someone with more money than they could conjure up.

The two new partners had enough between them to get a lease, Josh with three gold pieces--not greenbacks, and Katherine, with two casks of wine that were worth more here than in Titusville. There was a good reason for this difference in value.

At present, bottled water was selling at a higher price per gallon than crude oil. The water in the new town was already not-potable. The growing number of nearby oil wells had contaminated the underground water and it could not be used for drinking. With the thirsty and hungry throngs gathering here, wine would go at a premium price--a real treat in place of water in this slice of wilderness.

"Welcome to the first public land sale of this new town!" Josh looked up to see a dark-bearded man carrying a white cane. He was dressed out in a bright green suit with white spats and a green derby perched on his bobbing head.

"Five hundred valuable lots are up for sale. Get in on the ground floor of the Duncan and Prather development. A private city, folks!"

The man barking the advertisement paused for a quick drink

out of his pocket flask.

"Get your greenbacks dusted off and ready to plunk down for one of these spectacular pieces of property!" he hollered.

"And if you are lookin' to buy a lease, line up over on this side. Leases were sellin' at $50 for six months or $100 for a year."

Josh had read one of the leases yesterday. He discovered that the real catch seemed to be that the renter had to remove whatever structure he built on the property when the lease was done or sell the building to the owner at the owner's price. That made leasing a gamble. Nevertheless, he and Katherine had agreed to renting, if a lot were available within their means.

...

At the Holmden house, the noon dinner crowd had disbursed leaving stacks of dirty dishes, scorched kettles and greasy skillets. Katherine was literally up to her elbows in soapsuds and was employing a scraper on some stubborn stains. The kitchen was stifling hot.

Suddenly Josh dashed in, smiling and breathless.

"Katherine, we got it! We rented a lot, and for even less than we figured--used only one wine cask and two gold pieces, not three. The gold was an easier trade than paper, that's for sure. Good thing that I rented early in the day, 'cause the prices are risin' now."

She turned from the large metal tub of hot water, her hands wet and dripping with suds.

"Which lot did we lease, Josh?"

"The one we talked about at the corner of First and Brown Street. Closer than this place is to the U. S. Petroleum workers. Our restaurant will be right on the way to their usual dinner spot. Right on the corner--easy to find."

He went on.

"Those 500 lots are sold--just like that. It was a buyin' frenzy. Folks pushin' and shovin' to get to the cashier who was busier than all get-out. A bunch of money changin' hands, all right." He paused for a breath. "And most of the good leases are sold, too. Good thing we were ready--knew what we wanted."

He turned his flushed face toward her and spread a paper out on the table.

"Here's the agreement for you to sign. Then I got to run it back to them right away."

He pulled up a chair while she wiped her wet hands on her damp apron and signed the papers.

"You wouldn't believe what's happenin' out there. Once the lots are sold, the owners are just turnin' around and leasin' them for two and three times what we paid. Fancy figures, their gittin'. It's like stampedin' cattle, the way folks are jockeying to position for the best location for whatever business they are plannin'. And I overheard several men discussin' that fact that there are no restrictions or building standards. They were sayin' that it makes building' a whole lot easier--no requirements for such.'"

"Those people sound greedy--getting whatever they can from all this excitement."

She handed him the signed agreement. Sticking his cigar between his teeth, he grabbed it without reading it.

"I'll be back. You're almost done with this cleanup, right?"

"Well, if I'm not by the time you return, you can help me, 'partner.'"

He laughed and almost ran through the doorway and back to the auction excitement.

Katherine turned back to her chores. Maybe things were not as bad as they seemed the night she had heard about Booth's death and the trial of his associates. As a precaution, she had decided to return to a former surname--her alias, 'Gerrone' and to select the first name of 'Kate.' In this fast-paced place, a name-change would go unnoticed, especially since she was associated with Josh, a native of the area. In Pithole, the landscape transformed on a daily basis and was fast-becoming the heart of commerce, where opportunities abounded. Pithole was the center of the oil trade where money flowed like water.

Now, she had a chance to have money flow her way.

Kate's French Restaurant

June 1865

Josh dropped the hammer he'd been using to nail down the last of the tarpaper on the roof.

"Finished! It's done!"

As he clambered down the ladder. Katherine, who was sitting on the wooden steps of their new building looked around. Sawdust and end pieces of wood lay on the muddy ground. She liked to smell newly cut lumber, and for now, it replaced the offensive odor of crude oil that usually dominated the area. The aroma of newly cut timber came as a relief.

"So many changes have occurred since the sale of properties just weeks ago."

"Yeh." Josh waved his hand holding his cigar in the direction of the new structures that had come to dominate the hillside.

"First thing built was that board shanty of Henry James, that Nantucket cooper. He finished that thing in one day. And now we got the Astor House--that went up in a day, too. Two entire city blocks are complete--in just four days--and those businesses are open." Josh sat down beside Katherine. She noticed that his hands were black from handling the roofing materials.

"What are they sayin' about the number of people here in Pithole now? Two thousand white men, eleven women--you're one of 'em--and one Black man. And on top of that, the Homestead Well on the Hyner place came in big and is flowin'. Gonna make our restaurant a success, with all these hungry folks." Josh paused. "We gotta name it--our restaurant."

"I've decided on the name." She looked up and away from Josh.

"'Kate's French Restaurant.' I registered it at the leasing office yesterday."

Josh said nothing. Katherine gave him a sideways glance to see his reaction to her declaration. He turned to meet her eyes.

"I thought we would talk about it--what to name it, but you've already decided, huh?"

"Well, Josh, with the distinction of serving French wine, I

275

decided that the name should reflect that."

Josh studied the palm of his dirty hand. He seemed resigned.

"Well, let's get a sign made and I'll nail it up near the door to the dining room. Got to let folks know that we'll be open for business soon. All these newcomers in town gotta' eat."

"That's right." She paused. "Did you ask your aunt if she would sell us some of the produce she's raising?"

"Well, she said that since she's found someone to help her with the garden, she could agree. Said you'd been sucha' help that you deserved some of those vegetables you planted. She seemed relieved to get a helper since you left out from there."

"She must have found a worker who lives nearby."

"Don't know, but her garden has been doin' well, so good thing she found this woman with a young 'un. So many restaurants openin' up, she can sell everything she's growin.'"

...

In early July, the number of inhabitants of Pithole was mushrooming. Oilmen, teamsters, laborers, cooks, bartenders, farriers, and ne'rer-do-wells had converged upon the tiny town as soon as there were places to stay and meals to buy. Some of the accommodations were in place, but with such a rapid influx, the new village lacked planning for public services. It left the exploding population to do what they pleased. Push back against lawlessness soon followed.

Colonel Duncan, who along with Prather had purchased the Holmden Farm and leased lots in Pithole took it upon himself to police the new town. With no legal authority and in secrecy, he created a group of vigilantes, all volunteers. The growing citizenry grew to fear and hate these rough bullies who they considered were serving Duncan's interests, protecting his properties. When Duncan designated William Murray to be the leader of the fifteen-man rogue group, the high-handed Duncan and Murray arrested citizens at will. They held court, passed sentences and meted out punishments. When they arrested two newcomers for disturbing the peace and fined them $150 plus a gold watch, the strangers accused Murray and Duncan of usurping authority. Landing in the Venango County Court in Franklin, Duncan was charged with conspiracy when he failed to produce any document that authorized his reprobate practices. Although it appears that Duncan had worked to protect the whole community, the *Titusville Morning Herald* published acrimonious articles regarding his high-handed behavior. Due to the court ruling that restricted policing in Pithole, criminal behavior increased at will.

Early one Sunday morning, the bartender arose to investigate a noise in the barroom of the American Hotel. When intruders refused to leave, he screamed for help. A violent fight ensued and the robbers escaped, but threatened revenge--to destroy the hotel and murder the bartender. A group of vigilantes had not long to wait for the return of the gang leader, the notorious John Burke and his henchmen. Deputies fired their guns, subdued the invading mob of eighteen, and Burke was imprisoned at the jail in Franklin. Incidents of lawlessness and other revolting practices dominated the boomtown.

People tossed garbage into the muddy streets. Dead horses and mules lay in nearby bushes, putrefying. Hastily constructed privies were inadequate to meet the needs of citizens and visitors, and those that were in place lacked maintenance. Drinking water was non-existent--dangerous to human life. At first, a person could buy a barrel of water for fifty-cents, a pitcher for ten-cents, but the prices immediately escalated to fifty-cents a pitcher and ten cents, a cup. The ground water was unsafe even for bathing.

A visitor told a reporter from the *Titusville Morning Herald*, "The whole place smells like a camp of soldiers with diarrhea." Pithole was not for the faint-of-heart, nor anyone with a weak stomach. City-services did not exist.

As well, sleeping accommodations were stretched to the limits and beyond. Newcomers arrived by horseback, on stage coaches, in wooden wagons or on foot. They were men of every ilk--oil men, speculators, merchants, lawyers, doctors, blacksmiths, clerks, bankers, the homeless and thieves and they all came with one goal in mind--to make as much money as soon as possible.

While they poured into the epicenter of the oil excitement, the five planned hotels, Morey, Danforth, Chase, Metropolitan and the Duncan could not be hammered into shape fast enough to meet the mounting demands. Men scrambled for any accommodation and at $2 a night were packed in like sardines in a can, head-to-foot; or paid $3 for a hanging-hammock. One dollar got the weary a straw-stack on the floor.

The United States Petroleum Company saw additional opportunities to make money from these fortune-seekers with cash in-hand. To accommodate the influx of teamsters in May, a warehouse owner converted a portion of the large building, meant for oil storage, into sleeping quarters and named it, The United States Hotel. Now, this resting space was expanded and turned into a huge dining area by day. One hundred men a night lodged for $2 each, and 1000 meals a day sold for $4 a head. All of these lodgers and diners were looking to make a fortune, either using their own cash or someone else's.

Eye-catching newspaper advertisements circulated through big cities and swept over the countryside prompting hopefuls to invest in oil and get rich. Companies sprang up selling stock in new oil ventures--some legitimate--but with little experience in such enterprise. Others were fraudulent from their origins and with no plans to mine the "liquid gold" that was on everyone's mind. Oil speculation struck the war-weary nation like the incoming tide at full-moon on a clear night.

For the early months of 1865, oil companies reported that they had filed capital certifications with the Secretary of State in three jurisdictions. The figures testify to the excitement of the bourgeoning petroleum industry: New York, $350,000,000; Massachusetts, $160,000,000; and Pennsylvania, $145,000,000. The source of the money was people, some who had enough money to invest, and others, ordinary folks, who could ill afford such risk. In Pithole, buying one-sixteenth of a share was a common deal, and deciding which well showed the most promise was a gamble. The choices were many.

In July, six months after the Frazier Well had come in, a reporter from the *New York Tribune* climbed-up the supports of that well and reported that he had counted over 300 derricks on the Holmden property and nearby lands--lands that now were denuded of all things living and were blackened with oil. A few straggling trees survived on the hills stripped-bare of all former vegetation.

. . .

Katherine had been following the fate of Booth's collaborators. Every morning, she had purchased either the *Titusville Morning Herald* or the Erie newspaper. Sentencings of Booth's agents were announced to the public on July 5. Two days later, some of the accused were hanged, and others imprisoned. Each passing day after the executions gave her hope that the hunt for remaining conspirators--and for her--was over. No sign of detectives or federal authorities in this area of a rapidly growing population of strangers gave her confidence.

Once their restaurant was completed, she had felt secure

enough to move from Widow Lyon's cabin into one of the rooms Josh had built into the second floor above the dining area. She was busy, happily involved with her project and on the verge of making money.

...

At first light one morning in late July, Katherine carried her tin mug of hot coffee toward the front stoop. She enjoyed the cool air and a few minutes of relative quiet before the pounding and sawing of nearby chaotic construction commenced for the day. Since launching *her* restaurant, as she thought of it, she wanted time to reflect on its success.

Josh had reluctantly agreed to call the place, "Kate's French Restaurant: Dignified Dining and Fine French Wine." Hers was the only establishment in the mushrooming municipality that offered such an exclusive ambiance. As reflected in the name of her establishment, she had determined to change her first name from Katherine to Kate, to further confuse any pursuers.

She opened the door slowly to find someone sleeping on the board porch floor, rolled-up against the side of the building. A brown horse, gray around its muzzle was tethered at the watering trough. She was surprised to see the animal. No such critter was safe and likely to be stolen or turn-up pulling some teamster's wagon full of oil barrels over the muddy roads.

Just as the sun's rays beamed over the rise to the east, the sleeper stretched and opened his eyes. Kate saw that he was a young boy, maybe 12-years-old. He looked alarmed when he realized that he was caught spending the night on someone else's property. Abruptly, he sat up and ran both hands through his hair.

"Well, who are you?" She looked at him quizzically.

Just then the door to the dining room opened and Mabelle, a young girl whom Kate had recently hired, emerged.

"Oh, Miss Kate, this here is Luke. He asked me if he could sleep out here last night, so I told him it was all right. He had nowhere to go."

She gave Mabelle a hard look, but said nothing.

"Well, thank you. Thank you both for allowing me to sleep here. And for hitching my horse near me."

Kate thought he was well-mannered and not like some of the other street-urchins she had encountered when buying newspapers.

"What are you doing here in Pithole, Luke?" She was curious. He seemed young to be out on his own.

"I just got here last night. I'm looking for work. Just a job of some sort. I am answering an ad that was in the *Oil City Register*-- about jobs for boys my age--selling newspapers." He paused. "So, at 8:00 I am going to their office over there." He pointed toward a building up the street near the on-going construction. I have the ad here in my pocket--tore it out."

"Are you all by yourself?"

"Yeh, for now. Ma's gone to stay with my grandpa until our land in Oil City gets sold. Been a muddy mess there since that bad flood a couple of months ago."

"She'll sell some property?"

"Yeh, the railroad is buying up land right where we have lived since I can recall. It's called the Clarion Land and Improvement Company."

"So, it's just you and your mother?"

"Oh, no. I have a brother, my big brother, Elias and he's up in Titusville working on the new log road, just starting work on it."

"Your brother's name is Elias? Elias Kahle?"

Luke jumped to his feet in excitement.

"You know Elias?"

"Yes, we met in Titusville back in February. He was on his way home from the war." She paused. "So, you're his kin? And you're here in Pithole by yourself?"

She looked Luke up and down, wondering if he were strong enough to help out in the evenings, clearing tables, washing dishes, dealing with the trash.

"How would you like a place for the night and two meals a day in exchange for helping out at my restaurant?"

Luke's mouth dropped open for a few seconds.

"Sure! That would be fine." He paused and then frowned.

"What about Topsy? She's my horse. Is there somewhere that I can keep her?"

She shifted her gaze to Luke's steed, considering the dangers of horse thieves, while weighing the advantages of having access to a horse.

"I need to give that some thought."

Luke departed for the newspaper office and Kate waited for Josh to join her.

...

Josh chewed on his cigar as he listened carefully to Kate's

plan to employ Luke at the café. Having been blind-sided by her naming the restaurant without his opinion, he was on the alert. Nor did he miss the fact that she referred to the restaurant as 'hers.' It was his investment as well, but she seemed to be several jumps ahead of him with her schemes.

"So, if Luke could stable his horse at your aunt's place with Ellie, he could take care of both animals and sleep there in the barn, if he's not staying down here at the restaurant. And each morning, Luke could bring down whatever your aunt has to sell to us and then go to work at his appointed spot to sell newspapers."

Josh agreed that it would make things easier for both him and Kate since his travel into Plumer and Titusville periodically removed him from supporting their enterprise. He had to agree that it was a well-thought-out plan that appeared to help them all, Topsy included. In fact, the company of another animal might do Ellie some good. He had to admit that Katherine could make good plans without much effort.

After a cup of coffee and breakfast, he hiked up to his aunt's cabin to discuss the proposal.

. . .

Mike Mulligan exuded an air of confidence, when he entered Kate's French Restaurant for the first time. Kate had to admit that he was an impressive presence. He had a take-charge bearing that belied his average height. A red-faced visage with a thick body and muscular arms and shoulders gave anyone watching, the distinct impression that he was powerful. Not only did this Irishman from Galway Bay flash his blue eyes and quick temper, but he was a teamster, and like others in the same occupation, Mike flaunted greenbacks, lots of greenbacks.

Although he was not an imbiber of French wine, he became a regular, helping the fledgling restaurant get on its feet. No one appreciated Mike more the Kate. She basked in his attention and the way he looked at her.

Having Mike as a friend gave the new restaurant not only financial stability, but had the advantages of physical security, as well. One night when several customers, sodden with alcohol, became boisterous and then shoved their chairs aside with a clatter, Mike stepped between them to avert a brawl. He forcefully shoved the potential combatants out the side door while extracting from each, what they owed the restaurant. Kate felt secure in Mike's presence which was almost every evening.

Teamsters as a group were a powerful, unruly, rowdy, bullying bunch. They wielded power over oil producers who were dependent on their services, moving thousands of barrels of oil out of remote areas to some other form of transportation, train, steamboat or flatboat. Getting the petroleum from the well to refineries was the crucial link of the industry. Oil storage was dangerous and frustrating in an unregulated industry where prices soared and plunged. The teamsters formed an unorganized brotherhood to discuss their issues. Well aware of their importance and advantageous position, these drivers knew they were the lynchpins in the success of moving oil out of remote Pithole.

At first, transporting a barrel of crude the eleven miles from Pithole to Titusville cost one dollar, but the charge quickly rose to $3 a barrel. The more reasonable teamsters who chose not to over-charge the oil producers were soon bullied by their chums to adjust their prices to match the others. The usual load per team was five barrels, so haulers were in clover--$15 a one-way trip.

Teamsters' jobs were secure in the scramble to keep up with well production. There were not enough teams--usually two horses, a driver and a wagon--to move the thousands of barrels through the rutted, muddy Pithole roads to either Titusville or down the mountainside to the Allegheny River. Making monetary demands that seemed like extortion to oil producers, those haulers were in "the catbird seat," and they knew it.

The over-paid young men who drove long miles through inclement weather contributed to the prosperity of growing businesses in Pithole. They played rough, drank hard and raised hell, keeping the countryside in turmoil. Filling the barrooms, brothels and dance halls, they repeatedly wreaked havoc in a community struggling to attain some order and stability. Some of them joined Mike Mulligan at Kate's French Restaurant.

The men who frequented that restaurant were looking for more than a good meal and liberal amounts of libations. The young women who Katherine had hired soon realized that there were other ways to earn fast-money in Pithole. She had to strategize to maintain the employees that she and Josh needed to provide good service at their restaurant.

Kate found it difficult, in fact impossible, to discuss this new opportunity with her business partner, Josh. By late-July, she devised a scheme and confronted him with her plan.

"Josh, it is time for me to buy out your share of the restaurant."

Josh stopped in his tracks as he was clearing the last tables and the customers had departed.

"What? What did you say?"

"I think it's time for me to go on my own now. I've figured what I owe you for your initial investment and your fifty percent of this month's profits."

Josh looked stunned and she watched him sit down hard in a chair. It was two o'clock in the morning and they were both exhausted. She had planned it that way, so that he would have less time and energy to resist her proposition.

"The girls want to get work on the side at night--upstairs and I don't think you should be involved. They asked me to manage the business for them and I can't cut you in on that part of the deal. I am prepared to pay you your part now."

Just then one of the teamsters emerged from the second floor and headed for the door.

"Well, Mr. Cassidy." She moved to block the client's exit. "Let's you and I settle up now." When he saw that she meant what she said, he produced a wad of greenbacks.

Kate glanced at Josh who seemed astounded at her confrontive behavior and the results. No doubt, he was flabbergasted at the re-direction of what he thought was their business. After the customer had exited, he stood to leave.

"I see what you're talking about and I agree with you. I do not need to be part of this."

She felt relief at his quick decision. She was pleased. Josh was easy to manipulate and that made it simpler for her in this changing atmosphere where money readily flowed, at least so far, from the teamsters.

She handed Josh two gold pieces paid her by Mike for her attentions, and his half of this month's profit. He looked crest-fallen, but accepted the pay-off, dumped the stub of his cigar in the brass spittoon near the entrance door, and left without a word.

Her new business had eager customers who were loaded with cash. Just what she had envisioned--some easy money--finally. She had several wine casks yet in storage and one making her money by the glass, drunk by nightly celebrants with producing oil wells or good paying jobs. Besides that, she had experience in a trade, the brothel business, initiated by her step-father at the Red Lantern Inn, and trained by his loyal manager, Blanche de Brundt. She had the skills and the know-how. How fortuitous.

She would make this work for her. She would survive. In fact, she planned to live very well.   …

Josh lost no time in pursuit of getting his name off of the lease for Kate's French Restaurant. The next day when he had finished working in Auntie Gert's garden, he trekked down into town to conclude his legal affairs. Since his last visit to the offices of Duncan and Prather to pay the month's rent on the lot leased to him and Kate, his were not the only circumstances that had changed.

Now there was a Justice of the Peace and several deputy sheriffs, but community services yet lacked development. There was no city drinking water and the privies continued to be ineffective. Holmden Street did appear to be thriving with six hotels in business and Captain Vandergrift's Duncan House under construction. Lawyers, doctors, land offices and insurance agents shared crammed space, but managed their daily businesses. The place was teeming with people and activity.

As Josh approached the intersection of First Street, he noted the honky-tonk atmosphere mixed with good mercantile markets. Signs hung on various buildings--restaurants, bars and dancehalls including brothels--promising memorable experiences. As well, for the throngs who frequented this area, they departed with fewer greenbacks than when they'd arrived. He could see how Kate's new business fit into this frenzied area like a hand-in-glove.

Just then several women on horseback slogged into view, riding slowly down Brown Street to First Street across from where he stood in front of the Florence Restaurant, Emma's place. They wore broadbrimmed straw-hats with vails that flowed down their backs and on to their horses' rumps. In the bright sunlight, the vails gave off a shimmering sheen, one bright pink and another a light green. Their dresses were draped above their white legs to well above the knee. One was riding barefoot. Her low-cut dress exposed her cleavage of pale white skin. They sat up straight, smiling as they rode to the side of First Street where they stopped. Wreathed in smiles, they waved and called out to team after team of oil laden wagons as they groaned past them. The young male drivers craned their necks to get a good view of the beckoning beauties. The girls giggled and blew kisses at the passing teamsters. One called out.

"Come and have a drink with me this evening--right here--

corner of First and Brown Street! Right over yonder!" And she gestured with a swoop of her right hand pointing toward the intersection of First and Brown Street.

"I'll be waitin' for you!" She blew the closest driver a flirtatious kiss. In response, he raised his hat and stood-up in his wagon.

"Yahoo! What's your name, dolly?"

"They call me 'Sunny'! What's your name, you handsome gent?" Their banter continued as the horseback parade kept pace of the departing oil bearers.

Josh watched with fascination.

"Corner of First and Brown Street," he repeated aloud. Suddenly it hit him. That was the address of Kate's French Restaurant. He shook his head and turned his back on the scene.

He felt more relieved than ever to be severing ties with Kate. She was right, he did not need to be part of this business venture.

As he continued on First Street, he dodged the wagon ruts and pooled water. He stepped over a pile of sawdust near the construction of Murphy's Theater, and he noted the odor of green lumber, not unusual in this building boom. A newly painted sign helped him locate the offices of his former landlords: "DUNCAN AND PRATHER."

"What's the name of the business?"

"Kate's French Restaurant."

After a few minutes of shuffling through a drawer of files, the bespectacled, balding clerk shrugged his shoulders.

"Not in here."

"It has to be." Josh felt anxious.

"Well, so you have the papers for it?"

"Yes." He handed the clerk his documents.

"Here's the number for the lot. Let's see what I can do with that."

Josh sat down when the clerk left the room. He studied a large wall-hung map that marked out some 300 residences, fifteen to twenty blacksmith shops, ten hotels, the post office, mechanics shops and numerous other businesses. A notation on the corner of the map: "2000 POPULATION, July 31, 1865." He unwrapped a new cigar, gave it a good sniff, then planted it between his teeth and waited.

Several minutes later, the clerk, now beaming, lugged a heavy ledger to a table near Josh.

"Look'a here. No wonder I couldn't locate it. Look how it's named."

Josh read the ledger's line: "French Kate's Restaurant."

"Guess she'll have to change her sign to agree with our books. I'll be sending her a notice on that." He paused to adjust his glasses.

"Now, let's take care of your request."

As Josh closed the land-office door behind him, he ruminated about the error in the restaurant's name, and could not suppress a smile. Somehow, it seemed fitting, given the circumstances. French Kate's Restaurant was located in the right part of Pithole, right across First Street from Emma Fenton's place. Among the male inhabitants, Emma's Restaurant was an open secret. From what Josh had observed, Emma's place, the Florence Restaurant, often had a line of customers waiting to get in. Maybe 'French Kate's' new business venture could get started with Emma's over-flow. Well, Kate is a good business woman...

He smiled. He wondered what Jeramiah would have to say about this turn of events.   ...

Josh and Jeremiah sat on log near the United States Petroleum office several days after Josh had removed his name from the restaurant's property. Jeremiah removed his broad-brimmed hat and shook off the dust. He looked at Josh.

"Seems that Miss Katherine has joined the speculators and oil prospectors in regards to takin' advantage of this here oil boom." He grinned. "Guess I'm not too surprised at that. It's a way of life out here in Pithole--makin' quick money fast."

Josh picked the dried clumps of dirt off of his worn boots.

"Guess I was caught unawares--of how shrewd she is..."

"Well, she's not alone in wantin' to make money." He paused and lowered his voice.

"Guess you heard what Duncan and Prather paid. The Holmden Farm went for $25,000 and one-fourth royalties and then a bonus of $75,000 to the Holmdens." Josh nodded and Jeremiah continued.

"Now those guys are lookin' to make money by sellin' their entire operation for $1,300,000, and three gents from Titusville signed an agreement of July 24. Every last square foot of this here 200-acre farm is leased out. Just the town part here with all the buildings is leased for $60,000 a year. The Danforth House alone has a $15,000 lease."

Josh looked up from removing the clods of mud from his footwear.

"Gosh, I didn't know that."

"So now these Titusville men, George Sherman, Brian Philpot and Henry Picket have the first payment comin' due to Duncan and Prather thirty days after they signed the agreement."

"How much do they owe by then?"

"$300,000 by August 24, I recon."

"They must have lots of money."

"That's not what I hear. Sherman went to New York to raise the money for the first payment but nobody would bite. Too spooked by a big scandal there."

"What scandal, Jememiah?"

"Called the 'Ketchum Forgeries.' Some New York dude cheated people out of their money. So that apparently caused some of them wealthy investors there to back away from Sherman's offer. So, now I hear that Sherman is scramblin' to meet the deadline in a couple of weeks. I know because a possible investor named H.H. Honore came here from Chicago just two days ago to inspect the Holmden property. Guess no cash was possible so then a land-swap deal came up. I overheard that 'cause I was working nearby when they walked the property."

"Then what happened? Did that work?"

"Don't think so, 'cause the last I heard, that gent Sherman from Titusville was plannin' to find other investors. Doesn't have much time. That's a lot of money."

"Yeah, Jeremiah. It all sounds crazy. Just a year ago this land wasn't worth much. Hard to grow crops. Holmden's were doin' their best to produce much of anything of this rocky land. Now that oil's been found here, the land-value is way out there!"

"I agree. This place was nothing a year ago. In June, only a couple of buildin's and poof! Couple of months later, farms around here sellin' and leasin' for wild prices. Speculators roaming these parts like ants on a spill of honey. Hard to believe."

"So, does it sound like those Titusville gents will make the deadline of the first payment to Duncan and Prather?"

"Dun'no, can't say. Guess we'll just have to watch and wait."

"Yeah, probably won't take long. Things are a-changin' fast around here..."

_____

Unintended Consequences

July-August 1865

Luke shook the rain off of his new broad-brimmed black hat as he arrived under the high roof of the two-story Astor House. The inn, which had been built in one day stood at 50-52 First Street near the intersection of First and Holmden Streets, only one block from French Kate's place where he had spent the night. On a window ledge protected by the roof over-hang, he stashed his copies of the *Titusville Morning Herald*, then sat down on one of the hotel's wooden benches. At 5:30 in the morning, he could get away with perching there since none of the hotel's guests was around to occupy that space, yet.

He figured that it would take him until about noon to sell his allotment of newspapers. Prolonged standing, even for a thirteen-year-old was tiring. He had to take advantage now, or at least until the foot-traffic on First Street picked up. Except for the nonstop noises of the pumping oil wells just across the muddy street, the area was quiet. He closed his eyes but stayed alert to the sounds of potential purchasers.

Suddenly, a loud crash jarred Luke and he opened his eyes. The commotion of bulky barrels hoisted onto waiting wagons broke the comparative calm as arriving teamsters received their oleaginous loads at the U.S. Petroleum warehouse. In the gray dawn light, Luke watched horses being hitched, a team of two each, to a wagon loaded with five oil barrels. He observed the lead driver climb to his seat and with whip in-hand, signal his team to move. This hauler positioned his rig to lead a procession of a caravan of 100 loaded wagons headed for Titusville and the railroads, the next step in transporting oil out of Pithole.

When particular sections of the road developed impenetrable mud holes whose dangerous depths created necessitous detours, these determined drivers took the liberties of preventing damaged wagons or hurt horses. Taking matters into their own hands, they trespassed over farmers' fields at will with their tremendous tonnage, daring anyone to defy their numbers and their blacksnake whips, creating a sort of on-going guerilla warfare. Depending on well production or the availability of teams, this forced-march of conveyance was a daily spectacle in Pithole, Titusville and all territory that they traversed.

Luke thought it looked like a ghostly parade, these huge, once-elegant animals now were denuded of all hair from their eyes down to their hooves. They were splattered in mud mixed with oil, a perpetual paste that destroyed their capillary glands. Their hair ceased to grow. This cadaverous cavalcade of hapless horses that survived a short two-to-three months in these circumstances would continue departing from the wells until noon or later each day.

On this July morning, the temperature was cool and the dampness only exaggerated the chill and held close the odor of crude oil mixed with horse manure. Luke shivered as he watched the long lumbering line of transport slog into First Street and head north. The wagons' wheels were up to the hubs in wet, glistening glop, and the horses waded in mud to their knees. Luke felt sorry for these beasts-of-burden, hauling heavy liquid loads for eleven muddy miles.

His thoughts raced to Topsy who was stabled at the Widow Lyon's shed. At least she was out of the rain and wind. Hopefully, she also was safe from the horse thieves who ran rampant here. The Widow's place was not known to new-comers who were likely to be the filchers.

Suddenly, the mud-slicked walkway held travelers, men from The Lincoln House, a nearby boarding abode on Brown Street. Luke jumped to his feet, grabbing a folded newspaper.

"Get your morning news here! *Titusville Morning Herald* with the latest oil prices!"

Now, he was wide awake and hustling in his territory, the Astor House entrance and a semicircle of space along the hotel's street-frontage. He dashed across First Street when a man on the corner flagged him. The competition was stiff when working against a rising tide of youngsters who had come in small gangs from Rochester, Buffalo, Cleveland, Chicago and even Canada. The influx of growing groups of children with the average age of fourteen guarded their territory jealously while they sold copies of various news sources. New York and the Erie newspapers brought the seller four cents for each copy sold. Unfortunately for Luke, by the time he had arrived in Pithole, numerous paperboys had cornered the sales market for these more lucrative newspaper sales, but distribution of the local paper needed more hands. The *Titusville Morning Herald* paid each huckster two cents a copy, and Luke had happily signed on.

_____

289

For Luke, it was good money and he often earned five dollars a day, more than the earnings of some common laborers. As soon as people were up and about, he worked hard at sales. He was earning more money here than at his last job on the steamboat landing flats in Oil City.

In March, the monstrous inundation that had flooded so many businesses and homes had cost Luke and other workers their jobs. Now, he had to hustle. He was his sole support. He ran across First Street toward a boarding house where emerging men were exiting.

"Hear about it in the *Titusville Morning Herald!* Three-inch Oil Pipeline would bring cheap transport! Front page news!" Surprised workers gathered around him with their payments ready.

A week before, he had explained to Kate and Mabelle about a sales incentive.

"Mr. Prather. See, he owns the Prather and Wadsworth Bank up-the-way on Holmden Street. Well, he has made us newspaper boys an offer, one-sixteenth interest in one of the producin' wells. Gonna' go to the one of us that can first save $100--gotta be deposited in his bank. And I want to win."

...

As soon as his last paper had sold, Luke slopped through the mud toward Kate's place for his noontime meal. His feet made a squishing sound as he walked, but he knew he could clean and dry out his boots by six o'clock when he would report to Kate's kitchen for work. He scanned for a good place to cross the muddy street after the morning's traffic of oil-filled wagons had cut deep ruts into First Street. As he came around the corner, he looked up Holmden Street with its bare-boards buildings, half-dug cellars, and low-class barrooms and restaurants. Then a scene playing out directly in front of him caught his immediate attention.

A team of two horses was mired in mud. The driver was urging them to free themselves as they strained to pull their heavy load out of the quagmire.

The heavily bearded teamster got out and inspected the wagon wheels that were sunk well-over the wheel hub. Luke saw that neither horse had hair below its eyes, a sign that this team had been working at moving oil for several months. Suddenly, the hulking, frustrated driver grabbed his black snake. Spewing loud curses, he flogged each animal, but they could not budge the weighty

290

wagon from its ruinous rut. Finally, straining under the beating, one horse sank to its knees, fell forward, dropped facedown into the mud and did not move.

The futures of the horses and mules working in this industry were bleak. By the thousands, they were left to die if they broke a bone or when stuck in the mud of a hastily created roadway of bottomless muck. They were either destroyed on the spot, or deserted to perish alone.

Luke fled the scene, splashing his way toward Brown Street. Another terrible death of an animal... He had witnessed this tragedy too many times. He knew that the poor beast would be abandoned and left to die, suffocated by the mud. With tears in his eyes, he sat on Kate's porch and pulled off his muddy boots. He tried to erase the scene from his memory. All he could think of was Topsy and the terrible end to so many horses in this treacherous oil field.

It was common knowledge to those living in this area that no horses, mules or any other beast of burden were left within a radius of thirty miles. Railroad trains delivered horses and mules from nearby states. They were unloaded by the boxcar into nearby railheads. Considered a necessary means for transporting petroleum, they toiled over almost impassible roads from the inaccessible oil sources, and returned to the thriving town, loaded with lumber, building supplies and tools. Men depended on these beasts of burden for their livings.

Today, after witnessing the death of yet another horse, Luke felt sad and anxious about their harsh handling and dreadful demise. Sometimes, he sensed that the situation was hopeless.

What gave Luke hope was the future of corduroy or plank roads. He had heard discussions about plans for such a five-and-one-half-mile road from Pithole to Miller Farm, giving access to the Oil Creek Railroad. Two months ago, to the admiration of many, David Kirk, the oilman with the National Oil Refinery and Storage Company had hired a crew to chop a seven-mile roadway from the tanks of the Twin Wells at Pithole, south to the Allegheny River. At least that was some progress.

Luke felt proud that Elias was one of the men employed laying the plank-road from Titusville to Pithole. The project was under the management of William Webber, a Nantucket shipbuilder who directed the eleven-mile venture of laying four-inch wooden planks over "sleepers" that provided a solid foundation. The plank road would be the first visible link between Pithole and the outside

291

world. The last news Luke heard, the road crews had started work at the Titusville end and were moving southward. They were creating a hard surface for wagons, horses and men afoot who would pay a toll for its use. That made him able to continue living in this place, surviving the daily brutality and consequences created by the perpetual avarice of speculators and oilmen alike.

At least now, Elias was living in the area, and not fighting with his army unit in some place foreign to Luke. He was happy about that. His big brother was nearby at last.

…

Josh guided Topsy away from the deep mud ruts that confronted them at the end of the recently initiated construction of the plank road from Titusville to Pithole. Only two miles more and future trips between the towns would be easier, Josh thought. He judged from the length of the shadows cast by the few remaining trees in the area that sundown was about three hours away. He turned to view the progress of his client, a gentleman recently arrived in Titusville by train from Chicago. It was obvious to Josh that this bank president had not ridden a horse since his childhood, if then. Guess that's what happens when you're livin' in the city and you ride to work in a horse-drawn carriage, Josh mused. No wonder Mr. Sherman had hired knowledgeable guides to accompany the four citified gentlemen on this trip.

The tedious trek provided little shade over summer travelers and the new wooden surface of the plank road already was deteriorating, worn down by the hooves of teams pulling heavy loads of oil, day-in-and-day out. Here at the end of the hard-surface road, muddy holes challenged even the most observant horse-handler or sure-footed mule. The last portion of this trek would be the most grueling due to a heavy rain the day before. Water stood in puddles whose depths were unknown until some uninitiated visitor fell into one. Travel to Pithole was dicey.

Shifting in the saddle, Josh listened for any indication from the other portions of their party who were to give a distress signal, if attacked. Sherman had determined that each man be armed with a pocket pistol and be riding a horse worthy of galloping if necessary. Bandits infested these eleven miles from Titusville to Pithole. Josh knew them to be of a meaner sort--real highwayman who flung themselves at tired travelers at dusk, dawn and during the night. For the dozenth time, he reached to feel the loaded rifle that he had strapped under a blanket on Topsy's right side. He was relieved that this trek would soon be over for him.

George Sherman, a businessman from Titusville had hired a guide for each of his visitors and had ordered them to split up so as not to attract attention. The reason was clear to Josh after Jeremiah had provided the details when they had signed on for this trip...

'Ya' see, Josh, these oil speculators have big-money, and when they get here, they pay cash just like the oil companies. It's major money, $50,000 to $100,000. No banks here, so places like U.S. Petroleum have their own safes on the property. That brings us to Duncan and Prather who have made a killing on the leases in Pithole alone. Heard tell that one hotel lease fetched 'em $14,000. So now they're thinkin' big, or that's what folks are sayin.' Just think, only two months ago, they paid Tom Holmden $25,000 for the farm with a bonus of $75,000 later."

"Why did they pay the bonus?"

"With the wells puttin' out 3,500 barrels a day and 100 more wells goin' down... Now the money they were makin' on land leases just in town alone at $60,000 a year, guess they thought Holmden deserved a better deal. Besides those payments to Holmden, one-fourth of the oil royalties also go to that family."

"What's that got to do with us trekking to Titusville and bringin' these gents back with us?"

"That's where it gets interestin'." Jeremiah paused and looked around. "I think that Duncan and Prather see a golden opportunity to make even more money on their original investment. They put up the Holmden farm for $1,300,000. Now this guy George Sherman from Titusville and two others have agreed to buy the property, but they have to scare up some investors who have the money. So that's where we come in."

"Oh, I heard something about that. Said Sherman took the train to New York, but folks there got cold feet 'cause of some bank forgeries there, so he came back empty handed."

"Yeah, those were the Ketchum forgeries--been in the newspapers."

"Are these men from New York--that' we'll be protectin'?"

"No, these travelers are comin' from Chicago. A different bunch, but investors nonetheless. At first, these Chicago gents tried to do a land exchange, a real estate swap, the Holmden Farm for property in Chicago, but that didn't work out. So, they renegotiated and now they're comin' with funds for the first down-payment.

They have money…"

…

The group from Chicago was carrying a large sum of money, $400,000 in greenbacks, that for reasons of safety had been divided among and carried by each of the four businessmen. The host, Mr. Sherman had selected carefully, hiring only men known to him to be trustworthy and who knew the dangers and the territory across which they were required to traverse with such a large amount of cash. Josh felt proud that he was one of two selected from Pithole. Jeremiah was the second. The other two guides lived in Titusville.

Yesterday, leaving Ellie in her stall had been difficult for Josh as he trusted Ellie who was tried and true on every trip he had made. However, this assignment required a horse not a mule, so he and Luke had struck a bargain for Topsy's two-day rental: twenty-five per cent of Josh's take for this dangerous trip. This high-stakes journey involved the delivery of the first payment to Duncan and Prather for the 200-acre Holmden Farm, minus one-eight which they had set aside for themselves. Today was the deadline to make this down-payment, or the contract would be void.

Josh moved forward with the banker right behind him. Joshua Ellis looked uncomfortable with an expression on his countenance that could be described as pain. Josh took a deep breath and nudged Topsy forward. Since they were leading the trek, the other riders were spread out behind them for over a quarter mile. The distances were spaced between each pair of guide and guest so that they were within hearing range of a gunshot, the signal that they needed help.

Most of the teamster-traffic had preceded Josh's party back to Pithole and the road crews having completed their day's work also had departed, so the road became relatively quiet. Few travelers were around at the end of this hot day. Even the birds had taken to the bushes for shade, and the air was still and humid.

Suddenly, out of the periphery of his vision, Josh detected movement in the underbrush ahead. He watched two men emerge from their hiding place and they dashed toward him and the banker. Josh quickly unstrapped his Jennings rifle from Topsy's side, and took aim.

"Stop!"

The bandits split up, each charging toward a horse, Topsy and the banker's rented steed. The frightened banker clutched the reins and sat frozen in the saddle.

"Git off that horse!" The taller of the two thieves seized the bridle, then grabbed at the banker's right foot. The banker suddenly kicked the assailant, striking him in the face, and he fell back. Meanwhile, Josh aimed his gun over the head of the second highwayman who wielded a revolver in his hand.

"Put down your gun!"

Josh pulled the trigger. The sound of the blast rang out and echoed against the yet uncut forest. He took aim again, but this time, directly at the surprised attacker. The robber saw that his accomplice was covered with blood and was staggering away from the banker and his horse.

"Get away from us, or I will shoot you!" Josh nudged Topsy who moved as directed and brought him in shooting range of both of the thieves. The shorter of the two saw that he was out-gunned, holstered his pistol and led the bleeder away and off of the road. Josh shot the rifle again, over the heads of the disappearing men. He could hear them crashing through the underbrush, cussing loudly as they went.

In the distance, he could see the second pair in his party, galloping toward him and the shaken bank president. The signaling plan had worked, and soon the entire group had reassembled.

"Those robbers are thieves just lookin' for horses." Josh described the pair of attackers.

"Best we keep movin' as we're gonna' run out a' daylight soon." Jeremiah was the last to arrive.

Josh reloaded his rifle and talked to his assigned visitor.

"Good work, Mr. Ellis. You caught him just right and sent him to his knees."

Looking relieved, Ellis smiled slowly.

"Yes, I will have quite a story to tell them back at the bank, won't I?"

Several hours later, the weary party reached the office of Prather and Duncan. Josh accompanied them and stood by to escort them to their hotel once the deal was settled. He listened as George Sherman, from Titusville and the initiator of the deal introduced the threesome from Chicago.

"This gentleman is Joshua Ellis, president of the Second National Bank of Chicago; John LaMoyne and H.H. Honore, both businessmen from Chicago."

Prather nodded and gave a sign and all of the men had moved

away from the office entrance to a back room. Josh could see through the open doorway that the travelers were producing stacks of greenbacks and laying them on a table.

"No, this is not acceptable. We need payment in gold, not this paper money here." The harsh rejection cut through the still air like a hot knife through soft butter, and a deadly silence followed for just a few seconds.

"There must be some mistake. Judge Beckwith, our attorney advised that greenbacks are sufficient to make this here down payment." Josh could see Sherman's lean frame straighten to his full height.

"Don't care what Beckwith said. What we accept as payment is up to us, Colonel Duncan and I, not your attorney."

Sherman's voice rose in volume.

"But you never stipulated that the payment was to be in gold. I got the papers here to prove it. Your settlement terms are not specific, and to us, that means that you should accept the going currency."

"No need to argue, Mr. Sherman. The deal is off. Anyhow, sunset was thirty minutes ago. Business transactions terminate at sundown around here."

Josh could hear a shuffling of feet and then a loud bang on the table. Ellis, the banker, his fist clenched leaned over the table almost nose-to-nose with the Colonel.

"What kind of business ethics do you people in this wilderness practice? Sundown! Midnight is the end of any day, not sundown!"

The arguing went on as Josh shifted his position to gain a better view of the tense and disputing men. He thought that their carrying $400,000 in cash anywhere was risky, but to tote it all the way from Chicago to Pithole was foolhardy. And now it seemed as if they needed to endure further risk by Prather and Duncan's refusal to accept the cash. Were they going to carry all that cash back to Titusville by horseback, and then on to Chicago by train? He had never heard of such as this.

"You sons of polecats! What underhanded lowlife!"

Sherman and Honore restrained the banker who continued to pound his fists on the wobbling table.

"Not much we can do at this point, Mr. Ellis." Sherman's voice was shaking with rage. "No need getting' physical…"

Josh saw the Colonel move from behind the table with his

fists clenched. Ellis stepped backward several steps.

"You, Colonel Duncan and this shyster, Prather will be hearing from my attorney. This shady dealing of yours isn't over! We will expose your lousy deal."

"These businessmen traveled all the way from Chicago carrying a great amount of cash and now you are jiggerin' up the terms of this land deal—word will be getting' around about the ways of your slimy business practices!"

"This is not the last of this. We will see you in court!"

Josh ducked back to his earlier position near the outside entrance and the four men skulked out, breathing heavily. The tension in the air was palpable as he accompanied the rejected and furious-four to the Morey House on the north end of the town.

After seeing the men to their hotel, Josh sat inside the back entrance of the Morey where no prying eyes could see him. With his unlit cigar clenched between his teeth, he counted out Luke's twenty-five percent of his payment from the trip. He rode Topsy to the Widow Lyon's barn, then walked down the dark street to find Luke.

Pithole continued to support its reputation as the dominating oil field in the epicenter of Oildom. By the end of July, five Pithole wells were producing 2700 barrels a day. Savvy speculators and eager oilmen were in the process of putting down seventy more shafts with plans for more to come. The Holmden Farm was covered with wells, workers, and fervor for Pithole's boom.

For all the money that flowed from the oil industry and the ongoing enthusiasm for extracting petroleum, Pithole, the source of these riches went without necessities to the peril of the community. Cholera was sweeping the country and threatened thousands who lived in towns and cities with no real standards regarding health. With no water supply, nor sanitation, the population of Pithole was at risk. As well, for all the dangers of fires, no fire department nor any organization for fighting a fire existed. The situation appeared to be a perfect formula for disaster.

...

The entire town was buzzing with the news. Well number 77 came in on August 1st, followed on August 2nd by Number 19, named the Grant Well. Then on the third day of August, Well Number 63 struck. At first the Grant needed pumping, but after only four hours, it began to flow at the rate of 800 barrels. The thousands of additional barrels of oil caught the producers by surprise, and they scrambled to store the crude. Now Pithole was producing 7000 barrels a day with no end in sight. The excitement called for celebration and many did just that.

Men jammed the barrooms, toasting the town and its prodigious production of liquid gold. Dance halls were packed and fellows who could find a female partner swung then with gusto. Music emanated from restaurants and hotels. Things were hot in the oil boomtown.

Jubilance over the increased production, however, was soon suppressed. The sudden glut of petroleum sent the price at $8 per barrel into a depression of $4.50 and by August 10th, to $2.75 to $3 per barrel. History was repeating itself in this young and unregulated industry. The increase in production spun other consequences as well--dire consequences.

Oil storage created a fire hazard. Combustion continued to be the major threat to the industry and to the community. Guards were posted around the wells day and night in hopes of preventing incendiary events. Warnings were on clear display throughout the entire area: "NO SMOKING!" and "SMOKERS WILL BE HUNG!"

Two months earlier, two U.S. Petroleum Tanks of the Frazier Well, 2,500 barrels of oil each had burst. Five thousand barrels of crude oil had gushed into Pithole Creek. Word went out that two boys down the run had struck a match to see what would happen. They lit the oily waterway, sending yellow flames roaring up the valley. Two hundred men including teamsters had scrambled to build an earthen dam that contained the oil flow and stopped the conflagration below. With that concerted effort, a disaster was averted. The inhabitants of Pithole were well aware of the dangers of stored petroleum.

More recently on July 31, Lease Number 19 had a fire outbreak during drilling.

"Saw it myself. I was up there on the Holmden property when that thing caught fire. One quick-thinking gent forced the pipe down into the ground. Smothered it quick. Good thing. That burnin' oil could'a caught the whole place a' fire."

...

Teamster Mike Mulligan was sitting at the bar of French Kate's Restaurant, surrounded by the waitresses, Luke and Kate.

298

They were setting up for the dinner crowd just as he had arrived with his news.

"The price for a barrel o' oil has dropped to $2.75! Oil storage gonna be a problem again. These owners are gonna store more oil 'til the price goes up. That's a real fire hazard with the wells here puttin' out 7000 barrels a day…storin' more and more oil is a real fire hazard…"

Luke sat quietly, lost in thought.

Mabelle noticed his silence.

"Why Luke. What's the matter? Cat-got-your-tongue?"

Luke shrugged.

"Went through a terrible bad fire in Oil City. Don't ever want to see it again. River streaked with fire, oil barges blowin' up…it was awful."

They all fell silent.

Finally, Kate stood up. "Well, let's finish setting up so we can stay on schedule."

Mabelle put her arm around Luke and gave him a hug.

. . .

The next morning, August 2, Luke posted himself at the entrance to the Astor House and had only ten more newspapers to sell when he heard excited voices.

"The Grant was pumpin' fer about an hour when they said that all of a sudden it started comin' at a rate o' 800 barrels."

"Guess those producers weren't ready for a spouter at that rate o' flow, ya' think?"

"No! Oil just started pourin' out all over the place--on to the ground, glidin' toward the crik. Into the grass, all over the place."

"Let's go up and look…"

Luke knew what it looked like and knew what could happen. He stayed at his post until those ten papers were sold and he had the money in his pocket.

. . .

That night as Kate and her employees were closing down the restaurant, Mike arrived. His face was blackened, his shirt torn, and his boots, covered in mud.

Mabelle ran to get him a chair. He looked exhausted and was coughing. She brought him a mug of water as the cook prepared a plate of food for his late dinner. The group of Kate's girls stood around Mike in a silent vigilance, waiting for him to talk, to catch his breath from coughing.

When he finally tried to say something, it started out with a croaking sound--dry and crackly. He drank some water and stopped coughing.

"What happened? We heard there was a big spill up near the Grant. It musta' been bad."

"Yeah, it was bad." Mike managed to speak.

As the group waited patiently for him to recover further, several other teamsters came through the doorway. They, like Mike were regulars at Kate's. They looked weary as well.

"What happened up there at the Grant?" Jenny had just hired-on at Kate's and was new to the oil fields.

Big Sarge slumped down in a chair and accepted the mug of water handed him by Mabelle who remained at his side.

"A bunch of people came on up to see what was happenin' at the spill. The crowd got bigger 'n bigger 'til there must'a been a hundred onlookers there."

"And there was six or seven guys perched up on the derrick, too." Mike's voice sounded stronger.

"All the sudden there was this huge explosion." Big Sarge gestured with his hands.

"So, that's what we heard down here at the restaurant, about two hours ago?" Sunny poured water into the emptied glasses.

Big Sarge nodded.

"Yup." He took another drink. "Worst thing I ever saw, even havin' been in the war. That explosion set off a fire that leaped into the air in huge yellow flames. People screamin' and cryin'…like a scene out'a hell." He shook his head and looked down. Mabelle covered her open mouth with her hand. Her eyes were wide with horror.

"Worst of it was those guys sittin' up on that derrick. That sheet o' fire just rose up almost like it was after them. Awful…" Mike looked distressed. "Them poor devils didn't have a chance. Saw 'em fallin' like derrick apples. Must'a killed them all--burned 'em." Jenny put her arm around Mike's shaking shoulders.

"That whole area--maybe an acre--was a sheet of flames. Dense black smoke billowing all over." Big Sarge paused for a breath. "Come on outside here. You can see the smoke, and smell it, too."

They moved as one entity out into First Street and to the flat area near the creek. The waxing moon had just risen. Its usual golden-white light had turned an eerie red color. Clouds of smoke emanated from the area of the burn. Here and there, citizens were gathered in clusters, talking quietly. One woman was crying hysterically and a nearby newsboy stood stark still, his mouth ajar.

Luke had retreated into silence during the entire discussion. The explosion reminded him of the night that John Obadiah had disappeared and he, Uncle Matt and Jesse had searched while the fires burned around them. The Grant Well fire was different than the conflagration in Oil City.

At that location, there were no oil wells on the site of the initial explosion. The fire had started in an open barge filled with crude that exploded on the water at the mouth of Oil Creek and sent flames roaring from one loaded barge to another, destroying much of the large oil fleet. At the Grant, the actual well and surroundings were aflame, endangering other wells and storage tanks. Luke shivered. Fires are fires no matter where they are--dangerous, smoky, unpredictable and inevitable when oil was involved.

Finally, he spoke.

"Did some of the people there get to leave? Did anybody get burned up?"

The question seemed to stun the group as they huddled together in the red moonlight and the smoke.

"Let's go back inside. Maybe you can eat something."

Back in the restaurant again, Mike answered Luke's question.

"Don't know, Luke. So much confusion, smoke, heat and screamin'. Just don't know, yet."

"I can tell you that some of those folks on that derrick threw themselves into the crik to put out their burnin' clothes. One guy, Lucius Kingsley--they said from Syracuse--he was one of 'em hangin' on the derrick." He pause and took a breath. "He might'a been the attic hand on that rig. Don't know. He jumped from the supports into the crik to get his clothes wet. After that, he run through the fire. Tryin' to get to a safe place. On his way, he slipped and fell into a puddle of burnin' oil." Big Sarge paused and wiped his eyes with his singed shirtsleeve. He cleared his voice and continued.

"When he got to some of those people watchin' said he was so burned they didn't recognize him. He was a moanin', 'O my God, what shall I do? On, my God, what can I do?' By then, his clothes was burned off'a him, leavin' his back, arms, legs all blistered and burned. He was charred to the bones--'specially his hands. One of the workmen held him in his arms and showed the crowd of gapers his hands--just seared to the bones…." Big Sarge stopped and put his face in his hands and started to weep. "It was awful to see…"

By then, Mabelle, the cook, Jenny, Sunny and the other girls were crying softly. Mabelle went to comfort Big Sarge, and Jenny hugged Mike. A few minutes later, Mabelle took Luke's hand and they tried to soothe each other. After a few minutes, he spoke to his friend.

"The reason I asked if anybody got outa' the fire…" He hesitated. "Ya see, that Oil City fire I told you about…Well, my Pa' never was seen again--never could find him."

A stunned silence followed and then the sounds of their weeping got louder as Mabelle hugged him closer.

Later that evening, Luke rolled up in his blanket on the veranda at Kate's Restaurant and heard the adults talking. Sleepless, he listened while the consumption of alcohol seemed to change his boss's speech. Kate's words slurred and it sounded as if she fell asleep in the restaurant, instead of her bed upstairs. Luke thought he heard Mike and Big Sarge talking in their sleep. They almost sounded as if they were weeping.

The next day, word came down that twenty people were terribly scorched in the explosion and fire, and Lucius Kingsley died in the arms of his fellow worker at the scene. Various accounts appeared in newspapers across the country; some listed that seven people had died, but most of the victims leaped into the creek and saved themselves.

Luke's Luck

September 1865

With Pithole's population growing to nearly 15,000 by September 1865, no effective law enforcement, no potable drinking water, nor sanitation means had been established. The petroleum companies piped in their own water, but the general public had no such luxury. Pithole yet had no schools, no church buildings, no police, no theaters. Two preachers, one Methodist and the other, United Presbyterian arrived to start street-corner preaching, then held services in unfinished stables, hotels, and barrooms. Food was scarce and expensive; getting it required standing in a long line with other hungry people. Fresh food was especially lacking except during berry ripening season or apple harvest. When a barrel of oranges was shipped in, the arrival was announced as a news item since it happened so infrequently.

Of the sixty-two grocery stores, fifteen meat markets, and fifteen bakeries, only a few had much capacity. Prices in Pithole were fifteen to twenty percent higher than in Titusville. Every possible provision that was needed had to be packed in over abominable roads by a team and wagon or on horseback. Horses were a necessity.

Livery stables in both Titusville and Pithole had horses to rent. Businessmen and travelers could ride from one location to another since Titusville had twenty such stables, but Pithole lacked adequate facilities. Horses here frequently turned up missing. Thefts occurred nightly during the summer of 1865 and the ads offering rewards for their return documented these occurrences.

First Street was notorious for horse thefts, and those living in that area were well aware, sometimes from having experienced a theft. Luke had learned quickly, schooled by Kate the morning they had met on her front veranda. From that day on, Luke had stabled Topsy at the Widow Lyon's place, alongside Ellie, Josh's mule.

After his noon meal at French Kate's Restaurant, Luke usually hiked the mile up to Topsy's stable. Some days he would ride her, but not into Pithole. He followed a trail that led east and paralleled the Allegheny River. He did not want anyone to know that he owned a horse.

"I'll be back in time to set up for dinner." Luke picked up his plate and carried it to the washing pan. He saw Kate nod her approval, and once out the door and off of the veranda, Luke took off in a run up Brown Street.

As he approached the Widow Lyons' place, he thought something looked different, was not quite the same as during his previous visits. A wooden hoe lay on the ground at the side of the cabin. A half-full basket of beets was askew, near the hoe, as if carelessly dropped.

When he approached the entrance to the horse shed, Luke found it empty. Ellie's stall was vacant as well. Josh was on a regularly planned trip into Plumer that day, so Luke understood why Ellie was gone. She was with Josh. But Topsy, where was she?

Luke's stomach was flip-flopping and he began to feel sick. He walked around the cabin to the front door, and found it latched. Widow Lyon was not at home. Then he remembered. She was helping out at the Holmden's dining room at noontime on a daily basis.

But where was Topsy? He went back to the stall and looked around. Her halter was gone as well. Had Josh taken her with him? Luke couldn't imagine why he would do that without asking for permission.

He walked out of the stall and looked for tracks in the soft dirt. At first the strip of grass alongside the garden obscured the hoofprints, but then he saw them. They led out behind the cabin, away from the crest of the hill and the oil wells below.

Now the tracks were almost hidden by the wild grasses and bushes, but Luke stopped and started until he found the next hoofprint. He kept tracking for what he figured was a half mile. The sun was hot and he sat under a large oak tree to rest and cool-off.

Now, away from the hubbub surrounding the oil wells, the forest was quiet. He closed his eyes for a minute and then heard a noise. It sounded like someone chopping wood or hoeing a garden plot. Luke scrambled to his feet and followed the muffled thuds. The horse trail led that way as well, so he felt more confident in his search.

He moved forward quietly, not knowing what to expect, nor whom he would encounter. Horse thieves? Probably. When he came to the edge of a small clearing, he squatted on his haunches and waited. Just then the chopping sound ceased. Next, he saw movement near the left of a small log cabin, and a woman appeared with a hoe in her hand. She was wearing a checkered sunbonnet, a blue dress covered by a yellow apron, and knee-high boots. She sat down on a wooden bench near the door. He watched in silence. Why would the horse-tracks lead him here to this remote cabin, and who was this lady?

Suddenly, the woman scrambled to her feet and she stood with her back to the cabin door. Something had alerted her and she picked up the hoe as if it were a weapon. He watched intently, waiting. At the other side of the clearing, near the vigilant woman, the bushes swayed and shook. Now he could see something move out of the periphery of the cleared area.

The excited barking of an unseen dog broke the silence.

Slowly, a man stealthily emerged from the bushes and swaggered forward in a menacing manner. What was happening? Suddenly, the man laughed and lunged at the woman. She swung the hoe, hitting him on his shoulder. He grunted and stopped in his tracks. He swayed for a moment and then sprang at her with all of his weight. His opponent deftly side-stepped him but he caught her left boot at the ankle during his fall. She stomped her right heel on his wrist and he yelped.

"Get out of here, you fiend!"

"Not 'til I get a piece of you." He got to his feet and was holding his injured arm. He paused, glaring at her.

"Never mine. Where's the horse? I know you got one. Where is it?"

Hearing those words, Luke quickly picked up a downed tree limb, and plunged into the clearing. Both parties turned toward him when they heard him.

"You heard the lady. Get out of here."

Luke advanced toward the interloper who now had his eyes on him. He brandished his tree bough and ran toward his adversary, a man taller than he, but not so steady on his feet. As Luke got downwind of him, he could smell alcohol.

No longer the target of the intruder's aggressions, the intended victim silently approached the horse thief from behind and slammed the hoe over his head. As he staggered from the blow, Luke rammed the branch into his ribcage. He fell flat, gasping for air. Looking dazed, he crawled to a sitting position.

"Get up and get out of here!"

The woman then yelled something in a language that Luke

did not understand. Suddenly, a large snarling dog, bounded from the cabin. The woman gave the unwelcome bloke a swift kick in the buttocks that hastened his scrambling to his feet and running toward the bushes. The dog stalked him, growling and snapping at the intruder's boots and pantlegs.

"I want to be sure you're really leaving this time, instead of skulking in the bushes."

She pursued her adversary into the brush, whacking him with the hoe as they went. Luke followed her as she and her dog drove the man for a hundred yards or more. When they came to a steep incline and a boulder-strewn mountainside, she gave him a final crack on the head with a well-aimed hoe as he half tumbled, half crawled among the trees and rock outcroppings toward the Allegheny River below.

"Stay!" The obedient canine sat down abruptly and whined, his front paws treading the soil.

She picked up a large rock and threw it after the retreating interloper. Luke watched as it whacked the intruder on the shoulder. The pummeled man did not look back at her. He kept on running. The dog stood and barked ferociously.

As they watched the crook disappear into the brush along the river shoreline, the woman warrior paused to catch her breath, and her watchdog stopped woofing.

She turned to look at Luke.

"Thank you for your assistance." Then she bent forward and talked quietly to the dog. "Come." She started to reverse their trail, the canine leading the way.

"Do you have my horse?"

"Yes." As they slowed their pace to talk, she gave an order to the dog again.

"Home now!" Her animal-companion took off in a run toward the cabin.

"What are you doing with Topsy?"

"Keeping her safe from that thief and others. Widow Lyon's place is not so isolated now. More people moving into Pithole."

"So, you work for Widow Lyon in her garden?"

"Yes."

"So, you are the person who came to help after her renter left?"

"Yes."

"I'm Luke. Topsy is my horse. Thank you for taking care of

her."

"You are welcome."

"What's your name?"

Luke turned to look at the female fighter who had defended herself so well. She was younger than he expected. Her bonnet occluded his getting a good look at her.

"Susan."

"Nice to meet you, Susan."

She smiled and removed her head cover.

"I guess you don't remember me, Luke." They had arrived in the clearing around the cabin.

"Remember you? No, I can't say that I do. Never had made acquaintance with anyone named Susan." He looked at her quizzically.

"How would I know you?"

"I helped Elias pull you out of the Allegheny River four years ago."

Open-mouthed, Luke stopped dead in his tracks, confused. Then it hit him.

"Gala! Are you, Gala?" He gave her a hard stare and recognized the blue eyes and tan face.

"Gala! Oh, my goodness! It's really you!"

He moved toward her. Why was she dressed like that? His mind was racing.

A sudden rustling sound in the woods near the west side of the clearing startled Luke. Another horse thief? He saw Gala grip the hoe handle. He had abandoned his tree limb-weapon in the woods and looked for something else to use. Both stared toward the area of a disturbance in the quiet woods.

First Luke saw a black wide-brimmed hat, similar to his. A tall figure crashed through the underbrush.

"Luke, you here?"

As the man emerged, he thought he recognized the voice.

"Who's lookin' for Luke?" Luke widened his stance as the stranger approached at a rapid pace, his hat obscuring his face. The sun was in Luke's eyes, making it difficult for him to see.

"Luke? It's me, Elias." He took off his hat and Luke saw his eye patch and recognized his brother.

"Elias, what are you doing here? I thought you were working up on the plank road."

"I was. They let me off early because we are a bit ahead of

schedule and only two miles from Pithole. I told my boss that I wanted to come in here to see my family and see if there is any word..."

Luke looked at Gala who Elias seemed to have not noticed since she stood on his blind side.

"Elias, look who is here--lives here. Gala!"

Gala moved into Elias' vision, and he frowned.

"Gala?"

She turned her face toward him and stood smiling.

"Yes, Elias, it's me. I must look different to you than four years ago."

Elias seemed frozen, unable to move or speak. After several moments, he moved close to her, looked into her eyes, then wrapped his arms around her.

"I have been looking for you since I got back."

Finally, Gala broke their embrace and looked up at him.

"First, it was said that you had been killed in the war. That's what was being told down on the steamboat flats." She paused and took a shaky breath. "Then this man that I trade with, he works some at a hotel in Titusville. He told me that he had seen you there, but with a woman. Having dinner with her, and it looked...intimate. When I heard that, I thought you had brought someone back with you..."

Elias frowned.

"I had dinner with Katherine--Katherine Le Conte the night I got off the train. We met in a snow storm and she helped me get to a hotel. Couldn't see in the blowing snow." He paused. "She has a café in town here." Smiling, he paused. "No, she's not my woman. You are!"

Luke watched as the two held a long embrace, both weeping with joy.

"Now, I am home at last, really home." Elias broke the embrace and held Gala out to look at her more closely.

"What are you wearing? You look like a Pennsylvania farm girl."

She smiled through her tears.

"There is someone I want you to meet--both of you."

They walked with her to the cabin. She opened the door. First the dog emerged followed by a child. The canine walked protectively alongside a blonde-headed four-year-old who looked as if he'd just awakened from a nap. When the shy child turned away,

Mogwa nudged him toward his mother.

"Elias, this is little Elias."

With his arms out-stretched, Elias fell to his knees as his son hesitantly moved toward him. Mohwa remained beside the child. The dog sniffed Elias, then licked his outstretched hand, and whined softly. On her knees now, Gala put her arms around her son, his father and Mohwa. Both parents were weeping. Little Elias clung to his mother; the dog was silent.

Happy and excited, Luke sat on the ground and watched the long-awaited reunion.

Elias was really home now.

...

On September 25, Luke awoke with a start. He felt some urgency about this morning, but sleep-drugged, he could not remember why. As he pulled on his cold boots, he recalled that this was the first day of his new paper sales. Last night for the first time, The *Pithole Daily Record* had gone to press, and Mr. Morton had promised Luke the first fifty copies to sell at his post on Holmden Street near the Astor House, if he arrived by 5:00 A.M. He shivered as he buttoned his jacket against the early morning chill. He realized his sleeping accommodations were inadequate against the cold now, and he knew he needed to find another place. Kate's front veranda was fine for summer, but not so now that September was almost spent.

Dodging the wagon ruts and mud holes as he crossed First Street, he headed north on Holmden Street and ran the two blocks on a deserted wood-sidewalk to the newspaper office that was located across the plank-street from the Chase House. As he ran, he calculated his income. With two different newspapers to sell each morning, the *Titusville Herald* and the *Pithole Daily Record,* his income could double. Hopefully in several months, he could add money from his newspaper sales to the $20 Josh had paid him and buy a sixteenth interest in an oil well. He had been disappointed when he learned that he had lost out on the deal to be the first to save $100 in Mr. Prather's bank. Instead, another newsboy had won the prize offered by the banker.

Then his mind jumped to what he had overheard last evening when he was clearing tables at French Kate's Restaurant, Kate and Mabelle had been discussing the new hotel...

"I went up to take a look at the Chase House the day it

309

opened. I'd say it has it all, the post office on the first floor, the Western Union Telegraph office on the second, and a beautiful reading room and library. Oh, and the other good thing. They've just completed the plank-surfaced section of Holmden Street in front of the Chase House."

Mabelle had chimed in.

"They say that it's lit by gas lights and heated by steam, and can bed 500 guests. Then there's double verandas and steps leading to the second floor from the sidewalk. That's something,' ain't it?"

Kate had nodded as she wiped off tables, and Mabelle took it as encouragement to continue. "And, Miss Kate, they say that there is a huge dining room and plush--that's what my friend called it--a 'plush' ladies lounge."

Mabelle paused and looked around, then sidled-up close to Kate and continued in a conspiratorial manner.

"The taproom has a long wooden bar with pictures of women--almost no clothes on." She giggled and both looked toward Luke who appeared not to have overheard this description.

But Luke had been listening with interest. The only hotel Luke had ever entered was the Astor House, and from what he had seen, it was not grand, and did not seem to be any match for the Chase House. Now for sure, he wanted to get a look at the Chase House for himself, especially the taproom and those wall-hung pictures. He grinned, then pulled himself from the thought as he approached his destination…

Breathing hard, he pounded on the office door of the *Pithole Daily Record* with his freezing fist. Frank Spare, Morton's business associate opened the door immediately.

"You're right on time, Luke. I like that in a young lad." He thrust a pile of newspapers into the boy's outstretched arms. The gratified recipient of the stack noticed that Spare did not smile, but seemed weary, his eyes red, his hair disheveled, and his beard, harbored bread crumbs.

"Good luck, lad. Come back here when you've sold them all." Then he paused and managed a dog-tired smile of happy fatigue. "'Tiz a great day! Our first hometown publication for Pithole. This newspaper will bring the people together--people from everywhere, suddenly in Pithole." Spare's appearance belied his enthusiasm.

Luke thanked him and departed for his post at the Astor House. He determined that it was going to be a good day. His income was about to increase.

The advent of the *Pithole Daily Record* was a response to the growing petroleum production of the Pithole wells that attracted yet another wave of enthusiastic entrepreneurs and eager employment enquirers who washed into the area. In fact, so many folks overran the hotel capacities and other civic amenities.

During September, town leaders had initiated a petition to incorporate the expanding municipality. The increasing drinking water shortage had reached a crisis. Street peddlers sold water for fifty cents a barrel and hotels and restaurants paid to have water hauled in for their use. Early that month, the newly organized Pithole Water Company searched for an untainted water source, digging by hand to the bedrock for water near the top of the hill on the Morey property, a good distance from operating oil wells. After erecting a derrick and engine shack, they struck water at 189-feet on September 27. A spray of written applications washed into the office of the water company located nearby the United States Petroleum office and the water company took immediate action.

Crews laid water mains on First and Holmden Streets for customers who were mainly businesses and a sprinkling of private households. Connections were included as a means of fighting fires. However, the lack of adequate funding and absence of an authority to support the water company resulted in a failure to retain water in the modern mains at night. The citizen's conflagration concerns were only partially assuaged since water pressure was episodically inadequate for effective fire-fighting.

The burgeoning population of 15,000 prompted an attempt to meet not only the need for water, but the other city services as well. Charlie Highberger was sworn in as a justice of the peace. Several other men were appointed to provide policing in hopes of bringing some order to the teaming town. Restaurants and dance halls fronted flourishing prostitution and the number of barrooms were on the rise by mid-September. Gambling, the lifeblood of many adventurists and freebooters, included gaming opportunities that abounded at most drinking establishments. Faro banks were set up anywhere there was a vacated, turned-over box, fleecing the uninitiated of their money. Other forms of entertainment emerged when the construction of Murphy's and the Athenaeum Theaters neared completion.

Eager audiences anticipated potential performances. Posters advertising "Octaroon" featuring Billy Forest for the opening show, and other bulletins promised "Macbeth" for future viewing. Murphy's Theater became Pithole's most impressive structure with its three-story height, auditorium with 1,100 comfortable seats: 800 in the orchestra section and 250 in the gallery. The commodious construction paraded a half-dozen carpeted boxes, luxurious damask draperies, and included an orchestra pit designed to accommodate twelve instrumentalists. The stage curtain that depicting scenes of the oil region originated in New York City as did the Tiffany-created chandeliers that dazzled the theater-goers. Such cultural opportunities radiated the aura of community pride and possible permanence, amid the lack of practical improvements.

The importance of moving oil and dependence on countless teams of horses and wagons to perform this vital task created a paradox with the cultural advances of the community. Streets remained deep in the mud ruts of slick sludge and horse manure. Mabelle had complained to Kate about her difficulties when she attempted the navigate the Pithole's streets.

"Why, Miss Kate, it's getting' worse out there. I was tryin' to walk up to the post office. When it came to crossin' Second Street, I looked for a good place to try'en cross, but could spy not even one. So, with the mud so deep-I got out'a both my shoes and stockin's, then waded into it up above my knees. Just had to close my eyes to some of those fellas watchin' me, but then I thought maybe it was good for our evening trade here, if you know what I mean." She giggled.

Kate had smiled and continued to polish glasses at the bar. "I don't think you need to advertise, Mabelle. Business is steady every night."

Mabelle seemed unphased by Kate's comment. "Good thing we have a bucket of water right outside the door for folks to scrub their feet. Otherwise this floor here would be messed up with mud and smell like National Livery Stables right up the street."

There were some other signs of a promising future for Pithole. Visitors came to view Pithole, important visitors. Millionaires, bank executives, businessmen, war heroes and politicians. The continuous stream of serious investors, stockholders, wildcatters and those just plain inquisitive individuals stressed the services of the boomtown, and inspired the citizens to sign the circulating petition for organizing and making improvements.

As the request for incorporation of Pithole ground forward

at glacial speed, talk of voting and office-holding emerged from the shadows created by oil news. Candidates advertised in the newspapers, published brochures, and made promises of mainly "good government," their knowledge and compliance with election rules, questionable. Since Pennsylvania law read that only men of one-year residency were eligible to vote, some of the candidates for office failed to meet that requirement. The legality of their service in office, if elected, weighed heavily on some of the occupants of the flourishing oil town.

The fact that newspaper sales hit a daily high of 8000 and the recently-published Pithole Directory listed the city's businesses seemed to speak to the growing importance and permanence of Pithole.

Business is Booming

October 1865

It was true. Business was booming. Holmden Street, the longest of five parallel streets in Pithole had acquired the appearance of a prosperous business district. A half dozen hotels were under construction. Both sides of the street had large signs, Christy's Drug Store, William Stewart's Clothing and Notions, and Hubb House, to attract busy buyers to their successful establishments. Resourceful businessmen like Capt. J.J. Vandergrift had developed an entire city block that housed small shops, a theater, and a hardware store. Workers and visitors swarmed the muddy street, coming and going from the Chase House, the famous center of the growing community where new-comers arrived every day.

The influx of workers and visitors into Oildom increased the rising tempo of daily business in Pithole. One of the busiest services in the thriving town was the United States Post Office.

…

The early October day was clear and cool due to the steady rain that had cleansed the air the evening before. Kate gathered her skirts in preparation to cross the slimy street. As a matter of practicality, except for special occasions, she had given up wearing hoops under her skirts back in July when she moved into Pithole. The ungainly fashion seemed to agree with city-dwelling women who tread on solid streets and level walkways. In muddy Pithole, the hems of her skirts were constantly caked with mire. Here, unlike Titusville, there were no services to beat mud from women's wear. She adjusted her broad-brimmed straw hat with her left hand, pulled on the door handle of the post office, and entered.

As soon as this postal service was initiated on July 20, 1865, she had established a post office box for her business, French Kate's Restaurant. Finally, she had a means of communicating with Ebenezer and cousin Fredrick, instead of relying on telegrams or Barnswell Buchanan to forward correspondence that would come to Franklin. That came as a real relief.

As well, she seemed to have escaped any pursuers since the last of the Rebels operating in Canada and some of Booth's co-conspirators had been caught and executed. Now, she felt more confident moving about in the hubbub of this thriving oil town. Such an influx of strangers helped her keep out of the limelight. No more intimidating border guards; no more heinous headlines about the war, nor "wanted" bulletins bearing her name. Had her stepfather given up on his attempts to legally acquire her Brooklyn property? Things seemed to have calmed down. She had a thriving business. She was making money on her own from the proceeds of the restaurant and the payments—her cut—from the girls' evening pursuits.

As she emerged from the post office, she paused just outside the entrance. Her eyes swept the surroundings from left to right, a habit engrained in her surveillance precautions as a courier for the Rebels during the war. She spotted a familiar figure to her right.

Luke. She wondered what he was doing at the head of a growing line of people who did not have their own post office boxes as she did. They were compelled to stand in line for general delivery and await their turns at one of the two windows manned by Mr. S.S. Hill, the well-known postmaster, or one of his seven assistants to pick up their mail. The lengthy line snaked from the post office down the sidewalk for about fifty yards and was made up mostly of impatient young men who were roughhousing and shoving each other out of line and off the sidewalk into the murky mud.

Was Luke getting mail from someone? She walked over to talk with him. She thought he seemed surprised to see her standing beside him. He immediately answered her inquiry.

"Oh, Miss Kate, I am here to earn some money since all of my papers are sold."

"How are you earning money, standing here in line?"

"Well, some folks don't wanna stand here for an hour waitin' for Mr. Hill to open-up his windows for handin' out mail. So, some of us paperboys stand-in for 'em. They pay us to take our places in line. I can get ten cents just for doin' that. Fer, me that's like sellin' five copies of the *Titusville Morning Herald*. So, when I finish paper sales on time, I come up here and meet my friends and stand in line before they open the window inside. In 'bout an hour, I can sell my place and then go see Topsy and visit Gala and Little Elias, up yonder." He gestured toward the hillside behind them."

"Little Elias took his first ride on Topsy yesterday, 'afore the rain come in. Gala and I walked Topsy while Little Elias held on to her mane."

"Did he like his first ride?"

"Well at first, he was a bit a'scared, but after a few minutes, he was laughin'."

Two of the newspaper boys standing nearby walked over to Luke.

"You gotta a horse, Luke?"

Luke appeared surprised by the question. He glanced at Kate who had warned him about horse thieves. She watched as he put his left hand behind his back and crossed his fingers, as if to be forgiven for the lie that was coming next.

"Oh, no, Gustav. It's my brother's horse, and it's only up there for a short time—not there much longer."

He looked around to see who else might have overheard the discussion about Topsy. Did Kate know he was renting out his horse to some of Emma's girls across the street at the Florence Restaurant? Those waitresses paraded through town regularly, all dressed up, waving to all of the men they encountered. He wondered if she knew he was making money from their parades. He dismissed the thought and turned toward his friends, but addressed Kate.

"This here is Gustav, and this is Fred." Katherine nodded and was glad to change the focus of the conversation away from the horse.

"Yeah, we hold a place in line like Luke said. On a nice day like today, we make about ten cents, but on rainy days when nobody wants to stand out here, I've made twenty-five cents." Gustav turned toward Kate.

"Yeah' ya' gotta bargain with 'em. Rainy days are good for us' cause of that." Fred spoke quietly, looking down at his feet.

"It rains a lot here, just like in Buffalo—but not so windy."

"You're down here from way up there on the lake?"

"Yeah, my ma and pa are dead, and I got adopted by some people up there."

"Why are you here in Pithole? Do those people know where you are?" Kate was curious.

"Not sure. I left them a note, but don't know if they read it. They already had four chillens and I felt out of place." Fred looked at her. "You got chillens?"

The orphan's question caught her by surprise, and memories of her life in France flooded over her. She shook her head as if to clear away those thoughts.

"No, not here in Pithole."

"Where do you stay—sleep at night?"

Gustav spoke first.

"Well, I make enough money to stay at the Barton and Begerly Boarding House on Prather Street, and mostly, it's good."

Fred hunched his skinny shoulders and dug his toe into the mud along the edge of the plank sidewalk.

"I been stayin' in a hay loft, down at the Astor and Metropolitan Stables on Holmden. They allows some of us to sleep there." He paused. "I eat with Gustav at the Young American Restaurant."

"The boarding house don't include no breakfast, so I get my meals there too, like Fred said. Most of us eat there 'cause they give us paperboys a cut-rate. They treat us good."

"Yeah, I like that place 'cause you can have as many potatoes as you want. I love potatoes." Fred smiled shyly.

Kate said goodbye to the boys, then patted Luke on the shoulder and gave him an approving nod before she started for the restaurant. She thought that he had listened and learned about the danger of horse thieves. Often, it's not safe to tell the truth. Not in these times with so many strangers in town.

The numerous new arrivals in Pithole had pushed the U.S. Post Office out of its original location and into the Chase House where there was much more space. Sorting 3000 incoming and about the same number of outgoing pieces of mail a day required more commodious accommodations. Single men, many of them veterans of the now-concluded War of Rebellion eagerly awaited news from girlfriends or relatives back home. Over the past three months, 20,000 letters remained unclaimed and had to be held in the Pithole's dead-letter office that took up yet more space. All of that untaken mail was a sign of how some people came for a while and then left Pithole. The population was fluid. The *Pithole Daily Record* listed this unclaimed mail alphabetically in two columns: men and women. Mr. Hill's figures indicated that the Pithole Post Office ranked number three in Pennsylvania, only Pittsburgh and Philadelphia managing more volumes.

Kate returned to her place to find Mike Mulligan sitting at the bar with Big Sarge and Herman. After greeting her, they resumed their conversation that as she noted was subdued and she heard them laugh.

A line of ravenous men was forming outside for the dinner meal. Kate hurried to begin setting up for the onslaught of the hungry. She was listening with interest to the teamster's conversation, just like her prior life of ease-dropping for the Confederates.

"But Mike, like I said, those plank roads have been to our advantage, makes traveling with all that weight, easier. What I am concerned about are those pipelines that are bein' laid from here to Miller's Farm. Course it's uphill and they gotta pump it, but it's goin'a cut into the amount of oil that we're gonna have—for us to haul."

Mike shifted in his seat.

"You weren't on Oil Creek in 1862, Sarge. You were fightin' in the war. But the idea about oil pipelines has been around for some time. See, this Samuel Brown and a couple of other gents proposed to pipe crude from the wells up along the creek to send oil down to the Allegheny. Tryin' to get around the freshet system—good reason. It was mighty expensive and dangerous. They tried a section of pipes, but the joints were so defective that that oil leaked so bad that they gave it up—sold out. So, then Ole' Henry Harley gave pipin' a try—laid five-and-a half-inch pipes from the Nobel Well below Schaffer Farm to the railroad station—end of the line. Now, he used lead to seal the joints, but after layin' over two-mile o' pipe some of our drivers cut the lines and set fire to the storage tanks." He chuckled. "'Course the thing leaked—lost a lot o' oil. It was an expensive disaster. Ya' see, I look at what's happened, and just don't worry too much about pipes carryin' oil. Some of those inventor guys are squirrely—crazy ideas."

Sarge nodded.

"Well, Mike, I keep hearin' about that oil buyer, Van Syckel. I haven't gone over there to look—too busy hauling oil—but it's said he's got workmen layin' two-inch pipe from Pithole across to Miller Farm. Started that back, first week of this month. Lapweldin' fifteen-foot lengths."

"How far they gotta' go—how many miles, ya' think?" Herman took a drink of his whisky.

Mike laughed.

"Ya,' I been hearin' about that project. One gent I talked to said those pipes are layin' on top of the ground—most of 'em. Some parts buried shallow. Tryin' to keep the grade right." He slapped Sarge on the shoulder, then lowered his voice.

"Won't be too hard to get to those pipes, will it, Sarge? 'Course, that sayin' that the nutty idea of sending oil through a pipe works."

"Not with five-and-a-half miles of pipe to pick from, it won't. Not enough armed guards to keep it all under a watch."

"We'll be makin' them pipes leak real bad," Herman sniggered.

They looked around to see if anyone were listening to their discussion. The doors had opened for the evening meal, but the eager- eaters paid no attention to Mike and his comrades. They were focused on one thing—food. Amidst the swarm of hungry men, Jeremiah entered the crowded café. When he spotted Kate behind the bar, he decided to forego a vacant dining chair, and sauntered over to the end of the bar where she was working. He took a seat across from her.

"Hello, Kate. I'm still tryin' to get used to your name-change…" He looked around and then lowered his voice.

"I see you got some of those teamsters hangin' around your place."

"They got money, Jeremiah, lots of it."

"Well, we both know why. Those guys have a stranglehold on the oil industry. Gotta have them to haul the oil outa here, ya know. They been gouging' the producers for months. Prices are outta sight for some of the independent, small oil producers who can't afford their steep rates-$3.15 a barrel. What really got me was when they raised their rates to $4.00 when production was high and oil storage at dangerous levels. They really are in a powerful position."

"Yes, I know. What's important to me is their money. They gave my restaurant a good start. I don't know if I could have stayed in business back in July, if it hadn't been for Mike over there."

"So far, they're keeping ahead of the changes that are comin' soon."

"Changes, what changes?"

"Awe come on, Kate. You hear them talkin'—talkin' about the oil pipelines that are bein' built to Miller Farm. Next, I hear there's one planned for Henrys Bend—and that's all downhill, gravity-run, to the Allegheny, not pumped like Van Syckel's pipes up to Miller Farm."

"Yes, I am aware of that."

"I hear that with three pumps on the Miller Farm rig-up will amount to what 300 teams can move workin' ten hours a day. That much oil will be pumped a day!" He stopped talking, and looked around at the diners and then at the teamsters who were at the far end of the bar.

"Kate, that's gonna put these teamsters in a bad spot. They're gonna be outa a job. And then when the gravity pipeline gets workin', it'll be a crisis for these guys who have been gouging' the oilmen for over a year." He paused and lowered his voice even more.

"I know from the plank road revenuers that those guys even drove over the new plank road to almost the end, then got off into the mud to avoid payin' the toll. They're a bunch of greedy crooks."

Kate leaned toward him over the bar.

"I appreciate your information." She leaned close to his ear. "I've warned the girls that things could get rough—both monetarily as well as physical." She paused. "Just when my business is going well for me." She frowned and left to wait on two arriving customers at the bar.

When she returned a few minutes later, Jeremiah ordered a drink. She poured his and a shot for her herself. She smiled and toasted his glass.

"Thanks, Jeremiah." She downed her whisky, then departed to wait on her customers.   …

Luke met Gustav at the post office and they stood together in the growing line. It had begun to rain. They were expecting Fred, but after a half an hour, he did not show up as planned. Both boys sold their spots in line at the same time for twenty-five cents each.

"Let's see if Fred is at the restaurant."

They walked down the plank sidewalk to its end, then plunged into the muddy street. The rain increased and the mud grew more slippery. They ran to the Young American Restaurant, but Fred was not among the boys on the covered porch who were pitching pennies, nor was he eating dinner. Gustav looked perplexed.

"Where else would Fred be? He's usually with us."

Luke shrugged.

"Let's check the hayloft at the livery stable. He might be there. It's so rainy, he may have just gone to sleep early."

They slogged through muddy Holmden Street to the stables. The familiar odor of horses and damp hay spurred Luke on, and he climbed the loft ladder, leaving Gustav on the bottom rung. The overcast, rainy conditions made it difficult to see among the beds of straw and he requested a light. Gustav asked the stable's farrier to borrow his lantern, then climbed to the place where Fred and Luke slept during cold weather. By the lantern's light, they spotted a small figure lying in the hay.

"Fred, we found you. Come on to dinner with us."

Fred did not stir and Luke moved the lantern as close as he dared to the flammable grass. He shook Fred by the shoulder, but Fred did not awaken.

"Gustav, come look at Fred. I can't see him breathin', not movin' either." He paused while Gustav crawled up the short ladder and into the hay-bed.

"Fred, wake up. We want to go to eat now." Gustav waited for a response.

Still Fred did not stir. The boys looked at each other. Gustav spoke first.

"You wait here. I am going to get Doc Waring across the street."

A few minutes later, Gustav returned with a young physician, one of nineteen who were practicing in Pithole that fall. Dr. J.D. Waring clambered up the ladder and into the hay. He placed his hand on Fred's torso, then produced his stethoscope, and unbuttoned Fred's shirt. He held the scope to their friend's chest and signaled from the boys to be still. The doctor withdrew the instrument and sat back on his haunches.

"Boys, help me carry your friend to my office."

Once there, they laid Fred on an exam table. Luke thought Fred's face looked white and he still did not move. Several minutes after arriving, Dr. Waring told Gustav to knock on the next door and ask for Dr. Lamb to come to his office. Soon both physicians were bending over Fred's limp body.

"Boys, Fred is dead." Dr. Lamb paused, then asked, "Has he been sick?"

Luke remembered that Fred had been coughing for about a week, and told the doctors.

"Does he have family here?"

Gustav explained Fred's lack of parents and departure from the home of a couple in Buffalo who had adopted him. Dr. Lamb bowed his head at hearing the story, and signed.

"Too bad…"

An hour later, Luke walked slowly through the fallen leaves

that were swirling over the mud ruts on Brown Street. With a heavy heart, he arrived on Kate's veranda and sat down to scrape off the sticky mud that clung to his boots. Although it was yet afternoon, the overcast skies brought on the darkness earlier than usual. It seemed to Luke that today's clouds and sinking sun had cut short the daylight, like the untimely death of his young, frail friend.

Gustav and Luke broke the news to the other paperboys. At learning about Fred's demise, Nicholas from Chicago had crossed himself and others of the group had grown uncharacteristically quiet, for these usually ebullient boys. The downcast comrades, all of them struggling for survival had silently passed the hat among their number and collected money from anyone of them who could give. The funds were meant for a small coffin and conveyance of Fred's body to his adoptive parents, the Simmonds in Buffalo. It was Luke's job to arrange for transporting the body. Memories of the day's events sent shivers down his spine, and he hurried inside to the warmth of the restaurant's kitchen.

Mabelle looked up from eating a bowl of steaming Stew. Instead of joining her, Luke began to set the tables for dinner.

"Luke, this here stew is really good. Cook saved you some."

He just shook his head. Struggling for self-control, he could not trust his voice. Mabelle gently pulled him to a chair beside her.

"Luke, what's wrong?"

His friend easily extracted the story about Fred's death, and the collected money for his coffin and transport.

Trying to constrain his anguish, Luke finally trusted his voice and sought Mabelle's advice.

"Which teamster should I ask to take Fred's body back to his folks in Buffalo?"

Mabelle's sad expression showed her concern.

"Ask Sarge. He's from Tonawanda, near Buffalo."

Luke dug into his pocket for the money meant for returning Fred's body. His eyes filled with tears as he approached Sarge who was talking with Mike at the bar. He quickly wiped them away, cleared his throat, and stood beside him, waiting for Mike to recognize him.

Both men turned to Luke at once.

"Hello, Luke."

Luke stammered and then told them about finding Fred, and the doctors' conclusions.

"Dr. Lamb thinks that Fred died of pneumonia. Said his lungs must'a been infected and he couldn't breathe any more. Dr. Waring wrote a letter to take to Fred's parents. I've got money here that we paperboys collected." He held out the collection of greenbacks and coins.

He paused, choking back tears.

"Is anyone driving to Buffalo with a load, ya' think?" He waited, afraid that he would cry in front of these men. He swallowed hard, looked down at his mud-streaked boots and tried to think of something other than Fred's limp, lifeless body and pale, pinched face. Fred had been one of his closest friends.

After a minute, he felt a hand on his arm.

"It's settled, Luke. Sarge will take care of getting his body back to Buffalo. You keep the money for your friends. No need to pay. We teamsters will take care of the transportation. Just give me the information about his family."

Relieved and grateful, Luke carefully produced an envelope bearing the location of Fred's adoptive parents. Inside was Dr. Waring's consoling letter.

The next morning the dominating derricks bore black against the red streaks of dawn as the oil-stained wagon bearing the body of the boy from Buffalo lumbered over the rough ruts of First Street toward Titusville. Solemn newspaper boys gathered along the rutted route in a silent salute to one of their own.

Later as they returned to their respective newspaper posts, Gustav and Luke noticed that more men than usual were calling to them for newspapers.

"Seems to be a lot of people in town. Good for sales, and it's not raining, either."

Neither Pithole residents nor *the Pithole Daily Record* were impressed with visitors to the renowned oil town. Speculators, politicians, the well-known, and the curious as well as those seeking employment were a perpetual presence in the thriving market. However, this time, they did take notice. On this occasion, 200 wealthy men and tagalong newspapermen had accepted the invitation of Charles Vernon Culver, a thirty-five-year-old politician, banker, and speculator to visit the site of a proposed town. He called his planned town, Reno, naming it for Major General Jesse L. Reno who had been killed in 1862 at the Battle of South Mountain in Maryland. The site of his proposal was located on the Allegheny River between Oil City and Franklin, where Reno had spent his boyhood.

Claiming that large amounts of oil lay hidden in that location near Reno, Culver had arranged the sales and leasing of laid-out lots whose future oil production as well as that in Pithole would be supported by a railroad.

The second railroad proposed for the area that included Pithole was that of Charles Culver's assemblage. General Burnside, a Civil War hero was already employed as its Chief Engineer and President. This rail network would eventually be called the Reno, Oil Creek and Pithole Railroad. Within a month, this railway project was taking construction bids, hiring on thousands of men, and staking out the route. The plan to move both passengers and oil might come to fruition quickly, since work had already begun.

To prove that there was an abundance of petroleum in the area, Culver included Pithole in their itinerary. Unlike Pithole, however, the community Culver had conceived was a utopian dream with no drinking nor gambling, clean, with uncluttered houses, neat yards, and a pleasant place for the wealthy owners and oil businessmen to live while engaged in controlling their oil fields. Reno would relieve these important men of living in rough circumstances such as Pithole or nearby Petroleum Center.

All he needed were entrepreneurs who wanted a quick turn-around of their investment and a total of $10,000,000.

This tsunami of 200 additional travelers caused extra strain on already crowded conditions at the Morey House. Despite their wealth and renown, these men who had toured the working wells of U.S. Petroleum, heard speeches by successful oil men, and been wine-and-dined into the wee hours were crammed into accommodations where they slept eight to ten in a room so crowded that some were forced to sleep on the floor.

For all of his efforts, not only did Culver get seventy-five per cent of his guests to invest, but the newspaper boys had a hay-day with newspaper sales exceeding what most of them had ever experienced. All of this activity plus Pithole's October oil production of 8000 barrels a day was further proof that the town was prosperous and had a promising future.

...

With all the talk about the prodigious production of the Pithole wells, the continuing consternation about the cost of moving the surfaced oil was about to change. Thousands of teamsters, like

Mike, Sarge and Herman had been keeping an eye on the efforts of devising improvements in the method of delivering oil from Pithole to refineries.

The wagon drivers were well aware that the construction of the plank-roads was near completion, and that the improved roads would get them out of the mud. The plank roads did not alter the amount of oil they carried, neither diminished nor increased their work, but just made it easier. The distances remained the same. Railroads had been proposed and were under construction. Those too were not yet a direct threat to teamsters' traffic. However, when oil pipelines moved forward and threatened to be successful, the drivers paid attention.

They knew that oil pipelines had been tried and failed over the past three years, large amounts of money, time and equipment, lost or wasted, but when Van Syckel's persistent efforts appeared to be gaining ground, the teamsters sat straight-up in their wagons and focused on the issue.

That powerful group of teamsters was the one entity that brought forth pushback to pipeline plans. The earlier failures at attempting to send oil by pipe had reaped the ire and ridicule of many bystanders. Those who proposed such delivery of oil were considered dreamers, or schemers. Now with Van Syckel's project threatening to be successful, many considered that sending oil through pipelines was the equivalent of taking bread from the mouths of children, or of legalized robbery. Other dissenters claimed it infringed on the rights of drivers to earn a living, like striking a fatal blow in the head of those who moved oil by horses and wagon. Pipelines would kill their means of a livelihood, a lucrative job and control of their incomes.

As the pipeline from Miller Farm to Pithole moved ahead, the teamsters voiced their opposition. When their complaints and concerns went unheeded, their verbalizations progressed to making plans for taking action. Defensive strategies converted to offensive schemes. They were not about to stand helplessly by while a new technology might prove them to be behind the times, and useless.

Kate watched and listened carefully as this wave of new know-how swept over the boomtown. Her restaurant morphed from a friendly meeting place for Mike and several other drivers, to a teeming, testy atmosphere created by a rougher crowd than yet, she had experienced. She kept a close watch over her successful business.

___

One late afternoon in mid-October, a gang of thirty-some drivers arrived two-hours prior to the advertised dinner-seating at French Kate's Restaurant. They went directly to the bar, then sat in a group on one side of the dining room, drinking, smoking, chewing and spitting at random. An intense discussion quickly ensued, and she thought it too late to get Mike or Sarge's attention to setup ground rules to restrain this boorish bunch. By the time the tables were to be setup for dinner, several of the agitated men were talking loudly, making clear their intent to foment discord and show their anger about the endangerment of their jobs.

Finally, Kate's patience wore thin. The restaurant was heavy with tobacco smoke. It sickened her. These men's refusal to use the spittoon supplied at the end of each table or the oblivion of its function made her short-tempered. She pulled Mike aside and gave him an ultimatum.

"Mike, get this crowd out of here. I have customers to feed. Look at the mess they made. I hope Luke gets here soon. I need him to clean up after those ruffians. Where did they come from? I never saw them before this."

Without an argument, Mike complied, and within minutes, the noisy, drunken and agitated drivers departed. Just then Luke came through the door.

"Who are those men?"

Kate gave him a warning glance and he stopped in his tracks.

Stone-faced, Mike looked at Kate and then, Luke, Mabelle, Jenny, Sunny and the other workers, then addressed them as a group.

"Stay off the streets after dark. We just made plans to get the attention of the oil producers and the pipeline men. They are plotting to take our jobs away. That isn't gonna happen!"

He set his jaw, tipped his broad-brimmed hat, turned his back to his audience, and stalked out the door past the growing line of diners.

Luke winced when he heard the Mike's advice. How different Mike was than earlier when he arranged for Sarge to deliver Fred's body to Buffalo.

Luke shivered.

Trouble's in the Wind

November 1865

Luke descended from the rough wooden platform that held his straw bed at the Astor and Metropolitan Stables at 22 Holmden Street. A pang of remorse flowed through him. No more being with Fred. His feelings of loneliness were persisting every day since his friend's death, especially when he had dinner at the Young American Restaurant or climbed the ladder to the hayloft. He shook away the sad feeling, and pulled on his boots.

The air was brisk and to warm up, he moved faster along the muddy street toward the *Pithole Daily Record*. Upon his arrival, Frank Spare poked his head out at Luke's knock on the door.

"Here's the day's headliner for you, Luke. This is an important article. It's on the first page." He paused. "Come on in, lad. It's cold out there."

Luke sat on a wooden crate near the door in a room crammed with boxes of paper, a cluttered desk, and a potbellied stove that emitted a welcome warmth. Spare went on.

"A group of oilmen have banded together--met several days ago in Titusville to make decisions about stabilizing the petroleum industry. Their first big decision is about the size of future oil barrels. Before this, a barrel of oil was thirty-eight to fifty gallons. Now the coopers will need to comply with the new standard and make barrels so that they can hold forty-two to forty-six gallons." He paused and looked straight at Luke.

"So, that's a good holler-out for you this morning. 'Decision on the size of oil barrels!'"

Luke nodded and got to his feet.

"Thanks, Mr. Spare. How about giving me some extra copies of the *Daily Record* today?"

The need to reign-in the mushrooming oil industry arose from a number of issues. Since 1859, the ways of managing oil remained primitive. From the early practices of running a short wooden pipeline from a well to a barrel, or pumping petroleum into large, leaky wooden holding tanks for movement by bulk boats, or wooden barrels had made little progress.

Early on, barrels were gathered up from any source and the

sizes varied widely. Barrels remained the mainstay of moving oil, when they became available. These containers were high demand from the start.

Coopers, mainly from New England who had lost their jobs in the waning whaling industry flocked into Northwestern Pennsylvania's oil fields. Whale oil generally had been calculated at forty-two gallons a barrel or by the old English measurement, a tierce. A single cooper in a small shop could turn out six to twenty barrels a day. Coopers with larger manufacturing businesses located wherever the need for oil barrels was greatest, along Oil Creek, in Titusville, Franklin and Oil City.

Some barrel makers succumbed to pressure from oil producers or tricky teamsters to manufacture barrels with false bottoms, heavy staves, or bung-holes that required oil gauges to enter at an oblique slant and provide elevated readings. Oil traders of good repute stipulated that barrels measure forty-two or forty-four gallons a barrel. Deceitful barrel sizes were compounded by other dishonest practices that clouded the petroleum industry.

Withholding crude from the market when the price per barrel dropped, and dumping oil onto the market when the price per barrel rose had been a contentious custom since 1861. The small producers suffered the most during these fluctuations since many had limited storage facilities or their pine-plank storage tanks leaked, diminishing profits when they did sell. Pressure from creditors, laborers in need of work, and high fuel costs haunted many of them. The episodic withholding of oil from the market seemed illogical and fruitless for those with low production, limited storage, and few monetary resources.

Confusing measurements, creative bookkeeping, and exaggerated production estimates led to distrust. When a well slowed its production and the figures regarding the amount of oil produced were inflated, the inaccuracies led investors astray. The practice of fancy figures halted when the U.S. Congress leveed a tax on petroleum in September 1862.

The initial tax rate started at ten cents a gallon, then increased to twenty cents in 1864. For producers to pay taxes of $8 to $9 dollars a barrel worked a hardship on many. Oilmen banded together and pressured Congress to change the law. Finally, in April 1865, that distinguished body reduced the levy to $1 a barrel, and even that was too great a tax when oil prices dipped. To those in the oil business, being taxed at the equivalent of thirty-three percent seemed unjust.

As well, royalty systems were complex. Computations were tricky--fractions, and fractions of fractions. Subleasing small portions of land created mathematical challenges in determining the various sums of money owed to several parties. In the changing of hands as occurred with the Holmden Farm, U.S. Petroleum owed Duncan and Prather ¾ of ¼, the ¼ belonging to U.S. Petroleum. The re-sale of the Holmden property left the new owners owing 1/8 of their oil royalties to Duncan and Prather.

The monetary situation was further complicated when U.S. Petroleum failed to collect royalties from subleased land. These debtors, unscrupulous oil producers had their clerks create unethical bookkeeping that obscured the truth, like a fog over the land. These practices led to discrepancies between dividends and oil production. It did not take long for government auditors to start asking questions and computing taxes-owed that were based on inaccurate data. Indeed, standards of proper procedure were profoundly absent. However, the oilmen had learned a valuable lesson in cooperating and applying pressure to make changes, and standardizing barrel size was an appropriate start.

The written notifications had come twice, like warning shots over the bow of a ship at sea. The author who signed as "Oil Shipper" published two articles in the *Titusville Morning Herald*, one in late-August and the second in mid-September. Apparently, no responsible reader who had control over any of the three entities in question took heed. The author warned that when the plank roads, the railroads, and the oil pipelines all came to fruition simultaneously, none of them could reap a profit. The reason was startling and unfathomable during the prodigious Pithole petroleum production of the past six months. The article claimed that there was not sufficient oil in Pithole to create a reasonable return on such investments as were being outlaid.

Petroleum was the life-blood of this boomtown, and if anyone had read these editorials, they most likely would have denied the contents. Or, if they had spoken of their concerns stirred by the writings, they would have been the subject of scoffing and ridicule. Afterall, no one could repudiate the fact that business was booming.

...

Jeremiah was tethering his horse near the watering trough in front of Chalfant's Hardware Store on First Street.

"Jeremiah!"

He looked up to see Josh emerging from the store.

"How ya been? Long time, no see."

"Ya gotta minute?" Jeremiah gestured toward an unoccupied bench that rested up against the side of rough wood building.

They sat, and Josh, his unlit cigar scrunched between his teeth tipped his hat to shade his eyes from the late afternoon sun.

"Wondered if you are thinkin' of signin' on to bein' part of a posse."

"Posse? What's the occasion?" Josh became curious.

"We think there's gonna be a reaction in the next night or two to the testin' of the Van Syckel pipeline. So far, the watchmen that he's employed have managed to keep folks away from his invention, but I was at the testin' some days ago, and looks like it's gonna work."

"You were up there when they tried it out?"

"Yeah. The two Read and Cogswell steam pumps here in Pithole plus the additional one at Little Pithole put 900 pounds a-square-inch of pressure without leakin'--the whole five miles of it. Right up to the Oil Creek railhead."

Josh frowned. "So how much oil's it gonna push through to Miller Farm?"

"It was amazin'. In one hour of pumpin,' eighty-one barrels. So, if you figure it, in just one day, that pipeline can deliver the same as 300 teams slogging through an eight-hour day, chargin' $3.00 a barrel--dependin' on the weather, of course." Jeremiah paused. "When the weather's nasty and wet, of course, those teamsters boost their prices."

"Well, how much is Van Syckel chargin' a barrel-to move the oil?"

"Just one dollar--just one..." He shifted his weight. "When that fourth pump gets workin' at Cherry Run, then 2500 barrels a day will get moved. They say that'll be an increase of twenty-five percent."

"Well, how they gonna keep up with that oil-comin' through a pipe? Sellin' oil by the barrel is one thing--can count so many barrels, but in this pipeline and into tank?"

"They are preparing certificates to account for the oil purchases when it comes through these new pipes."

The two fell silent. Josh looked straight at Jeremiah and lowered his voice.

_____

"How you think the teamsters are gonna take that?"

"Well, all the oilmen are gettin' concerned."

"Yeah, that'll put those drivers out of business, won't it?"

"Think so…we're all expectin' trouble."

"So, now we're back to the posse. Is this volunteer or are they payin'?"

"Think they're payin.' They're hirin' additional pipeline guards, I know that. Trouble's in the wind fer sure."

…

It was pitch-dark when Luke awakened. He lay there wondering if it were time for him to head to the newspaper office. He looked up through an opening in the board roof of the shed. The moon was still high in the sky, not low on the western horizon as it was yesterday when he got out on the street.

Suddenly, he felt his straw bed shake and he heard a thumping sound. Was someone renting a horse at this hour of the night? He lay still, barely breathing. Then he heard two men talking in low voices.

"Gotta get movin' to catch up with the boys down by the crik."

"Yeah, I've gotta get the saddle on this critter before she lets out a whinny." That was followed by several soft grunts, some cussing, the creaking of the stable door, and then the fading squishy sounds of hoofs in mud. The two men had left.

Now, Luke was wide awake and curious. He fumbled in the dark for the ladder that was long enough to reach the opening in the low roof. Climbing carefully, at first, he saw nothing but a half-moon and some stars. Like a hunter in the woods, he stared into the dark, watching for movement and listening for the slightest sound. He stood on the ladder for several minutes, shivering from the cold.

Then coming from the west side of Pithole Creek, he heard low voices that seemed to carry for a distance. There was no wind. The air was still. Then the sound of horses moving away from his location caught his ear. Still he could see nothing. Taking one step higher, he spied a yellow light—no doubt a lantern. It bobbed around and then disappeared in— the darkness, as did the sounds. The cold was penetrating, so Luke came down from his perch and wrapped himself up in his mother's patch-quilt, then wormed his way into the hay for warmth. Soon he was asleep again.…

In pitch blackness, Josh stood at the ready near one of the Read and Cogswell pumps that were housed in a rude shack. He heard them--horses snorting and an undertone of deep voices--before he sensed movement in the blackness.

"Who goes there?" It was the voice of one of the deputized men several yards closer to the travelers. When no response came, a sound of a gunshot split the still night air. Josh and the other guards loaded their shotguns simultaneously. Next, the entire area lit up with lanterns, like fireflies on a hot July night.

"What's your business?"

Several armed men moved toward the silent group. Still no response to the guard's questions.

"There is no trespassing on this property. Get out of here, or you will be arrested."

Now Josh heard some indiscernible discussion, and the riders turned their steeds away from the challengers, heading back the way they had come. He listened to their retreat.

Breathing a sigh of relief, he looked at the positions of the guards along the pipeline. Their lighted lamps illuminated a pattern of one lookout every forty or so yards until the pipeline disappeared over a rise.

Several minutes after the intruders had departed, a tall, powerful looking man emerged from among the guards and their lights. He stepped forward with a lantern held high in each hand.

"Good work, men. That went well. We'll keep this plan in place tomorrow night too, and just hope that it continues to block travelers from the pipeline without any real trouble."

Josh recognized the voice of Charles Carner, the foreman of line walkers hired by Samuel Van Syckel. Great words, Charlie, Josh mused. They all knew that this was just the first of many confrontations to come.

The following day, Kate eaves-dropped on the discussions of the teamsters who showed up at her restaurant for the noontime meal. It sounded as if they were going over their attempt to attack the pipeline. She said nothing and acted disinterested in their talk. But she listened intently to the formulating of plans for that night.

"Like I said, now we have some idea of how many men they got on this end of the pipe."

"Yeah, around them pumps--expensive equipment's gonna

have more guards."

"So, that settles it. Tonight, we divide up and go into the pipeline several places about a mile out'a town. They laid it along Holmden Run, so we'll be followin' that crick for a ways."

"Yeah, probably easier to get to--less guards..."

"Let's get some shut-eye. Don't have no loads comin' outta the U.S. Petroleum tanks, so no work for most of us today."

Kate listened with interest. It was certain that trouble was brewing. She wanted nothing to do with any of it, as long as they did not target her business.

...

Luke had only two more *Titusville Morning Herald's* to sell when he saw Josh walking toward him.

"Ya gotta a *Herald* for me, Luke?"

"You just get up? It's near noon. You must'a been up late."

"I signed on to the posse and for most of the night we were up at the start of that pipeline that runs to Miller Farm."

Josh moved closer to Luke and spoke in a low voice.

"U.S. Petroleum fella's and Van Syckel think someone might try to damage Van Syckel's latest attempt to move oil out of here. Bunch of teamsters gonna be unhappy..."

Luke grabbed Josh's arm.

"I heard some men just below where I was sleepin'--over at Astor and Metropolitan Stables and something shook my bed and woke me up. Must'a been the middle of the night, 'cause the moon was right overhead."

Josh took the cigar out of his mouth.

"What were they doin' there, takin' a horse?"

"Sounded like it. They were quiet about it."

"Any idea who they were?"

Luke shook his head.

"Nope--too dark to see anything."

Josh told Luke about the silent men who approached the pipeline on the other side of the creek.

"Well, keep your eyes open, 'cause this is only the start of trouble, we think."

...

"Gotta stop the pumps to fix those two breaks in the line..."

The voices emanated <u>from</u> a closed door at the U.S.

Petroleum office where Josh was reporting in after another night of guarding the pipeline pumps.

Just then the door opened and George Etzel, the night watchman for the pipeline project emerged with an empty tin cup in his hand. His knee-high leather boots with his trousers packed into the tops were spattered with mud as were his pants. He looked at Josh and nodded.

"Gotta get me another cup of coffee…"

Josh looked at Etzel's enflamed eyes and tired face then decided to take advantage of the chance encounter.

"What happened last night, George?" He paused, waiting for the tall, lanky oilman to answer. "For my end of the line, things were quiet--just a couple of gents lookin' for a jug of whisky that they said fell off their wagon just before sundown. Come back lookin' for it. We just shooed them away."

"Had damage to the line partway up the hill--about a mile-and-a half outta town." He took a drink of his coffee. "Damn red necks! Just not enough line-walkers at that point. The angle of the hill hides that section of pipe from view from our man when he is walking at the other end of his area. Gonna take some time to get that part of the pipe replaced--chopped it up pretty good, they did. Came in there with pick axes. One break, appears they used chains to pull the pipe--hooked to horses. Oil all over the ground."

Josh listened and wondered about the other rumors he had heard. Encouraged by the conversation, he decided to ask Etzel.

"Any truth in what I been hearin' about some of your men being threatened?"

"Oh, yeah. We get a couple of letters a day, threatening to kill the chief engineer, William Snow and Al Smiley, the superintendent." He looked directly at Josh. "Busted glass all over the floor this morning too. Fred Jones' office, the only window on the side facing the creek. Found a big rock near his desk with 'Stop the pipe' scrawled on it with charcoal."

Josh shifted and pushed for more information.

"Any truth in you fella's who constructed the line for Van Syckel being pressured?"

"Well, keep this under your hat." He turned to see if anyone else were within earshot. "Van Syckel is moving out'a here today--going to Titusville to stay."

That news caused Josh to pause.

"What about the others, George?"

334

"Well, they ain't got the money that the boss has, so they're having to stay here. Most of them--Charlie Carner, Bill Tompkins and even Emmett Fleming who's in charge of accounts were living in one of the boarding houses over on Prather Street. So now, they've spread out--gone to other hotels, but are rooming in twos. George Coutant, too. Just gotta watch each other's backs, I reckon."

In the next several days, while the pipeline was pumping at full steam, there was talk of a second line planned to Miller Farm. To make matters worse for the teamsters, the word was out that the Pennsylvania Tubing Company had gathered enough capital to build a two-inch gravity line from Pithole to the Allegheny River. It was constructed with advanced methods.

The T.G. Gaylord Company in Cincinnati, Ohio employed a hydraulic jack with ten tons of pressure to ram together the R.C. Robbins joint, a further improvement to prevent oil leakage. Surveyors measured the pipe's projected pathway carefully with its 360-foot drop to the Allegheny River, and computed a fifty-foot drop for each mile. The pipe's pathway led down the Pithole Creek valley for seven miles to Henrys Bend on the river. Workers buried the majority of the pipe three to four feet deep, but other portions lay exposed at the twenty-one crossings over Pithole Creek. A huge 10,000-barrel iron tank at the Henrys Bend railhead required that oil be sold without delay in order to manage the deluge of oil running downhill from the Pithole wells.

The starting date for construction was scheduled for October 24 with a target of completion on December 10, a date that was projected to commence the movement of 20,000 barrels by gravity over a six-week period.

The success of the first pipeline, Van Syckel's line threw 500 teamsters out of work within a month. These drivers feared successful innovations and for the demise of their jobs. They were angry and some, hungry. Trying to discourage the emerging technology and its promoters, by night, they attacked with clubs, guns and stones, damaging the pipeline to Miller Farm. Until guards were increased in sufficient number to discourage many of these men, they set fire to oil tanks and smashed line connections. By day, they screamed threats of certain death and spewed torrents of abusive language, unacceptable in nearby towns, but now common place in the boomtown. Shouting out their rights to work and support their families, they blamed the pipeline planners of taking bread from the mouths of their children.

Finally, some of the drivers realized that their futures were undermined by technological improvements that could not be reversed. Many of the teamsters left town to find work at emerging sites of oil production in nearby communities, free of new inventions, so far.

...

The sun had set under a cloudy sky when Mike and his two companions ordered drinks at French Kate's Restaurant. Kate had interrupted the last of the dinner setup chores to fill their drink orders, and poured herself a shot of whiskey. Mike raised his glass and turned toward her and Mabelle who was re-arranging some chairs nearby.

"Cheers and farewell to the madam and the ladies of this great house!"

Surprised, Kate stopped moving her glass toward her lips. She saw Mabelle, her countenance as white as new fallen snow, whirl to face the teamster-trio, her mouth open in shock at the toast.

"What? You're leaving?" Mabelle sat down hard in one of the chairs. She looked imploringly at three of their best customers. Her eyes filled with tears as she looked directly at Sarge. When he failed to meet her gaze, she slumped in her chair and began to sob.

Kate stood to her full height and downed the shot of whiskey.

"Why so soon? Do you think that this fight against the pipes is over already?" Suddenly, she felt sick at the thought of the loss of regular revenue from these consistent customers.

Mike spoke for the them.

"Well, Miss Kate, we gotta feed our horses and our families."

"Families, you got families--wives and children?" Mabelle looked shocked. Kate could see her clenching her fists.

"Sarge, you never told me. You said that someday..." Her voice trailed off and she laid her head between her arms on the table in front of her and sobbed.

Kate watched Sarge shift uncomfortably on his bar stool, down his drink, slide off his seat, and head for the exit without a backward glance.

"See you at the stables."

Mike finished his drink quickly, and stood to go.

"Kate, it's been great, but nothing lasts forever."

He stepped toward her, and she felt him grab her by the waist

336

and gather her in his strong arms.

"Don't forget me, Kate. I may be back sometime."

She felt her glass sliding from her grasp and it hit the hard-wooden floor with a crash. She heard Herman crunch over the shattered glass, past her and Mabelle.

"Come on, Mike. Let's go."

She suppressed her anguish and her anger as she watched them leave. Just when things were going so well. What will happen now with her three consistent clients departing? Will she and the girls be able to make the monthly lease payments? How many teamsters were exiting? What would become of other businesses if many of these men left?

She looked toward the gathering crowd of diners to see fewer men than usual lined up outside for the late afternoon meal. She sat at the bar and gazed into space.

After a few minutes, she called to Mabelle.

"Show your grit, Mabelle. We've got work to do. My dear departed Pa-pa' always told me, 'It's always darkest before the dawn...'"

...

Lingering drivers, a tougher crowd and unemployed, hung around bars and gambling tables by day, and harassed the pipeline guards by night, often engaging in skirmishes. This blatant behavior of disregarding property and rising civil disobedience encouraged other ne'er-do-wells to take advantage of the deteriorating state of affairs.

Robberies and attacks on other property and people were on the up-tick. Under cover of darkness, men on horseback thundered through town, firing guns that terrorized residents. The dark, rutted streets became opportunities for evil, forcing men to travel in pairs or in groups to protect themselves and each other. Women dared not emerge without a male bodyguard or two even in daytime. Women feared being on the streets at night, even escorted. The rogues robbed drunks and those alone who happened to be abroad after the setting of the sun. It seemed that no one nor anything was safe.

In the wee hours of a Sunday morning, the bartender at the American Hotel on First Street awakened to noises. Following the sounds, he discovered three intruders helping themselves to liquor. His confrontation and commands for them to pay up and leave were met with a wild flinging of fists and the bartender screaming for help. As the three thieves departed, they hollered threats to return with the intent of killing the man who was ousting them.

So grave were the intimidations that the hotel manager obtained a warrant for the arrest of the gang and its leader. A hand-picked force of men assembled and laid in wait inside the saloon for the thugs' return. The next night when eighteen men broke into the tavern again, sheriff's deputies who lay-in-waiting fired their weapons as warning shots and subdued the toughs. Their leader was arrested. He was hustled out of Pithole and delivered on horseback to the county jail in Franklin, some twenty miles away.

...

"Jeremiah, I need a word with ya'."

Alfred Smiley, the assistant superintendent of the pipeline for Samuel Van Syckel walked confidently in his shiny new knee-high boots and black cap that was tilted at a roguish angle. He was emerging from the offices of the U.S. Petroleum Company. Jeremiah stood by a wooden watering trough near the entrance, out of the earshot of nearby workers. The early morning sun was a welcome relief in the cold November air.

"What's on yer mind, Al?"

"I have a proposition for you. I need your assistance. Just got a telegram from Mr. Van Syckel. He's looking to buy a large amount of oil from U.S. Petroleum and he wants it done as soon as I can manage it. Trouble is, U.S. Petroleum wants some of the money upfront this time, not after the oil's been pumped to Miller Farm. It's not the same as the times of the teamsters. If the money was not forthcoming then, U.S. Petroleum just stopped the barrels from rolling out of here. Now, it's in a pipeline and moving fast, so paying has changed too. They want their money up-front-cash on the barrel-head."

"Looks like a grand time, to me, for Van Syckel to buy--with crude dropped to $2.75 a barrel. And look at those huge tanks over there--twenty-four of them, each full-up of crude." He looked at Smiley. "So, that's a problem?" Jeremiah tilted his hat to shade his eyes from the sun.

"Well, it can be when you're dealing with Sam." He lowered his voice. "Ya see, Sam Van Syckel spends greenbacks fast and furiously. Not long ago, the National Bank of Titusville loaned him $30,000 to avoid debts and embarrassment. When I, being his oil buyer try to curb his spending...well it's nigh to impossible. And

338

that's the truth." He paused. "I feel like a racoon up-a-tree. All I can do is come down 'cause, of course it's his money. So, I have to put up or shut up." He held out both hands, palms-up. "I'm just trying to keep him solvent and paying his bills."

Jeremiah indicated that he understood Smiley's frustration with a nod.

"So anyway, this latest deal is the biggest one I've dealt with yet. He's aiming to buy a single lot of 100,000 barrels of crude at five dollars a barrel. So, the seller wants a $100,000 down on the deal before they'll start pumping to him. He's planning to come down from Titusville to meet me at Miller Farm tomorrow afternoon. He says he'll have the cash. Wants to purchase the oil by the next morning before the price goes back up." He stopped and looked at Jeremiah. "I'm planning to ride with William Tomkins, the dump boss and George Etzel, two of the most trustworthy and powerful men I know. And you're the third. Could you go with us?"

...

Jeremiah arrived at the Chase House on Holmden Street thirty minutes before the stagecoach was scheduled to depart for Miller Farm at nine A.M. These coaches had recently begun once-a-day-service to Pithole and were now a part of the stagecoach runs that radiated to Oil City, Rouseville, Titusville, Plumer, West Hickory and Miller Farm. He picked out the coach bound for their destination. It was parked amid an assemblage of hacks, stages, and horse-drawn carriages that were picking up travelers. Wearing heavy winter travel clothes, mainly men were jostling about with their bundles and carpet bags. Jeremiah felt for the Colt revolver that he had sequestered under his heavy trekking coat, and waited to greet his travel companions.

Hours later at Miller Farm, seated at a small table in the corner of a dining room, Jeremiah watched Samuel Van Syckel transfer the pack of money to Smiley. Van Syckel sported a closely trimmed mustache and wore a fine-threaded suit with a brown woolen vest and black bowler hat. The cash was wrapped in plain grocery paper. He considered the whole affair highly hazardous, but necessary under the circumstances. Hand-carrying $100,000 of greenbacks on foot seven miles through the night was risky, but required under the time constraints dictated by Van Syckel. The transaction completed, Jeremiah stood and looked around. He could see no one observing them. The crowd of disparate men in the spacious restaurant, heads bent forward, seemed intent on eating.

He did agree with Smiley on his plan to return to Pithole on foot. The plank road attracted bandits, and travelers who might appear to have anything of worth would be tempting targets. Just possessing a horse made the rider vulnerable to unwanted attention and possible robbery. Traveling at night would obscure him and his comrades from prying eyes, since they were following the less-traveled footpath along the pipeline. As well, the presence of line-walkers and sheriff's deputies who were guarding the line could provide some protection, if it became necessary.

After a meal of chicken, dumplings with gravy followed by a thick slice of crisp apple pie, the four men started out for Pithole. The sun had set, the light, gone. The night watchman, George Etzel commanded the lead followed by Jeremiah, twenty paces behind him. William Tompkins came next, carrying the package of cash in a long, gray travel coat with deep inside pockets. Al Smiley chose to bring up the rear. Each man was armed with a new Colt revolver provided by Smiley, and Jeremiah totted his rifle as well. In the inky blackness, they could locate each other by the sounds of crunching fallen leaves that were underfoot.

At the beginning of their trek, the half-moon emerged from behind the clouds and illuminated the area well enough for them go without a lantern. They chose not to use the one lamp they had among them unless necessary so as not to attract attention.

Off and on they would see lights through the trees in the direction of the plank road. To Jeremiah, they looked like lines of glowing fire flies, yellow-orange from a distance. He was surprised that so many people were afoot at night out here on the wooden highway.

Suddenly loud hooting reverberated through the dark, tall trees. A large shadowy bird glided silently across the trail ahead of them. A shuffling noise followed, and then the cry of some little critter that had just been snatched from its tracks. Witnessing the reality of the food-chain gave Jeremiah pause to reflect.

Was this a foolhardy mission? Those with money in this petroleum industry got to call the shots, but their employees took the risk. Smiley had planned well. So far, they were safe.

Soon they came to a section of the pipeline laid in close proximity to the plank road. Just as the four approached the narrow strip that divided the two paths, they heard footfalls on the hard-wooden road. The sounds caused the four trekkers to freeze in their tracks and with a signal from Etzel, they stooped to the ground next to a thin growth of brush. They could make out two men approaching on horseback. Jeremiah felt his heart beating against his chest wall. The horsemen were within a wagon's length of the hidden men. Unhurried, they moved on by Edzel and the other hidden men.

Just as Jeremiah and his companions were on their feet and creeping away from the road, gunshot thundered through the trees and horses whinnied. The foursome scrambled off the path and into the woods toward the pipeline. They hunkered down, wondering what the shooting was about.

A bolt of lightning split the air as clouds boiled over the half-moon. Thunder rolled overhead and through the valley in front of them. Jeremiah felt the rain as it swept over them. He pulled his hat down more tightly on his head when the wind picked up. Etzel signaled them to follow him.

Now, the downed autumn leaves were wet making their surfaces slippery. The path chosen by their leader was obscure and off of the footpath. Bushwhacking, they moved forward, the lightning illuminating the underbrush episodically. They paused at a deep ditch where Etzel cautioned them about mud. The muck lay on the other side of the trench and clung to their boots as they slogged across it.

They heard another volley of gunfire from out on the plank road. They came to a clearing and Etzel picked up the pace. They edged across the treeless, open space, then entered a tree-line and stopped for a moment.

"Got us to the other side of the pipeline, away from the plank road and that shooting. Don't think we're in danger over here. Walking won't be so easy, though."

The rain increased and thunder rumbled from overhead clouds. The downpour changed to hail that was beating on Jeremiah's coat and weighing down the brim of his hat. As they trudged another half-mile, the barrage abated and the clouds parted to reveal the moon. Thunder grew more distant and lightning no longer threatened to reveal them.

Jeremiah shook the ice off his hat and felt a trickle of freezing water flow down his neck and back. He shivered as they paused at the base of a huge tree and drank water from their canteens. Tomkins tried to work the clumps of mud from his boots on the exposed tree root.

"Stop." Smiley put his hand of Tomkins arm. They all froze in place, not moving.

As if on cue, an obscure figure loomed up about ten yards in front of them, blocking their route. They hunkered down behind a cluster of small spruce trees and waited.

Just ahead, another figure with a lantern came into view.

The yellow light bobbed about, then was joined by another.

"Who goes there?"

Etzel answered in a firm voice. "Etzel, George Etzel, night watchman of Van Syckel's pipeline."

The two lights moved swiftly toward them. "It's Cheeney and Richards guarding the pipe. Mr. Etzel, what are you doing way out here?"

Etzel rose-up from his position.

"You alone?"

As if in answer, Smiley, Tompkins, and Jeremiah stood and then walked toward the guards and identified themselves. They shook hands with the two watchmen.

"Did you hear those gunshots?"

"Just before the gunshot, we saw two men on horseback. We stayed out of sight. Don't know who they are."

Together, the six trekked the next half-mile to the limit of the two guards' area of the pipeline. Off and on they could see lamplights and hear muffled voices along the plank road. As they grew closer to Pithole, lanterns appeared more numerous, glowing out of the blackness, signs of the line- walkers. In the far distance, the torches burning gas from oil wells, flickered like fireflies.

The group had fulfilled its mission. Van Syckel's $100,000 payment in Greenbacks were now out of danger, but the future of Pithole was not.

The Turning Point

November-December 1865

On November 9, 1865, the President of U.S. Petroleum, W.W. Evans arrived in Pithole from New York to review the holdings of his corporation. His opinion of the status of the enterprise could determine the future of the oil fields in Pithole. Most locals, who had come to ignore the waves of visitors that flooded the boomtown, astutely noted the eminent visit of the President of U.S. Petroleum. Evans' keen observations and resultant opinions of the status of his oil enterprise could hold heavy sway over the life or death of their new town, only seven months old.

Had it not been for the importance surrounding his initial inspection, considerable concern and studied attention might have been paid to the sudden cessation of the actual oil well that caused such a big commotion in Pithole in the first place, in January of 1865. Only one hour after Even's arrival, the Frazier Well, the celebrated success of the first wildcat attempt to find oil in higher elevations suddenly had run out of oil—just stopped producing. This original well was famous for reviving the flagging petroleum industry at a crucial time. In the end, its demise was considered more sentimental than recognized as an untoward omen of things to come. Its expiry passed with little notice.

The price of oil had dropped to $2.75 per barrel and twenty-four huge tanks-full of crude stood on the U.S. Petroleum property on the bank of Pithole Creek. The company was withholding much of its production until a more propitious time to sell, when oil prices would rise. What Evans witnessed was the long line of wagons heavy with oil barrels that had to be moved since the storage tanks were full. As a result, some 200 teams lumbered through the mud-clogged streets of Pithole toward Titusville. What Evans may not have realized was that hundreds of team drivers had recently departed from Pithole for more favorable circumstances. The remaining teams that persisted were making money for the moment, but were now insufficient in number to keep up with the flood of crude from the wells.

Those remaining teamsters, frustrated by new technology, appeared insolent toward pipeline inventors and oil agents. They were frightened of losing their livelihood. Like dying bees in the late Fall that aimed to sting anything that slightly disturbed them, the teamsters continued to create havoc under the cover of darkness. They acted out their frustrations on anyone in their paths. Mainly, they targeted oil producers and their collaborators who had created a more efficient method of moving crude oil out of this remote location.

For the teamsters, industrial advances seemed to be non-stop. In fact, the day before W.W. Evans' appearance, the second Pithole-to-Miller Farm pipeline began pumping. In response, the teamsters cut their price for hauling oil from $3.00 to $1.25 a barrel, which instead of helping their cause, exposed to everyone how severely they had been bleeding the oil producers. The two lines pumping at capacity produced $2000 revenue a day, an astounding increase from previous losses to the expense of having oil hauled by wagon. The court of public opinion was confirmed. The teamsters' overcharging had hastened innovation of other methods of moving oil. The team drivers were consumed with anger.

...

"Fire, fire!"

Kate's head jerked up and she ceased counting the income from the day's diners.

"What! Luke put on your boots and go see where the fire is."

Grabbing her shawl from its hook in the kitchen, she ran to the restaurant's entrance and out on to the dark, frigid veranda where Luke was stuffing his feet into his cold, mud-caked boots.

"Look, Miss Kate! Those flashes and smoke are coming from up near Second Street. I can smell the smoke!"

Bright sparks and red-hot embers shot skyward high over the nearby buildings, like shooting stars on a clear night.

"What's on fire? Is it gonna spread?"

Avoiding the steps, Luke jumped off the side of the wooden porch and started running up Brown Street toward the smoke.

"Come back and tell me what's on fire."

Luke clambered through the partially frozen mud ruts of Brown Street until he reached Second Street, about a block from French Kate's Restaurant. Out of breath, he saw yellow flames leaping upward and gray smoke billowing from the Rochester

House, at the corner of Prather and Second Streets, one of fifty hotels in Pithole. As a crowd gathered near him, he watched as a number of men struggled to fight the fire. They lacked equipment since no fire hydrants nor adequate water pressure existed at night in the newly laid pipes of the town's water system. Nor did Pithole have a fire department with men trained to fight fires.

Through the smoke, Luke could see two muscular men wrestling a barrel of water. The two gents filled wooden pails that were handed down a line of volunteers to the those closest to the inferno. More water barrels appeared from somewhere, and bucket after bucket moved along the human chain for about an hour.

The anxious crowd stood in the frozen mud and watched warily. "You think it'll spread—like to that building on the right?"

"Look'a that! You can see the inside of the Rochester. Looks like the dining room. The wall paper's burnin'! It's on fire!"

"What started it, ya think?"

"Dunno, but those team drivers have been making threats. Surely not, though…"

Luke saw several of his paperboy friends, one with his mouth agape, staring into the glare. A late diner with his white napkin yet in place, faced the blaze, a drink in his hand. Luke wondered if those staying at the hotel had had time to rescue their belongings. The heat from the inferno felt hot on his face, and he moved back away from the snapping of the flames.

The furious effort by the all-volunteer fire fighting force finally staunched the blaze as the embers were dulled by the water. Smoke curled lazily from the remains of the building, a pile of burned rubble. Luke heard someone say that the hotel was a total loss, $8000.

"The hotel had insurance, they say."

"Yeah, but only for $5000. I heard the manager talking. He's standing right over there, ya see?"

Through the smoke, Luke spied several men pointing to the smoldering ruins of the hotel with its two walls burned down, and the interior gutted. Relieved that the fire had not encompassed nearby structures, Luke turned to go in the dark, back to French Kate's Restaurant and give her the news. He was relieved that it had not spread. He hated fires.

…

On December 10, the gravity pipeline from Pithole to

Oleopolis at Henry's Bend on the Allegheny River delivered its first load of crude. During the next month, some 20,000 barrels of oil traversed through the gravity pipe. For teamsters, that amount of crude would have been 4000 team-loads worth $60,000 payment to them. The effect of the pipeline's success was devastating to the team drivers. By mid-December, 1000 of these men had departed Pithole en mass and their money with them. As a result of this exodus, businesses in Pithole lost their chief source of revenue.

Another big blow to the lingering teamsters was yet to come. Titusville businessmen had been planning to lay an oil pipeline from Pithole to Titusville. The project had been delayed due to complications with the building of the Pithole- to-Titusville plank road. The Titusville Pipe Company anticipated the pipeline project's start in January 1866. The quality of these pipes was an improvement over the two previously laid lines and were even more expensive, $1000 per mile of ditching and forty-five cents for each foot of pipe. Engineers contemplated plans for digging frozen soil to lay the two-inch pipe in a single thirteen-mile-long ditch. These innovations would leave little work for the teamsters.

The modicum of employment that remained for the once-powerful team drivers was relegated to providing one missing link in the process of moving oil from the wells to the pipelines. Teams were yet required to do short hauls of oil barrels that were filled at the wells, then transported to oil dumps where the barrels were emptied by hand. From the dumps, oil traveled into the pipelines that carried the crude to the closest refineries in Henrys Bend, Plumer or Titusville, or railheads to be shipped farther distances. The success of two pipelines and plans for a third raised the tensions to a new high for not only the oil-haulers during the latter weeks of December, but for the citizens of Pithole as well.

...

"But Miss Kate, it's dangerous out there now that the teamsters are mostly out of work. Flossy-Jean over at Emma's place was comin' back from the post office yesterday, in broad daylight. And she got hit by something that whacked her right near her eye...it's all swollen and black 'n blue. Madame Emma's been puttin' snow and ice on it. Said Flossy-Jean's lucky to have her eye..."

"Josh told me that some of those angry men are using

346

slingshots to hurt people. Wonder if that's what hit her." Kate realized that Luke was listening as he cleared the last table of dirty dishes.

She had noticed that their customers for the evening meal ate in haste and did not linger to talk, as they had in the past. She overheard conversations about thugs and hooligans using clubs to beat-up drunks or unfortunates walking alone after dark. As well, there was talk about men with knives roaming the streets. Were these the teamsters like Mike and Sarge? She could not envision that. It had to be another element of evil-doers.

Now, she missed those two teamsters. They had been dominating influences at the restaurant, and seldom had anyone gotten out of hand, despite the lack of decorum that dominated the teaming town. Those two men had prevented all-out fights in her dining room. They held sway over the girls' evening trade, as well, and patrons knew that they had to answer to Mike or Sarge if any of them got rough in the rooms upstairs. All the patrons paid up—no bad debts. The waitresses' evening income had been guaranteed, and Kate got her cut. Now, things were changing.

All this violence and commotion now was affecting her income. Even the waitresses' night trade had fallen off. They were all asleep by 10:00 these evenings.

"Well, I think that Luke should stay here with us now that things are so bad after dark. Anyway, what could he do if somebody came after him in his stable-loft?" Mabelle looked from Kate to Luke.

Luke shrugged and said nothing.

"Well, Miss Kate can he stay here for the night, for at least while there is so much danger in the streets?" Mabelle turned toward her employer. When Kate felt Luke looking at her, and Jenny stopped sweeping to listen, she relented.

"Well, since after dinner business is lagging, I guess he could."

"Miss Kate, it's too cold for him to sleep on the veranda like in July. There's that little room at the top of the stairs. Why can't he sleep there?"

She considered.

"Better if he sleeps under the work-counter in the kitchen. In case the evening trade picks up, he doesn't need to be upstairs."

Luke felt relieved.

"Miss Kate, I want to go get my patch quilt from the stable

before it gets any later. That OK?"

She nodded her approval, and Luke was out the door like a flash.

The dark trees on the edge of Pithole Creek were silhouetted against the remaining light in the western sky as Luke made his way to the stables two blocks away. He climbed up the ladder to the loft and past two paperboys who had been sharing the space in the straw with Luke. One of them rolled over in the gloom.

"That you, Luke? Comin' to bed early, too?" He paused, and got up on his elbow. "Harry and me, we decided to get inside 'afor those riders come tearin' through town, crackin' their whips and shootin' again—like last night."

Luke felt around for his quilt, found it, and sat down. His friend went on.

"Harry and me and some other boys—we're thinkin' of leavin' here. Fearing for our lives. Besides, paper sales are off since so many teamsters have gone." He paused. "What's you gonna do?"

"Well, I live here—got nowhere else to go except back to Grandpa's place in Pitch Pine where my Ma's at..." He paused. "Except my brother lives nearby, but don't think they have room for me since they got another baby acomin'.' "

A long silence followed.

"Where you gonna go, Frank, you and Harry?"

"Donna' know. He's from Erie and I come here from Cleveland, but nobody there. My ma's dead and last I knew, my pa's got another woman who has her own babies. Guess I'll stick it out for a while longer—awful cold to travel now, anyway."

Suddenly, they heard the galloping of horses a block distant. Luke scrambled up to the hole in the roof and looked out. The town was pitch black by now and the evening star had risen in the west above the tops of the trees near the creek. The hillside to the East blocked all but a few wells and the yellow flames from their burning gas. He twisted in the direction of the noises and saw flickering lights moving toward the stables. The riders were throwing something that sounded like rocks at the buildings on either side of the muddy street. They hit with resounding thuds and he heard glass shattering. The ground vibrated and rattled their rough, shabby shed, their sleeping shelter. As the horsemen approached the stable, Luke could hear the distinct yelling of profanities aimed at U.S. Petroleum.

He shivered and kept watch. He relayed the rough riders'

348

progress to Frank and Harry. As the gang of ten or so riders passed the stables, Luke ducked his head so that the ruffians could not see him by their lantern light. Several of the riders pounded the buildings with clubs and the flimsy structures shook.

He heard one of the men pull his horse off to the side of the road across from their shelter.

"Otta set that damn thing a-fire. Fulla' hay. Sure would go up fast…"

Luke could feel his muscles tense and his breathing become shallow. Then he heard another voice caution the first speaker.

"Too many horses in there. Why kill horses when we can attack the bastards causing the problems?"

He heard a low response, but could not make out what was said. He peered out into the darkness and watched as their light disappeared into the gloom and down towards French Kate's Restaurant. Then, he let out his breath.

Mabelle was right. The streets were not safe for anyone…

…

The excitement of the small crowd was palpable. Everyone gathered in the clear, cold air on the border of the Rooker Farm and the Pithole Borough was talking enthusiastically, their hats bobbing and scarfs waving in the breeze. On December 18th, the landmark day had come. Three months of frenzied formation had come to fruition. The rail construction, under the loose authority of the Clarion Land Company had started in the summer. Progress was slow at first because the firm had been forced to recruit a thousand workmen from as far away as five hundred miles, there being no available locals to tackle the job.

Like all projects in the expanding oil territory, once begun, they progressed with undying energy and great haste. The simultaneous work of clearing trees, grading the terrain, building trestles and laying track were running a race with nature. Winter was coming on, and the Allegheny River would quickly clog with ice and obstruct boat traffic.

As the teamsters began leaving the area in late Fall, concerned citizens realized that their delivery services were leaving with those exiting. The conveyance of coal and other provisions by boat would diminish and the boomtown would be shut off from the essential supplies, unless the rail project were completed in time.

349

The rail company had purchased essential equipment in order to provide delivery service. Train cars had to be shipped from the manufacturer in Philadelphia to Pittsburgh then up the Allegheny River by steamboat. The river was so shallow during those Fall months that this major purchase had to be transferred on to barges for the last portion of the river trip. The cost of this effort to pierce the wilderness by rail was exorbitant.

Construction expenditures of the six-and one-half miles of railbed and rolling stock totaled $675,000 with a floating debt of $190,000. The standard gauge of four-feet, eight-and a-half inches had a mile of siding and a triangular turn-track. Traveling at twelve miles per hour, The Pithole Railroad from Oleopolis to Pithole crossed over Pithole Creek ten times on wooden trestles. The rolling stock comprised of two wood-burning Baldwin locomotives, twenty-five freight cars and a mail-car. Passenger service was promised for the future, though a train station was completed in time for the commencement of service.

The two-story wooden building was situated on two-and a-half acres of land together with other necessary maintenance and storage buildings. The upstairs of the railroad building housed the station master, and the downstairs accommodated the ticket office, telegraph services and a small waiting room. Pithole Creek bordered the building on two sides and necessitated a footbridge. Connecting steps were built by First Street merchants and linked rail service with the town. The station's one outstanding feature was the external yellow-ochre paint job that distinguished it from the colorless, bare-boards of most other buildings in Pithole.

Luke, Jenny and Mabelle stood together in the excited group of citizens who anticipated the first railroad train to enter Pithole. It was due to roll in at any moment.

"I've never been on a train, have you, Mabelle?" Luke looked inquisitively at his older friend, as he stamped his feet to keep them warm.

She shrugged.

"Sure would like to get a ride someday."

Jenny turned toward them.

"I rode a train a'oncest, comin' from Cleveland to Pittsburgh with my Pa and his new wife, after my Ma died."

"Was it exciting? How fast did it go?"

"They said it ran about thirty miles an hour…seemed fast to me."

"Fast as a horse can gallop?" Luke was curious.

"Depends on the horse."

Mabelle and Luke laughed, and Jenny blushed at the attention paid to her and her humorist answer.

Just then, a loud blast of the train's whistle pierced the morning air. All heads in the crowd turned, intent on catching a first glance of the smoky, wood-burning engine.

Everyone seemed to be talking at once.

"Look at that smoke stack—looks like a funnel—wide at the top and narrow at the bottom where it sits on that engine. And the shiny brass steam whistle."

"I like the looks of the bell, right behind the smoke stack. Ya see it?"

"What's that on the front of the engine?"

"That's a cow catcher—pushes cows off the track!" A young man wearing a Union soldiers' uniform hat had turned toward them.

"Rode on one of them com' home from Virginia after the war stopped."

"I'm going to save some money and buy me a ticket, just to get a ride to Oleopolis. I could walk back to Pithole if I had to." Luke looked inspired.

"I'll go with you, Luke. It would be so excitin'!" Mabelle smiled at the thought.

Here was living proof that they were tied into a wider world than Luke had ever known. And the town would have coal for the on-coming winter weather.

...

Despite the exodus of many workers and the negative effect on businesses, projects that had been in progress for some time reached completion in December. D.B. Danforth had leased a lot at the corner of First and Holmden Streets, strategically sited for the convenience of businessmen, across the street from the U.S. Petroleum office. Designed as an executive's hotel, the quality of the building far surpassed the built-in-one-day structures that predominated the boomtown.

The Danforth House was constructed in a more deliberative manner at the building costs of $40,000 plus $14,000 bonus payment for the lease. The three-story construction with a covered veranda on two sides sported painted-white porch pillars kept clean, relatively, by the plank street that fronted the main entrance. The hotel's name appeared boldly between the second and third floors in prominently painted letters on two sides: "DANFORTH HOUSE." The sturdy structure accommodated 140 guests who enjoyed a decent dining room, a friendly saloon and commodious meeting rooms. With H.W. Mabb as the proprietor, the newest structure in town opened on Christmas Eve.

For all comers who would tour the hotel, the owner offered a festive feast followed by a dance. All was free: food, dancing and liquor. The offer drew an excited crowd, eager to celebrate.

Kate, Mabelle and Jenny and several other of "Kate's girls," as they had become known were among the celebrants who imbibed in the offerings and danced with abandon.

"No need worrying about the situation." Mabelle seemed to have recovered from Sarge's sudden departure. "Too bad they left when they did. They're missin' a nice party in the midst of all this cold weather."

"I'm having another whiskey. Anyone want to join me at the bar?"

Just then, both girls were whisked away as dance partners, and Kate moved toward the bar. She was enjoying herself, so seldom did she get away from the business of running her restaurant. Mabelle had it right. Can't worry about the departure of their benefactors, the teamsters, Mike and Sarge.

She had been scanning the crowd since her arrival, as was her custom, and seeing no men who appeared to be detectives or federal agents, she relaxed with her glass of whiskey at the far end of the bar. Then, she noticed a lanky-looking man standing nearby with a plate of food, piled high. He seemed familiar to other attendees, stopping to chat, and shaking hands with his free right hand. Katherine frowned. Who was he? She signaled the bartender, whom she knew from his frequenting her place.

"Siegfried, who is this man, right over there with that plate of food. He's got a dark beard…"

"That's Darius Steadman, Reverend Darius Steadman. You don't know him? He seems to be acquainted with everyone in town. Been raising money since October for that Methodist Church that got the land on Duncan Street, given to them by Prather and Duncan. Church is 'most finished by now…" He nodded to her then moved off to make drinks for more patrons of the bar.

She could not help staring at the preacher who seemed out of place at such an occasion as this celebration--liquor being served and all. But then, she reasoned, it is Christmas Eve, and half of Pithole seemed to be here at the Danforth. She had heard of him, but had never seen him before. She recalled how someone had described him. He had been the chaplain for the "Wildcatters," the Pennsylvania 105th Volunteers and had contracted typhoid somewhere in the south, becoming so wasted that he resigned and returned home to convalesce. From the huge pile of food on his plate, it appeared to her that he was yet attempting to increase his weight. She shifted in her seat. So, he was the preacher that had been holding services on street corners, in stables, and just about anywhere there was a crowd.

Tonight, people seemed happy to see him. As he walked past her, she turned to see a sign stuck to the back of his coat, "Christmas Eve Carol-Sing! 11:00 PM, front of Murphy's Theater, Mm Brignoli leading. All faiths welcome." She smiled. Apparently, the reverend knew how to draw a crowd.

Just then, she felt someone touch her arm. She turned to find Jeremiah smiling at her.

"You seem engrossed with the reverend. I was wondering where his opposition is tonight--that young Catholic priest, Joe Finucane and Presbyterian, George Ormond. Guess his building fund never did recover from that slick talkin' gent, Reverend Hughes who absconded with the $10,000 he got from the share of that oil well."

"What oil well, Jeremiah? Don't think I know that story." He had seated himself next to her.

"One day Hughes was preachin' at Patchen's Hotel--they'd just opened. Had a big crowd since he was a convincin' speaker--people loved him. So, after the lecture was over, a man in the audience was so impressed with Hughes that he donated a 1/16th interest in an oil well on the Hyner Farm. Heard later that this Hughes fella cashed in that share worth $10,000, abandoned his bein' a Presbyterian preacher and skedaddled out of here. Rumor has it that he's studyin' law somewhere."

"So, that's why the Methodists have a church almost built and the others are dragging behind?"

"Yeah, think so. Let's dance. Come on Kate." He led her to the dance floor to the music of a piano, a banjoist and a cornetist.

"Jeremiah, if you're going to do your fancy clogging, you'll have to teach me how."

It was the first time she had celebrated Christmas since

leaving France.

Several days later, Kate pulled a letter from her mail box. Fredrick's discussion about her French family and the efforts to manage their infected vines filled the letter.

"I am looking forward to your return this next summer. Hopefully, you will no longer be pursued and free to travel. I miss you. We all miss you. Love, Fredrick."

She put the letter down and sat defocused, lost in thought. Her business was lagging without the teamsters, but she would survive.

...

Fire protection was on the minds of many concerned citizens and a meeting was called by the burgess to discussed the issues. The small group who attended voted to levy $2.00 per month on every household and business in support of fire protection, and a vote of the public was needed. The burgess announced the date of a public vote and the meeting was adjourned.

The next day, in opposition to the announcement of a public vote on the $2 levy, someone had published fliers, advising against it. They were handed out on the streets and posted on buildings.

However, that same afternoon, before the citizens had an opportunity for a final vote on the tax, an incendiary incident not only caught the attention of the public, but threw them into a panic. A blaze was discovered on the second floor of the Continental Hotel and burned so ferociously that all the buildings on Main Street seemed threatened. Hours later, a fire at Welch's Boarding House at Brown and Third Street propelled people into action. Although no definitive reason for the blazes was sited, folks knew that kerosene lamps had caused other such fires in Pithole.

Although 1000 concerned citizens flocked to an emergency meeting at Murphy's Theater and approved the purchase of firefighting equipment, the Council of the Borough had no such funds. The second mandate required every person holding property to have two barrels of water at the ready for fighting fires.

In mid-December, a kerosene lamp had exploded in the lobby of the Tremont House then caught the Cayuga House ablaze. Next the Continental Hotel and Welch's Boarding House burned, triggered by a scorched chimney. Fires were not the only cause to worry during the long, dark days of frigid winter weather.

A growing cynicism circulated among many citizens of

Pithole as winter enfolded the town. A post war depression enveloped the nation and even the once-booming petroleum business came under its influence. Although oil flowed through the new pipelines, oil prices remained low. The real concern was for the flagging demand for crude. The thousands of teamsters who had departed left businesses with few customers. The plank roads were in serious, deteriorating condition. The once teeming streets of Pithole were now almost deserted. Bars, brothels and other places of amusement sorely missed the free-spending young team drivers. Thousands of business and professional men disappeared with no plans to return. "FOR-RENT" and "VACANCY" signs were displayed throughout the snowy streets. *The Pithole Daily Record* advertised, appealing to customers for hotels, boarding houses, grocery stores, butcher shops and various services. Performers at the Murphy's Theater and the Athenaeum came less frequently and both buildings were advertised for sheriff's sale. Other properties up for tax sale interested few to no takers.

The Titusville Morning Herald summed up the dismal disaster: "…Pithole looks like a deserted village. It is possible to walk from one end of the town to the other and not be able to count twenty inhabitants."

The once thriving town lay quiet, blanketed in silent snow that reflected the yellow-orange flames of burning gas from hundreds of oil wells. By night, these ghostlike lamps noiselessly lit up the oil fields. By day, a suffocating pessimism subdued anxious inhabitants.

Pithole was crashing.

The Downward Drift

February 1866

Luke waded through the blowing snow on Brown Street toward French Kate's Restaurant. He was coming before the scheduled time for the lunch trade, and was hoping for a bowl of hot stew, something to warm him up. He was still absorbing the news from Elias.

Elias, Gala and Little Elias were staying in Pitch Pine where they had gone to celebrate Christmas with his mother, Molly. Instead of returning to Pithole, Elias and Gala had decided to remain with his family. Pithole was dangerous. Elias had taken a job with the Oil City and Pithole Railroad, because his prolonged absence from his family seemed ill advised. This was especially true since Gala was "in a family way" as his mother had put it.

Today, in addition to selling the *Pithole Daily Record*, he had an extra job of distributing fliers for Mr. Spare who had printed them, 1000 handbills announcing the arrival of an entertainment group that was scheduled to appear in Pithole. He laid the fliers on the dining table closest to the entrance, then grabbed the broom and quickly swept the snow off of the steps and veranda.

When he re-entered, Mabelle was reading one of the handbills aloud to Kate and Jenny as they set up for lunch.

"Here it says, 'Playing February 2 and 3 at 8 PM (doors open at 7) at the Athenaeum: Hagan's Dramatic Athlete and Pantomime Troupe.' Then they list the 'talented artists': Mrs. Lizzy Smith, Miss Isabelle, Mr. J.B. Smith, Mr. Ben Hagan, Mr. Hadley…"

Kate stopped laying out plates and turned toward Mabelle. "Who was the last name you read?"

"Mr. Hadley?"

"No, the one before that."

"Mr. Ben Hagan."

"Let me see that." She took the handbill for her own inspection. She read aloud, "Ben Hagan!" She felt a wave of pleasure wash over her. Benedict Hagan was coming to Pithole. She sat down in a nearby chair and re-read the announcement with his name on it.

Her three employees watched her as she seemed lost in thought.

"So, who is Ben Hagan? Somebody you know?"

"Well, yes. He worked for me when we were in the Baltimore, when I first came to America from France."

"You lived in France, Miss Kate? That must have been something!" Mabelle's eye danced with excitement.

"Luke, may I keep this handbill?"

"Yes, Miss Kate. You can keep it. I have plenty of 'em. You are my first customer!" And he headed into the kitchen to see what was for lunch.

...

Benedict Hagan looked down at the station master who ran the freight offices of the Pithole Railroad in Oil City. The small two-story building, constructed of bare brown boards lay at the bottom of a steep hill. He squinted in the mid-day sun at the scraggly, leafless trees that clung onto the rocky, snow-covered outcroppings just yards away. He could see why the residents of this forlorn-looking borough continued to describe to anyone who would listen to them about the historic flood of March 1865.

The raging waters of Oil Creek and the Allegheny River had caused a vast amount of damage. On the buildings that survived, muddy high-water marks told part of the story, along with the remaining piles of debris that citizens, fatigued with the enormous clean-up had learned to ignore. Heaps of broken boards and several huge uprooted trees rested on both north and south banks of the Allegheny River. Yet here in the center of these ruins, workers were laying tracks that led from the railroad freight yard on the north river bank, where he stood, and continued up-stream until they disappeared around a curve.

"You mean to tell me that passengers cannot ride this train into Pithole? It seems like the only reasonable way to get there from here."

The stocky station master shrugged his shoulders.

"Well, in a month or so, passenger service will commence, according to the schedule." He scratched his scraggly gray beard. "'Course it goes without sayin' that the weather may have ideas of its own." He revealed a missing front tooth as he smiled at his own humor.

357

"I need transport now, not in a couple of months."

"Tell ya what I can do fer ya, if'em you want. We can transport your gear, all the equipment you say you have on this here railroad. 'Course, you and your troupe will have to get into Pithole, otherwise. But you won't have to tote yer stuff there." He paused. "Well, of course that depends on them guys over there," and he gestured with his gloved thumb toward a gang of twenty or so workers who were hauling rails and ties from a freight car and carrying them along the railbed toward a location around the bend.

Benedict frowned and considered the offer.

"I need my baggage shipped tomorrow, no later. You mean the rails are not yet in place?"

"Well, yes and no."

Benedict shifted his weight. This seemed to be taking a long time, arranging for shipping to Pithole.

"Ya see, mister. Our fellas are layin' the track just fine, accordin' to the schedule set by Mr. Shirk, Jacob Shirk. He's directin' this here project--he and Mr. Fox, in charge of construction for the Oil City and Pithole Railroad. Got the right-o'-way from the Borough of Oil City and all that…"

"How much? How much will you charge me to pack our belongings onto the train?" Benedict's feet were cold and he was running short of patience.

"That's what I'm getting' to. You see the Warren an' Franklin, part of the Pennsylvania Central Railroad--well, they are disputin' Mr. Shirk's right to be layin' this line to Oleopolis. Ya' see once to Oleopolis, the tracks to Pithole are already in use--just a matter of hookin' them up. Been makin' trouble here for a day or so."

"Trouble? What kind of trouble?"

"Well, sir, as soon as our men grade the bed and lay the rails, them guys who's workin' for the Warren an' Franklin are bargin' in here--200-300 of them at a time an' fillin' up the road bed with rock an' junk and tearin' up the ties an' rails fast as our men can lay 'em." He paused. "They're even throwin' some of the rails and ties into the Allegheny!"

Just then, two men rushed past Benedict and the agent. They were dog-trotting toward the bend in the roadbed, but were close enough for Benedict to hear them.

"We got $30-$40,000 riding on this construction. These disruptions and disputations are costing us money, each day we're delayed. We've hired 400 men to complete this job." Then they passed out of earshot.

"That there is Mr. Shirk in the black coat, and the gent tryin' to keep up with him is Mr. Fox, both Oil City to Pithole Railroad managers. Looks like they're headed up 'round the bend there, where the commotion is today. 'Cuse me, I'm gonna have to go up there to see what's happenin'"

Benedict hesitated for just a second then impulsively followed the agent. As he ran forward, he heard a roar go up from a crowd, just as he was rounding the bend. Shirk and Fox were surrounded by dozens of men. As Shirk placed his booted foot on a railroad tie, the restive group got quiet. Shirk, a medium height gentleman, shouted.

"No one has the right to tear up the work of the track-layers." He turned and shifted his gaze to his left. "Mr. White, David White, you'd best get your men out of here and let my workers lay these rails."

The crowd rumbled and Benedict could feel the tension among the several hundred men. One group was attempting to lay rails but the other faction was armed with pickaxes, crowbars, and shovels.

Then White, a muscular-looking man stepped out of the crowd and confronted Shirk.

"You have no right to this roadbed!"

One of White's workers moved toward Shirk with a pickax poised over his head. A collective gasp swept the crowd. The aggressor swung the pick and planted the sharp end of the ax into the wooden tie only inches from Shirk's foot. A roar went up from the hundreds of workers from both railroad companies. The aggressors moved toward him, like an ocean wave rolling onto the beach.

Shirk appeared trapped, and he drew a pistol from his pocket.

White leaped up onto a nearby tool box and goaded his faction. An angry shout went out from those opposing the stalled railroad workers.

"Kill him! Kill him." White began the chant and his lackeys joined in. "Kill him!" The sound roared up the river valley.

Armed with tools of their trade, White's employees rushed Shirk and Fox. The construction engineers took off running hard, like two rabbits sprung from their hiding places. The menacing mob of several hundred men pursued them into the center of Oil City.

The construction crew for the Oil City to Pithole Railroad followed, lugging picks and shovels, ready for battle.

Benedict was short-winded as he followed the crowd back past the rail center. By the time he caught up with the rioters in the center of town, word passed through the crowd that Shirk had barricaded himself in his home.

"Somebody go get the police 'afore this here gets completely out of control."

"Wonder how much the Franklin to Warren Rail people are paying these Irishmen, fresh from the old country to harass the Oil City to Pithole workers. Looks to me like that White fella is the center of all of it."

"Listen! I hear that church bell that signals everyone to gather-up to help the police. Here they come now."

As the police were attempting to restore order, they herded the hoards toward the lock-up where they faced the borough's Burgess. White led his workforce, armed with shovels, picks and crowbars as they shouted obscenities and threats at the authorities.

"These police can't scare us. Nobody in this town can stop us from tearing up those rails! Let's go for them, men!" White's orders echoed off of the hillsides and the tool-toting toughs slogged through the mud toward the police in a threatening manner.

Benedict leaned against a building and pondered the situation. It reminded him of his days in New Orleans before the war, men besting each other about the side they were taking, North versus South. He could go in there and take care of White himself, no problem. But too many pickax-wielders. Could get himself killed, and for what? This was not his cause. He did not have a dog in the fight.

Word came through the crowd that the Burgess had issued a warrant for White's arrest. The police quickly quelled the rioting rowdies by handcuffing White and marching him to the jail. Benedict watched with interest. White dragged his feet and shouted to his followers.

"Burn down the freight station. Burn down this whole damned town!"

Benedict moved so that he could see the rebellious roustabout enter the jail. The noise of the threatening throng was muted by the lack of a leader, and the crowd slowly scattered.

Mulling over what he had just witnessed, Benedict removed his hat and ran his fingers of his right-hand through his hair. No wonder there was no rail service of any kind from Oil City to Pithole. The railroad companies and their employees were too busy fighting over the roadbed and rights-of-way.

Without a backward glance, Benedict headed toward the stagecoach ticket office.

…

Luke was lost in thought as he swept the dining room floor of French Kate's Restaurant. Looking out toward the veranda, he was relieved to see a line forming for 5:00, the first seating of the evening meal. Since the teamsters and many others had departed Pithole, the second seating sometimes was not needed and the line of the first appeared shorter than six months ago. He had heard Mr. Spare at the *Pithole Daily Record* say that the population was shrunken to 4000 from the 15,000 recorded last October.

Suddenly, Mabelle was at Luke's elbow and jolted him out of his thoughts.

"Luke, looka' there! See that gent that just jumped the line and is comin' up the steps? Who is that? Look at the way he's dressed! Never saw such as that comin' through this door!"

Luke looked toward the entrance and his jaw dropped. A muscular-looking man with a dark, closely-cropped beard opened the door. Before he entered, he shook the snow from his black beaver hat. His well-pressed dark suit and stand-up, celluloid collar bespoke him as a gentleman of high fashion, not a mud-spattered teamster or well-worker with thigh-high muddy boots and suspenders over-top a heavy, woolen shirt.

The arrival looked the dining room up and down.

Mabelle stepped forward.

"Can I help you? Dinner starts at 5:00-in just fifteen minutes…"

"I am in search of an old friend, Miss Katherine Garonne. Is she on the premises?"

Luke looked to Mabelle for an answer to this inquiry.

"Well, Miss Kate is the owner of this restaurant. Is that who you're seekin'?"

"Don't know until I see her. Is she here?"

"Yes. Who should I tell her is inquirin' after her?"

He smiled.

"You tell her that Benedict Hagan is calling."

"Benedict Hagan!" Luke blurted, then put his hand over his

mouth. He recovered. "You are the actor on the fliers that I handed out to folks!"

"Awe, and you must be Luke, the newspaper boy who is doing such a fine job for *The Pithole Daily Record*. Mr. Spare spoke highly of you. Said you worked diligently to distribute the fliers for my show, 'Hagan's Dramatic Athlete and Pantomime Troupe.' No wonder we had a full house last night!"

Hagan held out his hand to shake with Luke who could feel the enormous strength of his grip.

"Yes, I am Luke." He paused and turned to Mabelle. "And this here is Miss Mabelle. She works here too. We both do."

As if on cue, Kate appeared then approached. Hagan turned toward her and bowed deeply. "It is Miss Katherine! I am in the right place."

Luke saw Kate's face flush and her eyes lowered to midway as she looked Benedict up and down. He produced papers from his inside vest pocket, and held them aloft.

"Now that I have located you, Miss Katherine, I am inviting you, Miss Mabelle and Luke to attend our second and final performance while we are in Pithole." And he placed the tickets in Kate's outstretched hand.

"Thank you." Her eye-lashes fluttered as she spoke. Luke and Mabelle voiced their thanks as well.

"Benedict, let's you and I have a drink and catch-up. It's been years since I've seen you!" She turned toward Mabelle.

"You, Luke and Tilda can manage the first seating, can you not?"

"Oh, yes, Miss Kate!" As she guided Benedict toward the bar, her waitstaff prepared to accommodate the cold, hungry men who were lined-up outside.

…

The evening after the performance of "Hagan's Dramatic Athlete and Pantomime Troupe" performance, Kate and Benedict sat side-by-side at the end of the bar, a half bottle of whiskey between them. With only a kerosene lantern on a nearby table, the light was dim; the restaurant was deserted; and the girls were rid of their evening customers. Now, she could surreptitiously study him. Tonight, on the stage of the Athenaeum, his muscles bulged as he had hefted the heavy stone on to his chest and broke it. The audience was awed and she too was amazed. She had felt herself drawn to him.

He appeared more mature than when they had met on the Baltimore docks two years earlier. As she listened to his recounting some of his adventures, she realized that those intervening years had been two years of fast-living and hard-drinking.

"Yes, I gambled, played cards, made money, lost money. Always an opportunity to gain a few more greenbacks." He paused. "Matter of fact, I played fero bank in Mobile, dueled in New Orleans and gambled my way through the South to the North."

He took a drink of his whiskey and continued.

"I did come through Pithole last July and witnessed the wild building that had begun. It was then that I encountered Miss Emma who now resides across the street here. She was in the process of leasing her lot at that time. She and I struck up an acquaintance of sorts." He paused and gave Katherine a sideways glance.

"Were you around here then?"

"Yes, I was not staying in the town yet, just in the area."

"So, that's why I did not see you among the crowd that was trying to lease a piece of this place."

"You were looking for me?" Kate felt pleased that he had searched for her then. She remembered how she almost forgot her courier cover, and could have exposed herself to authorities when she had spotted him in the train station in Buffalo. She had wanted to see him then, to feel his strong arms around her, a comfort that she had so needed.

Kate was careful not to mention her entanglement with John Wilkes Booth. Even Benedict might think that she had taken one step too far, who knew? And she definitely did not want to scare him off now. This was her opportunity to attract him, to keep him near her. Was Emma yet of interest to Benedict? She would take care of that if it were so. She needed him.

Seductively, she leaned toward him to provide an enticing view of her breasts that the deeply-cut neckline of her Paris-made gown offered.

"You and your troupe are pulling out tomorrow? You've filled the house two nights in a row. Why not a third and fourth?" She poured another shot of whiskey for both of them. When he did not answer, and put the drink to his lips, she went on.

"The entire performance showed all of us a rollicking good time. I especially enjoyed Miss Isabelle's singing and dancing, and the high-flying Whettony Brothers were amazing on the flying trapeze." She paused and looked into his eyes. "Of course, you are my favorite act, Professor Hagan." She laid her left hand on his right arm and ran her fingers over his rippling muscles.

He smiled and took her hand from his arm and then placed her fingers on his lips.

"I have been giving my immediate future some thought since I've arrived here. Being on the road, especially in these parts, can be troublesome. No good train service and these rough, muddy roads can be tiresome."

What Benedict was not telling his former boss was his other reason for remaining in Pithole. The night after the last performance at the Athenaeum, as the manager, he had collected $1900 from the two-night's profit and he owed money to his performers. Before paying them, he had decided to use that sum to make himself some extra money. Easily finding a game of faro bank, he spent the next three hours playing. His gambling lost him the entire amount of money. The next morning, he confessed and suffered the ire his troupe that left town without him.

He turned full toward her.

"With a little persuasion, I might be tempted to put down roots for a while."

Katherine could feel her heart pounding and a stirring between her legs.

"What kind of persuasion could change your mind and keep you from the tour?"

Slowly, he pulled her into his arms, picked her up and carried her to a nearby couch. He eased the top of her dress down to her waist and touched her breasts with one hand while working his other hand up her skirt and into her pantaloons. She responded to his touch, and was aroused to the point of total submission.

He whispered in her ear.

"Every time I look at that scar on my right knee, I think about you…I have been waiting two years for this moment…"

She murmured and languished in the thought.

"It's about time…"

…

As he lay in his makeshift bed under the work table at French Kate's Restaurant, Luke was basking in the glow of the two-hours of exciting entertainment at the Athenaeum he had watched with Kate and Mabelle. He had never seen such acts, especially Benedict

Hagan breaking a huge rock on his chest. How had he done that? Nobody he knew had such muscles. Ben's muscles had bulged and gleamed during that strenuous feat. The crowd's yelling, stamping their feet on the wooden flooring, and clapping rang in his ears. He couldn't wait to ask Mr. Hagen about how he developed such strength. Maybe he could learn how to practice building such a physique.

He was falling off to asleep when he heard the clanging of a church bell. Fire! Another fire! Now where?

Jumping up from his bed, Luke pulled on his coat as he shuffled in his stocking feet toward the door. His boots, usually cold and stiff when dropped off outside, lay inside where he'd left them when he had arrived. Sitting on the cold floor, he quickly pulled them on, stood up and unlatched the front door.

Mabelle's calling to him made him stop.

"Luke, are you awake? Do you hear the fire bells?"

"Yes, I am going outside to see where the fire is."

"Come back and tell us, will you?"

He agreed, then headed out the door and down the snowy steps. When he stood in the center of Brown Street, he could see the yellow flames leaping upward in the sky to the north. In the fire light that reflected off of the recently fallen snow, his path was better illuminated and he took off running up the hill toward the flames. By the time he reached Fourth Street, he could feel the heat from the conflagration. Several walls of the Tremont Hotel were aflame.

On the opposite side of Holmden Street, men and women hovered together in the cold. He saw several girls who were wrapped only in government blankets, bare legs exposed to the cold night air. The men of the bucket brigade were working furiously, passing buckets of water to those nearest the fire.

Suddenly one of the men on the fire line dropped out, carrying a bucket with him. Luke watched him take off his gloves and stick his fingers into the water. The crowd viewing the firefighting stopped talking as they observed this worker.

"Harvey, bring that light over here, would ya?"

The two hovered over the bucket that sat in the middle of the street.

"Look at this! It's not just water. It has oil floating on the top!"

"Where'd it come from?"

"The water? From that well right over there, a neighbor's

well, Mrs. Ricketts well!"

"Holy cow! There must be oil in that water well. What the…"

"Here we thought we were dumpin' water on the fire, and now find out it's partly crude oil. No wonder the fire's not under control. We've been feedin' this inferno!"

Suddenly, onlookers disappeared, then reappeared with buckets, barrels and other receptacles capable of holding some of the "water" from Mrs. Ricketts' well. Despite the fire and its dangers, the boomtown folks had oil on the brain.

During the night, the blazes spread and burned down the Chautauqua Livery Stables and partially damaged The Buffalo House and the nearby United States Hotel. The Tremont House where the fire started was a total loss. But predictably, the incinerated buildings were not the most talked about event of the disastrous fire.

The really hot topic around town was the wells--water wells that flowed with oil instead of water. By sunrise, excited citizens spread the news about the three water wells and five nearby springs on the west side of Holmden Street and the backside of John Street that were flowing with crude oil.

For the next weeks, thousands of curious visitors flooded Pithole eager to see the remarkable sixteen-foot water well that catapulted the lease holder out of poverty. Widow Ricketts had been eking out a living by taking in washing. Now, zealous speculators had bid on her lease until it was worth $7000, almost overnight and she earned the name of "Mrs. Cinderella Ricketts--The Oil Princess."

"And the best part of the story about the fire and Mrs. Ricketts is those men, four Irishmen proposed marriage to her!" Mabelle laughed. "But she was smart enough to stay away from those gents who just wanted her money."

Neighbors speculated about why there was oil in those water wells.

"That pipeline to Miller Farm probably leaked that oil…"

"No, it happens when the ground water rises with a heavy rainfall, and the oil comes to the top. That's all."

Nobody was sure of why Pithole had crude oil in its water wells. What they were sure of was that those city lots where the wells were located were affected. Their value increased--doubled, and so did the number of fires in Pithole.

Ferocious Fighting

February—April 1866

Just days after Benedict Hagan decided to stay in Pithole, he placed an advertisement in the *Pithole Daily Record*. It announced that "Professor Hagan" would hold sparring exhibitions and gymnastic demonstrations at his new location on First Street. Touting himself as the "Eminent Master of Gymnastics and the Celebrated Champion of the Manly Art," he offered boxing lessons, fifteen for $10. When only a few inquisitive menfolk came to his establishment, he moved to re-invent himself.

In an ad that appeared several weeks later, Benedict Hagan had changed his name to Hogan, perhaps, some thought, to alter his Germanic name to a more Irish sounding surname. The many Irish immigrants employed by the railroads, and other oil country work might have thought the name, "Hogan," similar to their own names, and signed up for Ben Hogan's events. However, in early March, a different arrival in Pithole read the advertisements and answered pugilist-Hogan's challenge to take on all-comers.

Stonehouse Jack stomped up the steps of French Kate's Restaurant just as Mabelle, Tilda and Kate were cleaning up from the lunch crowd. He pushed the entrance door open with such force that it banged against the wall and startled the three women. He stood with hands on hips looking every inch of six-feet tall. His stringy black hair hung in an unkempt manner, and Kate thought that it had not seen soap and water in months. She said nothing, waiting for him to speak.

"I come by here to see what the competition looks like."

"Competition, what competition?" A cold chill shot down Kate's spine, alerting her to the danger that had just invaded her dining room. She put her right hand on the gun in the pocket of her skirt.

"Don't give me that twaddle. You know what I am talkin' about. They say that you run a cat-house here and I come to make a visit to see it."

Kate frowned and did not move.

"Well, my place is not on display. This is a private business and you've no right to come bursting in here, uninvited and unannounced."

"Well, let me introduce myself." His voice sounded menacing and mocking. She thought he snarled instead of talked.

"I am Stonehouse Jack, and as a name called by them folks in Cleveland, 'notorious champion of all devilry.' I am the new owner, the keeper of the Old Free and Easy, just a block over." He gestured with a sweep of his left arm.

Mabelle and Tilda stood stalk still, their eyes fastened on the intimidating intruder. Kate took a step in his direction.

"State your concern, Mr. Jack. Our noon-time trade has eaten and departed. You're too late for food."

"I come here to discuss the fights that involve the girls from my Free and Easy, called Heenan's Cottage. Just bought them out, but the girls come with the deal." He shifted his weight, staring at Kate.

"So, I am here to warn you that you need to keep your inmates away from my place. I don't want no hair-pullin' screaming match such as what I learned goes on around here. Those four bitches of the Rob Roy House messed up each other scratchin' and brawling. Got one of my girls in trouble, but she escaped bein' arrested with Mary Quinn and the other three."

"That has nothing to do with my place. What do you want?"

He sat down on the edge of a dining table with his arms folded.

"Well, I got word about the dead body, a baby's headless body being found over across the mud-patch to Emma's place. What's that all about? You know?"

"It's none of my business, Mr. Jack. I stick to my own affairs."

"Well, I know what went on," Tilda blurted out.

Katherine gave her a hard stare, and she could see Mabelle poking Tilda in the ribs with her elbow. Nevertheless, Tilda, the most recently hired of her employees gushed on.

"Somebody was out walking in back of Emma's when they come across the body. The police got wind of it and there was an investigation by the chief of police and the constable." She took a breath. "But nothin' come of it. Nobody got arrested or nothin'."

Stonehouse looked uncomfortable for the first time during his invasive visit. He tugged on the frayed collar of his soiled shirt.

"What I'm referrin' to is the big fight between Emma Hall and Charlotte…her last name escapes me."

"Orm," Tilda filled in.

"They claim that there was another woman who was in that fight where Emma and Charlotte were goin' at it...blackening each other's eyes and gittin' arrested."

"So, what's that have to do with my place?" Kate was ready for this frightening bloke to depart.

"Said that a person from your place was involved."

"Who told you that?"

"I ain't sayin.'"

"Well, then this conversation is over."

Stonehouse pushed himself off of the dining table and stood to leave. He stopped at the door-jam and turned.

"Oh, and by the way, I understand that the braggart, Ben Hogan is a special friend of yours." He looked straight at Kate. "You tell him that he better stop that braggin' 'cause I can bust him up real good." He stomped out and slammed the door behind him.

The next addition of *The Pithole Daily Record* ran an article about Stonehouse Jack, also known as Robert J. Vance, who had turned up in Pithole. They listed him as a fugitive of justice who faced a charge of murder in Cleveland, Ohio for shooting a man named James McCue. They noted that Stonehouse had accepted Ben Hogan's challenge to a fight. The paper editorialized, "We hope our police will prevent the fight from coming off."

That afternoon, Kate cleaned her pistol and reloaded it. Stonehouse Jack had come skulking around her restaurant once and could easily return. However, Ben Hogan kept Stonehouse occupied in the coming days and any thoughts of his returning to harass her were squelched.

...

On Saturday, March 10th, the arena at the Metropolitan Stables rocked with excitement. The fervent fans of fighting packed the area, some piling on to the wooden fence on the west side for a clearer view of the anticipated action. Many toted flasks filled with whiskey or containers with other alcoholic favorites. Kate and Jeremiah scored front-row seats with tickets from Ben, and they arrived early enough to watch him warm up prior to the fight.

Stonehouse made his appearance before the start of the event and strutted about the ring when his name was announced, waving both hands in the air and shadow punching as he swaggered. He made eye contact with Kate and spat on the floor within her view.

Jeremiah turned to her.

"He appears like an aggressive fighter, and has a mean, nasty look to him, too. Good thing you weren't alone when he came calling the other day."

"Ben said the same thing…he is an unpleasant person, very unpleasant."

After six breakneck rounds of punches and jabs, sparring and fancy footwork, neither contestant was the worse for it. The packed-in spectators were agitated to a heightened level of anticipation for the conclusion of the spectacle. By now, the arena reeked of a nauseating odor of human sweat, horse manure and stale ale. The outcome of the match was to be determined by a decision. When the crowd heard that, they became restless and some booed at the proclamation, apparently wishing for a more bruising battle. A hush fell over the anxious onlookers and when the decision declared Hogan the winner, a roar of approval swept through the arena.

Stonehouse loudly disputed the decision and with his jaws clenched and eyes like slits, he moved within arms-length of the proclaimed winner.

"I challenge you to a second match!" He shouted and glared at Hogan. "With or without gloves!"

Hogan consented to Stonehouse's contentious contest, and arrangements were made for the fight to follow with a $250 prize to the winner. The spot selected for the challenge was a clearing at nearby Balltown. The police wanted no such fight within the Borough limits.

However, days before the scheduled re-match, Stonehouse apparently was unable to contain his animosity. The sun was low in the west and the last of Ben's clients had departed from his newly acquired establishment. He was cleaning up the gym when he heard footfalls on the outside steps of his place. He looked up just in time to see Stonehouse fling the door wide and slam it into the outside wall of the building.

"You son-of-a-polecat! You think you're such a good fighter! Swaggerin' around the ring the other day…tryin' to make me look bad!"

Ben stood still, watching the intruder. Stonehouse's fists were clenched, his back hunched, and muscles of his face looked contorted.

"You're really a coward! Hidin' behind that fancy footwork you used to trick the judges. Think you're a pretty boy, do you?" He moved toward Ben. "We don't need no fight next week to settle who's the best. Let's do it now!"

When Ben failed to respond to his verbal blows, Stonehouse got into a boxing stance, both fists clenched, ready for action.

"Come on, you coward. Let's duke it out now, once and for all!" He moved closer to Ben, and took a swing near Ben's head. Ben stepped back to avoid being hit.

"I know you're tryin' to ruin my reputation as a fighter! And I ain't gonna let that happen!"

With those words, he lunged at Ben who sidestepped the assault. Red-faced and sweating, his eyes like slits, Stonehouse glared at Ben, holding the stare. Suddenly he lunged again, this time landing a punch to Ben's left shoulder.

Once hit, Ben moved from defensive to offensive, mentally and physically. He backed away from the assailant.

"Stonehouse, you came in here looking for a fight. You're on my property and trying to provoke me into fighting you. I'm telling you now, that's not a good idea for you. If I were you, I'd stop now."

Stonehouse ran at Ben who met him with a punch in the face. His opponent looked surprised at the blood that gushed down his face and onto his shirt.

Like an angry bull in heat, Stonehouse picked up a nearby stool and flung it at Ben. He ducked the wooden missile and rushed Stonehouse, knocking him to the floor, now awash with blood.

Just then, Ben saw Kate appear in the doorway.

"What's going on, Ben?"

From his position on the floor, Stonehouse continued to shout contemptable names at Ben. Ben signaled her to stay clear of the fighting. He knew he was winning this unsolicited skirmish.

"Get up off the floor, Stonehouse. You wanted this fight! Now we're going to finish it."

Ben stood ready as his opponent slowly regained his feet. Each time Stonehouse shouted an obscenity, Ben pummeled him. Finally, Stonehouse fell silent. His face was covered with blood and he was so battered that he staggered, and was unable to stand. He toppled over like a drunken sailor in port on payday. Minutes later, he revived himself, and slunk out of Benedict's gym.

By the time the police arrived at the scene, Stonewall had disappeared and Kate withdrew. Ben surrendered himself to the law enforcement. When He faced the Justice, Highberger did not hand down a punishment, but only reprimanded the pugilist.

Stonewall had departed Pithole.

The March 16, 1866 edition of the *Pithole Daily Record,* "complimented" Ben Hogan "for ridding the community of the undesirable Stonehouse." In a short period of time, Ben Hogan was becoming a well-known figure in Pithole. He had rid Pithole of one danger, but another appeared.

…

A week earlier on March 8, after most of the neighbors on Mason Street were in bed asleep, an arsonist set fire to the Star Bakery owned by William Douglas. Unfortunately, the bakery had fallen on hard times as the population of the borough waned, and Douglas immediately came under suspicion as having started the fire to collect the insurance. Further sleuthing by the insurance company and the police found the owner innocent and solved the mystery. A disgruntled former female employee sought revenge for being discharged as a "garrulous nuisance." Douglas received his insurance payment. Other fires were caused by arsonists as well.

Insurance companies directed their fire investigators to prove that some fires had been set by property owners looking for insurance payouts. Citizens who had discontinued their insurance due to skyrocketing costs were frightened and angry at the very thought of arson. There were threats of lynching such criminals who were endangering the community for their own greediness.

A clothing store owner, Joseph Levi had recently increased the insurance on his business. On the night Levi had departed for a business trip to New York, a passerby discovered a container of burning garbage on the outside wall of Levi's store. By the time firefighters arrived, a hot fire brought icy skepticism and suspicious insinuations against the owner. Levi hastily returned to Pithole and had to defend himself.

A few nights later, a kerosene lamp exploded in the National Hotel on Brown Street at 2:45 A.M. The lack of an alarm bell and the problems of awakening fire fighters resulted in the hotel being completely incinerated. The blazes claimed five nearby houses, the Wisconsin Livery Stable and the Lincoln House. This conflagration and others like it continued a deadly destruction of the boomtown.

These fire hazards, the same poorly assembled structures bereft of tightly tied timbers and lack of crack fillers proved to be poor protection against the cold winter weather and wild west winds.

The inhabitants of these breezy abodes suffered from various illnesses. Having survived the threats of cholera during the Fall and the rumors of dysentery from the lack of sanitary facilities, the people of Pithole were afflicted by catarrh, grippe, and pneumonia during the cold months.

The frequent victims of many diseases including infectious respiratory illnesses, prostitutes working in brothels were in close contact with countless men. The sixty to seventy-five establishments in the booming borough housed some 400 such female inhabitants. These anonymous young women seemed to appear from nowhere as the town thrived and money flowed. Despite Burgess Keenan's 1866 New Year's Day proclamation that such lawless businesses would be brought to justice, those in charge just turned a blind eye and silenced their tongues.

The editor of the *Pithole Daily Record*, however, spoke his mind. Earlier, on January 18, the author of a story had railed against "debauching and disgusting scenes at the 'Free and Easy...'" with "the females gliding among the patroons plying their trade."

In a later edition of the *Record*, an appeal appeared urging that a new law be passed banning "...pretty waiter-girls in concert saloons and other places of amusement in this county--if passed--will remove the only visible means of support of these places."

The girls from the brothels on First Street were notorious for their brawling behavior and frequent fights, and, in general, were not suppressed by the law. It was illness that struck them down and put some of them out of business.

A number of Emma's girls were stricken with fits of fever and bouts of coughing. Finally, someone summoned a doctor, but for several suffering young women, it was too late. The physician diagnosed the cause of their deaths as pneumonia, a condition that was ravaging the town. The number of deaths was rising. To make matters worse, rumors began circulating that other diseases were invading the boomtown, as well.

When several cases of diphtheria were diagnosed, contacts of those who were ill required quarantine. Warning placards displayed at their place of business or dwellings kept the public at bay. Talk of establishing a "pest house" confronted the borough, but funds to build this small hospital for containing contagious diseases never materialized. Not only was the Borough of Pithole broke; it was in debt by $3700. Subsequently, with the number of deaths increasing, the question arose again as to the disposal of the bodies.

With so many strangers in the boomtown, victims' families were mostly unknown and family burial plots were in far-flung locations, not anywhere near Pithole. However, when kin of the deceased were identified, town authorities shipped the bodies to their families. When some arrivals did appear to take root in their new environment, the burial question changed.

Since they now appeared to be citizens, where should they be buried? The Holmden's had a private graveyard, and some months into the establishment of Pithole, they expanded the burial ground for newcomers. The Holmden family enclosed their plot with an iron fence. Additional graves, many of them unmarked were dug in the area, outside of that family fence.

In March, another young girl from a First Street establishment died. Since her name and hometown were unknown, shipping the body out of Pithole was not an option. When the question of where to bury her was considered, certain self-righteous citizens rigorously objected to the prostitute's interment in the town plot. The holier-than-thou hullabaloo caused a reverberating ruckus.

When the objections to burying the dead woman on "hallowed ground" of the Pithole graveyard rumbled through the borough, Reverend Darius Steadman, the Methodist minister tackled the problem. He declared that saints and sinners alike were welcomed by the church. He and his congregation agreed on that argument and determined to bury the homeless girl in the Methodist churchyard. Some of Pithole's most esteemed citizens were her pall-bearers.

...

Five weeks after Benedict Hogan arrived in Pithole, the first passenger train transported 200 people from Oil City to Pithole on March 10, 1866. Despite the fact that side switches and tracks on the Rooker Farm were unfinished, the yellow railroad station at Pithole was teaming with the new arrivals as well as local on-lookers, many of whom had never ridden on a train before. It seemed like a great day for Pithole, but for Kate, it renewed the possibility of her step-father's pursuers finding easier access to the once isolated area, her refuge.

For Luke and Mabelle, the initial passenger service spelled excitement of a new experience for them. One day in mid-March after the noon meal was completed and the diners, departed, they sat at one of the side tables in Kate's restaurant. They were counting out the money each had saved for the special occasion of their first train ride.

Kate had overheard their discussion.

"How do we know how much to pay for the tickets?"

"Well, Mabelle, here it says the passenger rate is seven cents a mile. Glad we're not freight, 'cause it costs more--fifteen cents a mile." They both laughed, but Mabelle's laugh morphed into a racking cough. When she caught her breath, she continued.

"So, for that kind of money, we get to ride for seven miles each way?"

"Yeah, and the ride lasts for about a half an hour and goes about as fast as a horse can gallop, a good horse." They both laughed again, remembering Jenny's joke the day the three had watched the first freight train arrive from Oleopolis. Luke had planned to purchase their tickets to Oleopolis and back for next Wednesday when Mabelle could get that afternoon off of work.

A few days later, Mabelle did not appear from her room above French Kate's Restaurant, and Kate directed Jenny to check on her. When the young waitress reappeared, her face was drained of color and her usual sunny smile had disappeared.

"Miss Kate, come quick! She won't wake up! I can't see her breathin'!"

Kate had noticed yesterday that Mabelle seemed listless and been coughing at the end of the first seating. But Mabelle had not complained.

She mounted the stairs and entered Mabelle's small room. In the darkness, she thought the chamber seemed stuffy and cold. Mabelle was clutching the edge of a blanket that was wrapped around her feet and legs. Kate placed her hand on Mabelle's chest. She could not feel a rise and fall of any respirations. She shook Mabelle's shoulder first with one hand and then with two. When Mabelle did not respond, she turned to Jenny who had followed her up the stairs.

"Go get Dr. Waring. Tell him that Mabelle is very ill and that we cannot awaken her."

Jenny turned and fled, stumbling down the stairs as fast as she could go without falling. Tears, streaming down her face, she scrambled into her boots and coat and was out the door and into the snow in just a few minutes.

Kate remained at Mabelle's side, but finding no signs of life, she descended to the restaurant and retreated to her liquor storage.

She poured herself a shot of whiskey, downed it in one jigger, then poured another. Sitting at the end of the bar, she waited for Dr. Waring to arrive.

This death would leave her without Mabelle's efficient organizing and energetic work in the operation of the restaurant. But just where would she find another girl to wait table at her place?

...

The train's shrill whistle filled the air as the wood-burning steam engine approached the Oleopolis station. Luke waited until the other passengers on his coach departed, and then he arose slowly to leave. Luke mused...it wasn't supposed to be like this. Mabelle should be right beside me, getting off of the train. Now, instead, I am walking alone and Mabelle is lying dead in a cold coffin.

He moved toward the end of the last passenger car and watched as two train workers off-loaded the pine-wood casket that bore Mabelle's body. They transferred the pine-board box to a freight car that was sitting on a siding. Luke stood at the end of the platform, unable to move, staring at the boxcar bearing his friend's body to Franklin, to some kinfolk, unknown to him.

Now, he realized how little he knew about her--why she had come to Pithole and from whence. What he did know was that from the beginning, she always looked out for him, like a big sister might do. Would one of his own sisters have been like Mabelle? Johanna and Magdalena who died of diphtheria, whom he's never known? Had they lived, maybe Mabelle would have been about their ages. But now, Mabelle, too was gone. He was lost in thought.

Just then, a loud crash startled him. He looked toward the source of the disturbing noise. The car with Mabelle's casket was jolted as it coupled with other train-cars that were headed south, down the Allegheny River.

Long suppressed tears filled Luke's eyes. He whispered.

"Mabelle, this is not the train ride that you and I had imagined. I am so sorry that you must go on alone from here."

Luke turned away as the train began its journey without him.

...

Kate stomped the mud from her boots as she entered the post office to check for mail. When she opened the box, two envelopes lay inside. One was wrinkled and somewhat soiled. She thought that it must be from Fredrick whose letters looked worn by the time they arrived in Pithole from France. She flipped over the second piece of mail. A letter from Ebenezer. Looking around, she saw nowhere to sit and read in private. Tucking both envelopes into her deep left-hand skirt pocket, she decided that she would have to wait until she got back to her place before she could read them. She headed down Holmden Street toward the drug store.

A bell tinkled, announcing her entrance to Lee and Gould's Drug Store on First Street. The pharmacy was empty of customers and she was alone there.

The familiar odor of chemicals and powders filled her nostrils as she moved slowly toward the back counter at the end of the long narrow room. On her left, she passed glass cases and shelves holding heavy bottles of various shapes, sizes and colors-- white, clear, and brown. To her right, shelves bulged with labeled containers that lined the wall, extending almost to the ceiling. The glass cases in front held perfumes and toilet waters from France. Pausing at the display, Katherine breathed in the odors of a line of products she knew to be some of the best manufactured.

She settled herself on the familiar four-legged backless-stool that placed her directly in front of the large white mortar and pestle that Mr. Gould used to grind and mix some of his compounds.

The short, white-haired pharmacist entered by pushing aside the cloth curtain that separated the store from his office. Eyeing Kate from over the top of his rimless spectacles, he cleared his throat.

"Good day, miss. How can I assist you?"

She leaned forward and spoke in a low tone. "I am here to get laudanum that was recommended by Dr. Waring. I need four ounces."

The pharmacist gave her a long look, then opened the door of a large cabinet.

"Awe, yes, Miss. I have what you want right here."

He turned to an array of rows of drawers in a large wooden cabinet to his right, and retrieved the drug. Within minutes, Katherine paid for her purchase and left the pharmacy.

Since she needed a girl to replace Mabelle, she had decided to have the drug on hand in case it was needed. A new waitress who was unaccustomed to her employ in the evening trade might need a dose of her purchase to ease her nervousness. Laudanum or whiskey were the remedies that worked for others, to calm their anxieties on their first or second trysts with evening customers. She tucked the small bottle wrapped in paper into her left skirt pocket with her mail and headed across the street to her place.

...

On March 28, 1866, the news struck, like a bolt out of the blue. Culver, Penn and Company was failing. The grandiose scheme of Charles Culver to build an utopian city with a railroad connecting Reno to oil producing areas such as Pithole and Petroleum Center had hit an impenetrable wall and burst the financial bubble. Although it drew little concern, the first sign of trouble came with construction delays in the building of the railroad. Like a silent copperhead snake that had struck, the real surprise came from a chain of bank failures that ripped through the Northwestern Pennsylvania oil country from their main banking house in New York City. At close of business on March 27, Culver and Penn suspended operations. Patrons holding the currency of any of Culver's banks found themselves without recourse. That paper money, issued by Culver's banks was worthless now.

With that dire news, the two Pithole banks, Prather, Wadsworth and Company and J.R. Kemp and Company closed up for two days in an attempt to prevent damages secondary to the Culver fiasco. Failure of the Culver, Penn and Company rattled the finances of many locals when banks scattered throughout the oil region were affected by the company's closure.

In Pithole, agitated, angry men gathered to discuss the worrisome situation. Many people panicked, unable to retrieve their savings or cash checks from one of Culver's banks. That money would be lost to them. Rumors abounded, raising the tempo of the fallout from the banking disaster. Culver claimed that he would meet his obligations. To complicate matters, Culver was the areas' representative in the U.S. Congress, 20th District and a major spokesman for the emerging oil industry. As well, two of his banks, one in Meadville and the other in Titusville modeled themselves as national banks despite the fact that they failed to meet the federal regulations for such by the national bank act.

...

Jeremiah bought Luke's last copy of the *Titusville Morning*

Herald.

"What does this mean, Jeremiah, this bank failure? People are really riled up over it. Been hearin' them talk all mornin'. Is it gonna make the oil wells stop producin'?"

They walked together down the muddy street toward Dewitt's Oyster House for the well driller's favorite lunch.

"No, Luke. It's not that bad for most folks. It's really bad for companies that are owed money by Culver and his cronies. We may end up havin' to elect a new representative to Congress. He's the one in a real mess. Remember when he brought all those prospective investors here to Pithole last Fall? Well, the ones who invested their money with him won't get it back…"

Luke felt encouraged.

"Did you decide on a well for me to invest in yet, Jeremiah? Usin' the money Kate gave me that she owed to Mabelle and the money I saved, I will have $100 by next week, if the newspapers keep selling like they did today."

"Yes, I have a well in mind. Found one that I thought you would find interesting. It's been dug already and was a good producer until a week ago. Just quit. The other driller and I think that it's clogged, either with wax or something. We have plans to try to unclog it by blastin' it with a torpedo."

Luke stopped in his tracks.

"A torpedo! What's that? Does it explode?"

"Yah, way down in the well. It seems that the owner is in need of some cash to do the blastin', so that's your opportunity to buy a slice of his stock offering. I think that it's a good bet, or I wouldn't be suggestin' it to you. It was a good producer before it stopped, so I think we can get it back up and flowing."

"When are you gonna blast it? Can I give you the money next week?" Luke was excited.

"Can I come to see it get blasted?"

"Oh, yah. I'll let you know. It will be several weeks, I reckon. We gotta get the torpedo and some supplies." Jeremiah paused. "You know we haven't blown more than one or two wells here in Pithole. It'll be something unusual for this place."

…

Ben and Kate sat at a table in the corner of Ben's boxing arena sharing food that she had brought for their late lunch. With the restaurant customers having been served at her place, she had left Jenny in charge with Tilda assisting in the cleanup. Now with Ben's next boxing student not due for an hour, they had time to talk in private.

"The letter from Ebenezer just brings up the old hatred and horrible memories about Petrus Plugge. I can't believe that he came by the Brooklyn Navy Yard, snooping around again. Ebenezer thinks that he gets a bit tipsy each time before he arrives…said he had liquor on his breath, and staggered some. Kept asking about my whereabouts…trying to get information out of poor old Ebenezer."

"Why is your friend so concerned?"

"The letter said that this time, that horrible stepfather of mine is waving a train schedule in his face. Says now that there's a way 'into that wilderness' that he's going to find me…make me sign those papers to release my property to him."

"Guess he needs the money, now that Ebenezer says he's remarried."

She was pensive.

"I hadn't thought of it until now, Ben, but I'll wager that woman, his new wife, wants a clear inheritance, in case something dire happens to Petrus."

"Sounds like that might be it, Kate. And what did Fredrick have to say? Anything new with the vineyards?"

"Yes, the treatment for the fungus seems to be working and he needs to meet with an arborist as well as several of his largest customers. He still plans to sail as soon as the North Atlantic is calmer. Probably in May or so."

Kate shifted her weight on the hard surface of her seat.

"I am overhearing some of the men at lunch say that you're being bearded by Jack Holliday. That he's been around town bragging about besting you in the ring. That true?"

"It seems that he's trying to get something set up for a fight. Problem is being the police, of course. They are not wanting a fight like this in town. Too many excited fans for them to contend with."

"Who is Holliday? Where'd he come from?"

Ben took a swallow of beer.

"I think he's from Rochester. Gained his fame for the strangest feat I've heard of. They say he wheeled a wheelbarrow all the way from Rochester to Buffalo, without stopping.

"What…?"

"Got him a lot of attention at the time, and now he's claiming to be a great fighter. So, guess he wants to prove to himself and anyone interested that he is what he claims to be--an unbeatable boxer."

"You planning to fight him?"

Ben reached over his empty plate and stroked her cheek.

"Of course. That's why I advertised in the newspaper…to bring attention to the sport of fighting and get some men interested in learning from me here at my gym." He paused. "I've decided to promote myself as 'the German Benedict' for this fight. That should catch some people by surprise…make them interested enough to come to the match.

…

On April 18, 1866, the sun broke through the gray clouds in time for the 2:00 P.M. fight between the German Benedict and J.J. Holliday. Just as Ben had predicted to Kate, a good-sized crowd of spectators were willing to pay one dollar for admission to this well-advertised fight. Avoiding interference of the Pithole police, promoters had staked off a fighting arena in a vacant field near Balltown.

Kate stood at the ring boundary, on the opposite side of the ropes from where Benedict was warming up. A mob of 800 encircled the staked-out area, pushing and shoving for the best possible view of the big fight. They were mostly men who had gathered, and she scanned the crowd, but saw no one she knew. Jeremiah positioned himself behind her, buffering her from the press of zealous fans of fighting. She felt protected by his presence.

He leaned closer to her left ear so he could not be overheard.

"Looks like most of these fellas are supporters of Holliday. They're a bad-mannered bunch, armed with rifles and pistols. I heard several threatening to stop the fight if they think it's unfair. This is not a friendly crowd for Ben."

Adjusting her hat to shade her eyes from the afternoon sun, she turned to look up at Jeremiah.

"If Ben wins this fight, I don't know what might happen…especially if his victory is by the judges' decision again. Look what happened in the match with Stonehouse."

She produced her whiskey flask from the left pocket of her skirt and took a drink. She could feel the familiar burning in her throat. But today, she reasoned, she needed the alcohol to calm her nerves. She had great faith in Ben's fighting ability, but who knew how this hostile, armed crowd would respond to the outcome of the fight.

Just as the match was about to begin, a dozen of men, clad in black hats and mounted on horseback, fringed the outer ring of the crowd. Their sudden appearance made her feel uneasy, and she took another drink from her flask.

At the appointed time, a dark-haired J.J. Holliday swaggered into the ring, holding his muscular arms in the air, and the crowd roared their approval. When Ben was announced, a few people clapped, but the lopsidedness of the crowd-support was blatant. The German Benedict faced a hostile situation. The six-foot-tall Holliday seemed to tower over Benedict's five-foot-ten height. Kate took another swig from her flask, ready for this competition to start.

At the signal, the match was on, Holliday swinging and Benedict outmaneuvering him for some minutes. Suddenly, Benedict swung into action, landing a punch which decked the big six-footer and round one ended. The second, and succeeding rounds were similar until the eighth round. During that bout, Holliday landed an illegal blow on Ben and the officials stopped the fighting.

In the remaining minutes of the contest, Holliday appeared to be waning, and Benedict took advantage. He lifted his opponent, threw him in a somersault, then with a one-two punch knocked Holliday flat. Now the outnumbered Hoganites cheered and chanted, "German Benedict," so loudly that the supporters of Holliday were muted and reluctantly ceased their verbal threats to disrupt the contest. Benedict had won fair and square, and not by a judge's decision. Holliday's henchmen knew it.

Kate watched Ben pick up a towel and mop his sweaty face. Just when she thought he was coming over to where she and Jeremiah were standing at the ropes, she spotted Emma. The red-haired madame from the Florence Restaurant leaned into the ropes and grabbed Ben's arm. Despite her having downed the entire flask of whiskey, Kate watched carefully, and felt blindsided by Emma's performance. What did Emma think she was doing? And in public? Benedict was her man, not Emma's.

"What's that about, Kate? Is Emma a friend of Ben's?"

"I'll see about that." She pushed her way past Jeremiah and through the departing mob until she reached the antagonist's side.

"So, Emma. I didn't know you are a fan of J.J. Holliday. That is why you're here today, right?"

Emma appeared surprised at the statement.

"No, Kate, I am here in support of Ben."

"Is Benedict a special friend of yours? I was not aware..."

Emma stared Kate straight in the face.

"Has it not come to your attention until now? Everyone in Pithole knows that Ben and I have a relationship." She paused, mocking her. "Where have you been?" Then she turned away with a whirl of her skirts.

Consumed with jealous rage, Kate grabbed Emma by her shoulder.

"You know that's not true. It's a lie, and you're probably the one spreading that rumor!"

She was furious at feeling publicly humiliated by this woman of such a reprehensible reputation. She leaned toward her target, hiked up her long skirts to above her knees, and kicked Emma as hard as she could--just like Jacques had taught her. She watched with satisfaction as Emma lay sprawled, face-down in the mud.

The End of an Era

Spring—Summer 1866

Conflagrations remained the scourge of the Pithole community in the Spring of 1866. The stench of burned wood and crude oil hung over the boomtown waiting for a spring breeze to cleanse the foul odor, until the next fire. With runoff from fire-fighting and each rain storm, Pithole's streets deteriorated into masses of mud that slowed both pedestrian and animal traffic to a near-halt. Since the downturn of the economy, many leases in Pithole were abandoned and when the businesses moved out, the buildings which they had occupied stood derelict. They were fuel for the future infernos.

Another in the series of catastrophic combustions began on the north side of First Street and spread, enveloping eight nearby buildings--a $30,000 loss with no insurance money forthcoming. One week later on April 3, Zinnegan's Hardware Store ignited and flames spread to a shoemaker's shop, a grocery store and on to the Franklin Hotel. During efforts to contain the blazes, the Utica House caught fire, but volunteers doused it with water and prevented that hotel's destruction. Then, the same week, another fire consumed the Old Homestead, a rooming house, the Holmden House and J. Shieve's bathhouse. Victims of that fire gathered their courage and money to begin rebuilding along First Street.

The problem of fighting fires not only continued, but escalated as the economy worsened. The two previously organized fire-fighter groups had lacked leadership, discipline, and community support. By now, they were non-existent. With no central location for equipment, no trained volunteers, and inadequate water pressure in the city pipes at night, the situation appeared hopeless. With the number of neglected buildings growing, the Borough Council offered support to anyone who could organize means to fight fires.

Finally in desperation, the Borough Council passed a law fining any able-bodied male occupant of Pithole, five dollars for refusing to assist other fire-fighting volunteers at the scene of a fire. Conversely, some citizens did step forward to control fires, even single-handedly.

The manager of the Oyster Bay Saloon was passing by the Waugh and Satterfield Grocery Store one evening when he saw a blaze inside the store. A lamp was on fire and the door to the store, locked. That did not deter Seth Crittenden. He broke into the building, and at his peril, grabbed the burning lamp and heaved it into the street. The *Pithole Daily Record* lauded him as a hero for his brave actions. At least one fire had been prevented, but unfortunately, further fires threatened the besieged boomtown.

...

"I am here in answer to an ad in the Buffalo newspaper."

Benedict came from behind the bar at French Kate's Restaurant to welcome the arrival, a slim, attractive girl dressed in a dark travel cloak and muddy black boots. She carried a carpet bag.

"Welcome to French Kate's place."

Kate heard the discussion and appeared from the kitchen carrying a large platter of potatoes, on the menu for the first seating.

"What have we here, Ben?"

"This is...what is your name?"

Speechless, the anonymous girl stared at her and Ben.

"Well, you must have a name. What is it?"

"What kind of place is this?"

"It's a restaurant."

"I was expecting a house...a home like the letter said... 'a respectable private family.' You are the people who sent the letter, aren't you?"

"Take your things upstairs and come right down to help serve dinner. Here's your apron." Kate was impatient.

"I didn't sign up to be a waitress. My mother would not have approved if she'd known that...and you serve alcohol here?" She turned toward the door.

"I'll be going. I've made a mistake."

Benedict grabbed "Anonymous" by her arm.

"You've come all this way. At least stay for the night. The stage won't go out to Titusville until 9:00 tomorrow morning."

Outside, men were beginning to line up for dinner. The girl saw them, and Kate thought she seemed to be considering their offer. But, she thought their applicant did look like trapped rabbit.

"Oh, it will be OK. We've a bed for you, so you don't need to pay for a hotel tonight. My name is Kate and I own this restaurant.

Benedict is my business associate."

Their frightened arrival seemed to be resolved.

"Well, all right. Just for tonight." Her voice sounded shaky. "My name is Cassandra." She turned toward Ben and burst into tears. "I'm so tired after that long trip…"

Kate placed the platter of potatoes on a table and led Cassandra to her room. When she returned, Ben looked at her quizzically.

"Think she'll stay?"

"I doubt it. She said she is hungry, so I'll fix her a plate."

"Kate, we need her if we're to stay in business, at least until your lease runs out in July." He rolled his eyes at Kate. "Let's make sure she stays…"

"How?"

"Give her laudanum."

"She's not going to take it."

"She will if we mix it in her mashed potatoes…then lock the door of her room until she calms down and decides to cooperate. We'll tell her she will not get any more food unless she joins our staff. Hunger will make her do almost anything." He smiled his wicked smile that she loved. She felt his hand on her buttocks as she exited to the kitchen.

Under the influence of laudanum, Cassandra finally capitulated and agreed to work. She began in the kitchen where she could be kept under close supervision.

About ten days later, after the noon diners had come and gone, a woman appeared at the restaurant entrance. She was wearing a travel cloak and a handsome hat with pheasant feathers. Kate thought her a rare female here in Pithole, a middle-aged woman unaccompanied by a husband who might be here on oil business. Apparently, she was alone, but she made it clear that she meant business.

"I am here to take my daughter home with me!" Her voice was shrill and her neck and face, flushed bright red. she appeared frightened.

"Your daughter? Who is she?"

"You know very well who she is. Cassandra. My daughter is Cassandra and she came here for a job. Where is she?"

Ben came from washing glasses behind the bar.

"You must be mistaken. There is no one here with that name." He positioned himself to show off his muscular chest and arms.

"No! I am not mistaken. She is here! Where is she?"

Ben moved slowly, like a lurking lion, toward the visitor.

"Madame, it is clear to me that you are at the wrong address. Let me help you out to the street."

The woman began to cry and refused to budge. Ben applied a firm grip to her arm and forcible guided her toward the exit. She pulled his hand from her arm.

"Let me go! I am here to take Cassandra home with me!"

Ben pushed her out the door and on to the street.

"I want my daughter!"

He turned his back, reentered the restaurant and locked the door. Kate watched while the distraught mother looked about, then turned to trudge up Brown Street.

Kate downed another shot of whiskey and sat at the end of bar.

Two hours later, she heard loud knocking on the locked restaurant door. She left the kitchen to answer it. In front of her stood the bewhiskered Methodist minister, Reverend Steadman whom she had seen on Christmas Eve at the celebration of the new Bonita House.

Kate smiled and greeted him in her most soothing voice.

"Hello, Reverend Steadman. What a surprise." She saw that he was accompanied by three males, all of whom were armed.

"We are here to see Ben Hogan."

Ben emerged from the kitchen.

"How can I help you?"

Kate quietly exited the room. She listened from behind a closed door as an argument ensued.

"Yes, a woman did come here looking for her daughter, she said. When I told her that no such person was here, she got hysterical and started screaming and crying. I had no choice but to encourage her to look elsewhere."

Further discussion got more intense and Kate heard Ben's raised voice.

"I have to ask you gentleman to leave. I cannot help you find this missing daughter."

Suddenly, she heard the multiple clicking's of revolvers followed by a determined declaration.

"We are here to take Cassandra to her mother, now!"

"All right, all right! Take it easy."

"Where is she, Mr. Hogan?"

Next, she heard the heavy footfalls of the four men and Ben climbing the stairs to the second floor. A loud burst of crying and sobbing of the drugged Cassandra filled the restaurant as Ben freed her from the locked room. Kate followed the noise of many feet descending the stairs, then crossing the dining room and out the door. It closed with a bang.

At the bar, she poured herself a shot of whiskey and mused aloud.

"That foolish girl should have known better than to answer an ad in a newspaper."

The story got around town about Cassandra's escape from French Kate's Restaurant. She had written her mother a letter regarding her dire circumstances, dropped it out of the window of her "prison" and somehow, without a stamp, it was delivered to her mother in Buffalo.

There were no repercussions from this situation which may have been of a low priority and of little legal interest. The plight of this young woman in this back-woods, anything-goes atmosphere would have been just one more prostitute in trouble. The money-minded men of Pithole were focused on making a quick fortune, not responding to the complaints of an hysterical mother.

...

On April 30, 1866, out-of-control blazes consumed yet another portion of First Street. Eighteen structures went up in flames taking with it five hotels--the Oil City, Cumberland, Eckert, Globe and Center all fueled by vacant buildings in their midst. The estimated loss was figured at a discount from the earlier values in the borough, $30,000.

This time, many disheartened folks walked away from their leases and left behind the smoldering ruins and the odor of burned boards mixed with crude oil. The stench permeated the town for days. Now, no one bothered to clean up the mess nor to rebuild. The devastating destruction left gaping gashes in the failing fabric of the dying borough. The depressing nature of the former boomtown reflected the condition of the local economy as well.

The fiasco of the Culver and Penn Company collapse dragged into broad daylight, some long-hidden, sobering facts. In January, the practice of publishing untrustworthy data came to the attention of the public. Oil producers had been reporting inflated figures to the newspapers and in other media. Petroleum companies had stated that Pithole wells delivered 3,685 barrels per day. The *Titusville Morning Herald* published the accurate data-only 2,240 barrels were actually produced, 1445 barrels less per day.

The federal tax assessor, M.V. Swift calculated the production of the twelve pumping wells on the Rooker, Morey, and Holmden farms, and his data were presumed to be more accurate than the figures from the oil producers, especially since their taxes were based on the assessor's data. The inflated oil production numbers of the past months were meant to entice speculators and investors. The economic downturn and emerging truth about the misleading statistics took the wind out of the sails of the outlandish oil speculation and inflated real estate prices. The news negatively impacted the entire petroleum industry and real estate values in Pithole.

By the end of April 1866, the older Pithole wells were producing fewer barrels per day, and more recently established wells brought forth only small quantities of oil. They totaled only 1800 barrels per day. To make matters worse, the price of oil gradually sank from a January high of $5.50 a barrel to $3.50 by June. But the persistent publishing of inflated information continued to fuel the instability of oil prices.

The price of a barrel of oil could recede or advance as much as a dollar in one day. Informal oil exchanges took place throughout the early oil fields wherever men gathered at local hotels or businesses. Wild speculation and excited gamblers gained and lost fortunes in just minutes. The advent of the first organized Oil Exchange in Titusville, five years in the future, damped-down the widely varying prices and chaotic speculation, calming the oil market.

Only a few citizens seemed to understand the bigger picture of the economy of Pithole. As soon as the downward trend became apparent, those businessmen began withdrawing their companies and investments from the boomtown. Pipelines and the trains now carried crude oil directly from the wells to the refineries without the need of thousands of teamsters, and myriads of other workers. The profits made in the sale of petroleum were leaving the area that actually produced the oil. That income from the sale of crude was flowing into the hands of companies and their investors who were located elsewhere--Pittsburgh, Cleveland, Chicago, Boston and

New York. The money was gushing away from Pithole, not toward it.

Theaters and hotels were the hardest hit from the lack of visitors or locals with money to spend. The Bonita House, despite its renowned clients such as wealthy Oil City financier J.J. Vandergrift, and the esteemed editor of the *New York Tribune*, James G. Bennett, and others of fame and fortune, never turned a profit. The Murphy Theater stopped performances in April and later held a competition concert with the grand prize to the winner being the theater.

Later, the Bonita House followed suit and created a competition event. They sold tickets, not only in Pithole, but in communities far and wide. However, after 700 tickets sold to the public, sales fell off. Efforts to revive the project included inventive schemes--offering gold watches and giving away interests in oil wells. Nevertheless, the venture died. The winner of the grand prize would have won the elegant three-story Bonita House, unencumbered.

The failings of these and other Pithole businesses caused the floundering Borough government to suffer. The treasury lacked income from property taxes. The municipality was in business for only three months, but complications over a contested election slowed the wheels of the young government. By the time the authority was sanctioned, six months later, much of the property to be taxed had been destroyed by fire, abandoned by owners, or out of business. The once bourgeoning borough was not only broke, it was in deep debt.

. . .

As soon as he had sold the last of his newspapers, Luke hurried up to Gala's cabin that he now occupied. With the snow gone and the weather warmer, he had moved out of his sleeping quarters under the work table in the kitchen of French Kate's Restaurant. Since Mabelle was no longer there, it was not the same for him and he was ready to leave for the cabin, a place of his own, away from the fires.

He cut some cheese and broke off a chunk of cornbread then headed out to meet Jeremiah at Lewis Smith's well on the Holmden Farm. Luke was excited to have an opportunity to learn more about oil wells. Since he had lived along Oil Creek, Luke had a keen interest in the oil excitement. Uncle Matt and Old Mac, the relative of farmer-turned oil producer, Hamilton McClintock had inspired him by providing opportunities for his visits to some of the first wells up the creek.

Now, four years later, Jeremiah took Luke's continued interest seriously. Luke found him sitting on a bench, his back against the pumphouse, eating his lunch. He pulled out his own food and sat down beside the lanky oil driller.

"Glad you came, Luke. I want you to see this well and understand what we will be doing here tomorrow, to get it opened up. The Holmden 129 was a good producer for a few weeks—about 100 barrels a day. Then it quit. Several things could be wrong with it. The first thing that we did was check to see if any equipment was clogging the bottom. So, I fished it—used a mouse trap to find out if there were no broken drill bits or whatever. There weren't. Then Lewis decided that it must be hung-up with wax or heavy grease, like several others in this area."

"Is this the well I'm going to invest in?"

"Yes. Lewis and I think that this well can be unblocked."

"How do you do that? With a torpedo you told me about?"

"Right. Lewis is a shooter. It's taken some time to get the things we'll be using tomorrow. You see, Luke, we cased this well right after it was drilled, so we know that it is not water flooding that made it quit producing." He paused.

"Matter of fact, this gent named Benjamin Tupper cased the first well here in Pithole a year ago—the Holmden Number 149. He had a great idea and we've been casing wells since then."

"How do you do that...casing?"

"By drilling a larger hole, big enough for a 3-and-¼-ʾinch tubing-artesian tubing—artesian tubing. Then we drop it down to the first sand where we put a seed bag to seal it off from any ground water. After that, we lowered 2-inch tubing inside the casing clear down to the bottom of the well." He paused and took a drink. "Yah see, we can pull that 2-inch tubing out whenever we want to without causing any flooding. It's made of twelve-to-fourteen-lengths of wrought iron pipe that's been threaded at the ends so more can be connected—depending on the depth of the well. I've retubed some of these wells ten to twenty times."

"How long does that take, Jeremiah, to re-tube?"

"Lewis and I did this one in just a day. So now we think that this well is clogged with something, most likely wax or heavy grease." He paused to take a drink from a tin cup.

"Is that why you're gonna put down the torpedo?"

"Yup. And that's another story…A couple of weeks ago, they experimented with a torpedo made by George Mowbray, a Titusville chemist. He's in a disagreement with another inventor named Roberts, Colonel E.A. Roberts who claims he has the only right to use nitroglycerin in torpedoes, that it's his invention. Anyhow, they tried blowing the Clara Well over on the Morey farm."

"I heard some folks talking about it. What happened?"

"The Clara is a 610-foot well and the torpedo went off all right—big roar!" He gestured with both hands in the air. For the first time since knowing Jeremiah, Luke noticed that his middle finger on his right hand was missing, but said nothing.

"Throwing off a lot a steam—clear to the top of the derrick. But it did no good."

"Why?" Luke looked at his friend's hand as Jeremiah talked.

"Not sure. These things are so new…Lewis has ideas about making a better explosive device. He has a design of a torpedo and went to a place called Phelps, New York with the draft of it—in his head—not on paper. Amazing!" Jeremiah smiled. "Some young mechanic there built him a torpedo outa galvanized four-inch tubing five-foot long. It's charged with blastin' powder, not nitroglycerine. Tomorrow, we're going to try it here on Smith's well."

Luke felt special, being told about an experimental device like this torpedo.

"So, what time should I come back here tomorrow?"

Jeremiah seemed lost in thought.

"I didn't tell you how Lewis got that big thing back here to Pithole." He paused, looking at Luke. "You see he was 200 miles from here with this forty-pound explosive. Now Lewis weighs only 130 pounds, so that torpedo was a heavy thing and dangerous to carry." He smiled. "He didn't want to alarm folks or get thrown off the train so he disguised it--put it in a tin tube made for carrying surveyor's maps. It was a piece of good luck that he got back here safely on that crowded train."

Impressed with Lewis Smith's invention and his courage, Luke pulled a wad of greenbacks from his pocket, all of his savings. Suddenly, he thought about his father.

What would John Obadiah have thought of his investment? He imagined his father's voice…

"This oil business is just a fluff in the pan…don't be foolish and waste your money…don't gamble in the risky oil business…"

Luke pushed the old warnings aside.

"Here's the money for the 1/16ᵗʰ of a share in this well." He handed it to Jeremiah. "I will be here tomorrow to get the papers for it." Then he stopped. "Oh, I gotta tell Mr. Spare I need the day off."

"We're planning to start at first light."

. . .

As the sun peeked over the bluff to the east, Luke watched Jeremiah and Lewis Smith lower the experimental explosive within five feet from the bottom of the well. Despite the early hour, a crowd of about fifty onlookers were on hand. Jeremiah gave Luke a thumbs-up sign, then turned to trigger the explosive. Unlike other earlier well-blasting experiments, Smith's torpedo went off at the first ignition.

Luke heard a loud roar and felt the ground shake under his feet. Steam shot skyward from the depths of the well, up and over the top of the derrick. The vapor rained down on him and the other spectators. He shivered with excitement as he shook the water off of his black, broad-brimmed hat.

Hours later, he listened to Jeremiah and Lewis as they assessed the effect of the torpedo.

"The tubing is back down. What's it lookin' like, Jeremiah? Let's get the pump started…" The men lapsed into silence as the continued to work.

Jeremiah broke the quiet.

"Lewis, it's comin' in! A good flow! Ya-hoo!" The two oilmen shook hands and smiled. Then Jeremiah motioned to Luke. The young investor ran to join them at the derrick. Excited, he watched intently as dark crude flowed into the wooden retaining tank.

. . .

Benedict Hogan, "German Benedict" was taunted by several fighters who were looking for a match, a gent known only as Elliott, and John Dennely from Montreal, and several others. As before, they were prohibited from holding public matches within the borough.

Now, dubbing himself the "Eminent Master of Gymnastics and Celebrated Champion of the Manly Art," Benedict opened some rooms at 76 First Street. He advertised fifteen boxing lessons for ten dollars. When that venture failed to draw in students, he hung a sign, "THE BEST PITTSBURGH LAGER BEER, PRETZELS AND GOOD CHEESE." In order to pay the rent, he changed his gym business sign to HOGEN'S LAGER BEER SALOON, BUT WITHOUT "WAITRESSES."

"When you're looking for an amorous evening, French Kate has the waitresses, just two doors over."

...

Meanwhile, the animosity between Kate and Emma erupted episodically. Still chafing from the public humiliation of being kicked into the mud after Ben's match, the owner of the Florence Restaurant kept an eye on the shrinking clientele of her business, and jealously guarded her "regulars." Making it her business to monitor the diners who frequented French Kate's Restaurant, she spied two men departing Kate's place who usually spent their evenings with her girls. Emma was irate.

"Of all the nerve…"

The next morning, she waded across the muddy street to Kate's restaurant.

"What do you mean luring two of my best customers to your place?"

"What makes you think that any of these men belong to you and your ilk? I say they go where they like and where they get what they're looking for." Kate paused and looked Emma in the eye.

"Guess you can't stand the competition, can you? No wonder. You've got such a bunch of floozies."

"They're not floozies! You're the one with the floozies." She could see Emma's face reddened and her eyes flashed with anger.

"Emma, you had better get out of here with your angry talk-now." When Emma stood her ground, Kate took Emma by the shoulders and shoved her back toward the door she'd just come through.

Physically forced onto the veranda, Emma grabbed a broom and swung it at her head. Kate wrenched the weapon from the angry madam and poked her in the back with the handle.

"Well, you and Ben have taken up against me!" Emma's face was flushed with fury.

"What?"

"I know that Ben is givin' his boxin' clients some coupons

394

for your place. You're drainin' off my business."

"What we're doing is none of your affair, Emma. Go home!"

Like a cat, Emma pivoted quickly and caught hold of Kate's dress, ripping the bodice to the waist."

"You whore!" Emma turned and quickly departed.

Just then, Ben appeared on the street, directly in Emma's path. She marched past him spewing expletives and shouting back at Kate who stood naked to the waist, her dress with a huge tear in the front.

She watched while Ben followed Emma into her place, demanding as he went the reason for the squabble. The door slammed shut, but Kate could hear shouting. Just minutes later, Ben arrived in the dining room.

"Emma punched me and I wacked her."

...

Once again, the prize fighter stood before Justice Highberger at the end of a jury trial. "Benedict Hogan, this court finds you guilty! You are being fined $25 and court costs."

Kate jumped to her feet.

"Ben's being fined? Emma Fenton started the whole thing by coming on my property, making accusations. She damaged my dress and called me names. And you and this jury are fining Benedict?"

The Justice of the Peace pounded his gavel for silence and the crowded court room buzzed with excitement.

"Order! Order!"

"Benedict was defending himself and me from this ornery, aggressive crone who doesn't know her boundaries and lives to aggravate her neighbors, like me!"

Emma was on her feet, her lawyer trying to restrain her.

"Lies! Lies! All lies!"

More pounding of the gavel.

"Order, order! Madame, please sit down and be silent."

As the court finally emptied, Kate felt mollified as she took Ben's arm and in a dignified manner, departed the scene.

...

Late that night, an arsonist set fire to half a block of

buildings along First Street including Benedict's gym and saloon. They were burned to the ground.

So frequent were the attempts at arson that the borough council on May 22, 1866 finally assigned night watches to guard parts for the community from 10 P.M to 8 A.M. Frank Austin hired on to cover First to Second Street and Jim Coat was posted at Second to Third street.

A month later when Special Officer Wiley arrested two men for attempted arson on First Street, the outraged Pithole public met at the Chase House and authorized a $500 reward for the arrest and conviction of pyromaniacs. As well, the city water company agreed to keep adequate pressure in mains to fight fires, a $5-a-night charge.

...

In the wee hours of June 15, Kate awakened to loud pounding on the door of her restaurant. What time was it? She looked around for her wristlet and realized that Ben still slept undisturbed. The haze of alcohol from an evening of heavy drinking clouded her thinking and made her head ache. She lay back down. Maybe the caller would go away. Her girls did not perform amorous congress after midnight, so anyone wanting their services was arriving at the wrong time. The noisy knocking resumed and was accompanied by audible declarations.

"Police! Open up!"

Now, she was wide awake and gave Ben a firm shake with her left hand. On her right she was groping in the dark for some clothing. What did the police want at this hour? Maybe it was another fire in the neighborhood. At that thought, she put on a dress, shoved her feet into her cold shoes, and shook Ben, who finally roused himself.

"What's all the ruckus?"

"The police, Ben. They have been banging on the door for five minutes."

Upon hearing that, he sat up abruptly and pulled on his trousers that were slung over a nearby chair. He preceded her to the restaurant entrance and was facing three policemen carrying lanterns.

"What's wrong? Is there a fire somewhere?"

"No! This is a raid. The Borough has ordered these dens of prostitution be closed. We are taking you in. You're under arrest.

Who else is in there?" He motioned with his wooden baton toward the restaurant.

"Only Kate, I think. Go take a look for yourselves."

Just then Kate emerged from the entrance with Jenny and Tilda.

"Where's the fire?"

She looked around at the crowd on the street in front of her place.

"What's going on? Why are all these people out here on the street at this hour? There's no building ablaze?"

"Where have you been, Kate? The Borough Council has given orders to put a stop to our businesses and this is the start of it."

Even in the dark, Kate recognized the taunting voice of Emma Fenton, her nemesis who had designs on Ben. She had more than one reason to despise Emma. Their businesses had been running competition for months. Emma's Florence Restaurant had waitresses who plied the evening trade, just as Kate's girls did.

What Emma had broadcast was true. On May 26, after months of ineffectively dealing with the blatant problem of prostitution, the Borough Council "...declared prostitutes a nuisance and banned them to parts unknown..." according to the *Pithole Daily Record*. The borough police were following orders. They gathered names and addresses of those they had rousted from their beds, and walked them up toward the borough offices on Holmden Street. Along with a few johns who were caught at one of the speak-easies, the police scooped up Fanny White, Miss Mary Shane, a proprietress and a number of occupants of the Star Restaurant.

By the light of various lanterns, Kate could see that she was part of a motley crew who were dressed or undressed in various garb, a few wrapped in blankets. Those seized in the raid formed a long line that stretched from First to Second Street and beyond. Now a crowd of people were gathering on the opposite side of the street. These were so-called "reputable" townspeople who had been awakened by the commotion. They gaped at the accused. Some of those apprehended began cursing epithets at the onlookers, and an across-the-street yelling match ensued. The unsuccessful efforts of the police to control the crowd was a spectacle in itself.

For Kate, who minded her own business and had made an effort to keep out of sight except for rare occasions, being exposed, arrested, and paraded about in front of half the citizens of Pithole constituted a new low point. To be seen with this company, disheveled and disordered made her angry. This, she reasoned was the result of her stepfather's treatment of her. If her Pa-pa' or Ma-ma' had been alive to see her through her formative years, never would she have been in such disgusting circumstances. Her head ached and she pulled her flask from her pocket.

The next day, the *Pithole Daily Record* ran an article that was partly tongue-in-cheek about the night's raid. It described young women who took refuge under beds, dashed through the nearby woods, and somehow managed to escape the police dragnet. The up-shot of this attempt to enforce an ordinance was much to do about nothing, like a tempest in a teacup. A few inmates were fined. That night, it was business as usual and the great night raid was considered disgusting by many, and a demonstration of the impotence of the Pithole police in their attempts to carry-out the unenforceable ordinance.

...

On June 18, 1866, another device for moving petroleum out of Pithole drew a large crowd of curious onlookers. Two massive wooden tanks mounted on a flat-car rolled into the borough for the first time. Each wooden structure on the tank-car held eighty barrels of bulk oil, and with four trains a day from Pithole, these innovative Densmore tank cars had the capacity of moving thousands of barrels oil in a short time. James and Amos Densmore of Meadville received a patent on April 10, 1866 for their "Improved Car for Transporting Petroleum," using flat cars from the Atlantic and Great Western Railroad in the invention.

Although there were downsides of this innovation, danger of explosion and the loss of oil through leakage, did not impede progress. Within a year, a total transformation in moving oil out of the rugged wilderness of Pithole, oil tank cars and petroleum pipelines had revolutionized the oil delivery process.

...

The one-year lease for French Kate's Restaurant expired in mid-July, and left her with few options. But other factors changed her circumstances as well. Over the past six months, the borough council had passed ordinances, staged raids, and leveed fines against

Pithole's prostitution establishments. Those efforts had little effect. The end finally came for most of those businesses due to the decrease in the borough's population and dwindling brothel patronage. When the money eventually dried up and buildings that had housed the prostitutes burned down, the majority of the soiled doves decided to move to more lucrative oil fields. Kate's waitresses planned to join them because their evening trade had fallen off.

Early one July morning in 1866, Tilda and Jenny packed up to depart with some 240 prostitutes. Kate listened from the bar where she was having a whiskey.

"Tilda, let's drag your bed down the steps first, then mine."

"Do you think that flimsy mattress will fit through the front window, just throw it to the street?"

"Good grief, Tilda! It will get all muddy, if you do that!" Jenny seemed perplexed.

"Well, Jenny, I think it will be faster to push it out. The wagon is loadin' up fast with so many of us leavin' at once."

"Throw yours out if you must. Didn't your mama teach you anything? I'm dragging my down the steps."

"Never knew my mother. I think she died when I was small. Just my older sister and me, and Pa when he was around…"

"Come on--less talkin' and more movin.'"

Finally, they dragged their belongings down the stairs, out the door, and onto a waiting wagon. Kate walked to the entrance of her defunct restaurant and stood on the veranda to get a better view of the gathering girls.

A crowd of citizens was congregating to witness the massive movement. The prostitutes of the pleasure palaces were disbanding, just as the borough decree had mandated. However, it was not the police raids and continuous threats of fines that disbursed the occupants of the numerous brothels. It was the waning economy and the shrinking population of the fading boomtown. Like other departing businesses, the ladies of the night followed the money.

The muddy street was lined with teams hitched to wagons piled high with feather beds, straw ticks, linens and large travel trunks with brass closings. Kate watched the weighty wagons silently proceed, one-by-one down First Street and up the hill to the plank road.

Then as if prompted, carriages, two stage coaches and more empty wagons arrived, lining up along First Street. Giddy girls, laughing and talking loudly climbed on board the passenger vehicles and arranged their long, fancy dresses, colorful carpet bags, and tins of food. In the crowd, she spotted Jenny and Tilda talking with Belle and several of Emma's girls. Then she thought about Mabelle and her not being with the others. Well, it was not her fault that she had died. Mabelle should have spoken up and asked for a doctor. Slowly, the two loaded stage coaches took the lead followed by the carriages then tailed by the wagons.

One of the occupants of a dray, suddenly rose to her feet, her wide-brimmed hat fluttering in the breeze. She shouted.

"We're off! Here's to the boys of Pithole!" With that, she lifted a metal flask that reflected the beams of the morning sun. She put the drink to her red lips, took a long swig, then started to sing a local ditty.

"We are the girls from First.
You think we are the worst
Because we show our knees
And do just what we please!
You just don't know the facts:
Men pay to feel our backs--and more!"

The rollicking rhythm spread from wagon to stagecoach until their en mass departure became a virtual chorus.

"Row, row, row your boat
Down the oily creek,
Merrily, merrily, merrily, merrily,
Things are looking bleak!
Good-bye Pithole!"

The celebrants waved at familiar faces and blew kisses to the borough police who had arrived at the sounds of the gathering crowd and the musical exit.

As soon as the girls had disappeared and the crowd disbursed, Kate took down her sign for French Kate's Restaurant. She took a deep breath and poured herself another drink. Now what would she do? Where would she go? She sat down at the bar and contemplated her immediate future. At this point, staying with Benedict seemed to be her best choice. Like other businesses, her profits had plummeted over the past three months, and liquidating the contents of the restaurant seemed like a means to restore some of her shrunken savings.

She began organizing the eatery equipment that she planned to sell. Her carpet bag was packed with personal belongings, and was out of sight behind the bar. The building was an empty shell without the sounds of diners and the tiddling of the staff. A feeling of loneliness enveloped her. "It's always darkest before the dawn..."

It was late afternoon and the sun had disappeared behind the derricks at the edge of Pithole Creek as Kate was leaving her place with a box of glassware. In the dimming light of dusk, she spotted a well-dressed man in a travel coat and black hat who looked out of place along the burned-out buildings of First Street. In the waning daylight, he appeared to be reading street signs and lot numbers to get his bearings. Not wishing to engage anyone in conversation, she ducked back inside her empty restaurant with its bare tables and chairs.

Something about the visitor seemed familiar, but in the failing light, his face was obscure. Instinctively, she felt for her pistol and the knife that she kept strapped to her right leg. From the shadows, she watched as he passed her place, then crossed the street toward Emma's location. When he moved up the darkening street toward the Chase House, she decided to return to her packing project.

She was on the second floor, folding up her dresses and skirts when she heard a sound. Was someone entering the restaurant? With Ben at his new gym preparing for a match against one of his many challengers, she was alone. She had hung a sign on the front door that projected a clear message to anyone approaching: "CLOSED."

A scraping noise alerted her, and she walked to the top of the stairs. When she looked down into the unlighted bar, she could see a form sitting at the far end. She squinted for better vision and made out the profile of the stranger she had spotted on the street earlier. A chill went up her spine and she put her hand on her gun. With so many adjacent buildings abandoned or burned to the ground, and the brothels mostly emptied, few people now inhabited the area.

The intruder turned toward her and she took a step backwards into the shadows. The board she stepped on let out a audible squeak. The man looked her direction, got off of the bar stool and was walking toward the stairs. Kate froze and held her breath.

"Katherine, are you up there? I know you live here. Your neighbor, Emma told me all about you."

Now Kate recognized the voice. It was Petrus Plugge. Adrenalin shot up her spine. She could feel the hair raising on the back of her neck. She felt trapped, like a cat up a tree. Ebenezer had warned her that her stepfather had threatened to search her out, but it seemed unlikely. It was a long train ride from Brooklyn to remote Pithole. She looked around for an avenue of escape, but knew there was none. If he came up the stairs, she would be forced to face him, and she was alone.

She shrank back into her bedroom. A footfall on the steps frightened her. Better to answer him and confront him now, not boxed into this bedroom...Stop him before he comes up the stairs.

Suddenly, a long-suppressed memory took form...

Petrus Plugge dragging his trousers, one boot on, one off. The silver flask in his hand, he was climbing the polished stairs of her childhood home. He kept moving up the steps as she escaped into her bedroom. She slammed the door and tried to lock it, but he pushed his corpulent body into her room. His engorged appendage poked from between his thighs. She screamed...

Trembling, Kate shook off the memory of the terrifying trauma. Wishing she had a lamp, she took a deep breath and moved to the top of the staircase. It was now dark inside since the sun had set.

"Who is it? We are not open of business tonight."

"Katherine, you can't bluff me. You know well who I am."

"What do you want?"

"Information."

"What?"

"Where is our son? I know you had a baby and it's mine!"

"You repeatedly raped me, you bastard! I was a helpless child! I want nothing to do with you!"

"Where is he?"

He started to move slowly toward her. She could hear him climbing up one step at time--one, two, three, four. Only a few more to the top.

"Stop! Don't you come near me!" The sound of his footfalls ceased.

"I have papers for you to sign."

"I won't sign them."

Darkness enfolded them like a blackout curtain. She could hear his breathing. She tried to focus on him in the dark, but her eyes had not adjusted. Suddenly he sprang at her, grabbing her skirt. She kicked at him but he caught her right ankle.

"Get your hands off me!"

Blindly, she kicked at him. He grabbed her left ankle with more strength than she had anticipated. She felt her legs get yanked out from under her. Then her head hit the top step as he dragged her down the steps to the bottom. Her back throbbed. The room was swirling around her. Now they were in semidarkness on the first floor. She could make out his silhouette poised over her. Watching him pull a bottle from his pocket, she lay momentarily dizzy and immobile. He crouched on one knee, removed the stopper and poured a portion of the ingredient onto a rag.

The throbbing of her head and the pain in her back were excruciating. Her skirt was twisted under her with the gun lost in the fabric. She could not move to retrieve either of her weapons. She watched him feeling around on the floor for something. She wiggled her fingers and toes to assure herself that they functioned.

When she struggled to get to her feet, he held her down with one hand and pushed the tainted tatter to her face, over her nose and mouth. She held her breath and raised her right knee, striking him in the groin. The intended pain knocked him off balance, sending him sideways into the wall, head-first. She rolled to the right and kicked him again. The sodden cloth fell away from her face and she took a breath. The odor was sweet.

He lay on his back writhing with pain. She jammed her knee onto his chest and stuffed the permeated cloth into his open mouth and held it there. He kicked and bit but she pinched his nose shut while he tried to push her off. In several minutes, the chemically-soaked rag did its job--on him instead of his intended victim. She felt for the bottle and dumped the remainder of the liquid onto the rag and his nose. The liquid burned her hand. He lay motionless.

She retreated to her front veranda and strained to breathe in fresh air. How long she sat there on the deck with her back propped against the outside wall of building, she could not tell. Dizzy, and disoriented, her head throbbed with each beat of her heart. Through the daze of her semi-consciousness, she thought she heard someone walking between her building and the one adjacent. She tried to focus in the blackness, but the only light emanated from the burning torches of the distant oil derricks.

She had no sense of the passage of time when she gradually regained her awareness. She was so tired that she could barely move. Finally, her head began to clear from the exposure of the fumes, and she recalled the struggle against her enemy. She had intended to escape, but had only made it to her own front porch. Apparently, he was still inside.

By sheer force of will, she got to her feet. Walking slowly

and keeping her balance by holding on to nearby dining chairs, she crept to the spot where he had fallen. An amorphous form loomed at her feet, a large dark lump. At this distance, she caught a whiff of sweet-smelling liquid, the contents of his bottle. Not wanting to get too close to him, she listened in the dark for his breathing. She could hear none, and moved even closer. Finally, she gave him poke with her foot. Nothing moved. Was he unconscious or even dead? Whichever it was, he remained on her floor at the foot of her stairs.

What to do? What would she do if he were dead? The problem of disposing of him, slowly entered her addled brain.

Suddenly, she smelled smoke and peered into the dark. Then she saw flickering light through a window. Fire! Remembering her belongings and her Papa's mirror and Fredrick's flask, both gifts that she cherished, she moved to the back of the bar and grabbed her bag. By the light of the growing fire, bright lapping yellow flames, she could see smoke coming through the cracks from the outside. Her unconscious nemesis forgotten, she rushed to the open door with her carpet bag in hand. The room was lighted now by the growing fire. When she reached the exit, she turned to see the dark figure that laid lifeless, sprawled on the bare floor, the rag yet protruding from his mouth. She hesitated for only a second, then ran out of the open door and onto the veranda.

Now flames were leaping at the porch roof and she scrambled off of the far end and into the muddy street. Buildings adjacent to her place blazed bright yellow against the dark sky. The heat from the fire felt hot against her face and distancing herself, she crossed the street. In just minutes, the west wall of her former restaurant burst into flames, then collapsed with a loud crunching sound, as the yellow flares lapped against the night sky.

She was mesmerized. As the infernos billowed before her, the oil-soaked lumber exploded, first the walls, and then the roof timers ignited. Her eyes defocused as she remembered her stepfather's hateful treatment of her…

…

She was back in her bedroom again, fighting the pressure of the silver flask and the burning liquor that he forced on her. His terrible appendage forcibly penetrating her—raping her at will--his will.

Overcome with emotion at the memories of the Red Lantern

Inn and his plans to sell her "services" to wealthy men, she screamed and held her aching head. The flames rose higher and were so hot that she had to back away farther from the conflagration. She sat on a tree stump across the street. She was crying hysterically as the memories of Petrus Plugge flooded her--slamming her head against the table at the Brooklyn Brothel--her excruciating pain in child birth--and the threatened loss of her intended inheritance arranged by her father, Captain Van De Meer...

...

Quietly, the rain began. The first icy drops splattered on her aching head and ran down her face and neck. Like being hit with a cold bucket of water, she was pulled back to the present.

Men bearing buckets of water appeared near her, and she retreated from the activity. Neighbors were gathering to gander and gossip. Then, she remembered the body of her attacker.

Would these men extinguish the fire before it cremated her stalker? Neither she nor Benedict were in good standing with the borough police. How would she explain the human remains in the ashes of her restaurant? She shivered with the thought of apprehension, of a trial by jury and the prying eyes of the public. How would she ever explain herself, her circumstances...how?

Suddenly, muscular arms encircled her and she looked up through her swollen, tear-soaked face into the eyes of Benedict. He just held her until she stopped sobbing.

Minutes later, the rain grew to a downpour that dumped a deluge onto the blazing buildings. The firemen who watched the beaten flames die before them, cheered. They gradually gathered their buckets, shovels and hoses and slogged up muddy Brown Street toward the Chase House.

...

Later that night, the clouds cleared. The waning moon shed light on the smoldering ruins. Quietly, Benedict and Kate raked through the rubble. Finally, he motioned to her. Under a pile of charred remains of the collapsed rooftop, they uncovered the remanence of Petrus Plugge. First, they spotted a partially melted silver flask covered with ash. Then, she poked a stick into a pile of cinders and uncovered the shards of brown glass, fragments of the bottle that had held the substance meant to harm her.

"Most likely was chloroform he used." Ben squinted at her through the darkness. "It could have been you whose remains lay in this rubble."

She shivered at the thought.

He kept digging.

"Here's what's left of him--not much, but it is human remains." He paused and turned toward her in the dark.

"While no one is around to inspect this fire, let's get him out of here. That bastard caused you enough agony and discord. His death does not need to create questions and a police investigation." He backed away from the body toward his tools.

She pointed to a turned-over oil barrel, commandeered-water-barrel, for fire-fighting. Benedict nodded in agreement. Without another word, he righted the round receptacle and shoveled what was left of the vile villain, her terrible tormentor. He rolled the container to a nearby horse and wagon he had rented for their move from Pithole, and hoisted it on to the dray.

An hour passed and with the moon in the western sky, Benedict and Kate watched the oil barrel float down severely swollen Pithole Creek. Affected by the recent rain, the gushing torrent swept away the final traces of Petrus Plugge toward the Allegheny River and beyond...

On to Babylon

Kate stood in the U.S. Post Office at Pithole for the last time. She had pulled out a single letter from her mail box. It was from Fredrick. She quickly opened it and read the message. Fredrick had left France over a month ago and should be in Brooklyn by now.

Although Benedict was waiting for her, she quickly composed a telegraph message for Fredrick and Ebenezer: "Leaving Pithole and bound for Babylon with Benedict Hogan. I will be in touch."

Then she mounted the steps to the second floor, entered the Western Union Telegraph office and paid the telegraph operator to send her message.

…

Late that afternoon, Benedict slid his hand over Kate's sleek satin skirt and squeezed her thigh. He turned to her and smiled.

"Here we are…still daylight. Made it in good time, despite the muddy roads."

As Kate prepared to climb off of the wagon seat, she hoisted her long skirt to above her knees and gave Benedict a long lustful look, and smiled.

"So, this is Babylon?" She looked around. "Does it have a post office? Where do we buy food?" She paused. "You know, Ben, this place reminds me of Pithole when I first arrived there. Just a bunch of oil wells and thrown-together buildings."

She put her hand of Benedict's thigh.

"Where are we staying?"

"I will know shortly."

Benedict lifted her from the front seat of the wagon. She could feel the strength in his hands and arms as she landed lightly on a dry spot in front of a building whose sign read: GENERAL STORE. She spotted the outhouse behind the unpainted structure.

"I'll be right back."

A few minutes later, she returned from the rear of the store to find Benedict unpacking the wagon. It appeared to her that he had stopped to talk with a woman whose back was turned away from her. As she approached, she recognized the voice, Emma Fenton.

She was stunned. What was Emma doing here? How could

407

this be? She was sure that she would be rid of her nasty neighbor when she left Pithole.

"What are you doing here, Emma?"

The red-headed madam abruptly wheeled in her direction.

"What are you doing here, French Kate?" She detected the edgy, challenging tone to her voice.

"Well, obviously, I am traveling with Benedict." Kate turned to him and gestured toward the nearest house.

"Are these our quarters? I am ready to get settled."

When Benedict hesitated, Emma chimed in before he could answer.

"Ben is staying with me, right here." She gestured with her right hand to the same small unpainted house.

"What!" A shock of adrenalin jolted Kate. With clenched fists, she took a deep breath, trying to calm herself. She felt her face flush and another bolt of energy race down her spine.

Emma looked at her wrathful expression.

"I told you that I had a special relationship with Ben, but I guess you didn't believe me."

Kate spun to stare at Benedict who failed to meet her eyes. When he said nothing, did not deny Emma's words, she was outraged.

"Do you mean to tell me, Benedict, that you are planning to live with Emma, not with me?"

"No, I will be living with both of you. There's enough room. Having two beautiful women is every man's dream and for me, that's just fine."

Astonished, Kate stared at him and Emma. Then reality hit her. Her future with Benedict—up in smoke like a burning oil well. Speechless with fury, she kicked him hard in the knees. As he bent forward with pain, she shoved Emma off balance and sent her sprawling into the muddy street.

Turning on her heel, Kate retrieved her belongings, one carpet bag, from the unloaded pile of luggage. As she stomped away, she reviewed her worldly possessions, the mirror, her Papa's present and Fredrick's gift, the silver flask with "K" embossed on one side. Her Mama's wristlet she wore strapped on her left wrist. Anything else, any other possessions had been destroyed in the fire. She calculated the number of greenbacks in her purse, and continued marching along the rutted road. She had enough cash to buy herself dinner and a room for several nights.

All around her in the rays of the setting sun, she saw the familiar oil derricks, sprawled across denuded fields. From their black, greasy engine houses came the creaking of the oil pumps and connecting rods that provided accompaniment for the few surviving crickets chirping in the deadly oil turfs. Several open torches burned yellow in the fading light. The familiar odor of crude oil mixed with horse manure filled her nostrils.

"Here I am again in the middle of this oil-country wilderness with nowhere to go, and no money coming in." As she contemplated her current situation, her eyes filled with tears of self-pity. Realizing that her weeping was making it impossible to safely continue on the rutted road, she stopped and took a deep breath.

"It's always darkest before the dawn…it's always darkest before the dawn…"

Up ahead in the dim light of dusk, she saw a lantern that marked a hotel in this oil derrick-wilderness. As she negotiated the mud-ruts and surviving clumps of grass, she heard singing. She stopped to listen and then could discern the sound of a piano that accompanied the songsters.

As she entered the bar of this distant outpost of Oildom, she surveyed the room, the habit that had stayed with her since her days with John Wilkes Booth. She spied a man who looked familiar, and she stopped in her tracks. She squinted, trying to get a clearer view in the smoke-filled room. She could see that he stood behind the bar and was preparing drinks for patrons. She smoothed her skirt, took a deep breath, then glided into the center of the activity.

The singing stopped, and a dozen men's eyes were on her. The bar tender looked her way as well.

"Katherine! Is that you ?" He paused. "It's me, Barnswell, here, from Franklin." He stared at her from behind the bar.

When she smiled and nodded, he quickly poured her a shot of whiskey.

"Have a drink! It's wonderful to see you again!"

She moved slowly toward him, then leaned on the bar. She downed the drink. She could feel it, burning its way from her throat, downward. She reached out her hand to her friend. It seemed like old times in Franklin.

"Play us a tune for old times' sake!"

She saluted Barnswell with the gesture of a toast, then, downed her second drink. A cheer went up from the spectators as she was escorted to the piano by a burley oil worker in greasy

Rosemary Neidel-Greenlee

trousers and muddy boots. She set aside her travel bag and spread her voluminous skirt as she perched on the piano stool. The room was fell silent as she launched into several favorite tunes and then concluded with "Oil on the Brain."

"'…Stocks par, stocks up, Then on the wane. Everybody's troubled with oil on the brain...'"

The crowd cheered. Enjoying the limelight, Kate turned toward them, nodded her head, and smiled. When she rotated back toward the keyboard, she sensed someone standing beside her. She glanced up and glimpsed a tall, muscular man who did not reek of tobacco. He had shiny brown boots and an expensive-looking suit with a cellulose collar.

She looked up into a handsome, smiling face.

"Bonsoir, misère." No response emanated from him, so she rose slowly and extended her hand. He took her fingers, put them to his lips and bowed. She felt a thrill of excitement shoot through her body as she stared into his beautiful blue eyes.

Finally breaking their eye contact, she looked around at the enthusiastic crowd and the familiar figure of Barnswell Buchanan, behind the bar. Her left hand felt Fredrick's letter in her skirt pocket.

A sense of calm enveloped her.

"Will you join me in a drink?" His voice was deep.

She lowered her eyelids and fluttered her eyelashes.

"Well, I'd be delighted."

The dawn had come again…

410

Epilogue

The wild speculation of gaining an overnight fortune in Pithole during the 1865 oil boom had ended by August 1866. The reality of this major shift in oil commerce left the formerly thriving Pithole settlement of 15,000 people with a population of only 6000. Written records and oral accounts tell us that the dwindling town simmered down.

Historian and author, William Culp Darrah in his book, *Pithole, The Vanished City* stated, "Like an alcoholic, sobered after a prolonged bender, weepingly renouncing his old ways and promising reform, throngs in the oil region joined temperance societies, flocked to revival meetings and turned to the courts of justice to punish offenders."

Major players in Pithole, the teamsters, speculators, wildcatters, independents, prostitutes, slick businessmen and the gamblers mostly had departed for more fertile fields. They left behind folks who seemed determined to keep the town alive. Oil workers-drillers, roustabouts and well owners remained at the U.S. Petroleum property to keep the operations going. Otherwise, those remaining were citizens who never had anticipated that they would gain--with little or no effort--an overnight fortune. In particular, they were the now-waning businesses that had supported the basic needs of thousands of oil field workers, visitors and occupants of Pithole. They were the grocers, meat cutters, druggists, doctors, attorneys and owners and workers of the numerous restaurants, bars, dance-halls and saloons.

Among the dregs of the declining town included hotels with few renters, derelict buildings with for-sale, for-rent, and sheriff-sale signs. In the midst of this depressing sight, the *Pithole Daily Record* was cautiously optimistic that someone somehow would revive the once vital borough. Despite the fact that several new wells were producing, the amount of oil pumped continued to drop, as did the price of oil. The cost of maintaining equipment, buildings and employees overwhelmed the income of the some oil producers.

Over the next eleven years, Pithole waxed and waned in numbers of population. Fires continued to be a scourge of the remaining buildings. Ne'er-do-wells came, were arrested, and expelled from the borough. With devaluing property, some destitute families survived among the ruins. The common annoyances of thievery, drunkenness and hogs running wild in the streets challenged the weakened government. When businesses departed, fewer job opportunities remained and the population drained away.

As leases ran out and the owners prepared to depart, some of them dismantled their buildings and took the structures away with them. In 1868, the Chase House, so admired by Mabelle and Katherine, the former site of the U.S. Post Office, and one of the best hotels in the area was removed to Pleasantville, just six miles down the road from Titusville. As well, Murphy's elaborately decorated, three-story theater that had offered opportunities of culture and entertainment in the rustic settlement sold to Pleasantville's J.T. McCoslin who rebuilt it in another location. Dr. F.S. Tarbell of Titusville purchased the Bonita House for $600, for its lumber and built himself a mansion. As well, the Pithole Presbyterian Church, so slow to materialize, eventually was removed to Oil City for use. By 1870, the landscape of Pithole had changed drastically and then gradually disappeared. Pithole had dwindled to 281 people.

Following in the path of many of the borough's former temporary occupants, some of the town's more resilient citizens reluctantly departed for new thriving oil fields within the region- Babylon, Tidioute, Triumph Hill, Tionesta, Pleasantville, and Shamburg. Finally, for Pithole, the end came.

In 1877 at the request of those remaining in the borough government, Pithole's charter was revoked by the courts. Two years later, only three families lived at the abandoned site. The gloomy scene of dark, ramshackle houses constructed from rough wooden boards would have shocked some of the previous residents. Dilapidated buildings of the once prosperous borough displayed cracked, faded signs of once bustling businesses. They dangled in the wind from broken boards, the last remnants of the formerly frantic and energetic boomtown.

In 1883, the Holmden property now completely deserted of occupants--the site of the Frazier Well that spurred the 1865 oil rush- -was up for public sale. Instead of the September 1865 active oil- laden plot that had sold for $2,000,000, the same property went for a measly $175 to the sole bidder, a former Pithole citizen, Edwin Twitchell.

Many former occupants and area residents celebrated the history of the place with a twenty-five-year reunion in November

412

1890. A second reunion set for 1891 failed and was not attempted again. Nevertheless, the concerned citizens and historians of the area amassed letters, photographs, many by well-known photographer, John A. Mather, legends, books, records and multiple mementoes from the oil hay-days of Pithole and those who lived there. Those memorabilia are now held at the Drake Well Museum in Titusville.

In 1930, the Daughters of the American Revolution had cleared undergrowth that was enveloping Pithole and placed markers at the notable sites. In 1957, James Stevenson, editor of the Titusville newspaper, purchased the property and cleared the area to reveal the remains of the old buildings, marked important sites, and made the area a pleasant place to visit. In 1961, Stevenson gave the ghost town of Pithole to the Commonwealth of Pennsylvania to be a preserved historical site of importance. The construction of a visitors' center created interest in preserving some of the foundations and cellar depressions to assist tourists in imaging the once vibrant boom town. Volunteers labeled the streets and locations of various businesses, and the grassy slope--the site of the town--was mowed on a regular basis.

At what appeared to be the peak of local interest, the ghost town, Pithole even had an elected mayor. Fred Sliter, one of Pithole's most supportive volunteers held this title for a number of years.

What had become of the former inhabitants of Pithole and the adjacent oil fields? Documentation is available on those who prospered greatly in the petroleum and related industries as well as citizens famous from their service during the Civil War. Colorful figures who played their historical hands have become the focus of a few writings, scattered legends, and shared stories. They are the fabric of folklore of the Pennsylvania oil region. The history they lived has created a sense of place for visitors to explore and for those of us from the region to savor.

A little about what became of many of those included in this saga:

French Kate, AKA Katherine Grant, or La Conte, or Granger etc. Local lore in the mostly vacated oil fields says that no one really knew where French Kate had come from. Hearsay has it that she had known Benedict Hogan in Washington, had a mysterious relationship with John Wilkes Booth, and used several surnames during her life, prior to coming to Pithole. It was said that she had a "magnetic personality" and was a beauty. Nor did anyone seem to know where she went after her time in Pithole, except that she had made her exit in the company of Benedict Hogan. I found that fascinating.

My interest in French Kate has lasted me a lifetime and ignited my curiosity years ago. When I learned about a portrait painting of her, I wanted to see it. Since I no longer lived in the area, I spent vacation time with friends who were familiar with the oil territory and local lore, attempting to track down the image of the mysterious madame. Around 2005 on one of my visits, I inquired of the whereabouts, then located the painting at what was then the Oil City Holiday Inn. (It was located at the very site of the ruins of the 1840's Oil Creek Iron Furnace.) A framed nude French Kate image hung over the bar at the restaurant of that hotel. Covered during the day by a heavy red curtain to hide her nakedness, the drapery was opened and the painting put on display at night when the bar was heavy with customers. Later, I learned that when the hotel ownership had changed, French Kate had moved on, just as in some of the legends about her--she just moved on. As well, folks told me that the painting was a product of a modern artist's imagination, not a relic from 1865. However, that information failed to deter me, and my interest in her story and those of other oil pioneers lives on.

Pugilist Benedict Hogan departed Pithole in the Summer of 1866 for Babylon. Throughout his life, he participated in many boxing matches and exhibitions of strength. Following his short time in Pithole, he labeled himself "The Wickedest Man in the World" whose self-declared feats of strength, gambling and various occupations are considered by many to be fascinating, but questionable, since he had a hand in writing about his own adventures in an 1887 book, *Ben Hogan's Wild Life in Both Armies*. Many stories abound about his life, and one of the most acknowledged of his escapades occurred after his departure from Pithole. He created the "Floating Palace," an elaborately decorated river boat that held gambling tables, dancing girls, and abundant alcohol. When town's people would complain about such a floating establishment of degrading debauchery that had tied up near their Allegheny River settlement, Hogan would either move to the center of the river where the town had no authority, or float down-stream to a new, untainted territory until forced to leave again.

In his later years, Hogan reported that he had gotten "religion" and subsequently preached for the redemption of others. He did marry, but the identity of his wife remains conflicted. Some say he married French Kate while others name his wife as having another identity. A copy of his death certificate indicates that Hogan died on October 28, 1916 in Cook County, Illinois.

Gen. Matthew Henry Avery arrived in Pithole just as he was completing his military service in the 10th New York Cavalry. In May 1865, he organized many of his cavalry unit to answer a request for help in moving the glut of oil emanating from the Frazier and the Twin Wells at Pithole. Avery soon became involved in the oil business as a broker in the Bradford fields and in the Parker Oil Exchange. For years, he was a well-known figure on the floor of the Oil City and Titusville Oil Exchanges. Due to poor health, he retired to Geneva, New York. On September 1, 1881 at age 46, he succumbed to dropsy.

California Sam AKA Samuel Crawford had been trained as a carpenter before he departed for the California gold fields in 1854. He moved on to Idaho in 1862 and returned to Pennsylvania about 1864-5. He eventually became involved in the oil business, lived in Emlenton, married and had four children. At least one of his offspring profited from business in the Pennsylvania oil fields. Harry J. Crawford, his son, was engaged in the banking business. "H.J.", as he was known, was the first president of the Quaker State Oil Company

Charles Vernon Culver, a financier with dreams of building a railroad and an utopian city that was suitable for oil executives, attracted many investors. In only months from his appearance in Pithole, he was discredited. A string of Culver's bank failures in thirteen cities brought about the collapse of his grand scheme. This financial disaster propelled some oilmen out of business and created chaos in the financial world.

Suspicious Franklin creditors charged Culver with conspiracy to defraud and he was arrested and imprisoned in May of 1866. The catastrophe of his failed ventures spread throughout Culver's firms and some of his associates were charged with embezzlement and fraud. The embarrassment of this adverse publicity and impending imprisonment forced him to resign as the

Congressional representative from the 20th District of Pennsylvania. By August 1866, an audit of assets and liabilities revealed that Culver had more than $650,000. Creditors pressured him and plans for payments were worked out. In February 1867 after a lengthy trial, a jury acquitted Culver and associates of any illegal activities.

Once out of prison, he recovered portions of his businesses, but the plan to build the second railroad to Pithole was scrapped. Following his acquittal, numerous claims against Culver, many of which were considered false, mounted to over $40,000,000. These numerous lies and endless greed shed light on the insane speculation in petroleum and finally brought it to a halt.

Culver returned to the oil business and lived in Franklin until his death in January 1909 at age 78. He is buried in the Franklin Cemetery.

Col. A.P. Duncan, the tough-minded businessman of Pithole's Duncan and Prather had purchased the Holmden Farm for $25,000 in 1865. Subsequently, he amassed a fortune in the Pennsylvania oil fields, including significant monetary gain during his time in Pithole. He had donated the property in fee simple to the Pithole Methodist Church where he had been a prominent member while living there. The colonel moved away from Pithole in 1866.

His father, T.C. Duncan who also made money from oil, left $10,000 to the same church that was finally dedicated in May 1866. Upon Duncan's death, his un-sympatric kin contested the will. The outcome of legal action left only $4000 to the little church that was in need of big repairs in 1873.

Henry Harley built an oil pipeline from Benninghof Run to Shaeffer Farm, the terminus of the Oil Creek Railroad in 1865, only to have it attacked and damaged by teamsters. He persisted by having twenty of the assailants arrested and went on to pump 800 barrels a day into iron tanks at Shaeffer Farm, ready to transport to oil buyers by rail. By 1867, he and his partner, William Abbott controlled the Western Transportation Company that had the legal rights to pipe oil to railroad heads. Various business ventures provided Harley both status and wealth. Years later, legal entanglements destroyed his prosperity and he drifted to New York. He died 1892.

Capt. William Hasson had drilled an oil well on Oil Creek

nine days after Col. Drake's successful venture. He and associates purchased 1000 acres of land that was to become the northside business and residential area of Oil City. He opened a hardware store, but with the onset of the Civil War, he enlisted in the 142nd Pennsylvania Volunteers, Company I. Surviving combat at the Battles of Fredericksburg and Chancellorsville, he was severely wounded during the Battle at Gettysburg. The army discharged him in October 1863 and he recuperated to return to the oil fields of Venango County.

Hasson and others formed the First National Bank of Oil City in which he eventually assumed responsible positions to become the bank's president. He married, raised a family and lived in Oil City. As well, he was involved in many civic activities including organizing the building of the first bridge across the Allegheny at Oil City, serving as the first burgess after working to get a charter for the new borough, acting as a state representative to the Pennsylvania state legislature for several sessions. He also was involved in presidential campaigns.

Hasson's generous philanthropy led him to donate fifty acres of land for the creation of a public park, land for the local hospital, nurses' home, and several churches, all for the good of the community. (As a child, I and my friends lived on Hasson Heights, played in Hasson Park, swam in the Hasson-Ramage Public Swimming Pool and had friends who lived on Hasson Avenue.) Capt. Hasson died at age ninety in Oil City and is buried at the local cemetery.

Alexander Keenan, the first burgess of Pithole had been studying law and was later admitted to the bar. He continued his residence there for some time despite the decline of business.

Gen. Ambrose Burnside, an 1847 West Point graduate had a number of opportunities for leadership during the Civil War. He resigned from the U.S. Army in 1865 and is sometimes remembered for his distinctive "sideburns" and unique beard. During the oil rush, he was recruited by Charles V. Culver to build and run a railroad from Reno to Pithole for exporting oil. Following the collapse of Culver's financial schemes, Burnside served as a U.S. Senator and the Governor of Rhode Island. He died in 1881 at the age of 57.

Col. E.A. Roberts arrived in the oil area at the end of the

Civil War. He claimed the rights to the development of a torpedo for use in unclogging oil wells. Although several other men had independently invented similar means to clear wells, Roberts filed his plans for a patent. In 1868, after extensive litigation, he was awarded the patent on his torpedo.

Alford W. Smiley remained active in the oil business, facilitating the buying and selling of crude. He eventually moved to the settlement of Foxburg, Clarion County and wrote the book, *A Few Scraps, Oily and Otherwise* that highlighted some of his experiences and people he knew during the oil boom.

Samuel Van Syckel designed the first successful oil pipeline from Pithole to Miller Farm in 1865, breaking the stranglehold of the thousands of teamsters who carried oil by horse and wagon from Pithole to Titusville and Miller Farm.

At age 81, Van Syckel died in Buffalo, New York in March 1894 and is buried in his native New Jersey.

Frank Spare, the newsman, who originated the *Pithole Daily Record* and worked with Luke, the newspaper boy, died of a heart condition in 1866.

In July 1867, Rev. Darius Steadman moved to Fredonia, Pennsylvania at the direction of the Methodist church.

Stonehouse Jack AKA Robert Vance was arrested a week after his 1866 fight with Benedict Hogan. He was charged with drugging a dancer who worked for him. Following his release on those charges, he again was arrested for picking the pocket of Karl French at the Terrapin Lunch in Pithole. Again released, he was brought in on assault charges, but acquitted.

Capt. J.J. Vandergrift had been in the steamship business before re-locating to Oil City in the early 1860's. His landing flat on the muddy banks of the Allegheny River were well known and much used during the exporting of oil by barrel and by bulk in the early 1860s. He stored oil when the price dropped and sold and shipped, when the price was high. Among one of the most productive businesses in purchasing and shipping petroleum from the Oil Creek Valley, Vandergrift eventually served as a director of the First

National Bank, the Oil City and Pithole Railroad, and was a member of the Borough Council. Local historians described him as being a "high-toned gentleman of strict integrity, energetic, and enterprising."

Vandergrift made his home in Oil City. In 1881, he and business associates created a pipeline system to facilitate the gathering and storage of crude which became the United Pipe Line Company. He served as their president for seventeen years. In nearby Siverly, he built the Imperial Refinery. Standard Oil incorporated that refinery and Vandergrift was elected to Standard Oil's board of directors in 1875. He organized the Forest Oil Company that evolved into the major pipeline company in the country. Vandergrift died in Pittsburgh in 1899.

J.D. Waring, MD remained in Pithole longer than any of the other nineteen physicians. He was the youngest of the doctors who practiced there. In the early morning of February 24, 1868, his house burned when his wife accidently knocked over the glass chimney of a kerosene lantern. In bitter cold weather, his wife escaped with their infant, and the doctor dropped their 2-year-old son into the arms of Adelbert Lewis, a bystander, then the doctor jumped to safety.

These historical figures are just a few of the people who took part in the dramatic events that birthed the oil industry. Following the first commercial extraction of crude from a wedge of wilderness in Northwestern Pennsylvania, oil forerunners created what was necessary in the infant industry. They adapted equipment, transformed transportation, built refineries, and created products while surviving the unexpected consequences of their own success--floods, fires, accidents, ice jams and an erratic economy. These tumultuous times of a nation divided by a civil war were wrought with the wild rush of speculation, greed and ambition.

Despite the chaos, the most powerful industry in modern history was born and flourished far beyond the imaginations of most, launching the petroleum trade that would drastically alter the world economy and global environment.

Acknowledgements

My many thanks to friends and family who encouraged my writing this historical fiction. My nieces, Linnah and Betsy Neidel, and my nephew, David Neidel all of whom read portions of the manuscript and offered sage advice. Beth B. Neidel, my sister-in-law and my brother, John provided me with a key resource, *The History of Venango County, Pennsylvania 1879* and other materials that are noted in the bibliography, as well as their encouragement. My longtime friend, Merry K. Strohm encouraged my efforts and gifted me the *John A. Mather, The Legacy of Pennsylvania's Oil Region Photographer,* a valuable resource.

Brandon Boocks, Executive Director of The Venango Museum of Art, Science and Industry granted me permission to include their map of Oil Creek Valley, Pennsylvania.

The Drake Well Museum archivist, Susan Bates guided me to online resources and important publications. Drake Well Museum's Executive Director of Friends of Drake Well, Emily Weaver; and Curator, Sarah Bell assisted me in obtaining the street map of Pithole and the permission to use it.

My friend and author Jamison Borek patiently guided me through the self-publishing process.

I greatly appreciate their help.

The book's original cover was created from paintings by my friend, artist Yana Merrill. Her daughter, Riva Merrill expertly laid out the cover with the assistance of Colin Bridge.

My writing friend, Sara Ford cheered me on.

And to my partner, Paul Pedersen, who was untiringly supportive of my efforts, I am forever grateful.

About the Author

Rosemary Neidel-Greenlee, a veteran of the U.S. Navy has co-authored several books about the service of women in the United States military. With co-author, Evelyn Monahan:

A Few Good Women: America's Military Women from the WWI to the Wars in Iraq and Afghanistan, Alfred A. Knopf, 2010.

And If I Perish: Frontline U.S. Army Nurses in WWII, Alfred A. Knopf, 2003;

All This Hell: U.S. Army Nurses Imprisoned by the Japanese, University Press of Kentucky, 2000;

Albanian Escape: The True Story of U.S. Army Nurses Behind Enemy Lines, University Press of Kentucky, 1999.

Regarding women's military history, Ms. Neidel-Greenlee has been interviewed on television and NPR radio, appeared on Book TV, C-Span II, and provided presentations at book fairs, history museums, and veterans' and military programs.

She is a native of Oil City, Pennsylvania, has two sons and lives in Santa Fe, New Mexico.

List of Characters

Historical Figures:

Primary characters:

Benedict Hagan/Hogan, "Big Bad Ben Hogan, Wickedest Man in the World"

John Wilkes Booth, famous Shakespearean actor and assassin of President Abraham Lincoln

"French Kate" AKA Katherine Van De Mer, Katherine Grant, Mrs. Katherine Le Conte, Madame Antoine G. Garrone, Elizabeth Louise Granger, Betsy Granger

Secondary Historical Characters:

Gen. M.H. Avery

Gen. A.E. Burnside

California Sam AKA Samuel Washington Crawford, farmer/oilman

Cassandra, answered Hogan's ad for a waitress

Charles Vernon Culver, businessman

Col A.P. Duncan & son businessmen

George Etzel, night watchman

Emma Fenton, owner of Florence Restaurant

William Hasson, Businessman in Oil City

Charles Highberger, Justice of the Peace

A.A. Hill, Pithole postmaster

J.J. Holliday, pugilist

Charles and Thomas Holmden, original owners of the Holmden farm

Stonehouse Jack, pugilist AKA Robert J. Vance

Walter R. Johns, editor *Venango Spectator*

Alexander Keenan, Pithole Burgess

General Edwin Lee and Susan Lee, Confederates in Montreal

Lee & Gould Pharmacist, Drug Store

Widow Lyon, lived near Pithole

One-Eyed Pete, AKA D.H. Peterson

George Prather, businessman

Widow Ricketts dubbed "Cinderella Rickets"

A.W. Smiley, manager for Van Syckel

Lewis Smith, torpedo inventor

Frank Spare, *Pithole Daily Record* editor

Rev. Darius Steadman, Methodist Minister

J.J. Vandergrift, businessman
Samuel Van Syckel, oil pipeline inventor
J.D. Waring, MD, one of the youngest physicians in Pithole
Jonathan Watson, oilman, successful intrapreneur

Inmates at the Rochester House of Refuge are taken from actual inmate cases, but the names have been fictionalized.
Administrative authorities at the House of Refuge are historical figures.

Main Fictional Characters:
Barnswell Buchanan, bartender
Josh Carpenter, local guide; partner in Kate's French Restaurant
Jeremiah Duff, oil driller, friend of French Kate
Ebenezer, Assistant Harbor Master, Brooklyn Navy Yard
Amos Elias Kahl, son of John Obadiah
John Obadiah Kahl, manager, Cornplanter Landing
Luke, Allison Luther Kahl, son of John Obadiah
Molly Margaret Degleman Kahl, wife of John Obadiah
Petrus Plugge, Barrister, Katherine's stepfather
Fredrick Van de Mere, cousin of Katherine Van de Mere

Minor Fictional Characters:
Big Sarge, teamster
Blanche de Brunt, manager of the Red Lantern Inn
Gala AKA Susan Red Fox, Seneca Indian, Elias' lover
Jacques Guyto, vineyard worker
Andrus Mathias Kahl, brother of John Obadiah
Jesse May, friend of Kahl family
Maybelle, waitress, prostitute at French Kate's Restaurant
Mike Mulligan, teamster
Old Mac, relative of Hamilton McClintock, farmer/oil well owner
Rufus Stoops, Confederate conspirator
Captain Emile Van De Mere, father of Katherine Van de Mere
Sarah Wilson, widow of Thomas Wilson-KIA)

Terminology

Attic Hand: worker in a drilling or a production crew, employed in the derrick, often climbing to the top.

Black Gold: early term referring to petroleum.

Bulk Boat: on Oil Creek in the 1860s, an open flat-bottom boat used to transport crude in an open boat rather than in barrels.

Cash on the Barrel-Head: term alleged to have originated in the early Pennsylvania oil fields. According to *Oil & Gas Dictionary of Historical Terminology,* Major Adams, manager at Clapp Farm on Oil Creek, demanded payment of $10,000 owed for the first 1000 barrels of oil be made in cash. As the story goes, Adams kicked the nearest oak barrel upright and counted out the payment on the barrel's head.

Crude: term for unrefined petroleum-unaltered.

Crude Skinners: early teamsters who replaced boatman during a pond freshet.

Derrick Apples: derrick parts that would fall from the top of an oil derrick to the base: nuts, bolts, pieces of wood etc.

Doghouse: on early oil leases, a small shelter-a single room or closet that could serve as a place to sleep for someone-a worker on a rig or a lease.

Guiper: Oil Creek oil boat with a flat bottom that was towed up the creek empty by horses, then loaded with 25-50 oil barrels and floated down the creek.

Greasers: clothing worn by oilfield workers consisting of a flannel shirt, warm trousers and heavy boots.

Gusher: a flowing well with natural gas that under great pressure propels some of the oil up and out, high over the derrick.

Johnny Newsome: A new arrival in oil country.

Kicking Down: method of drilling a well using a spring pole of 10-15 feet long, arranged over the well, working over a fulcrum. Stirrups attached to the end of the pole on which 2-3 workers each place a foot, and using a kicking motion, brought down the end of the pole and worked the bit, thrusting it into the well-hole.

Mouse Trap: a tool designed to fish small parts from the bottom of an oil well.

Oil Fever: a malady of enthusiastic oil speculators.

Pond Freshet: a method of releasing dammed up water to increase the amount of flow in a creek.

Red Neck: a reference to teamsters in the early days of oil transporting.

Rock Oil: an early term for petroleum to distinguish it from other oils, i.e. castor oil, linseed oil.

Seneca Oil: Crude oil so called because early pioneers had learned about it from the Seneca Indians.

Shooter: The worker who used nitroglycerin to increase the flow of an oil well.

Snake Oil: a term that refers to oil having medicinal properties; usually bought from a traveling peddler.

Soiled Dove: a prostitute.

Spouter: a term for an oil well with an uncontrolled flow.

Spring Pole: a tool that is an essential part of the equipment in kicking down a well.

Toolie: A tool dresser, responsible for sharpening a drill bit.

Wildcatter: A driller who drills for oil in an area where no oil has previously been found.

Yellow Dog: a teapot-shaped vessel used on early oil rigs with a saying that the light is adequate to see a yellow dog.

Reference: Roxanne Hitchcock. *Lube Lingo, Oil and Gas Dictionary of Historical Terminology.* Oil Region Books: Oil City, PA, 1999.

Bibliography

"Action at Mount Zion Church." Wikipedia.org.

"Ads for Rooms to Rent." *Pithole Daily Record*, November 29, 1865, Vol. 1, p. 4.

Adomites, Paul. *Oil Fields, Oil People: Re-imaginings of the Great Stories of the Early Days of Pennsylvania Oil*. Emlenton, PA: Adam Midas Press, 2012.

Alford, Terry. *Fortune's Fool: The Life of John Wilkes Booth*. New York, NY: Oxford University Press, 2015.

"Allegheny Valley Railroad. " Wikipedia.org.

Amsler, Allison Luther. *History and Records of the Rickenbrode Family,* Venus, Pennsylvania: unpublished, 1935.

"American Enterprise in the 19th Century." nautarch.tamu.edu.

"Anglican Book of Common Prayer, 1662." seaservices.com.

"Arnold's Complicity and Confession." *The New York Tribune,* May 19, 1865.

"The Assassins." *Philadelphia Inquirer*, May 19, 1865, P.1. genelogy.com.

"Atlantic and Great Western Railroad." wikipedia.org.

"Baltimore Riot of 1861," wikipedia.org.

Bates, Samuel P. "Forty-Second Regiment, Bucktail," *History of Pennsylvania Volunteers, 1861-5; prepared in compliance with acts of the legislature, Making of America Books.* quod.lib.umich.edu.

"Battle of Atlanta." wikipedia.org.

"Battle of Kennesaw Mountain." wikipedia.org.

"Battle of Pace's Ferry," wikipedia.org.

Becker, Matthew. "Women's Wristwatches Began in Early 1800s." October 16, 2017, beckertime.com.

Bell, John. *Rebels on the Great Lakes: Confederate Naval Commando Operations Launched from Canada, 1863-1864.* Toronto: Dundurn, 2011.

Bells, Mary. "History of the Electric Telegraph and Telegraphy." inventors.about.com.

"Ben Hogan is Dead." *Oil City Semi Weekly Derrick,* November 9, 1916.

"Ben Hogan—The Evangelist." *Oil City Derrick*, August 14, 1971.

Bjorklund, Karna L. *The Indians of Northeastern America.* New York: Dodd, Mead and Company, 1969.

Black, Brian. *Petrolia: The Landscape of America's First Oil Boom.* Baltimore: The Johns Hopkins University Press, 2000.

"Boom Town Vocabulary." petroleumhistory.org.

Bone, J.H. A. *Petroleum and Petroleum Wells With a Complete Guide Book and Description of the Oil Regions of Pennsylvania, West Virginia, Kentucky, and Ohio.* Philadelphia: J.B. Lippincott & Co., 1865.

Bonta House Pithole, PA, (Photo), VCGC#415.JPG, mail.google.com.

"Wine at Winterthur: Samuel Francis DuPont, 19th-Century Collector." June 14, 2012, museumblog.winterthur.org.

"Bounty Jumper." wikipedia.org.

Brewerton, G. Douglas. "May God Save the Union," (Civil War Music.) civilwar.org.

"Brooklyn." wikipedia.org.

"Brooklyn Navy Yard." wikipedia.org.

"California Sam." *History of Venango County Pennsylvania 1879.* Franklin, PA: Venango County Historical Society (reprint 1979), p 939.

"Canada in the American Civil War." wikipedia.org.

"Castle Thunder (prison)." wikipedia.org.

Chaconas, Joan L. "The Old Capitol Prison." *The Surratt Society News*, April 1977.

"Chronology of the American Civil War." civilwarhome.com.

Civil War Exhibit. Atlanta History Center, Atlanta GA.

Coates, M.W., Clive. *The Wines of France.* London: Century Editions, 1990.

"Cornplanter." wikipedia.org.

Cone, Andrew and Johns, Walter R. *Petrolia: A Brief History of the Pennsylvania Petroleum Region, Its Development, Growth, Resources, Etc. From 1859-1869.* New York: D. Appleton and Company, 1870.

"Confederacy's Canadian Mission: Spies Across the Border." historynet.com.

Crocus AKA Charles C. Leonard. *The History of Pithole.* Pithole, PA.: Morton, Longwell and Company, 1867.

Cruise on the Erie Canal. Lockport Locks & Erie Canal Cruises, Lockport, NY.

Darrah, William C. *Pithole: The Vanished City: A Story of the Early Days of the Petroleum Industry*. Gettysburg, PA: Self-published, 1972.

The Derrick's Hand-Book of Petroleum: A Complete Chronological and Statistical Review of Petroleum Developments from 1859 to 1898. Oil City, PA: Derrick Publishing Company, 1898.

Dickey, J.D. *American Demagogue, The Great Awakening and the Rise and Fall of Populism*. New York: Pegasus, 2019.

"Dispossession and Disruption." Erie Canalway National Heritage Corridor. eriecanalway.org.

Dolson, Hildegarde. *The Great Oildorado: The Gaudy and Turbulent Years of the First Oil Rush, Pennsylvania 1859-1880*. New York: Random House, 1959.

"Dramatic Oil Company." American Oil & Gas Historical Society. aoghs.org.

"Drinking on the Go." uncorked.winterthur.org.

"Early Crude Oil Production Levels and Pricing." oil150.com

Eastburn. "Oil on the Brain: A Comic Ballad." Philadelphia: J. Marsh's Music Store, 1864. (Sheet Music copyright 1864).

"Ebenezer Crawford's Ancestors: The 4th Generation." Courtesy of Beth B. Neidel, family archives, Carmel, CA.

"Edwin Gray Lee." wikipedia.org.

"Epigaea reopens." wikipedia.org.

Erie Canalway National Heritage Corridor. (**http://eriecanalway.org/learn/history-culture/native-americans.org**)

———

Etzel, Judy. "A Voluptuous Redhead of 'Slight Morals.'" *Oil City Derrick*, March 11, 1970.

Etzel, Judy. "Hogan Teams Up With French Kate.'" *Oil City Derrick*, March 12, 1970.

Etzel, Judy. "Ben and Kate in Pithole." *Oil City Derrick*, March 13, 1970.

Etzel, Judy. "Hogan and French Kate Part After Violent Quarrel." *Oil City Derrick*, March 16, 1970.

Etzel, Judy. "French Kate Displayed Jealousy And Vanity But Still Was Loyal." *Oil City Derrick*, March 17, 1970.

Etzel, Judy. "The Story of French Kate." *Oil City Derrick,* June 27, 1985.

"France in the American Civil War." wikipedia.org.

"Faro (card game)-Rules." wikipedia.org.

"The First Pipeline War." nautil.us.

Fitzgerald, Peter. "List of Brooklyn Neighborhoods" (and map.) wikipedia.org.

"French Intervention in Mexico." wikipedia.org.

Giddens, Paul H. *Early Days of Oil: A Pictorial History of the Beginning of the Industry.* New York: The Colonel, Inc. 1964.

Gilfoyle, Timothy J. "Prostitution Densities in Manhattan, Map VIII-Blocks with Houses of Prostitution 1870-1879." *Undergraduate Economic Review*, Vol. 3, (2007) Iss. 1, Art. 8.

"Governor Blacksnake." wikipedia.org.

"Greenback 1860s Money."wilipedia.org.

Dawson, Kay, Mong, Margaret Anne and Smith, Taunee. "Grove Hill Cemetery." Oil City, PA: Heritage Society of Oil City and the Venango County Genealogical Club, 2017.

Head, Constance. "J.W.B.: 'I am Myself Alone,'" *The Surratt Society News*, November 1980.

Historical Sketch of Oil City: 1871-1971.

"Historic Ferries of the Atlanta Area." wikipedia.org.

"Historic Pithole City: Oil's Vanished Boom Town 1865-1877." Oil Region Alliance. drakewell.org.

"Historic Seneca Leaders." sni.org.

"History of Brooklyn: From Village to City," thirteen.org.

"History, Port of Bordeaux." bordeaux-port.fr.

"History of French Wine." wikipedia.org.

"History of the 42-gallon Barrel." *American Oil & Gas Historical Society*: aoghs.org.

Hitchcock, Roxanne. *Lube Lingo, Oil and Gas Dictionary of Historical Terminology*. Oil City, PA: Oil Region Books, 1999.

Hogan, Ben. *Ben Hogan's Wild Career in Both Armies*. 1887, Oil City, PA: Re-printed 1998 by M.A. Mong.

"Hogan's Short Political Career." *Petrolia*, October 30, 1874.

"Holmden Farm Oil Interests for Sale Cheap." *Pithole Daily Record*, November 27, 1865, Vol 1, # LV, p.1.

"Hotel Arrivals." *Pithole Daily Record.* November 28, 1865, Vol. 1, p. 2, col. 4.

"*Humbolt.*" user.xmission.com.

Hunt, H.H. "The Oil Dorado." *Business Directory*, Titusville, PA, November 1865.

"Iron Smelting Furnace Was Initial Industry in Oil City District." *The Derrick*, Tuesday, June 28, 1955, p. 29.

Ivy, Kyndal. "Illegitimate Children in France in the 1800s." prezi.com.

"Jacob Vandergrift—Transportation Pioneer." oil150.com.

"John A. Mather Historical Marker," explorepahistory.com.

"Johnson's Island." ohiohistorycentral.org.

"Justice! The Findings of the Military Commission." *Philadelphia Inquirer*, July 7, 1866.

Karns, Steve. *Images of America: Cherry Run Valley, Plumer, Pithole, and Oil City*. Charleston, SC: Arcadia Press, 2000.

Kauffman, Michael W. *American Brutus: John Wilkes Booth and the Lincoln Conspiracies*. New York, NY: Random House, 2004.

Kelly, Jack. *Heaven's Big Ditch: God, Gold and Murder on the Erie Canal*. New York: St. Martin's Press, 2016.

"Kingdom of Wurttemberg." wikipedia.org.

Kingsley, Nancy, Long, Joanne, Newton, Arch. "Synoptic History of Emlenton." 1977, courtesy of Beth B. Neidel family archives, Carmel, CA.

Klein, Philip & Ari A. Hoogenboom. *A History of Pennsylvania.* New York: McGraw Hill, 1973.

"Knox Oil Boom." Published by Knox Glass Inc. 1966. courtesy of Beth B. Neidel family archives, Carmel, CA.

Langguth, A.J. *Driven West: Andrew Jackson and the Trail of Tears to the Civil War*. New York: Simon and Schuster, 2010.

Leonard, Charles C. "History of Pithole," *Pithole Daily Record* pub., 1867.

Levin, Alexandra Lee. *"This Awful Drama:" Gen. Edwin Gray Lee and his Family.* New York: Vantage Press, 1987.

"List of letters uncalled for at the at Pit Hole City Post Office Up to September 12, 1865." *Pithole Daily Record*, September 2, 1865, Vol. 1, p. 2, Column 4.

"The Lure of Laudanum, The Victorian's Favorite Drug." mentalfloss.com.

"Lyrics ca. 1861: John Brown's Body Lesson," civilwar.org.

"Major U.S. Immigration Ports: 1851-1991." gncestry.com.

Martens, Charles D. *The Oil City: A History.* Oil City, PA: First Seneca Bank and Trust, 1971.

Mather, John. *The Legacy of Pennsylvania's Oil Region Photographer.* Titusville, PA: The Colonel, Inc., 1995.

"Matthew Henry Avery, BG." geni.com.

McCall, Marilyn. *Ben Hogan's Wild Ride.* New Wilmington, PA: Glode Printing Co, 2009.

"McClintock Petroleum Company, Venango County, Pennsylvania (story)." scripophily.net.

"McClintock Well #1: The World's Oldest Continuously Producing Oil Well." drakewell.org.

McElwee, Neil and Lois. "Oil City, Pennsylvania: Northside Historic District Downtown Walking Tour." Oil City, PA: Oil Heritage Region, Inc., 2002.

McLaurin, John J. *Sketches in Crude-Oil.* Harrisburg, PA: Self-Published, 1896.

"McNeill's Rangers." wikipedia.com.

Miller, Ernest C. "Warren County and the Civil War." *Warren County Observer*, May 27, 1961, p. 18.

Minard, Charles Joseph. "Minard's Map of French Wine Exports for 1864." wikipedia.org.

"Mob Law and Rioting." *Pithole Daily Record*, December 1, 1865, vol. 1, #LVIX, p. 2 column 2.

Morrison, Alice. "Ben Hogan, A Synopsis of Autobiography." Unpublished.

"Music of the 1860's—Patriotic Songs of the Era." civilwar.org.

Newton, J.H. ed. *History of Venango County Pennsylvania and Incidentally of Petroleum, Together with Accounts of Early Settlements and Progress of Each Township, Borough and Village with Personal Sketches of Early Settlers, Representative Men, Family Records, Etc.* Columbus, Ohio: J.A. Caldwell, 1879.

New York House of Refuge. (**http://www.archives.nysed.gov** research/res_topics_ed_reform_history.shtml).

"New York House of Refuge." wikipedia.org.

"New York House of Refuge-Parole Registers, 1882-1933." Microfilm, New York State Archives Cultural, Education Center Albany, New York.

"News of the Day." *New York Times*, April 21, 1861, p.4., newspapers.com.

"Nineteenth Century Turning points in United States History." DVD series.

"Noted Drug Emporium Served Local People." *The Derrick*. Derrick Publishing Company, June 23, 1955, p. 29.

"NZ related BDMs and Burials at Sea."
freepages.genealogy.rootweb.ancestry.com.

"Our City Charities: The New York House of Refuge for Juvenile Delinquents." *The New York Times*, January 23, 1860.

"Oil Creek: map and history." Pennsylvania Department of Conservation and Natural Resources, 2017.

"Oil City: The Town That Grew Up with Oil." Oil City, PA: Venango Museum of Art, Science and Industry, 1989.

"Oil City, Pennsylvania, Northside Historic Downtown Walking Tour." Oil City, PA: Oil Heritage Region, Inc., May 2002.

"Oil City, Pennsylvania, Northside Residential Historic Driving Tour," Oil City, PA: Oil Heritage Region, Inc. May 2002.

Oil City and Venango City Directory. Oil City, Pennsylvania: L.D. Kellogg and H.B. Pratt, publishers, April 1866.

"Oil Creek Railroad." wikipedia.org.

"Oil Discovery Marvel of Age." *The Derrick*, June 23, 1955, p. 23.

Oil & Gas Dictionary of Historical Terminology.
(http://www.oil150.com/about-oil/oil-gas-dictionary/)

"Our City Charities: The New York House of Refuge for Juvenile Delinquents." *The New York Times,* 1860.

"Oil was Struck at Well No. 3, Holmden Run. " *Pithole Daily Record,* November 29, 1865, Vol. 1, p. 2.

Pelaghi, Clarence. "Coal Oil Johnny Was More Than a Legend." *The Derrick*, July, 1976.

Pelaghi, Clarence. "Looking Back: Oil City Was The Terminal For Huge River Traffic." *The Derrick,* April 2, 1974, p. 12.

"Pennsylvania Geology." Bureau of Topographic and Geologic Survey, vol. 29, no.1, Spring 1998.

"The Pennsylvania Oil Regions: 'Rich as Mud'—The Route to the Oil Regions." *The New York Times*, December 20, 1864.

"Pennsylvania's Oil Region: Discover Pennsylvania's Oil Region-The Valley that Changed the World." Oil City, PA: Oil Region Alliance, Date unknown.

"Penobscot Bay History Online." penobscotmarinemuseum.org.

The Photographic History of the Civil War: Soldier Life and Secret Service Prisons and Hospitals. Vol. 4, Secaucus, NJ: The Blue and Grey Press, 1987.

Pickett, Robert S. *House of Refuge, Origins of Juvenile Reform in New York State, 1815-1857*. Syracuse, New York: Syracuse University Press, 1969.

Pilewski, Walter John. "When Pithole City Became a Ghost Town," (Song and story). Titusville, PA: Pilewski Enterprises, 1990.

Pithole City 1865-1867 map. Drake's Well Museum, Titusville, PA.

"Pithole City, Oil's Vanishing Boomtown (timeline) 1865-1877," Pennsylvania Historical and Museum Commission, 2015.

Pithole Directory, ed. and publisher: J.E. Barker, Pithole, PA, 1866.

"Pithole's Rise and Fall." wikipedia.org.

Poems of the Oil Country. Butler, PA: *Oil and Gas Man's Magazine*. Date unknown.

"Poker Hands." thesprucecrafts.com.

Preston, David. "The Trigger." *Smithsonian*, October 2019, pp.30-78.

Price, Pamela Vandyke. *Wines of the Graves*. London; Sotheby's Publications, 1988.

"Professional Friends of Wine: Wine History." winepros.org.

"Province of Canada." wikipedia.org.

"Public Notices." *Pithole Daily Record*, November 30, 1865, p. 2.

Pumping Jack Museum & Visitor Center, Emlenton, PA.

"Put Yourself in the Picture in the Valley that Changed the World*." Oil Country Gazette,* Vol. 8, No. 1, 1996.

"Recruits Wanted." *Raftsman's Journal*, May 29, 1861, p. 3. newspapers.com.

Reilly, Robert F. "Medical and Surgical Care During the American Civil War, 1861-1865." Dallas, Texas: *Baylor University Medical Center Proceedings*, 2016 April, 29(2): 138-142.

"Remains of Bog Ore Iron Furnace Near Cooperstown." *The Derrick*, Tuesday, June 28, 1955, 29.

Schama, Simon. "Abolition of the Slave Trade: United States and Britain Two Diverging Destinies." Stanford University lecture, 2000.

Seagraves, Anne. *Soiled Doves: Prostitution In the Early West*. Hayden, ID: Wesanne Publications, 1994.

"Seneca Nation of Indians." wikipedia.org.

"Seneca Nation of Indians-Clans." sni.org.

"Ship Motions." wikipedia.org.

Smiley, Alfred W. *A Few Scraps, Oily and Otherwise*. Oil City, PA: The Derrick Publishing Company, 1907.

Snodgrass, Chris. "A Chronicle of Some Victorian Events." users.clas.un.edu.

Souvenir of The Oil City Derrick in the Year of 1890. The Derrick Publishing Company, 1896.

"Special Edition Featuring the Oil Heritage Region." *Pennsylvania Geology*, vol.29, No. 1, Bureau of Topographic and Geologic Survey, Department of Conservation and National Resources, Middletown, PA: 1998.

Spicer, Edward H. *A Short History of the Indians of the United States*. New York: Van Nostrand Reinhold Company, 1969.

"St. Albans Raid." wikipedia.org.

"The Raid: The Northernmost Land Action of the Civil War." stalbansraid.com.

"SS Arctic," wikipedia.org.

"Steerage Passengers-Emigrants Between Decks." norwayhertiage.com.

Stephens, David T. and Bobersky, Alex T. "Transitory Accommodations in a Transitory Landscape: Hotels of Pithole City, Pennsylvania and Its Environs." *Oilfield Journal*, 2006-2007.

Stewart, Anne W. *John A. Mather: The Legacy of Pennsylvania's Oil Region Photographer*. Titusville, PA: The Colonel, Inc.

"Stobbs, Mike. "In Nation's Opioid Epidemic, a Chilling Sense of Déjà Vu." *Santa Fe New Mexican*, October 29, 2017, p. A-1.

Stocking Model 1850 (Pepperbox) Specifications. **Http://www.militaryfactory.com.**

Stowe, Harriet Beecher. *Uncle Tom's Cabin, Dover Thrift Editions*. Mineola, New York: Dover Publications, Inc., 2005. (original publication date, 1852).

Swetnam, George. "What's New in Pithole." *The Pittsburgh Press*, August 20, 1972

"Success at Oil Creek, August 27, 1859." U.S. Department of the Interior, Geological Survey, U.S. Government Printing Office:1980-311-34-52.

The Surratt Society. *In Pursuit of Continuing Research in the Field of the Lincoln Assassination*, unpublished, 1990.

Szalewicz, Steve S. *Oil Moon Over Pithole: A Story of a Phenomenon in an Oil Town.* unknown publisher, 1958.

Tarbell, Ida. *The History of the Standard Oil Company, Vol 1 & 2,* (reprinted). San Bernardino, CA, 2017.

Titone, Nora. *My Thoughts Be Bloody, The Bitter Rivalry That Led to the Assassination of Abraham Lincoln.* New York: Free Press, 2010.

"Treaty of Canandaigua." wikipedia.org.

Trainer, George F. *The Life and Adventures of Ben Hogan: The Wickedest Man in the World.* Chicora, PA: Mechling, 2009.

"Trial of the Conspirators." *Connecticut Courant.* May 20, 1865, p.1, genealogybank.com.

Tucker, Henry, composer, 1863, "When This Cruel War is Over," wikipedia.org.

"Uncivil War—General Meade in Northern VA, 1861." clevelandcivilwarroundtable.com.

"Union Blockade." wikipedia.org.

Upton, Sinclair. *Oil!* Albert & Boni, Inc.: New York, 1927.

"U.S. Timeline—1850s." americasbesthistory.com.

"U.S. Timeline—The 1860s," americasbesthistory.com.

"The Valley that Changed the World (history and map.) Oil City, PA: Oil Region Alliance.

Verge, Laurie. "The Baltimore Plot." *The Surratt Society News*, September 1980.

"19th Century Mourning Clothing. 1850 t0 1860 Fashion-timeline." vintagefashionguild.org.

"Victorian America." wikipedia.org.

Walking Tour of Pithole City with Directory of Some of Pithole's Sites." Drake's Well Museum, Titusville, PA.

"Western fashion, 1860s." wikipedia.org.

"The Western House of Refuge." rochester.lib.ny.us.

"When New York was the Prostitution Capitol of the U.S." nypost.com.

White, Thomas. "United States Early Radio History." earlyradiohistory.us

"William Hasson." Beth B. Neidel personal history archives, Carmel, CA.

"William Hasson, Capt." findagrave.com.

"Women's Fashions of the Victorian Era: From Hoop Skirts to Bustles." bellatory.com.

Yergin, Daniel. *The Prize.* New York: Simon & Schuster, 1991.

"13th Regiment New York State Militia, New York National Guard, Civil War." dmna.ny.gov.

"14th Brooklyn Regiment-'Red-Legged Devils.'" wikipedia.org.

"14th Regiment to Occupy the Marine Barracks." *Brooklyn Daily Eagle*, April 30, 1861, p.2.

"1800s Mourning Clothes and Traditions." victoriandress.blogspot.com.

"18th Century Turning Points in U.S. History-1701-1800." Ambrose Video Publishing, Inc., discs 1-4.

"19th Century Turning Points in U.S. History—1800-1900." Ambrose Video Publishing, Inc., discs 1-4.

"19th Century Mourning Clothing." 19thcenturyartofmourning.com.

"35th Regiment Massachusetts Volunteer Infantry." wikipedia.org.

https://io9.gizmodo.com › 1846-the-year-we-hit-peak-sperm-whale-oil-5930...

www.ingramcontent.com/pod-product-compliance
Lightning Source LLC
Chambersburg PA
CBHW061508020726
47502CB00006B/1979